Terrarium

Terrarium

New and
Selected Stories

Valerie
Trueblood

Counterpoint
Berkeley, California

TERRARIUM

Copyright © 2018 by Valerie Trueblood
First hardcover edition: 2018

Grateful acknowledgment is made to publications
in which some of these stories first appeared:
"The Finding," *The Seattle Review*; "The Magic Pebble," *One Story*;
"The Llamas," *Thresholds* (UK); "His Rank," "Cherries," and "Dogs of War
and Peace," *Southword* (Ireland); "Crisco," *Glimmer Train*; "The Tamarins,"
"Forced Entry," and "Flag of the Nude" (as "The Speech"), *The Northwest Review*;
"The Bull," *The Saturday Evening Post*.

The passage about trees read aloud by Diana in "Beloved, You Looked
into Space" is from Donald Culross Peattie's *A Natural History of
North American Trees*, vol. 2 © 1953 by Houghton Mifflin.

Library of Congress Cataloging-in-Publication Data
Names: Trueblood, Valerie, author.
Title: Terrarium : new and selected stories / Valerie Trueblood.
Description: Berkeley, CA : Counterpoint Press, [2018]
Identifiers: LCCN 2018001954 | ISBN 9781640090736
Classification: LCC PS3620.R84 A6 2018 | DDC 813/.6—dc23
LC record available at https://lccn.loc.gov/2018001954

Paperback ISBN: 978-1-64009-248-8

Jacket designed by Donna Cheng
Book designed by Wah-Ming Chang

COUNTERPOINT
2560 Ninth Street, Suite 318
Berkeley, CA 94710
www.counterpointpress.com

Printed in the United States of America

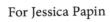

For Jessica Papin

Contents

From *Marry or Burn* (2010)

Invisible River	5
Choice in Dreams	22
Trespass	33
Phantom Father	51
Beloved, You Looked into Space	61

From *Search Party: Stories of Rescue* (2013)

The Finding	105
The Magic Pebble	111
The Llamas	130
The Stabbed Boy	141
Later or Never	146
Who Is He That Will Harm You?	160

From *Criminals: Love Stories* (2016)

Bride of the Black Duck	181
His Rank	193
Astride	196
Da Capo	208
You Would Be Good	228
Sleepover	234
Novel of Rose	267
Criminals	271

Terrarium (2018)

1. Cherries
   Aliens: Saving the Child ... 289
   Helen of Troy ... 291
   Dogs of War and Peace ... 295
   Book Review ... 297
   The Witch ... 302
   Crisco ... 305
   Cherries ... 309
   What We Found ... 311

2. The Infralife
   The Tamarins ... 315
   Ghost ... 318
   Stay ... 321
   Tarp ... 326
   Two Dogs ... 329

3. Earthly Love
   Hero ... 337
   Afternoon Tango ... 343
   Two Birthdays ... 346
   Whiteout ... 348
   Forced Entry ... 351
   Seurat ... 354
   Raccoon ... 359
   The Flag of the Nude ... 363
   The Bull ... 365
   Orogeny ... 369

4. What We Found
   Where We Grew Up ... 377
   Harvest ... 378
   Visiting Revivalist ... 379
   The Girl Who Told ... 381
   Advice ... 382
   Freeway Rescues ... 383
   River Boat ... 384

Terrarium

From

Marry or Burn (2010)

Invisible River

A woman stands at the mirror in a train station bathroom. Next to her a dark-haired girl is blending the shadow on one eyelid with a fingertip, while the woman marvels at the black pressed-down lashes, thick as a pocket flap. When both lids are done the girl pulls down her lower lip with two dark nails, perfect ovals, and examines her teeth and gums. Now she's making an *O* of her lips to cream on red lipstick, furiously round and round, not pausing at the corners. *All right, all right,* thinks the woman, *you're a beauty but that's too much lipstick.* The girl goes on a little longer and then without blotting her lips drops the lipstick in a little velvet bag and roughly cinches it tight.

She grabs the handle of a black leather suitcase on scuffed wheels, with a strap around it, and drawing her black eyebrows together yanks it on one wheel through the door a fat girl coming in holds open for her. *Whoever's out there waiting for you,* the woman at the mirror thinks, *he's in for it.* Or maybe there's nobody. Maybe that's the problem.

Of course nobody paces outside the door waiting for her, either. What train would she board, to what destination would someone accompany her, a woman of fifty-some who has laid a big brown purse in a puddle on the counter and seems content to daydream in a public bathroom? Finally she takes her hands out from under the water and pulls down the groaning belt of towel. She looks at herself. Despite her open stare, she didn't get a fraction of a glance from the girl. She isn't old. If she were, a quick smile might easily have passed both ways between them, a small bow across time. She is unsure, herself, about applying lipstick, which may in this light have the effect of a label stuck on an orange, but eventually she does it anyway.

Unlike the girl, whose big eyes were red-rimmed under the makeup, she is happy. Or very close. She sees the possibility.

2

Groundless near-happiness doesn't do anything for the Reader, if she comes across it on the page. She is looking for something with an edge.

The Reader is blond, healthily pretty in a laissez-faire way. At first glance her clothes look casual too, but they are carefully chosen. Two years in the city have taught her where to find clothes, which colors are hers, how to minimize her breasts. Intelligence and determination have won her the job she holds, not her first by any means, despite her youth. Having worked on publications for years, ever since high school, she has a long résumé that belies her wide crooked smile and her accent. Those in the ranks above her rely on her to hear a certain range of notes, in particular the notes struck by some of the newer writers, and convey it to them in the way of someone quickly transposing a tune. Some of her enthusiasms make them scratch their heads. "Take a look at this," they say. "What can I say, the Reader likes it."

When she has kicked off her shoes after work she stands on one foot with her knee on the painted tin cover of the radiator, leaning a shoulder on the glass. The sky narrows to a dark blue cone between buildings, with its tip in a river that can't be seen from here. But she relaxes. It is close by: a river. Full against its banks and then walled in, moving heavily alongside the streets with its own slow purpose.

The Reader grew up in a mining town with a river running the length of it. Until the age of twelve she lived in a house overlooking the river, which brought a shallow whitewater and a six-foot falls right into town. Two parents, three children, dogs, cats, trees, porch. Then her father died. After that she lived in several smaller houses, and finally, when her mother was getting into serious difficulties, an apartment above the café where her mother sometimes worked. No one called it a studio, it was one room, for just herself and her mother by then—her brothers were gone—and one cat. You couldn't see the river from the café but you could always hear it, hastening past the town where, with her mother, the Reader lived what she calls the sad part of her life. From time to time it rose out of its bed and flooded the town, drowning people's goats and pets and occasionally people themselves, sucking them through culverts, upending their trailers and wallowing away with them before they could wade out to a rowboat—the peaceful golden-brown river that gave them fish and black soil and green vegetable gardens.

Now she has made a second river her own, welcoming its tugs and barges, its measured progress into the heart of a city fit to be the destination of water.

Yet Nature has not been banished here, as people in her hometown would claim; it haunts the city, especially in this season. Wet leaves plaster the sidewalks, some as big as the pockets of the yellow slicker she wears in defiance of all the city black. She springs down onto the yellow carpet every morning thinking, *My wedding.* Should she have included a flower girl, one of her nieces, to give more of an aisle-feeling to the space? *The space*—that's what the hotel's wedding consultant calls the long airy room where the wedding will take place. The same was true when she was looking for an apartment: everything, even the closet, was a space.

She doesn't miss houses with rooms, or anything else about the town she came from. Too much was known there. Even her mother is gone from the town, no longer on her stool in the café lounge late with the regulars and the two floozies and an occasional girl in overalls from the highway crew. Too much was seen in that town, too much gone over in stores and church circles and on the telephone. A widow didn't go on and on in the sloppy condition permitted in the first weeks; a widow remarried or took an interest in the church or the lives of the next generation, or all three, ideally. To do otherwise, to let a bad habit get the better of you, to drink cheap wine for months on end, certainly to be picked up out of wet grass before dawn and have the snails pulled off you by your own child . . . to do these things was to imply that your loss had exceeded the losses of others. That your husband had been somehow superior. That you, yourself, had been uniquely struck down.

The daughter, the Reader, was another story. In all likelihood people in town still speak of her, persist in expecting her. There, homecoming queens are remembered for a generation. But no one she would want to run into is there. Her brothers left early and never went back.

She can call the brothers or not call them. Her boyfriend is on his way over. Her fiancé, now. *Husband*: sober word. But her boyfriend has nothing sober about him. He's like a dog, she tells her friends, a dog in a movie. Everyone on the set is making a movie, but the dog is at a picnic, sniffing, peeing on the grass, called back again and again to flop down, relax. Rewarded for it, for lying there panting. The dog thinks the picnic is real. And it is real. It's real when her boyfriend is around. That's partly because he's rich. *The story of Midas is wrong,* she thinks. *The rich touch things to life. They think what they're doing is real, and so it is. They don't get stuck in the wet mud of* was. Nothing had to be over, for people like her boyfriend, teased and admired for his appetites—too many green olives at the tapas bar, too much duck breast, too many girlfriends until she came along. True, new to the city he had gotten himself involved with girls who were not as easygoing as he. But he meant no one harm and his good nature always rescued him from these episodes, adventures on the way to her.

At the thought of him, and filled with the promise of blue, early evening, she does stretches at the window. All day she has read, taken notes, typed short, courteous letters that will go out under signatures other than her own. The stack she has left to read before the honeymoon is on the scarred steamer trunk where she props her bare feet when she sits on the couch. One panel of the old chest bears a Cunard White Star label.

It was a trunk she saw in an antique store, under a table. She knelt down, bumping her head, ran her hands over it, lifted the lid and saw it was full of moldy magazines. She could hardly breathe. She bought it.

Just before that she had broken off with a man, a married man who had taken her with him to England on the *QE2*. He wasn't rich but he knew how to do things like that. He gave her books and jewelry, a big dinner ring and pearls that had been in his family and should have gone to his daughters. She knows that now, though at the time she took the heavy pearl brooch from his hand carelessly, like a piece of fruit. And the fact that the big pearls were pears, spilling from a basket of gold, didn't charm her. The intricate basketwork, the braided handle—she didn't want these things out of a drawer in his house. She wanted him. "I bet this was your mother's," she said.

"It was. She had it from her grandmother."

In a way she had won after all, shaken him to the point that although he had sworn not to, he still called her from time to time, a year and some months later, just to hear her voice. She talked to him. She could do that now. A man older than her own father would have been had he lived, tall and half bald like her handsome father.

But certainly not, as her boyfriend claims, a father figure.

She doesn't hold it against her boyfriend that he can't *judge*. Why should he be able to? That, he always says of her long affair, was a bad deal. But—this can't be explained to him, ever—the disguise in which the older man moved, of someone unapproachable, trapped in his own power, the surprise of him when he rose up and showed himself, streaming some element of his hiding place, as if other men were logs and he a crocodile, *that* had had a charm almost fatal to her. Finally she shook free of it, just in time. She met someone who could soothe her, free her from her concentration on the charming, intent, eroded personality of the man, and from his body—though athletic and graceful—so capturable by hers, so quickly made tense and still. A body marked off into distinct regions, unlike hers, that has one surface like a heavy coat of paint. The dry skin of his face so unspringing-back, almost as if you could strip off patches of it by pulling, or leave fingerprints. The thin, dark, almost transparent skin around his eyes . . . maybe she would describe the skin as like the unwound cassette tape you saw for a while, shifting along the sidewalk or caught around the base of a fire hydrant. But she wouldn't go on and on. "Thin skin, bluish," she might write if she were the editor she intends to be, striking out lines of prose.

There was a time when creases, baldness, a graying mustache were things that acted on her heart like a drawstring. Probably he was one of many men his age she saw around her now, now that her eyes were opened, men getting out of taxis, crossing lobbies, who might laughingly admit to each other that they were learning in secret, from someone like her, how to be adored.

Thus also in the manuscripts she is reading: always the possibility that such a character, while feeling himself sad, his life-ardor waning, can be startled into explosive action. Especially with a guide—a Beatrice or a Tadzio. Maybe as he strides along the sidewalk with his hands in the pockets of his overcoat his heart is pounding from the cigarettes he can't give up. Or from longing, mortally pounding. Maybe he has children who are almost grown, almost not his any more, with no interest in how wild he is inside. A crocodile, she called him. But not one of the "new" men, gratified by their ability to produce tears; no, his tears are real, his sad half-closed eye has fallen on *her*. But he won't stay long, mired in this sort of love. He'll saw the murky waters aside and swim away. Maybe the motor of his soul is idling with fast jerks, maybe he is sleepless with readiness for the new. In some scenarios he will burst out in another hemisphere, in Africa or Australia. Anything could happen to him. He may not know it. In plots of another kind, all that is needed is for someone who does know it to lay her hand on his and lead it to the new continent of herself.

These possibilities are not the same thing as a romance.

As for women: Often, the Reader says, it's simply that they're predictable. They're embarking on this or that, lowering themselves into unfamiliar waters, testing their freedom. Behind them there's always some ruin, some man has ruined everything, and then they surmount the ruin. You have to be wary of this material, now there is so much of it. It would be better if somebody gave us a devoted wife. That would be something.

So many ex-wives come streaming across her desk. So many half-crazy plotters, cast-offs, matriarchs without a household. Or the brainy tough talkers, the intuitives, the solvers of murders. Rarely, a murderer. Revenge is of other kinds. So much revenge. Most of it imagined rather than carried out.

The bookstores are filled with these women. That's the strange thing, the Reader says regretfully: They're the readers.

3

The bride's mother in blue silk. The groom's mother in a linen suit of a fawn color that doesn't agree with her skin—she knew it with certainty as she was having her hair done—and a necklace of small emeralds set in old coins, to redeem the unlucky color of the suit, because she is a doctor married to an executive, and has good jewelry, while the bride's mother is practically a street person. The bride bought her the silk dress and jacket and altered them; she got her on her feet and dried out and sober for a week, to arrive at this moment of standing with a fine tremble and a set jaw, in the grip of what is not yet dread, more an apprehension regarding the reception: whether she is going to put her lips to a glass of champagne. Whether, despite her promise to her daughter and her daughter's faith in it, she will tilt her head and swallow.

When the bride draws near on the arm of her brother, she turns opposite her mother and stops dead, swaying a little off her careful balance. This causes the brother to just miss stepping on her hem, and frown a warning that any delay could collapse the whole occasion on top of them like a tent. The bride smiles at her mother, a studied, down-turned smile of acknowledgment, like a child's stiff stage curtsy, for the guests to see. When she starts to move again the mother raises her hands to her cheeks.

In actuality she is pressing her fingers into her ears to stop their ringing, but the groom's mother beside her turns, sees the hands cupping the face in a classic maternal gesture, and smiles her agreement. She does this in spite of knowing her son said goodbye to another woman in his apartment last night.

In the pocket of his morning coat he has the squat figure of Yoda. Silly, but his mother was determined; she climbed on a chair to rummage in the *Star Wars* box in the top of his closet at home. Why should the bride be the only one to walk down the aisle knowing she had with her some invisible, unbroken tie to the past? As they got ready for bed she found the figure in her suitcase, and at her insistence they dressed and took a cab back over to his apartment quite late, without calling. When he came to the door there was a woman behind him sliding into the bedroom, tossing dark hair forward over streaky, made-up eyes and red lipstick. In the middle of his living room was a black suitcase with everything tumbled out around it, cosmetics strewn under the coffee table, a bra caught on the chair arm along with the cord of a hair dryer, clothes in a heap on the rug, as if somebody had hurled the suitcase at the table or gone at it with an ax.

But it's too late to make anything of that, to question her son or help him extricate himself from either thing. His mother has poured out the last of what she can pour into him. When she first saw him with his best man rather grim beside him this morning, he was pale and tired; she herself is tired and wondering if anyone marrying anywhere in the world during this particular hour could possibly see the thing through to a day like this, a child's wedding, thirty years down the road.

Her husband's glasses are foggy. She takes his hand. Few at the company he owns are among the guests today or have ever seen this side of him, with cold hands and sweating nose. It's too late for either one of them to finish all they were intending with this son, their only child. Although they have not put it into words between them, they see him as hopelessly distractible, already swept away by the intrigues of his accidental job at a magazine—after so many applications to business school and medical school—and having no time for hard work, or for friends or sports or anything much other than the woman of the moment.

Was there something they did that made him turn out this way? Heaven help this girl he's marrying, pretty as she is. Is she pregnant? How nice she is, despite her one-upping of some of them at the table last night about this article or that book, despite those officious brothers— or one of them officious and the other withdrawn—at the rehearsal and the dinner, and the wives trying to pretend they're on good terms with the poor mother who didn't seem to know them apart. For the groom's mother knows, from her son—who is in the flush of an explorer's admiration for this brisk, unsuspicious girl with her brains and her ideals, an admiration his mother worries would be subtly altered by the absence of thick yellow hair twisted up on the head in a chaste braid, long waist, breasts verging on heavy—that the bride's brothers have repudiated their mother. Or one of them has and the other just follows along. They don't have anything to do with her. One of them has her power of attorney, she couldn't be trusted with a check if she had one to endorse; the other pays the rent on the room she has at the moment and is lucky to have—without it she would be little more than a street drunk—in a boardinghouse in Baltimore. A hole, the groom calls it, though he never saw it, or met the mother before this week, having stayed behind when his bride-to-be flew down to Baltimore to bring her back for the wedding.

Out of the hole into this hotel, old and fine, with its pleasing sconces and buttery sheets. The sons have seen to it that she move into a better hotel than the one their sister had been able to afford for her. Now she's staying in the one where the wedding and reception are to be held. Her sons are uptown in yet another, with their wives, having left all the children at home.

She ate her costly breakfast in the coffee shop. The groom's parents too are in the wedding hotel, but they didn't come into the coffee shop for breakfast. She didn't want to think they might have been instead having breakfast with their son and her daughter, who announced last night that they didn't believe in the prohibition on seeing each other before the wedding, and would meet in the morning. "Not tonight. Tonight we need our sleep," her daughter said.

They have dispensed with some of the wedding rituals. The reception is going to be free-form, but for the ceremony itself they've kept traditional music—a keyboard with an amp for the organ tones of the recessional—and language, phrases such as *Dearly beloved* and *keep thee only unto her*, which they would never, the bride said sternly, attempt to improve upon. For after all, as she argued to her boyfriend, whatever state her mother was in now, she had been the model for "till death us do part." And they would not get into composing any special vows to close loopholes or leave them open, whichever, the bride said with a laugh.

The old, the new, the borrowed: these she has gathered. Her mother was to provide the blue. Instead of a blue garter she brought a blue glass bead from a broken necklace, a gift of her husband, a bead she had carried in the pocket of whatever coat she owned from the time her daughter was a baby, so that now it was rough and almost colorless, as if salt had etched it. "I can't believe you still have this! I used to go in your pocket after it and put it in my mouth! I loved to feel the little nick, see? But of course now little kids can't have anything this small, they could choke." Some of her friends already had children; the rules they lived by frightened the Reader a little even as she saw them as perfectly correct. They were what awaited her but did not yet have to be concentrated on. "Oh, but where will I put a bead?" Miraculously, the maid of honor knew that some wedding dresses had a tiny flat pocket, sewn into a seam somewhere or hanging on a silk cord for just that purpose, the storing of some talisman, and this one did, inside where the gores of the heavy skirt swung open.

Tomorrow before the airport taxi comes, the mother thinks, *I might just disappear.* Her younger son has slipped her an envelope and she has enough cash. She could take the train to Baltimore. It wouldn't have to be the fast one. She could make the trip last hours and hours, among the snores and smelly socks, sleeping or just looking out the window. Stay out of the club car. Get off in Philadelphia for air, and board another train later. Wander in that off-the-train daze in which for minutes, to the eye, even the marble walls of stations creep faintly, like the near land out the train window moving at a different rate from the far. What would she do in Philadelphia? Walk, look around her. Everything in cities was changing for the better, the maid of honor on her right had told her at the rehearsal. She was the best friend, who had a job in the mayor's office. Is everything changing? The mother has a TV to keep her informed but the changes are far away from her room, her path to the mini-mart.

It would be good to be carried along tracks, instead of miles in the air with the destination rising up from below to stop her dead. She likes feeling herself pulled slowly away from where she has been, and all the steps of postponement.

The last time she took the train was six or seven years ago, to stay with her older sister in Baltimore. It was when she was first alone. Her daughter had left for school. A daughter, her sister warned her, had to get out. She had to go to college; she couldn't stay behind to manage for her mother. A daughter had to leave off being the steady little girl with an eye out for everything and everybody, steering her mother through the days into the blind evenings. This sister had stepped forward with an unexpected determination to get her straightened out, and she had agreed to it. It was something to try.

For a while, at her worst, after the quickly ruined time with her sister and before her sons stepped in, she shared a place not far from the station in Baltimore with two women whose names she doesn't like to remember, nor their red faces squashed in sleep, who tried to convince her to pack up and hop on a freight with them when spring came. They might know the switchman, but what did they know about her? She was still major steps away from that.

4

Stately as the deep organ chords issuing from the keyboard, a little prow comes forward against her breastbone, or it may be the bone itself pressing there as she is borne to the heights of tenderness for her daughter. It doesn't matter that two men, her sons, are in the row behind, with wives beside them who had been carefully seated too far down the row of wineglasses at the rehearsal dinner to make themselves heard if they spoke to her. It doesn't matter that in their wallets are pictures of children who have not been told of her, and better so.

Next she is escorted under the arbor of woven ferns and ribbon and led down the wide hall to the reception, the groom's mother following on her usher's arm with clear taps of her beautiful fawn pumps, not quite catching up. They are the first to arrive in the big echoing room; the bridal pair are behind a door in a private space where newlyweds can spend a few minutes getting their bearings before the reception. At the far end are waiters, with a forest of green bottles and the cake.

A tall man stands apart from them at the long table laden with candles and real autumn leaves, banked platters and swirled fabric, red and gold. Instead of greeting them when they came in, he turned his back. He may be the wedding consultant, passing a hand over his bald scalp as he scans the table.

The guests will serve themselves and find tables of their own choosing. The real planner of the whole thing was the maid of honor, her daughter's best friend, who works for the mayor. It was to be a little like a church supper in the bride's hometown in West Virginia, she declared. But a sophisticated church supper, with wonderful food. This girl could imagine her way into a bride's intentions better than any hotel wedding consultant. Everyone agreed she should start her own business.

"Ohhh . . . ," the mother had heard herself groan from the velvet couch in the bride's dressing room. "Oh, I didn't pay for anything." What a ridiculous thing to say, in anguish or surprise, to the daughter who came for her and flew her here and groomed her like a child, and got her dressed and pinned jewelry onto her.

"Don't worry about that," her daughter said quickly. "You're here." Then her daughter pulled her close against the big white rustling dress and hugged her as if she were a little thing with stage fright.

She knows the bride and groom are to enter and greet everybody and then give the band a sign and just dance out onto the empty floor. There is not to be a receiving line; why should anyone "receive" anyone else? her daughter had said, over the groom's mild protest. It was exactly that, his assuming certain obligations could be laughed at but would be met, that got the best friend going with her changes.

A receiving line seems to be forming up anyway, with the bride and groom trying to present to his parents various young women in black dresses with thin straps. Then the lights go down and the bridal pair starts the inaugural waltz, in which they are to dance until some signal allows a tide of couples to rise around them. Alone on the floor they dance slowly and beautifully. She is proud of her daughter's dancing. On the porch of the house by the river, she had been the teacher, dancing with a thirteen-year-old stiff with grief, as she had danced with her husband in the evenings in summer before he was sick, with the record player lifted through the window and lightning bugs in the hedge, up and down the pine boards they had stripped and varnished themselves, around the corner and back, laughing and carrying on while the boys, joining in, jumped on and off the glider, bouncing the needle on the record, and the baby girl tried to climb up after them. Tipsy parents—waving to the neighbors. Tipsy, that unknowing pair, yes, but not drunk. There was no need to be drunk.

Over by the bandstand she can see her second son, the shyer, less successful one who pays her rent, but he's looking at the band and listening carefully to something his wife is saying. He's a big man, tall, but not handsome like his father; he has a disappointed, fallen face. She thinks, *I did favor your brother, just like you said. I did. I'm sorry. I'm sorry, but he was so much ours. The first. I didn't know. I didn't know anything that could happen.*

Finally after a long time during which she can see only the bountiful rafts of stemmed glasses sliding among the shoulders—for they are not going to hoard the champagne for toasting, they are going to drink champagne all night—a few couples venture onto the floor and step carefully into each other's arms, and begin to rock slowly and move their feet in small squares, with concentrating smiles. As she watches them she feels a familiar sinking that means she needs a drink immediately. She will have to leave. Now. She's trying to retreat, but slowly, feeling behind her with one hand as if she's already had a few too many, or backed into one of the dreams she used to have, when each slow step led a few more inches back from some cliff or animal. She is suddenly so played-out and heavy in the arms and legs that she thinks she might actually have to go to her room and fall down and sleep.

She plays with the idea. She thinks, *Then if I wake up it'll be morning and I'll hear the river. I'll wake the kids. I won't have this life on my hands.* But of course she's playing a game, a game of tempting herself. She knows she wouldn't wake up in her old house but she thinks in stubbornness and perplexity, *If I can't I'll die.*

But someone is asking her to dance. It's the tall, thin man, the wedding consultant. He crossed the room to her, shook hands, told her a name like Rodney or Sidney. He must have identified her as a member of the bridal party because of her gardenia, and seen that no one has spoken for her. Perhaps that is his function.

She has not danced in years. When she gets out on the floor with him she is surprised at her memory of it, the alert that runs through her forgotten muscles. Some of that might be the man's doing. But here are her limbs stretching themselves, giving up some of their weight. In one of the smooth turns he executes, something catches, attaching her to his dark suit. At first it seems to be the corsage pin, but then she sees it's the other lapel, it's the brooch, her daughter's gift. Her daughter insisted that she take it, wear it, a big thick cluster of pearls in a setting the shape of a vase or basket with handles. "Lands," she says, "my daughter gave me this pin and it catches on everything."

He holds her away to look. The bruised eyes don't match his elegance. They seem to mock something, whether himself or her she can't tell. He says, "Looks like a loose prong. My mother wore one of those, and it was always getting her into trouble." Then, so as not to place her in his mother's generation—for he is roughly her own age—he says, "And now they're all the rage again."

She decides he's not the wedding consultant after all. "Which side are you on?" she says.

"Which side . . . oh, the bride's. I had the pleasure of working with her at one time." The tray of champagne is tilting their way. He dances her away from it, bracing her firmly as his steps lengthen. The brooch catches again. "Uh-oh. Here." He pauses, and one hand secures her back as two long fingers of the other press her collarbone, lightly, while with the others he bends a tiny wire in the setting.

She is flushed from the exertion and from having to arch backwards because of his height, and stick with the conversation and keep her balance in a sequence that began simply but has grown more unpredictable as he feels her follow him. They start again, whirling a path through the crowd. "My daughter says it's junk, but I don't know, these don't look like any pearls I ever saw, they could be real."

"I wouldn't be surprised. Are you going to sell it?" he asks in a friendly way.

She almost trips. "Why do you ask me that?"

"Forgive me, I'm thoughtless, I was joking." But he isn't a smiler. He has her close, where without her glasses she can't really see him. He seems to steer her with something small, maybe the wristbone. "I must be carried away, dancing with the mother of the bride."

"How do you know? You weren't at the wedding."

"I wasn't?"

"You were here in this room when we got here."

"Well, I'll confess. I said to myself, *The prettiest dress. Eyes bluer than the bride's.* And I heard you speak to Mr. Weller there, the young groom, and I thought to myself—*Voilà! West Virginia!*"

"Well, what about you? You're just as bad. You're not from here, you're from down south."

"So I am." With his mustache and sad eyes he could have been another of those soft-spoken Southerners you ran into in boarding-houses, always polite, showing you some pocket watch or worn-out leather book they carried around. He could have been, if you didn't notice the halfway-mean pride that belonged to certain males looking to tease you into something—she was surprised to recognize it—and a kind of barely-held-onto patience.

He spins her into the center of the parquet floor, three times, so that she lies this way and that like a dress displayed on an arm. "What took you from West Virginia to Baltimore?"

"Things happened," she says, trying not to show that the burst of energy is deserting her and she is losing her breath. "I had enough of the place. My sister—how do you know where I live?"

With both arms he holds her in, against the strong outward pull of his wide steps in the turn. "I suppose I know everything about you," he says.

"I guess my daughter turned into a talker." Out of the corner of her eye she keeps seeing the white dress of her daughter, wide skirts sloshing up and back. Even in this first dance, the dance to complete the wedding and start the new, married life, her daughter is keeping an eye on her.

"No."

"She worked for you."

"Yes, she did."

She tries to lean back to look at him, but with his forearm along her back and fingers to her ribs he keeps her where she is. By now she needs her breath and doesn't try to speak.

Her ears are ringing so that she can't hear much more than the big double bass thumping. That, she could feel even if she went deaf. The man seems calmly, even selfishly, attached to the idea of circling the dance floor with her for the length of this waltz, so long-drawn-out that other couples have finally started to fall back and gather at the round tables with their champagne.

"Well," she says, raising her voice to be heard as they whirl to the bandstand, where the mute on the saxophone is opening and closing, "you never know." She repeats it with each fluid triangle their twinned feet describe on the smooth wood. "You never know." The dulled feeling has moved off again and she's really dancing, breathing heavily but with ease. A wind has stirred up around them, holding the other dancers at bay. Even in stiff new shoes her feet move as if a current flowed under them, or from them, swaying her this way and that with little need for effort on her part. "You never—never—know."

"That's right. My, my. I thought so. You must have been born dancing."

She is getting used to his unsmiling gallantry. She is past making the effort to smile herself. There is a pleasure foreign to smiles, coming out of nowhere and going again, just as there is the opposite, for which tears are just decorations. With closed eyes she says, "As a matter of fact I was."

•

AS SOON AS SHE COULD, she left the ballroom purposefully, holding the slim black satin bag, her daughter's, with both hands like a dowsing stick. She looked over the brass rail of the mezzanine down into the lobby where a boy of nine or ten was waiting for the elevator, repeatedly jabbing the button. He kept his back to her; he had a thin neck tanned amber pink, with a small cloud of bone coming and going just above the neckline of his sweatshirt. She played a game that if he turned around she would see the fixed eyes of her first child, the one who had just taken his sister up the aisle. He thought he had escaped her but he hadn't. No, he had returned to her long since, un-grown, gazing over fat cheeks like a judge, or kicking with imperial joy, a baby again, on whom everybody stopped to congratulate them, tall husband, blond wife, and sturdy golden baby, because of the seal on the three of them of his having been born at the earliest height of love.

She herself is steady for the moment. She has made it through the wedding, she has danced, at the edge of the floor a man has placed her hand in her daughter's, bowing. Her daughter has caught her in her arms and whispered, "My Meery." Nothing so tender as this old nickname made out of her name by her daughter as a toddler, whispered on a soft breath that warmed her ear, has been said to her since an AA meeting years ago, back at home. Three or four years after her husband died—or it might have been five—she was feeling the stirrings of a deep terror. Her daughter was applying to college. A seedy old guy was looking at her, on the bleachers in the high school gym where she and a dozen others made their confessions. Of course some of them might recognize each other, even though the meetings took place in a bigger town across the county line. He said, "I seen you and your hubby a few times dancing at the lounge." They weren't supposed to allude to any possible connections they might have. "I told my wife, I had my wife then, I said, 'That's a sweet gal.' She said, 'Yes she is, and I know you wish we was all like that.'"

For that little space the tension had left her. She remembered that, leaning back until the knees of the person behind her on the bleachers cradled her for a second, and saying something like, "Oh, right, that's all we need. More like me. More drunks."

"Just hear what I say," the old fellow said. He was on his last legs. He had years and years on her, in the life she would have if she wasn't careful.

A cloud of gardenia encloses her face as she looks down at the boy until the elevator comes and he gets in. She stays with her hands on the rail, glancing neither left nor right as people come in and out of the reception hall. Her eyes, in which her daughter has put soothing drops, blaze the blue of her dress, her feet clench in the new shoes, she vows, as at her own wedding, eternal beginning.

Choice in Dreams

Molly was hoping to have a dream in which she didn't disgrace herself, in which she got to be an innocent tourist. There would have been solace in seeing her parents alive again, in one of those dreams that accept grief as a kind of heavy, immovable scenery but scour it of the peeling paints, leaving the sweet bare wood. Or she would have liked to ride a horse, as she had done effortlessly in childhood dreams. Or to see her beloved high school boyfriend and tell him she'd changed her mind, she didn't have to stay a virgin after all.

So many choices in dreams. But instead of seeing her parents or riding a horse, she dreamed the usual dream, the one saturated in shock, relief, delight, and shame. In the dream, she did what she had only dreamed of. In abandon and selfish joy, thinking all the while *At last!*— she did disgrace herself. She dreamed of Mike O'Meara.

Awake, she turned over and pressed against her husband's back, as if he might have looked in through the window of his own sleep at her acts with Mike.

Why dream of someone else's husband? A man whose wife dragged him out of bed on workdays because he couldn't get up, he was hung over. A man who couldn't fix the washer in a faucet, and left his towel on the good bedroom furniture in their run-down house, pieces that had belonged to his wife Alice's grandmother, because Alice came from a prominent family in their city, from one of the hilltop mansions of the philanthropic Catholic garrison, and Mike, a Catholic of a different sort, had carried her off. A man now bald, with legs atremble from chemo and radiation. A dead man. Is this a choice one would sensibly make, even in a dream?

On the positive side, a man who adored children, who could give you the hour of birth and the distinctive biography of each of his five kids. A man who made his living writing about crime, and had been seen to shed tears in the morgue. A man who put his arm around his wife when she was telling the story of how they had to get married when she got pregnant, a man who said, "Thank God things used to be that way," and whose oldest, smiling son stood up at the table and took a bow. A man who went out on his own and bought his wife a garnet necklace he could not afford, because she loved red and all she had left, she said, was a good neck.

MOLLY AND JEFF GOT TO know Mike O'Meara when he was dying. Jeff knew him for some time before Molly ever met him, because he showed up one day at the hospital to interview Jeff for an article about a corpse, and they liked each other. Jeff was a pathologist and Mike needed anatomical details. They got along so well that Mike took to stopping by the path lab whenever he felt like it.

Eventually they took such a shine to each other that they made a plan to meet for dinner with their wives, and then the friendship of years—the five Mike had left to live—began. He got his diagnosis soon after that first dinner, so almost all the time Molly was in love with him his death was on the way. She says *almost all the time* to herself because he seemed perfectly healthy the night they all crowded together into a booth and raised their glasses.

This was the period when food was first being served in a mound. Even in bars—they were in Mike's favorite bar—a plate arrived like a bed piled with coats. If you ordered fish, you would have to go in with a fork tine and give a tug, disrupting the mashed potato in ruffs of chard, with slices of seared tuna forming praying hands on top. Jeff said it helped to be a pathologist. Alice was the first to plunge in and dismantle her pile, as Molly, laughing, picked up her fork without a thought and looked directly at Alice's husband for the first time since they had sat down. All she had noticed as he slid into the booth and shook her hand were stooped shoulders and dark mussed hair, like his wife's.

At what exact point did she put down her wineglass and feel a flowing engagement with all that was going on in the bar, downstairs in the street, and beyond that on the waters of the Sound where ferries were passing with their lit windows, because she was looking at Mike O'Meara?

A few weeks later, Mike served out the first of Alice's casseroles with a big silver spoon that had belonged to her grandmother, and they began on their friendship. At the O'Meara table everybody interrupted and spilled things and sopped them up with the grandmother's linen napkins, and tilted back in the rickety chairs to laugh, distracted from whatever Alice was serving by the talk about crime and politics and religion, spun out of Mike's pronouncements and backed up by Alice's facts, and distracted too by each other—the three boys and two girls, the youngest already half grown, allowed from their earliest years to stay up late and shout their own opinions, or when they were older, to state them quietly with the irony of those newly back from college. And wine—Mike had to have a lot of wine, and Alice let him have it because she couldn't stop him and she wasn't one to fasten her hopes on somebody else's improvement.

Alice was a woman, Molly saw right away, in whose presence people including herself felt themselves amiable and worthy, at their best. Perhaps because of having been reared as she had been, in a kind of material and religious Oz, as Mike described it, and without seeming to will the condition on herself, Alice lived in a state of approval. She had known Mike since they were first graders at Saint Joseph's School. "She was the good girl," he said. He looked at Molly. "I bet you were the good girl too."

"I was," Molly said. "But not any more." They all laughed, Jeff threw his arm in front of her to restrain her, and for a moment she was safe inside the tent of marriage.

In the ninth grade, at a retreat in honor of the Blessed Virgin, Mike had handed Alice a joint and she had taken a deep drag.

"That did it," he said. "I was in love."

"In love," Alice said with a sigh. "I was the one. I was the proverbial slave. I had a lot of penance to do. They had me pray for him. Wasn't that smart?"

"And then the families got involved," Mike said. "I was too good for her."

Mike had not gone off to college when Alice did; he had skipped up a ladder of city jobs into the police department, where his way with witnesses and his regard for details worked themselves into his file and landed him in Homicide. But he lost heart for the work. He knew something about crime, and because he could write, they took him on at the newspaper. You could do that then, hire on with promises instead of credentials.

Even though eventually he wrote a syndicated column on crime, and appeared every so often on TV, few people in town would have recognized Mike or known where to find him if they had something to say about a crime. He wasn't at the paper, he was out and around, in courtrooms and jails and morgues. And bars, of course; he had a lot of drinking to do in the course of a day.

Molly had seen the danger in liking Alice too much, but it was too late for that; in no time she and Alice were in and out of each other's houses and Molly was reading through the youngest girl's poems because she, Molly, had once published poems in magazines—though sometimes the four of them did not get together for months. As couples, they had the kind of friendship in which regularity and obligation were kept at bay. Jeff was always saying what good friends that made them.

"That may be what men look for in friendship," Alice said. "Us girls want a commitment: Call me every day or else." How could anyone harm Alice?

ONE NIGHT MIKE MENTIONED IN passing that he was being treated for a disease. He had a lymphoma, a mild one. Hardly breathing, Molly looked at Alice. "They think it's the kind that can be relatively benign," Alice said after she took a drink of her beer. But if it was that kind, Jeff said when they got home, it didn't sound as if it was taking a benign course in Mike's case.

Five years went by. In some of them Molly was able to put Mike out of her mind for days at a time. In others it seemed she stood for half the year with her hand on the phone. *It's Molly. I have something to tell you.* Of course he would answer sometimes, when she called Alice. At those times her own voice surprised her, greeting him with normal concern, asking questions about the chemo, the steroids, the possible dietary measures. Of course she saw him. He was getting sicker. She began to let her thoughts of him take her where they would. As for dreams, she no longer hoped for them. She would have kept him out of them if she could, because as often as not the man finally drawing her to him was breathless and thin, the chest like an egg carton when she finally lay against it.

In real life he was not yet that bad. This condition of his did not appear to worry him. Early in chemo his hair fell out. His daughters gave him a cashmere ski cap, which he wore a time or two until they went back to school. "Half the men we know are bald," Alice said. Nevertheless, Molly had a recurring dream of holding him, comforting him, enclosing his scalp in her hands.

His eyebrows and lashes did not fall out. Gradually his cheeks sank in an unpleasant way, though, high up under the cheekbone where it didn't look like the normal hollowing you might acquire in middle age if you went on a diet, but like an excavation, as if tissue might have been siphoned out. Molly knew his face so well by then that she knew where every cell belonged, and she was seeing them change, shift, vanish. She wanted to ask Alice how she could stand it. Of course Alice was watching. Then he was on steroids, and when his cheeks filled out the strange little hollows were still there, like thumbprints in dough.

ONE DAY THE DOORBELL RANG. When she opened the door, with the chime still hanging in the air, there he was. "Come in," she said after a second. He walked in unsteadily—nobody knew any more which caused the gait, illness or liquor—and sat down at the kitchen table. He asked if Jeff was there, but of course Jeff was at work, it was daytime. Like many people who work on their own—like Molly, in fact—even without alcohol Mike often forgot whether it was the weekend or not and where people were who did go to the office. It wasn't that he didn't work hard. He was always on the track of somebody who could put him on the track of something before his deadline, and his big eyes, too big for a man really, almost in a class with Peter Lorre's eyes, were always searching down a street or around a room or over the planes of a face. If it was your face, those eyes were a snare. They were the famished, dreaming organs you see on posters of ragged children. They had down-sweeping lashes, black and thick, that acted on Molly the way the forest in a cartoon draws the scared kids in on tiptoe. Her body followed her eyes, her mind swayed, she stepped closer. Even a man—Jeff, for example, ordinarily a man of few words—would talk more freely, and in a more fervent way, with Mike as his listener.

"You've never had a friend like this," Molly said to him.

"He comes down there, he finds me," Jeff said humbly. Jeff was well liked, but nobody much hung out in the path lab or saw a lot of him. But Mike would get him out of the basement and make him eat lunch. "Drinks his lunch," Jeff said. "I keep warning him. But you can't tell him. He drinks because of the things he deals with." Molly had never heard Jeff, who kept at a remove the worst of life that he himself dealt with, plated out on glass and magnified, make a psychological assessment of another man.

"Why deal with those things?" she said, clinging shamelessly to the subject.

Jeff said, "Fate. Fate put him there. Look at the guy. His whole life. What's he going to do? No money for school, smart." Another first for Jeff, generalizing about another's life. Usually he stuck with facts. In that way he resembled Alice, who read every page of the newspaper and knew what was happening in the world without any wish to remake it in her own words. "The guy should be teaching. When he's done with chemo I'm getting him in to talk to the students. Why not? They all watch TV, they all want to do forensics. Smartest guy I know." People said that all the time, because Mike had not gone to college.

Jeff could say that.

Molly could say, "Did you see his column today?" And so on. Nothing more. She couldn't say, *What is it? What has happened to me?*

Not for years could she ask anybody for confirmation of Mike's effect. Finally she brought it up with her friend Rita, who had known him. Even then Molly couldn't say anything about how she had felt. And what Rita said . . . but that came later.

On the day he came to her house Mike said, "Are you really busy?"

Molly had been working at the computer but she said no. She said it several times. He said, "I've just seen something terrible. I don't even want to think about it."

She knew this must be the child everybody had been looking for. A six-year-old boy. They already had the man who had been seen with him. It had been in the paper for days, as helicopters circled above the woods of Seward Park.

Mike closed his eyes and made a tent over his forehead with his hands, as if he and Molly were sitting in the sun, and for a minute the eyelashes slept on the skin of his cheeks and drove all thought of what he might have seen from her mind. She supposed if he had been her husband she would have gotten used to the sight and maybe even been mildly irritated by it, as we sometimes are by a thing that once bewitched us.

Right away she thought he must have come from the morgue. Alice had told her his visits to the morgue figured in his drinking.

"I wish I could talk to Jeff," he said as Molly poured coffee. His eyes had opened. He shook himself like a dog.

She could have said, "Why didn't you go to the lab if you want to talk to Jeff?"

He and Jeff had a little contest as to which one had seen worse sights, though by then Jeff was out of the county hospital, where gruesome events from the newspaper drew to a close in the cold rooms of Pathology; he was back at the university and spending most of his time looking at slides.

"Do you want to call him from here?"

"No . . . no." He swirled his coffee. "This was a kid. I can't mention this to Alice."

Oh? How come you can mention it to me? But she leaned forward sympathetically and cupped her mug in her hands. His attention swiveled down to her hands. She saw it. His mind would narrow like that.

In a low, despairing voice he said, "Your hands . . . they're nice, they're . . ." She set the mug down. He took hold of her hands. He folded the fingers in to make fists, and raised the fists to his face and ground them into his eyes. A solemn shock ran through her, as if a comb had been dragged through her body.

All the blood had run out of her brain and into the skin and muscles of her hands, which were like invalids given up to a drug, and at the same time she had a marvelous clarity of thought, of almost disinterested pity for him. But that was quickly replaced by the familiar dazed longing. It seemed to her that he must know, having forced her hands to be the envoys of the secret, and yet something told her not to move, because assuredly he did not know, and would not want to know. When he stopped grinding her knuckles into his eyes and let go of her hands, it would shock him, she knew, if she spread them on either side of his head and pulled him across the table to her. No, he was like an animal that had come up to her in the wild, trustingly, and she had to be still.

"That's not really what I came about. There's something else I need to talk to you about," he said, still in the despairing voice. "Because of Alice." What was coming? She had to steady herself, try not to let her chest display the speed and shallowness of her breathing.

What is love? What is it? What is it? How can it be what it seems to be, nothing? A vacancy, an invisibility, a configuration of the mind. But with a weight, perceptible to the body. And a married woman with a husband she loved and liked, caught under the weight, unable to breathe? And it wasn't even a *person* for whom she felt this nothing, this love, not a personality, a self, a man who drank too much and wrote for the newspaper and had five kids, but the face and eyes of a *being* of some kind who lived in the body and looked out of the eyes of Mike O'Meara. A being from an earlier life trapped in the layers of this one. Or a primitive version of a human being, say a Pleistocene man off the northern grassy plain, looking for the first time into the eyes of a rough creature on the same plain, herself.

It wasn't even that she wanted all that intensely to go to bed with him. Or it wasn't primarily that—though she knew a lot of people would have said so. "Lust," Alice herself would have said in a minute, hearing of these symptoms.

She wanted to see him. Just that. Year after year she had remembered and rehearsed and desired the sight of Mike O'Meara more than the sight of Jeff or her children or her dead mother or anyone else. She had wanted to know she would see him and for as long as possible each time and with some promise that he would come back so that she could see him again. It was a primitive feeling without very much of herself in it, like the wish to get warmer when you're cold.

She had other friends, who, if she had called them and wailed out what was happening to her, would have kindly said, "You pity him. He's dying."

"Tell me," Molly said to him. But again the doorbell rang.

It was Alice, at the door. "Hello, Molly," she said. Her voice was that of a school principal who stands up by degrees and comes out from behind a desk. "I'm surprised." She walked in. "I'm surprised."

Mike was coming out of the kitchen. "Hi," he said to Alice with a benign tiredness.

"Hi, I saw the car," Alice said, looking no different from the way she always looked, with her rosy cheeks and thick half-combed hair and her chin tucked into her neck in a motherly way. She had on her red necklace; her fingers were touching it. She didn't look angry. "I just didn't know *where* you'd be. *Who*."

"Don't tell me you think I'm here with Molly." Mike sat down heavily on the bench in Molly's hall. Alice didn't answer, she just stood there. Molly can still hear what he said next. "Don't tell me you think that," he said. "It's not Molly."

"Sorry," Alice said, without looking at Molly. It was not like Alice to leave off the *I'm*.

It wasn't very long after that that Mike began to go downhill fast. He had to go for outpatient transfusions. Molly was one of those Alice invited to drive him and sit with him while the blood dripped in.

AFTER THE FUNERAL THERE WAS a long period when Molly contrived to have his name come up. Her friend Rita, who was a reporter at the paper, said, "O'Meara. Jeez, the poor guy. Something about him. He had that way. He never acted on it. Whoa, don't get me wrong. But he was always kinda playing. Those eyes. I know a couple of women who—"

"Oh, don't tell me that. Don't tell me that, Rita."

"Don't speak ill of the dead?"

"I don't mean that. I just don't want to know who. Who?"

"I think Marian. Yeah. She taught their kids. And Cathy Daley at the paper. They were always flirting around. She actually tried to get him to meet her someplace. He didn't, of course. He never would have."

Molly had never seen Mike flirt with anyone. Never. Was there a world for each pair of eyes? Like a private screening for each person, and yours was tailored to you?

She tried to ask Alice about this, delicately. Maybe the woman was just a fling. Obviously his heart was still with his family. Was he a man who had flings? "No," Alice told her. "No. That, he would never do. This was serious. He was in love. He thought we could separate, for God's sake. He was trying to figure it all out. Whether I could take it. That's probably the worst thing he said. 'You can bear it, can't you, you're so strong.' He was in love. He could barely walk at that point, his counts were so low, and he was talking about *getting an apartment.*"

"Oh, Alice."

"To be with her."

"Oh God."

"I know. I know. But he didn't get to, did he?"

"No."

"He never got to. And I have to think it was because of her, because she wouldn't. And I never knew who it was. It was a freak thing. Oh, he had his deal, with women. That was just his way. But you know him, Molly. You know how he was, about his family. But one day . . . he said he just looked up one day and there she was."

"Oh God."

"It was love. He couldn't think about anything else. She was younger than we are, of course. But she broke up with him at one point. When she told him she wouldn't see him any more he said that was like what he sometimes felt in the morgue. He would tell me these things. If he saw something unbearable in the morgue, his legs started to hurt. So I knew I had to let him. Oh, first I said, 'Maybe your legs hurt because of the lymphoma.'"

"Oh, Alice. His legs hurt. You thought it was me."

"Only that one day. Unbelievable. Sorry. I used to ask myself whether it was this person or that person, how young she was—I never could ask him her exact age—was she some friend of the girls'—but she was too sad-sounding to be all that young, she wasn't so ruthless, was she, or wouldn't she have gone off with him? Or whether she was somebody I saw in the grocery store, or at church. He liked Catholic women, you know, they were the kind he really liked because of filling the time at Mass when he was a kid, lusting over all those kneeling legs. But of course he didn't go to Mass now, so how would he have met them? Molly—" She gave Molly a wolfish glare. "You would tell me if you knew, wouldn't you?"

Jeff said the same thing to her. "You must have known who it was. Women always know." He was angry at Mike; he wanted to have been told. He was Mike's best friend. "Think she came to the funeral?" But at the funeral, only Alice was watching. None of this was spoken of before he died.

Alice never apologized for saying "I'm surprised" to Molly, in her front hall. That one "Sorry" was for having even dreamed it could be her.

Molly got through the funeral. As a friend, she could be forgiven a choked sound when the priest said, "Receive our brother Michael." Alice held herself together, though she gave a little laughing moan a couple of times when they were all eating and drinking afterwards, and let tears run down her cheeks without wiping them. But she didn't stutter or gasp or double over; she hugged her friends; when she wasn't doing that she kept her arm around whichever of their children was near, or held on to Molly.

And who was she, the one Mike chose? Who leans on the car door when the thought of him stabs her, who loses her cart in the grocery store? Who lets out a groan in the shower? Who can't go into the part of the cemetery where he is buried, in case his family, his friends have come to visit the grave?

They would not despise her. Why will she not make herself known to them? Why won't she answer to them, Alice, and Jeff, and Molly?

Trespass

Stark Bonney was listening to a patient's heart when the woman took his hand in hers and placed it, stethoscope still in the palm, on her breast. He would have said he drew back, as a doctor accustomed to the occasional inappropriate comment or gesture from a patient, though in fact his hand stayed where it was. She took the other hand, placed it.

"Three times I have come here." The scope was still in his ears, the voice in it muffled and rather deep. The breasts seemed at the bursting point. "The orange aura that you have, I see it." She had some kind of foreign accent with a relaxed, insolent sound in it. "From one time to the next I wonder if you recognize me? Why do you think I am here?" She let go of his hands.

Of course he recognized her. "We're looking into your heart block," he said, holding her now by the waist. "By itself, it's nothing."

"No, no. Because of you. I am not Mrs. So-and-so like you call me. My name is Katya. You said that you were going to take care of me. That is what I want you to do."

A long stormy affair followed, interrupted by her death.

KATYA HAD BEEN A VIOLINIST. But she was not good enough, she said, to play with any of the ensembles for which she periodically auditioned, so she worked in a bank. She was good with numbers; numbers and music went together. "I play too much," she said. "Not the violin. That, I do not." And in truth he rarely heard her practice, though he had heard her cry in the locked bathroom after one of these auditions. "No, I play, you know, in life. I am not serious. Though I love most of all the serious musician. I am always dreaming about this one with the violin, this one with the cello." From the start, she could hurt him. "Oh, you must not worry. A serious doctor—that is the same thing. I adore him, with his blue eyes"—she kissed his eyelids—"his clean skin."

He went into the bank, not his own bank, to see her behind her window in her loud silk and tight leather, her streaked hair pulled back from the small, carved face. "What do you do all day when nobody comes in?" Because everybody used the ATMs now.

"I talk to the guard. This man is very sad. Not a good American. I gaze out to sea."

In Russia she had been a child of promise, taken from her village to school in Moscow, set apart for the study of the violin. But the collapse of the Soviet Union left her with no sponsor, no clear course to follow. She had no parents. Her mother had died in her thirties of an undetermined ailment, her father, "my beloved," in the war the Soviets waged in Afghanistan. At ten, she and a friend lived and worked with the cook at their school; after the cook caught them taking rubles from her tin, they lived in a man's office and in a downhill series of hideouts. The list shifted with each telling. "Don't ask me this! We fell through the cracks. As you say." She laughed. "Cracks! You know nothing." At sixteen, she came to the U.S. with a man three times her age, and quite soon she had left him, but of course, she said with comic despair, he was still on her doorstep. Still plying his Katka with gifts. "Katka": in Russian that meant someone more . . . more fun than "Katya." The gifts she threw into a drawer, where even Stark could recognize the touch of a pawnbroker— engraved spoons, medals from the Napoleonic campaigns, lacquered brooches, old pendants of amber.

After two years of a dizzying rhythm of jealousy and reconciliation, Stark had arrived at a new stage with her, in which the baring of reasons for their trespasses against each other went on in a kind of calm. His, now, were merely rote flirtation, undertaken more to retaliate than for any interest another woman could have for him; hers had more weight: confessed cravings, late-night phone calls, disappearances. He was out-done in what his ex-wife had called his "ways." Now he had no ways, only the relics of an old habit.

"I have good luck," Katya would say, on a day when she was soothing him. "Women look at him, this doctor." She had a rare smile, wide, with the mouth closed. He watched, with a dawning hopelessness, the slow elongation of the curved lips. It was a smile he thought of as Russian, the expression of a pleasure half savored, half scorned.

Gradually she came closer. The chases down the sidewalk—during which he gave thanks for his hours in the gym—the recriminations and avowals, the shouts and even slaps: all these, he told his partner Bernstein, had been leading somewhere.

"Right," Bernstein said. "Go for it."

Twice she had moved in with him and out again, but this third time her mood as she lugged in her houseplants was sober. She closed the door, leaned on it with her eyes closed, shutting out whatever had been going on with somebody he had not been able to identify, though he knew it was not the Russian or the ex-husband. She threw armloads of clothing onto the couch. "I will stay, now."

This final return came at the beginning of the second year, the brim-ming year when he told his friends, "Seriously, I know what they mean by 'a new life.'" They walked holding hands, or even with arms around each other. They produced, she said, an energy field of their own. "I won't even ask what you're talking about," he said. If his daughter Lynn had said such a thing in her New Age phase, he would have given an irritated chuckle. Katya said, "It is how we are, in my country. We are not closed to the great world, like you. We have souls. Look at you. *And*"—her homesickness, her simmering nationalism could surface at any time, out of the schoolbooks of the child she had been when she left—"if *we* fight a war in Afghanistan, everyone is thinking, talking about war. All the time. We do not let our little sons go to the war while we have a picnic. You don't know about this. You have only daughters." He did not remind her that she had no children at all.

He was not going to pretend to perceive an energy field, but his senses had indeed unsealed themselves. Backing out of the garage, in his own alley he caught the smell of paint, roses, individual Dumpsters, lilac. "Louder!" She turned up the radio. "This doc-*tor*! He must have quiet, that is what he likes, so he can hear little sounds with his—what-is-it. Loud, forte, he does not know. Music! What is that, to him?"

He found her a ring with a chunk of emerald set in ruby chips. She said she would marry him at Christmas. Early in the new year, at the latest. "Right now is early in the new year," he said, for it was still April.

"Next year. But it will be a bad year. Another of your wars is coming."

He caught himself; he had almost said, "What does that have to do with us?"

Then, impossibly, absurdly, he was in a cemetery, walking alone to his car. He was at his door, fitting his key in the lock. He was on the stairs, he was in the bedroom opening the double closet she had taken over. He was stepping inside, he was standing draped in silk sleeves.

Impossibly, he was once more a man with a good car and a gym locker. Messages on his voicemail from women. The packed referral list of which he had once been so proud. Yet he was not that man. It was as if he had gone up the Amazon, or to Borneo, or some unvisited place where he had landed without the labor of travel, and once there found every tie cut but the one to Katya. He felt as if he had been taken inside a cave, one where an unknown organism lived that had not yet entered civilization, whether poison or cure. Because Katya was gone—one minute she had been with him and the next gone, with her death somehow part of the cave—he found himself alone with what had happened. No one could see the organism in him, the way you could see a tan or a loss of weight when someone went away and came back. Death—of course everyone around him in the hospital and the medical school was familiar with death. Nothing exotic there. Yes, his girlfriend, his fiancée, had died, and they were sorry. No one knew he had not come back.

A shame came over him. In her harshness, her casual insults, Katya had been right: to be an American was to be a fool. To hear no warning. To have no idea what was wrong with you. To be overtaken by events you had never foreseen, and to smile. Others in the world did not smile.

She didn't mean anything political; she had no politics.

He saw that the word *adore* could be used for something unrelated to love. Could it really have been he, Stark, who had tried in his heedless contentment to convert another person to decent, domestic, reliable love? At night he sat up in bed and grasped his head.

In the daytime he was filled with a dull apprehension, as if something were on its way that he must avoid. He had to hunch his shoulders and wait, the way he had seen so many do after an MI, not filling their lungs.

He didn't postpone any appointments; he went in to work every day. His clinic manager, Shawna, looked away from his eyes.

At home he would be standing in the light of the giant refrigerator Katya had chosen, in her love of appliances, and it would dawn on him that there was no food in it and the house was pounding with her music—audible no doubt to the neighbors—to which he had forgotten to listen.

"He does not know Dvořák from Debussy, the foolish man. The jerk. The musical jerk." She loved American slang. "It is all you have, in your language. I love this word you have, *jerk*! Of course we have such words! But we have so much more that you do not have because you have no souls. Oh don't argue. You are nothing but—jerks! Listen, Doctor, what you call the bug, the ladybug, with your no imagination, we call *bozhya korovka*, Little Cow of God."

He had opened the case and taken out her violin, and now it lay on the bedroom chair. Something held him there scraping a string vertically with his thumbnail to produce a thin squawk.

At the funeral he had met her ex-husband, the man she had stayed with in that year, twice that he knew of. His hand was shaken by a man with baggy eyes and a paunch, who had come to the service in an open-necked shirt. He looked like a drinker. What did he do? Stark could not remember, though he could remember tearing at the phone book looking for the man's number, trembling with hatred. The man seemed to be sizing him up in turn, and finding satisfaction in what he saw.

After the funeral, Stark called his daughter Lynn. "You were talking to him. What did he say?"

"What do you care, Dad? He said she would have wanted to die while she was pretty."

"Pretty! Jesus Christ she was never *pretty*."

"He said 'pretty.' Dad, I came to the funeral, OK? Katya was not my favorite person but I feel bad for you. But this is not what I want to be talking about. I do not appreciate—"

"Did he say she thought she was going to die?"

"No. God, Dad."

"What else?"

"He said she was about to come back to him. The guy's a mess."

"I guess she mowed him down," Stark said with a kind of pride.

STARK HAD AN EX-WIFE, ROSALIE, but the years of getting through medical school and a residency and raising two children were far behind them both. Nevertheless, when their younger daughter, Kelly, was in town, Lynn got them all together. On a Friday three weeks after the funeral, early in the afternoon, he called Rosalie and asked her to meet him for a drink. "No, not after work," he said. "I'm leaving now." He saw his stiff face glaring at him in the window glass.

He told his clinic manager, "Shawna, I'm going to have to call it a day."

"You should, you're getting that flu," Shawna said obligingly. Long ago, before her marriage, he had had a weekend or two with Shawna. She had suffered, liking Rosalie. But later he had seen her through her first son's atrial septal defect, and she was loyal. He tore off his white coat. He had never before left with patients in the waiting room.

Glimpsing the changes in Rosalie, he always felt a jab of protective dismay. Still, recently she had become involved with a fireman who, it turned out, was hardly any older than Katya. Rosalie had met him when, all alone in the old house, she had a chimney fire. Since taking up with the fireman she was using more makeup, and her dark eyes had gone small and sparkling. When she leaned forward the skin at her low neckline formed crisscross lines. There was no way to warn her not to lean across a table when she was with the fireman. "She's talking about fires," Lynn said. "She quotes him. She's a nutcase."

Rosalie said, "What are you telling me? Is the family suing you?" From Lynn he had heard that when the fireman was around Rosalie had a new, careless tone. She knew the pride he took in having had no lawsuits. Where was her soft heart? He felt tears come into his eyes.

"Good Lord, Stark. I know you didn't miss anything. I know you took care of her. I'm sorry, honey. Oh, dear." Rosalie had always cried when someone else did, even the children at times. She wiped her eyes; she had one of those manicures with white at the tips. "OK, look. Here's what you do. Go to the cabin. Go, and take it easy for a few days. Just lie around. There's a TV now. I got a satellite dish." The cabin was hers now; he hadn't been there since the divorce.

She said he didn't look good; he looked as if he had just crawled out of a cave. "Here." She dug in her purse. "Here's the key. Make sure you get it back to me because it's the only one I have now." In the old days they would have had three or four keys to the cabin, on hooks and stashed in drawers. But he couldn't inquire. Her tears had made him worse—and hadn't those eyes once seemed to fill her whole face when they shimmered with tears? He got up abruptly and went to the men's room. What was he doing leaning on a bathroom door with his eyes fixed on a hand dryer? With a diffuse spasm in his chest, a need to bear down after catching a breath, as if to keep something where it belonged. The dryer had a stiff logo of joined hands. From the wall the urinals gaped with their stains. How easily people ignored the real acts of the body, even people like himself, doctors who saw into the interior clenching, the explosions and expulsions. To how many people had he said the word *spasm* over the years, in reassurance?

When he opened his fist the key fell onto the floor. He picked it up and washed it. He dried his hands under the gasp of the blower.

"We haven't been over there in a month," Rosalie said when he came back and sank into his chair. "Somebody needs to check on the place. We were going to go this weekend but I can't, I'm off to lose weight."

We were going to go. She liked to hint at that part of her life.

"You don't need to lose weight," he said. Her hips had squared a bit, but she was small and still compact.

"Oh, now I do. Now I do. Lynn's taking me away to a spa. We're going to eat spinach leaves and do yoga and meditate. We'll have four days. So promise me you'll go. I mean it, Stark."

He thanked her in the parking lot. "Just go over there and take it easy," she said again, as if she were one of their daughters, looking out for him.

He didn't go home; he drove straight out of town and into the mountains. He hadn't packed anything; he would have to wear what he had put on that morning. His feet hurt, in his good shoes. At Washington Pass he pulled in and changed into the running shoes he kept in the trunk. He left them untied. *Because he's a bum*, he said to himself, in Katya's voice. He walked on old snow that still, in May, covered the short path to the overlook, and gazed down at the dizzying switchbacks. If you climbed over the fence and dropped, you would go straight down hundreds of feet before there was a thing to stop you.

On the way back he made new footprints, in the grip of a childish, sentimental urge to point himself out to somebody.

At the cabin—which was not a cabin at all but a log-and-timber house built with the first real money he had made, with five bedrooms and a river-rock fireplace, quilts Rosalie had found in country stores, scattered floor cushions still in their buttoned denim—he realized he had brought no food. He found a potato to slice, and fried it in olive oil in a familiar pan. He was not one who advised his patients not to fry. How would anyone who lived alone not fry? And Katya—who liked to present herself as a peasant and believed, or said she believed, that a fried potato was a meal if you had a glass of vodka to drink with it—Katya could have fried everything she ate. What use would any curbs have been? Should he have said more than he did, when he sent her to Bernstein? This was a young woman. A woman with nothing, seemingly, the matter with her. Before the day she seized his hands, she had come to his office twice with the complaint of having lost or almost lost consciousness. Something about the lazy way she related this history made him doubt it. Nevertheless he proceeded, because persistence and care were what he was known for. He uncovered a common thing.

He must have suspected, by the time she made the third appointment, that she came only to see him. Over the years he had accumulated a few patients who did that. And had that affected his judgment, made him less careful? Exactly what had she said, that first time? And what about afterwards, with Bernstein?

"Nothing. Nothing but what we saw," Bernstein said. "The thing might have shown up the next time, it might not have. Could we have induced it in the lab? You didn't do that; I didn't do that. One whole year she was my patient. Don't beat yourself up."

He should never have put his weight on her, with that heart inside her that was going to stop. He should never have raised his voice. What had he been thinking of? She had slapped him. He had thrown her down on the bed.

But he had not killed her by throwing her on the bed. She had stood up to slap him again, and lived another year. Standing in the kitchen eating his potato from the pan, he groaned.

He made his way along the downhill path, overgrown now, to the river, which was running so high it had carved out a new branch. He couldn't see in the semi-dark whether the branch veered back to the river where the woods began, or tore on into the trees. In the middle of the two courses was an island, with a big cottonwood at either end. Loud, tumbling water had claimed so much ground that he could not be sure exactly where he was. It blocked his way to the sand between the two trees, where he wanted to sit. Once he and the girls had dragged a picnic table all the way out to the river's edge. The table was long gone—stolen, Rosalie said. Bikers. They snooped around the empty vacation places now. A picnic table taken away on a motorcycle? "They scout stuff out and they come back for it," she said defensively. He had to consider the question of whether he had encouraged this kind of thinking in Rosalie, who had been so ready to take his word. How conventional he had been, despite his "ways."

"Thiefs should keep what they get." So Katya said, haughtily. "Or how can we have balance? Not like those guys in the movie." They had seen a movie about a heist. "Real thiefs, I mean."

"So should they get this ring? If they don't hurt this hand?"

Why had he said this? She had hidden the hand with the emerald on it behind her.

The branch was running fast, too deep to wade across. Deep enough to be black. You could see tall grass being rushed and flattened. There was no real bank. He put his foot in. Instead of dragging at it, the current lifted it like a leaf and pushed him onto the other leg, making him totter. Had the river ever come this far? He shook his wet foot, his body creeping with goose pimples.

His ears were full of the loudness of water, and for a moment on the path he had the sensation the river was moving up behind him. Lifting his head he saw, standing in the kitchen, a woman. Tall. *God, God . . .*

Of course it was not her. This woman was heavy. The woman was just standing in the kitchen without a sound, even though she must have seen him coming up the steps. She must have seen him at some distance, a figure approaching the house. She had his spatula in her hand, and she was holding the other hand out as if to soothe him. "Hi there," she said.

"Hello," he said. "Who are you?"

A man stepped into the kitchen. "I'm Ray Rollins."

"I said somebody was here." The woman held up the spatula with a surprising calm. "We were out there admiring your car."

"Whoa!" the man said. "I don't know, man, this is—here I thought we—thought we *had* the place. This weekend." So they weren't burglars. Or probably not. But then the man said uneasily, "What's the date, anyway?"

"Well now," said Stark, "it's the twenty-first, and I'm pretty sure I'm supposed to be here." He wasn't going to say "Goddammit, I built this house," or anything like that. He wasn't going to say Rosalie had given him the key because that would give away her name, if they were burglars.

"Whoa," the man said again. Ray. Ray something. He had a crew cut. He looked like a football coach. "So now, did you . . . You must know the owner?"

Stark said, "I do."

The man came forward with his hand out. "Ray Rollins," he said for the second time. He gripped like a blood-pressure cuff.

"Phil Bernstein," said Stark. He wasn't going to get into any explanations.

"This is Beverly," Rollins said after a second.

The woman said, "Beverly Lanier," and held out her hand. She smiled as if the situation struck her as nothing out of the ordinary. She turned to the man and because she was big herself, Stark saw for the first time how large and muscular were the arms, now folded, of the man standing beside her, how thick his neck. Not somebody he could tackle, if the two were there after all to steal from an empty house. But wasn't the guy too clean-cut to be a thief? The girl, surely, too simple. "Well," she said cheerfully to Stark, "you were here first."

"Right," said Ray Rollins. "Right. So you're a friend of Rosalie's. Jeez, I'm embarrassed."

All right. He knew her. Stark said, "Drive over from Seattle?"

"Yeah, we did."

"Quite a way," Stark said. It was a three-and-a-half-hour drive if you did it fast.

"Had to leave in rush hour, had to work."

Stark could see the man placing him: older guy, white-collar, someone who left before rush hour.

"Well, hmm, what shall we do?" said the woman, Beverly. She had sat down on one of the stools Rosalie had had made to line the counter. The stools had arms, you could swivel in them and see the whole house spread out with its comforts. *Open plan.* For months the words had echoed in their lives as they made trips to watch the place go up. "Not my room," Lynn had said, at twelve. "I want to be downstairs. I want the closed plan." Now Lynn was what, twenty-six? Twenty-seven? Older than this solid girl on the stool.

Stark waited for Rollins to answer her. He was going to back down, Stark could tell. He was the one who had made the mistake; Stark had received the key from Rosalie's hand that very afternoon. She couldn't have already lent it, if that was the only key she had.

It came to him slowly, as he was thinking of the key. He was bending, in his mind, to pick it up from the sticky floor of the men's room. It came to him who the man was. He raised his eyes from the counter, where the girl had wrapped her square hands around the basket of river rocks Rosalie kept there. The man had stepped away from her, scowling. It was the fireman.

We were going to go this weekend.

So he had come anyway, the fireman. He had come without Rosalie. With a girl instead. He must have his own key. He had brought a girl to Rosalie's cabin.

Beverly said, "I'm sure we can find a motel in town."

Hearing the word gave Stark a rude pleasure. *Motel.* Where this kind of thing belonged. Not in Rosalie's cabin, where Rosalie must have come more than once with the fireman, the bastard.

Ray slapped his hands together. "I need a phone book." His moment of shame and confusion was over. "And more important, where's the bathroom?" He grinned. Of course he knew where they were, phone book and bathroom.

"Oh gosh. But it doesn't matter." Beverly stretched and smiled. "I know the area, I worked up north of here one summer, with the Forest Service. I was a smoke jumper."

So. It was out. Firemen, both of them. Firefighters. The bastard had brought a girl from work.

Hey, want to go over to a great place on the Methow River?

Hey, why not?

"No kidding," Stark said. He never said *no kidding*. But he was Phil Bernstein. "That must be rough work."

"I liked it. I was young," she said, in the nostalgic way young people had of saying that. "They kinda made me prove myself a few extra times. But I like that." When she smiled the plumpness of her cheeks made the lower lids spring up and almost close her eyes. On one side she had a deep dimple. "You don't even want to know how much retardant is up there in some of those stands of Doug fir."

Without deciding he was going to do it, Stark said, "Why not just stay here? This is a big house. I have the room down the hall, there." It was Lynn's room. He hadn't wanted to go upstairs. "There's a big second floor. Four rooms."

She said, "Really? That would be great!" Ray was coming back. He walked with his hands on his legs, on the seams of the tight jeans, and a dreamy, private look on his face.

"Did you hear that?" the girl asked him. "Mr. Bernstein doesn't mind if we stay here tonight, if we want. It's late maybe, d'you think, to get a motel? We could do it tomorrow?"

"Jeez, I hate to do that. I don't know how I got this so turned around. What a dumbshit thing to do, excuse me." As if Stark were an old fogy.

Stark said nothing. He was doing it for the girl, with her dimple. It was the kind of thing Katya would do, and if he stopped there, if he didn't expose the guy, punish him, he would still be in the region of the kind of caprice that was Katya's. Katya did harm, but she tended her victims. When she had her accident, for instance, a few days later she tracked down the driver of the other car. Not because the man was hurt;

he was up and around and he was the aggrieved party, since Katya was a danger behind the wheel. She was trying to find out what the connection was between them.

"I don't know, Bev . . ." Stark could see the guy wanted to be let off the hook for bringing her here when somebody else had the place. He wanted persuasion, the bastard. "That would be . . . I don't think we . . ."

"I bet your neighbor just got confused about who was when," Beverly said.

"So Rosalie's your neighbor, is she?" Stark said heartily.

"No, no, I'm the one," said Ray, ignoring him. "I'm the one who screwed up. I bet it was next weekend. Jeez." He grimaced.

Stark was tempted to let him go on in this vein, getting himself into trouble. But Beverly said, "So, can I go get my stuff out of the car?"

"OK, I guess," said Ray, with a defeated look at Stark.

"HEY, LOOK WHO'S HERE." SHE had come down the path in the dark, by herself. "Look at this river."

Stark said, "This isn't the river. This is a spur. New."

"*Well, it's not deep nor wide*," she sang, "*but it's a mean piece of water, my friend.* You know that song?"

"I do not," he said.

"'Kern River.' Merle Haggard. *I'll never swim Kern River again*," she sang. "*It was there that I met her, there that I lost my best friend.* I was awake. I looked out the window and I saw you out there. Then I didn't see you. I thought, *Gotta be a path goes down that hill because he's gone.* I don't know, I got a creepy feeling. You can hear this thing really loud in our room. The room we're in, at the front."

"The river's high," he said patiently. He was going to have to talk to her. If a woman got up in the middle of the night, you would have to talk to her. "It's made a whole new channel."

"Look at that moon. Ah." She held up her arms. "You've been here before. A new channel, you say."

Clouds had swept apart to show the lopsided moon, hanging at the top of a cottonwood, so bright it seemed it had arrived with a hiss, like a lantern. The woods were thin here, and the moon was so bright it had dropped black shadows into them.

"There are pictures of you, in our room." She had to raise her voice to be heard over the water.

"What's that?" he said, as if he couldn't hear.

"Pictures. Under the glass top of the dresser." So the guy hadn't taken her into the master bedroom, where he must have been before. They were in Kelly's old room. Kelly, the little one, the sentimentalist, with her photo collages and scrapbooks. "You know the ones I mean?"

"What ones?"

"All these family pictures. Two kids. Girls."

"Is that right?"

"They look like they live here. The man looks like you, a younger you." He sighed.

"It is you."

"If you say so."

"Is this your place?"

"No."

"Whose place is it?"

"Rosalie's."

"Rosalie who? I don't know her, Ray knows her."

"He appears to."

"Why do you say it like that?"

"Rosalie is a good friend of mine," he said.

"Why did you come down here?" she said sternly. He could hear the voice of the firefighter. *Climb down. Do as I tell you.* "Were you going to jump in the river?"

"Was I—? Maybe I still am."

"I have my EMT," she said.

"That's good, if I do."

"I told Ray I got the feeling you were going to jump in the river."

"And what did he say?"

"He said you weren't. He said you probably came to finish some report."

"And that would be pretty lame, in his opinion," Stark said, "for a guy to do. Only you decide the guy is going to drown himself."

"You never know what somebody will or won't do. I used to guide on the Colorado. Some people—seems like they fell in on purpose. And fur-ther-more, ha-ha, I figured it out. You're the husband, right?"

"I was. You're on the case. Are you a private investigator?"

"Yeah. I'm what's-her-name. *Prime Suspect*. Actually I'm a firefighter."

"I'm willing to bet he is too."

"Yeah. It'll be hard on our kids."

"Your kids."

"We're getting married."

"No kidding. Congratulations."

"Thank you," she said with a tuck of the dimple. "How about you? What do you do, Phil? It's Phil, isn't it?"

"I'm a lawyer."

"I knew it," she said.

"Is that a fact?"

"How do you know when a lawyer's lying? He's moving his lips. Sorry. Lawyers can't get a break. But hey, the ones I know are great guys."

The dimple kept coming and going, but a girl like this, however she carried on in her own life, could be suddenly, mercilessly intolerant and proper. Yes, his daughters had taught him this, and a young woman or two who had turned on him.

"Lying would be something you frown on," he said.

"Not really," she said airily. She was getting into the spirit of things. She was not as simple as he had thought.

"Did Ray see the pictures?"

"No. I put my stuff on the dresser."

"Why didn't you show him?"

"I didn't feel like it. Why didn't you say you were married to Rosalie?"

"I'm not."

"She has a different name. I've heard it. I don't know what it is but it isn't Bernstein."

"I know that."

"So she took her own name back?"

"You're a very curious young lady."

"Nosy." She grinned. "I am. I'm what's-her-name." She put on a British accent. "Get me everything we have on the Bern-steins. And a shot of Scotch." Then she said, "You were down at the river when we got here. You used to come here a lot, I bet. I know you did. It's in the pictures. There was a beach."

"Out there, underwater. The river is supposed to be on the other side of that, where you see the cottonwoods. It's still coming up."

"Snowmelt. We had that hot week. That's all it takes, up in the snow-pack. River ever get all the way up to the house?"

"It never got anywhere near *this* high. Global warming."

She eyed him. "Ray doesn't believe in global warming."

"Why doesn't that surprise me?"

"What? You just now met Ray. Everybody likes Ray. Everybody."

"Especially you. You're going to marry him. You're going to marry a jerk." He was as surprised as if Katya had come up behind them and growled the word.

"Wait a minute. You don't know Ray, and you don't know me. What is this? What's your problem?" Still she didn't walk away.

"The guy's a jerk."

"You better explain that."

"Just ask him. When you leave tomorrow. Ask him if he's a jerk. See what he says."

"No," she said.

"You're asking for it, if you marry him."

"Wait a minute, buddy. You know nothing about this man. You have no idea how brave he is, how he'll risk himself. Why am I talking to you? Hey, you're a lawyer. What do you know about anything good?"

"He's a jerk."

"Quit it."

"Jerk."

"I don't like that," she said. She stepped close, the way a man in a bar would, to start a fight. He knew that from movies; no one had ever squared off with him in a bar. "I don't like that one bit." She poked him in the collarbone with her fingers straight, as if she were playing a scene in a movie. She seemed to be kidding, or at least half kidding.

"Nevertheless," he said.

"*Nevertheless?*" she said, crowding him. "*Nevertheless?*" She was bigger than he was. She poked him again. He stepped back, off-balance, and the next thing he knew he had stepped into water knee-deep and slipped. He had gone sideways. How had that happened? But he was getting his footing. Then he couldn't get his balance at all and he was off his feet, going over.

His whole body gasped at the cold. First floundering and then rolling and then the thing swallowed him.

"Your feet!" He could hear her yelling. "Get your feet out front!"

That was it. So the feet would hit and not the head. The time it would take to turn himself bore no relation to the speed of water. Ahead, this water was going to join the full force of the river. Something whacked him in the shoulder but it was too late to grab for it. He couldn't see, and water had filled his throat. He was a thing to be filled. His legs crossed and recrossed, the feet were wrong, not in front of him. His shoes were off. Something with an edge tore past one leg. Tree stumps. The draw was where the stumps were. He knew where he was but now he was choking. It was too late. His shoulder ran against something loose and clashing, snagged on it.

A weight bore against him, rolling him up. She was in the water with him. "Gotcha!" she said. With arms like pliers, she was dragging him. From the splashing she seemed to be wading.

"Beaver dam!" At least she was out of breath. She had him splayed on the ground, with stones under his back. "Old beaver dam! So—yeah! So hey, the river has *so* been up this high. Beavers!" His eyes were glued shut. From the sound of it she was hanging over him panting, stripping water down the legs of her jeans with her palms. She sat down. "I beat you to the dam! You had some close contact. Got some scratches. That's fast water."

He lay there with his limbs contracting and letting go. He wasn't cold. He got his wet eyelashes apart. He was in a half circle of flagpoles. No. Aspen: slim trunks pale as X-rays. Against the dark pines—the river had come up to the woods and some way in—the aspen showed tiny half-clenched leaves. The moon straight up was so bright he squinted.

"Hey, don't sue me," Beverly said, vigorously rubbing her arms. "Hey, Phil. Don't say I pushed you in a river and you lost your ability to earn your living as an attorney-at-law."

Why should a remark like that have a steadying effect? It seemed a way she might have hit on to comfort him.

"My shoes," he said.

"Forget the shoes," she said. For a moment it seemed there might be enough comfort in the world to get him through

"Jesus!" It was Ray, running and shouting. "What's going on? Are you all right?"

"See? I was right," Beverly said calmly. "He jumped in."

"I mean *you!*" Ray yanked her up and against him. "Bev! You *lived* out here, goddammit. Flood stage, baby. You heard the radio. There's range cattle going down that river. You could both—be in there—right now." He was rocking her from side to side. "Jesus," he said finally, holding her at arm's length. "Jesus, Bev. You had to do it. I know that."

He let her go and squatted beside Stark. "Hey, fella," he said. "You. Hear me?"

Stark coughed and rolled his head. Water ran out of his ears.

"Sure, cough. Puke. You're OK. Thanks to her. Do you know that? I want to say something to you. Do you see what you were up to here? You don't *do* that. No. You got it all wrong."

"Ray," said Beverly, not really chiding him. She smiled down at Stark with a bold cheerfulness. She had gone in, after all. She had done that, gone into fast water, pulled him out. With the little pit in her cheek she smiled at the matter of the beaver dam that would have caught him anyway, the matter of her having pushed him.

"I don't know," said Ray, shaking his head. "Jeez. You need help."

Now Beverly had squatted too, to rough his wet hair back and forth, the way a coach might after a game.

Ray rocked back on his haunches. "Nothing's so bad you have to jump in a river, buddy." He squeezed Stark's shoulder.

Stark let out a moan. Now he was cold, but he wasn't going to get up. He was going to lie there a while before he made any effort. He was the one on the ground, the one in trouble. He couldn't think how long it had been since he was the one lying down, with somebody bending over him, figuring out what the hell was wrong.

Phantom Father

She was a young married woman who fell in love.

The man desperately wanted to take the place of her husband. He made scenes: he pled, commanded, threatened suicide. The trouble was that although she had fallen in love so suddenly, she also loved the man she had married, who was in the dark about what was happening and didn't even know the time had come for scenes.

Love, love. The same word for different things. Who can be sure what it is that is being felt? Love, like so much helium blown into a balloon. The further trouble was that, of three balloons, her husband had been blown fullest, stretched thinnest.

Having no way of knowing this, and weighed on by the truth, she confessed everything to him, even her suspicion that the miscarriage they were grieving, away in his family's place by the lake, had been the lover's baby and not his.

It was summer, the war was going on, and she was away for a last weekend with her husband before he was to go overseas. But in the morning, when he put on his uniform, instead of leaving for his train he drove the car down the boat ramp, where it lolled onto its back and sank to the bottom of the lake.

After the funeral, filled with horror, grief, and a remorse that overpowered her feelings for her lover at first, she asked for six months to go away alone. When she came back, her lover had married someone else.

Those were the elements. All of it happened in the space of those few years around the age of twenty, when one is barely out of childhood. All three—the wife Annette, the husband Alonzo, and the lover—still had parents helping them with checks and advice, parents who had come through a world war themselves and carefully planned that the children born after it would live unscathed and happy. The three, themselves wanting to be happy, went through these events while another world war was raging.

In time Annette married again, and the three children she had with this husband would find bits and pieces of these old events in themselves, like tea leaves.

The first child, Michele, inherited her mother's looks: olive skin with pale eyes and pronounced dark eyebrows, round placid cheeks in a narrow face, lips full and crinkled like sunned grapes, her father said, lying back with her, his first baby, on his chest.

He was forty years old, a surgeon. He had been a poor boy and now he had plenty of money—though never as much as Annette's first husband, Alonzo, would have come into—but he didn't care for money, he cared only for the wife and the child who dogged his steps, learning the fruits and plants, minerals and sea creatures and geographical formations that gave their names to parts of the body.

The child was impatient with books, though she liked to turn the pages of his surgical atlas with him and let him show her the cherries and mulberries and bulbs, islets and pillars and spindles. The body is old, older than the mind, he told her, and she got ready for a boring fairy tale. Because the body is volume, it is stubborn, he said. Its rules are those of water. Most of medicine is keeping water in or out. And for the most part the body, in its ancient way—here the child began rolling her eyes and banging her heels on the chair rungs—goes about its own business disguised from the mind and without consulting it. She gave a haughty laugh and ran away from him, out of the house.

But waiting for her in high school was a certain boy. He was a boy with a grudge: as a small child he had had polio. Although he recovered, and suffered very few of what her father called 'the sequelae," he had a limp, and having been one of the last to get the disease, just at the time the vaccine appeared and saved so many others, he was bitter. When he got well he was wild, ahead of the boys his age instead of behind, known in the high school for his outbursts in the classroom, his stormy liaisons with older girls, even women, clerks or waitresses in their twenties, in places where the high school kids hung out.

MICHELE WAS SUNBATHING WITH HER parents. Her little brothers played in the coppery foam of low tide while the three of them lay talking about her mother's marriage. Her first marriage.

Michele said, "It's funny, when you first told me about Alonzo, I remembered him!" Indeed, she could remember the conversation, the slowly arriving, affronted surprise, at first, of the discovery that her mother had had another husband, and then an odd feeling coming over her, a recognition of the man they were talking about, as if he had come around a corner into view. "I remembered him!"

"You did?" her mother said musingly. She rarely contradicted her children or imposed an attitude on them that might be from another era, her own era.

"I know I couldn't have," Michele said, sitting up and leaning on her mother's legs. Her mother lay back, slightly overflowing the top of her bathing suit with the straps down, in her low beach chair. She had lost the narrow, bony shape that was her daughter's, except in the face. She was one of those women who keep a thin face. Men who passed glanced at her, the breasts, the plump tanned legs, tight-skinned and gleaming with oil. Michele looked down the legs to her mother's long, reaching toes; elegant and indefinably pitiful they seemed to her, the very keys of her mother's self. She leaned across and moved the pliant middle ones back and forth.

Michele was on the blanket, and her father had a hammock that separated him from the sand by just a few inches. He lay on his stomach on a yellow towel, idly running his fingers along the sand. They were all obliged to cover themselves and each other heavily in oil every hour because he feared skin cancer. He brought oranges to the beach to protect them from dehydration. He would cut them in half with his Swiss Army knife and expertly squeeze the juice into his mouth and theirs, from above, the way people drink from a wineskin. Then he would eat the pulp, because it was good for you, and urge them to do the same. Once he had it on his hands, the bags and towels and sandwiches, even the skin of their own arms and shoulders, had the smell of oranges.

"So tell me what he looked like," Michele said. "Alonzo. Didn't he have thick brown hair?"

"She told you that." Her father's voice was muffled against the towel. All of this was talked about in the family, not hidden.

"Did you tell me?"

"Oh, I probably did, Mish."

"Well, before you told me I knew. I knew what he looked like."

"Pictures," growled her father, consenting to appear jealous.

"I never saw one, did I, Mommy?" All her life she called her mother that.

"I don't know that you have," her mother said. "Eddie, has she seen pictures of Alonzo?"

"Bound to have."

"I have not!"

"Well, they're in the desk with everything else."

"Why was he named *Alonzo*? And did you know him, Daddy?"

"It was a name in his family," her mother said.

"The rich dream up names like that," her father said. They all knew he was proud to have been poor, himself, to have worked his way through college and sent money home to his mother. Yet he respected Alonzo, that was apparent to Michele. It was not Alonzo, it was the lover her father looked down on, the one who came on the scene and did all the harm. The man who had married somebody else after causing Alonzo's death. That man had no name.

"Anyway, I knew he had brown hair, Alonzo, thick and standing up, and growing down his forehead in a point, right? Right?" she cried, excited, as her mother dreamily, frowningly watched the boys drag a tree branch to a deep hole they had dug in the sand, their trap.

Her father sat up. "Somebody's going to fall into that," he said to nobody in particular.

"Did he? Did he or not?" Michele arched her foot and flipped sand onto her mother's legs.

"He did."

"Like mine."

Her father said, "Annette, you don't suppose—she's his daughter by celestial insemination?"

"She may be," said her mother thoughtfully. "But actually I think she's got your nice lips." Though they all said her lips were her mother's.

"Really?" Her father lay down again on his back and pressed his mustache up with his fingers. "These?"

Her mother leaned over and kissed him. "Oh, you're burned. Your shoulders right at the neck," she said, kissing him there.

"Where's the oil?" he cried, sitting up. "And the boys—! Tommy! Eddie! Come up here! Michele, where—?"

"It's in your bag, Dad. It's right there. And he had one of those chins . . ."

"I couldn't say," said her mother, becoming aloof as she poured oil into her palms.

"My phantom father," Michele said.

Her father got to his feet, shook himself, and ran down to the water's edge to oil the boys' shoulders, fair like his own, not olive and immune to sunburn like Michele's.

Michele thought she did not just pity the stricken young husband with the rare, sad name Alonzo, but knew him as kin. Now she was only six years younger than he had been when he walked out of his family's summer cottage in the early morning, got in the car, and drove to the end of the boat ramp, where the bank fell off sharply into a cave of water that sent up a slow, obscuring cloud of mud. No one had ever said precisely this; she had imagined it for herself.

She felt she was like him, proud but easily defeated. She was more like him than she was like her own father, who had real power and could not be defeated. She would have to be very careful that she did not love too single-mindedly (and that in doing so she did not, as her mother had, destroy anybody), and that the life she might have to lead because of the intensity, the near-uncontrollability of her feelings did not overwhelm her. She would have to be careful, and already she had not been careful.

Just down the beach from the pit her brothers had been digging, a group of hippies lay on the beach. In a year or two Michele would be on a beach in Europe with just such a group, but at the time she was suspicious of them. They had stuck two poles in the sand and tied on a banner that kept coming loose, with a peace symbol on it.

The war in Vietnam had worked its way into everything, lifting many of the restrictions on what people wore and how they talked, even bringing a draft resister up onto the stage of her high school to disrupt the assembly. The girls had their bathing-suit tops off, and the boys were stretched out on the sand without towels, letting the girls rub lotion onto their backs. One of the girls waved broadly at Michele's father when he was loping down the beach, her dark-tipped breasts spreading apart and then flowing in the direction of her arm. He waved back with the same broad, lazy motion, and Michele could see that the girl had dropped her teasing face and was smiling as he got to his sons and scooped them up with their thin legs dangling. They clamored to show him their digging, so he put them down and fell to his knees in the sand.

Michele oiled her own legs. She shook her mother, whose eyes were shut and whose forehead would tan unevenly if she kept it soberly wrinkled the way it was. "I don't know why, but I'm not interested in the other guy," Michele went on. "Your *lovah*. I'm interested in Alonzo. I mean, you were married to him. He seems like part of the family."

"And the other one?"

"He seems like the other one."

"And so he was," said her mother. "If you think you might be pregnant, we should go to the doctor rather than wait."

Michele lay back on her towel, slowly. "I don't think so."

"But you love him. You say you've been sleeping with him."

"I love him. I love him. I love him." She didn't want her mother to have to picture the car, the friends' cars, the logistics, so she said, "Just a few times."

"And so you'll want to have the baby," her mother said decisively.

"I don't think I'm pregnant. I'm thin."

"There's something about you that makes me think you might be. My first pregnancy—"

"With *me*! Or, no, I mean . . . no."

"No," her mother said. No, the first pregnancy had been the miscarriage that set in motion all they had been recalling.

"Here comes Daddy."

When her father had thrown his reddened body down again her mother began to speak thoughtfully with her eyes closed. "I was unfortunate. By that I mean I brought misfortune."

"Are we on that again?" Michele's father muttered.

"I learned my lesson very early, though I can't say what it was exactly. You'll find that. You can't say what you've learned, exactly, and whoever does—well, don't trust it absolutely. I learned too late for him, for Alonzo. It wasn't 'Don't play around,' or anything like that," she said, with dignity. "I wish I could tell you what it was."

"I'll tell you what it was," her father said. "It was 'Don't play around.' An ironbound rule. If you're married to a surgeon, especially. Because we are much more likely to do evil things to another than to ourselves."

Her mother said pensively, uninsistently, "It had something to do with life."

"Life is better than death, was that it?" her father said.

Michele said, "Aha, you're making Daddy jealous!"

"He's not jealous."

"I am too."

Her father had taken her mother's ripped-apart life and sewn it back into a piece. Her father was able to do that, Michele always said when she told the story, because in the 1940s and '50s men had the power to alter everything for women, or were thought to, and because life was better than death.

MICHELE HAD A BABY AND gave it up for adoption because that was what happened then, in her own era, even though her parents were more free-thinking than most; they had lived in Europe, and her mother, in particular, thought anything could be accommodated within the family, any number of people and memories of people.

Years later Michele would find herself telling her friends about the way her mother had suffered over the giving up of the baby, the son Michele had had at sixteen.

On the day Michele "relinquished," when she had gotten up out of the bed where they kept you for days at that time, and dressed herself in the clothes she had worn into the hospital, and they were signing her out, her mother had taken hold of the counter at the nurses' station and then, almost gracefully, let go and folded onto the floor. She had fainted.

When she came to, she got up clumsily, with all of them to help her, but she didn't say she was sorry; she withdrew herself from any talk about it. The nurse who took her blood pressure while she was lying on the polished floor gave her face a little stroke. Then the nurse hugged Michele, who had not been able to kneel all the way down because she was sore, and she gave Michele the baby's hospital bracelet.

The nurses told everyone standing around that it happened now and again, a dead faint like that. Her father had seen it in a medical setting, but Michele had never seen a faint. She had never known anyone who even said they had fainted. It was not an act of the time.

MICHELE GAVE UP THE BABY because of the time she was living in and because the boy she loved believed it was the right thing to do. He was powerful in argument. His disease had confined him for more than a year, and made him the boy he would be when he got up again: unbending, peremptory, greedy for every satisfaction of his will. To her, on the other hand, the polio explained everything, gave his bare leg in the back seat of the car, almost undetectably thinner than the other, a paleness that hurt her, his angry voice an echo of supplication.

She never forgot the absorbent force in this boy, shocking her with its drag, the *wick*—that was what it was—that had transferred her to him. If she were to see him again, it would still be there, she knew, if she saw him on some street ahead of her with his limp, or in a crowd, as she persistently imagined she would, out of which one of them would follow the other into a dark room—a room briefly illuminated and then lowered like a bucket into a well—and shut the door, and feel for a bed or lean back against a wall, and draw the weight of the other down.

Polio was a neurological disease, but as far as she could see it had not affected his nervous system, which was tuned high, to gradations of pleasure not familiar to very many men she was to meet, men twice his age, and to pleasure given as well as taken, pleasure that seemed to have to do with the body her father had told her about, that was all dammed water.

How would this boy, for all his harsh charm, his casual domination of her and others, know what the right thing to do was? How would he know what she should do? Why would she, so independent all her six-teen years, brought up to be, submit to his opinion?

You would have to be wiser than most of them were in high school, or for many years after that, to know what to do.

A YEAR AND A HALF after that, she was lying facedown on a beach in France. With her were some hitchhikers who were translating for each other across her, one of them tracing letters on her steaming back. They were talking about their parents, the ways of parents in the various coun-tries they came from. One of the French boys was already twenty, and the others teased him for calling his parents every week. Their packs were spread out on the hot sand all around them, and one or two of them were rummaging for pictures.

Michele didn't have any. She had come away without finishing high school, carrying nothing that might hold her back. While they were talking on the beach she thought of her father's face, with the suntan oil on it defining all the wrinkles of the smile he had had, the day they were talking about her mother's past and he had said he was jealous.

She had not written to her parents in months. She had put them, too, out of her mind. She did not join the conversation; she had withdrawn herself. She was just beginning to see how she was going to have to labor to find the way back. This was the period she had been warned about, nearing the end of the first year after the birth, nearing the anniversary.

She was not even sure she was going to live. Sometimes at night in a hostel bathroom, she would think she wanted to be annihilated, the way the birth had been. The baby existed; his birth did not. His birth-days would come; his birth would lie farther and farther behind him, unclaimed. And she who had never seen him, never been shown him: unclaimed.

It would have been impossible to open her mouth on this hot, anes-thetic foreign sand and tell what had happened, and no one pressed her. But she had begun to think about her parents. She thought, *My father is a man who cuts into people if they make a move to leave life. To capture them and bring them back into life.* Life was better than death.

He was no kin of the phantom father.

There must have been a picture of that man, the first husband,

Alonzo, and she must have seen it, to give her the vivid idea she had of him. Turning over to get the sun on her face, and then letting the others pull her up by the arms so she could smear more cocoa butter on her thighs, she saw with a detached, sad approval how dark and taut the months of backpacking in shorts had made her skin. It had taken on a textured sheen like tent nylon.

She wondered, scratching white lines on it with her nails, why she had no idea of the other one, the lover, the one who had come into her mother's young life and then defected, like a driver swerving out of the way of a crash he had caused: the one who so suddenly, shockingly, *ordinarily*, after setting off the chain of events that was to color her mother's life, had *gotten married*. And yet that man was nothing but the precursor of her father, probably even like her father in some way. Probably in reality she was, herself, more like those two who went on living than like the phantom father. Ordinary. Likely, after all, simply to marry and have children as her mother had done, and as her son would do—she bore down on herself to imagine it—her son, a child just now setting his foot down on the ground somewhere and taking a step. If that was when babies walked. Didn't they walk when they were a year old? And then they fell down, they got up, they went to school, they went to high school; they fell in love and nothing mattered that had come before. That was what they thought as they married and had children of their own. As he would do in his time, her son, having no conscious idea that somewhere in him were the boy's limp, the girl's ardor, the grandmother's body falling to the hospital floor.

Beloved, You Looked into Space

Our father married a woman who took an ax to a bear. She did it to save her first husband. The bear that charged him was blond at the neck and had enough bulk there that she saw it as a grizzly, a thin one. Later she knew it to have been a black bear, with half a paw shot off and a slug in its shoulder. A hunter told the papers there had been word of a problem bear in the area. The couple had no way of knowing that; they were staying in a remote cabin, and although the husband was a hunter himself, he had no gun because they were there to fish and take it easy. So our father said later.

The wife was a little distance upriver casting her own line when the bear grappled him down. Twice she heard a growl she thought was a plane overhead fading in and out. That was before he made a sound. He was trying to get under the water. When he came up he screamed for her to get away. Of course a bear goes into water, and it swatted him back to the rocks where it could straddle him.

They were fishing catch-and-release, late in the winter season, really the spring melt, when bears are lean and ranging for food.

Grizzly: anger. Black bear: hunger. Something to keep in mind about bears, our father said. He was a veterinarian, but bears were a new interest. His warnings were for my sister Shelley, the one who hiked and camped alone. Shelley had worked for the Forest Service and knew more about wildlife than he did, and by this time she had her own veterinary practice, so she could have expressed an opinion, but she didn't. The subject was his now.

Earlier the husband and wife had been taking turns splitting wood for the stove. *The ax.* She ran uphill and skidded back. The first blow she struck was a true one, splitting the ear and causing the bear to drag its head off her husband, turn a blood-filled eye on her, and stand up. The head swung, a paw swiped her arm and knocked her down. But the bear dropped back to her husband. Unaware she was hurt, she pulled herself onto her knees, her eyes level with what was going on. She felt for the ax, got to her feet. Like a batter, she swung it into the neck.

"I mean that next swing picked her up off the ground," our father said. It was he who was compelled to repeat the details, from the time he met her until the time we did, at their wedding. "I think I'm the first person to hear it," he said proudly. "From her."

Gerda. She was a small woman, he said. But she was a rock climber, with arms on her. Scars—although she was not one to spend time in front of a mirror—made her cover them up in long sleeves. I could picture her, short, wind-burned, one of those sturdy, gray-headed, big-wristed women you used to see looping cord or portaging kayaks on the ramps of the old REI, with a look in her eye like Mother Jones, or like Ripley in the cargo loader in *Aliens*. And what in that look would make a man, and not just any man but our peaceable father, savior of animals, decide in one week to marry her when he had mourned another woman for decades?

Our mother's sister Karen had met her. Ordinarily Karen would have gone into detail, but she had agreed that she would not. "I promised. Your father made me promise. You'll meet her."

"But not until the wedding." Gerda was in the Midwest settling things. "Come on, Karen. Tell."

"Let your father describe her. He wants to."

This was something new. Our father didn't describe people. Persuaded to speak of our mother, even long after her death, he had never put so many sentences together. "In that situation, most people would be lucky to get an ax blade through the guard hairs in the coat. Thick as rope, at the neck." He was eager to confirm these things. "I mean man or woman. Just wouldn't hit true, nine times out of ten. This girl cut clear down through the strap muscles, just short of the carotid."

For the bear was tracked and shot, examined and photographed. The old embedded slug, missing toes, abscessed teeth, ax wounds—these reached the Seattle papers.

It was three years afterwards that Gerda Hagen and our father met, saw each other every day for a week, and decided to get married. To the best of my knowledge our father had gone out with two women in the twenty-three years since our mother died. "I tried," Karen always said. "I had friends waiting in line. Kathleen made me promise her." Karen smiled across the table at Shelley because it was Shelley who remembered the personality of our mother, the powers of tolerance she had displayed, for almost everything that had come to pass.

And Gerda—Gerda had never gone out with anyone but the boy she married at eighteen. "It's true," Karen said. We were in a restaurant, talking over the situation. "So these two, somehow . . ." Karen had her wallet photos out, flipped to the picture of her sister. "Two virgins," she said to the face.

ALL THROUGH GRADE SCHOOL, WE got off the bus at Karen's house. We called her Karen, though our uncle was Uncle Cal. Karen didn't like the word *aunt* because she didn't think it expressed her relationship with us. "I know you're not my daughters," she said. "I know that. But I have my feelings and I don't like the word *aunt*, and for that matter I don't like *niece*. *Niece*. It's the sound. *Penis*. There's another one, same sound. That *niceness*. *Phallus* is a different thing."

"Stop right there," said Uncle Cal.

"Well, *geese* and *piece*. And *p-e-a-c-e*," said Shelley, who was the smart one. It was said in the family that she had read the newspaper at three. Our mother had taught her. In the second grade she was reading our father's home copy of *The Anatomy of the Cat*.

Karen worked half days; at home she took care of her sons and of us, and fought the nuclear industry. She talked on the phone as she stuffed envelopes and assembled casseroles and cleaned as far as the telephone cord would go. Or Shelley would set up the board and beat her at Scrabble while she talked. It was the height of the antinuclear movement. Nuclear fuel rods stood in a hot pool just across the Sound from us; a couple of states away, underground silos hid Minuteman missiles in the wheat fields. In our minds Karen had some kind of official standing that required her to call people up and warn them. Or her next-door neighbor Lois would come over and the two of them would take turns calling people who already knew the danger, to strategize. With Lois there, the talk usually worked its way around from missiles to alarming or disgraceful stories in the newspaper: freeway crashes killing whole families, cuts in food stamps, and kids found chained in basements.

It was Lois who introduced our father to Gerda. Lois had known Gerda and her husband Bob for years and years; she had known them when they were holding hands in the corridors of Garfield High School. It was no surprise to hear that at the time of the bear attack, Lois had spent hours in our aunt's kitchen going over the details. When Gerda came back into town, Lois invited Karen over to meet her. Inside of an hour Karen had it arranged that Lois and Gerda would come over for dinner, and so would our father. That very night. Just a casserole, Karen said. And really nothing would please Cal more than seeing his brother-in-law John and his neighbor Lois, and so on. And Lois's friend of course. Gerda.

"NOW, DON'T YOU GIRLS STEP on a spider," Lois told us more than once in the early days, waving her cigarette at Karen's frog poster. "Not in this house." The frog presided over the kitchen, crouched in a spiral of print that read SENTIENT BEINGS ARE NUMBERLESS; I VOW TO SAVE THEM. I remember Karen explaining *sentient* to Shelley. It meant that a frog took an interest in its kind. It meant spiders had fears. Hiding, waiting for food to draw near, driven by thirst down porcelain inclines, they feared us. The last thing they wanted, before their intense lives of waiting shriveled to gray lint in the basement, was to run into one of us. To this day I don't think Shelley and I see a spider without wondering whether it has had enough to eat and drink. And the poster didn't sound like a rule but it was one, a Buddhist rule. Karen explained Buddhism. I tried to listen the way Shelley did, but Karen's explanations took time and you were supposed to ask questions. Questions did not come to me the way they did to Shelley. What about bacteria? Sentient or not? What about the ones you cremated along with a person? Our mother had been sick, there must have been a lot of bacteria. No, bacteria were not at fault in our mother's case.

The cremation occupied Shelley's mind for a long time. She wanted to see where they cremated the dogs and cats at the clinic, but our father wouldn't take her. She took the encyclopedia to her room and made her own study of the subject of fire on flesh. Because what if the person being cremated was sentient? How did anyone know what went on when you were dead?

"SHE SET FIRE TO HERSELF!" Karen told Lois on the phone.

"I did not," Shelley said. "I didn't catch on fire, did I, Jenny?"

But she had not let me in the room when she rolled up her sleeve, struck a match, and held it to the skin of her elbow long enough to raise a blister. The blister opened and reopened in the ensuing weeks, being on a moving joint.

After that she went to see a therapist, an old woman from Karen's meetings and marches. In the therapist's bathroom, where Shelley once went to throw up, there was a cartoon of a naked woman on horseback. The woman carried a flag with a broken bomb on it. Shelley told me about it. Hearing us, Karen explained that the woman on the horse was Lady Godiva, who, being in fact an early activist, had ridden naked through a town in order to make her husband lift a tax on his people. "How come?" Shelley said. "Why would that make him do it?"

For once Karen had no explanation. Shelley got the encyclopedia and reported that it was a legend.

"Shelley, honey, lighten up," said Lois. "Somebody did something like that or there wouldn't be a legend."

When Lois was told a bad enough story from the newspaper, she crossed herself. I noticed that; I liked to see the little shake of the torso she gave once she had brushed off some threat. Nobody in our family had a religion except Karen, with her one rule, but we were allowed to have one if we wanted to, and I prayed to everything, from the stars to the giant statue of a dairy cow on the trip to Carnation Farms. I prayed to our fish circling the bowl with its gracious trailing fin, and occasionally to the point of light on the old TV when you turned it off. On camping trips I prayed to the tent flap, arched like a church window when the flashlight shone on it from outside. I prayed to all possible candidates for messenger to or from our mother. For what did I pray? A prayer was not so much a specific petition as a mental drone, unsought and surprising in its arrival, a fit of abjection with a luxury to it, a drama attaching to oneself, however invisible it might be to others. *Tell her to come back. Just once to see Shelley.*

Any number of women at home with their kids answered the phone in the dark afternoons of Seattle. So a lot of us heard the things talked about in Karen's kitchen in the eighties, and I wonder how many think about them the way Shelley and I do when we see kids get off a school bus in the rain. In our minds nuclear war existed in a kind of Magic 8-Ball, coming to the surface along with the numberless sentient beings, the ozone hole, Scrabble words scattered by the phone cord. Stevie Wonder on the stereo singing "Higher Ground," or when Shelley started piano lessons, Glenn Gould playing and humming an infinity of ascending and descending notes that never quite turned into a song but made Shelley roll her head and goggle her eyes and sing them in a way we agreed was the right match.

She was seven. I was four. I wished to become Shelley, reading words and music, knowing how to find out what people meant, when to argue, when to be unafraid, when to grow cold and faraway. But without tears: Shelley wouldn't cry the way I did, even when she hurt herself. She remembered everything, as I did not. I did not connect a repeating vague bleakness in certain rooms and at bedtime with any condition of my own. I thought I would always have to look for a sign and ask, *Are we sad?*

Rain streaked the windows; our father, stooped and silent, was somewhere sewing up a dog; our mother's body had gone up in flames; warheads could melt the flesh off your bones—yet Karen laughed, she cooked, she followed her rule. Why? Why protect the spider?

What about the things the spider had to trap and eat alive or it would starve?

"Hoo, you got her there!" Lois crowed.

"Shelley, we can't save everything we want to."

At the end of the day when our father came to pick us up, Karen would open the oven to let out the smell of her casserole so he would stay for dinner. "Oh, John, just let the girls finish their game," she would plead. Or, "Shelley's almost finished her homework. And Jenny's so cozy. She's under the table in the fort. Shh, I think she's asleep."

I liked to think our mother would have been the same way, had Karen been the one who died.

Uncle Cal liked to tell people he had spent years in a commune with four hungry guys and two sisters who wore feathers in their hair, painted their toenails, played the guitar, and knew how to cook. "Those two," he said. "They would make enough food for ten people, and you better go out and find ten or it hurt their feelings. So they could feed 'em *to-fu*."

Karen said Cal was the reason for the women's movement. She said the place was not a commune but just a big student house with rooms rented out and a shared kitchen.

They each had a day to cook the meals, but our mother, Kathleen, had been the best, Karen and Uncle Cal agreed. She was the youngest, but she could put a big meal together in twenty minutes, and every so often she broke loose and cooked *meat*. They argued about who in the house had eaten it openly and who in secret.

I could picture somebody at a skillet, spatula in hand. Meat sizzling. Her feet were bare, her back was to me, the hair in blond braids. *What did she look like?* Pictures of her had turned into something lined up on the bookcase with the goldfish bowl and the cat anatomy book. In the big, framed one, our father's favorite, she stood in the snow on her cross-country skis, waving a gloved hand. But the hair was pushed up under a wool hat and a blot of glare took out the eyes behind the glasses.

Once when I was lying in the upstairs hall dangling my Slinky through the banisters, into my ear on the floorboards came her voice calling up the stairs: "John?" When I told Shelley, she said the sound was not a voice, and if a voice, not our mother's. But she got down and put her ear on the spot.

When I was four it is said that I would demand the commune story. "Talk about meat!" I saw them all laughing and I couldn't figure out why the person who had singled herself out, the best and fastest cook—why the one who had known they all wanted meat was the one who died.

Also, at that age I couldn't figure out where our father was, in the house story. I didn't have the concept of marriage getting started in a specific place and time, with separate lives leading into it, and some choice involved. At the same time, I knew there were weddings. When the obligation was laid on the bride and groom I wasn't sure.

Even today I find myself thinking something of the sort, about Karen and Cal and others. People their age. Nobody our age. Maybe this is what everybody feels about the previous generation, and it isn't that something has changed.

Straight out of the commune they had their kids, so that by the time Shelley and I were in the house, our cousins were in high school. No one would have expected Dylan and Ricky to sit down at the kitchen table in the afternoon and talk about bombs and kidnappings and hikers lost in whiteouts. And at home, although he would hear us out on the news of ill-treated dogs who partially ate the baby when some infernal relative left them alone with it, our father gave no sign that these things held even enough interest to make somebody want to dispute them.

In time Shelley, too, no longer sat and listened. "Oh, dear, I've done it again," Karen would say when Shelley backed away from the table. I could tell she worried about Shelley, whose report card said that while she read at a tenth-grade level in the second grade, she took no part in the majority of activities and picked her hangnails until they bled. We knew some of this to be true, but Karen said, "This makes me mad." She called the teacher. "I'm her *aunt*," Karen said, making a face at the word for our benefit. She held the phone away from her ear so we could hear the pitch of the teacher's high, explaining voice. "Well, I wondered," Karen answered her. "I wondered if you were familiar with that."

The day came when we both had an interest to take us out of reach of the phone cord. Our cousins gave us their old *Donkey Kong*, one of the early versions that froze on the screen and had to be shaken and blown on until you spat, which Shelley played so much she could see the little geometric gorilla running up ladders in her sleep.

"In a dream," she told me, "you play a whole lot better. I can get him to do stuff. I can get him up a ladder"—her eyes narrowed over the control pad—"that *keeps going*." Her mouth stayed open with the lips bound over the teeth, which was a sign that she wouldn't stop when it was time to feed the dogs—that was our job after school, because although he lived mostly at Karen's now, one of them, Ben, was our dog—and she wouldn't stop to read me *Wonder Woman* in the fort under the table, where we would have spent every afternoon if the choice had been mine. There I had sworn that once, at the edge of the blanket that hid us as she read, two bare feet had come to stand, with toenails the color in the bottle of polish that still sat on a mirrored tray in our bathroom at home.

"They did not."

"They did so. I saw."

Then I felt bad, because while I had not made up the voice in the floorboards, I had made up the feet, and into Shelley's eyes as she tried to force some proof of the vision came the blank look I hated. The day was over. Now she wouldn't do anything except advance through the levels of *Donkey Kong* until our father came from the clinic to take us home, where she could go to sleep and follow the ladder up to wherever it went.

"He's not supposed to get away," I reminded her. By this time I too was in school, finally I knew something. "Mario's supposed to catch him." There was a hammer in the game that I could hardly ever pick up, though Shelley could, every time. Mario was supposed to use it to save the girl from Donkey Kong.

"This ladder just keeps on going," Shelley said. "I'm going to see."

Even awake she was good enough that our cousins—coming and going with their quick feints as if to sock us, their grins, their loud soccer cleats—would stop to watch her play. Up the ladder the gorilla went, clasping the girl. When they were watching, Shelley played so fast that our dog, Ben, would look up and whine, and I would have to get up off the rug and hook her sweaty hair behind her ears.

SHELLEY GAVE UP THE ADVANTAGE of having learned to read at three, and quit high school. For a while she groomed trails in a couple of state parks, and then she got a job with the highway department, driving a survey van. Then suddenly she was so thin she had to hold up her jeans with a belt, and talkative, always scratching her head and revising some plan. On weekends she helped out at our father's clinic. She was good with the dogs in particular, but she had developed a theory that people should not own them. An animal should not have to live indoors with people, doing their will. "Where should it go?" my father asked gently, the way he talked to owners when they were distraught. She didn't know where it should go. Because the wild dog had been changed by us, so that it was no longer safe without us. "You're putting too much energy into this, honey," said Karen, who had taught us to think about these very things. She tried to hold Shelley's hands to keep her from scratching her head, where you could see scabs in the part.

Then Shelley was going to learn to play the drums. She drove all the way to Portland to buy a set of drums you could get anywhere, and soon after that she fell prey to something.

We got a call from her survey team. The guy on the phone said they were in an emergency room in the suburbs and Shelley was with a nurse, describing for the third time the scrambling legs and thumping tail of a dog they had found run over beside the road. It was not as if this was the first dog they had come upon on the state highways. In the background I could hear Shelley's voice raised over another, quieter voice. "It wouldn't be a bad idea for you to get over here," her coworker said.

After that, she gave up talking and spent six months curled up in a facility where I went with my father and Karen to see her whenever they would let us.

A label might have contained what was wrong with her within two borders, and made it clear that others had had the same thing happen, but nobody provided one. As it was, the thing wrong seemed unlimited, and hers alone. A private effort, a tiring, unnecessary pioneering, fiendish in a quiet way, like hiding while people searched for you, or going to bed to dream about a ladder.

And then, as the doctors had said she would, she got better. She woke up, left the low, quiet building, went for her GED, and applied to college because she had to do that before she could go to vet school. And she did learn to play the drums, and played in a serious band made up of surveyors, the ones who had taken her to the emergency room.

Once she was out, she got back the energy she had had for doing a thing without stopping. Only now she was practical; she was going to get her hands on the severed paws and the crushed spines.

I was more like my mother—or like the woman Karen told me had been my mother, who although she had wanted, with Karen, to consider the worst that can happen, had never for a minute wanted to be on intimate terms with it. "You girls are both like her, in your ways," Karen said. "She felt things. She was not at peace. But who says we're supposed to be, in this life?"

If we were not, still Karen liked to go over the past at enough length that it lost the force of secrets and misery and diffused itself in words, like the words that spiraled protectively around the frog. "Your father was an awful mess. I didn't know what he might do. A poor old guy had just been in the paper, driving off the floating bridge into the lake. You don't remember."

I was always saying I didn't. I said those days were a blank, but I did have a couple of memories. One was of Shelley at the bathroom keyhole. "Go away," she said in a harsh whisper.

"I can look too."

"He's in there. Go play."

"I don't have to."

"*He's crying.*"

He must have heard us and backed up against the wall by the toilet, because when she let me look, I couldn't see him. Finally he came out, rubbing his face with a towel as if he had been in there washing.

FOR OUR FATHER'S WEDDING, SHELLEY and her partner Diana flew in from Chicago two days ahead of time. They stayed with me in the apartment I had shared with my boyfriend Eddie before he moved out. My ex-boyfriend. When she got up the first morning, Diana sat down at his piano in her silk pajamas and began to play, with a few wrong notes but a flowing style. After a bit you could tell it was "Stairway to Heaven" she was playing. When I laughed, Shelley said, "She taught herself."

"No, no, I was just thinking of that sign in the guitar store, NO 'STAIRWAY TO HEAVEN.' And backwards, remember Ricky told us, it was satanic? And we didn't know who Satan was?"

"Yeah . . . she just now got the sheet music," Shelley said, scanning the few CDs Eddie had left on the shelves.

Shelley was driving us over the pass because we had Eddie's car and it was a stick shift. I didn't like to drive it in the mountains. The wedding was taking place at a bed-and-breakfast in the Cascades, on the east side. The car was a hatchback with room for three of us, luggage, flowers, presents, a cooler of champagne and the cake. "I'd trust Shelley with it before

I'd trust you anyway," Eddie said. In our laughing days, he had laughed at the way I popped the clutch on the hills of Seattle.

Since then he had been rethinking things. My driving wasn't funny any more, and maybe I myself wasn't as entertaining as I thought I was. At one time my interests had had a comic flavor, for him. He would tell our friends, "We used to get the *New York Times* but they didn't have enough obituaries."

Eddie taught music and language arts in middle school, and at night he played the piano in a bar where I went with my friend Kitty from work. Kitty and I were both at the paper, condensing stuff off the wires into those two-inch-long items Karen used to read to people on the phone. Fillers, they were called.

If we stayed far enough into the evening, Eddie arrived, sat down, put a brandy glass on the piano for tips, and played for two hours without looking up or asking for requests, so hardly anybody put anything in the glass. He did smile to himself, once or twice in a set. The first night we saw him, I thought about him later when I was at home in bed. I thought he was a man who smiled privately, a man whose eyebrows would go up in pained transport during certain passages, like Glenn Gould's. A man with thick black eyelashes.

His hands stayed low over the keys, no flourishes. They looked lazy, but the sound was crisp. Up close, when Kitty and I invited him to join us the first time, he looked more like a boy, grinning and making jokes, quoting movies. It turned out he had graduated a year after we did. Still, there on the table were the large-jointed hands from the keyboard, lying at rest as the talk went on, as if what came out of his mouth was no concern of theirs. I don't know why I liked to look at them, and to hear his laugh-choked voice, when he really wasn't saying anything, only repeating stories and quoting Comedy Central, or why I waited for Kitty to go to the bathroom and leave me alone with him when what I wanted was an established grown-up, not solemn but on the melancholy side, with a few creases in his forehead, and convictions.

Eddie avoided convictions. He came from a big Catholic family, with priests in it. I said he should be proud, the Catholic bishops had come out against the war. Furthermore, he should be glad he was raised with a religion to comfort him. He laughed at that, but every so often he would sneak off early on a Sunday morning to go to Mass. He didn't offer to take me with him. "You'd give me a hard time," he said.

That summer I had been to his brother's wedding, a big Catholic affair with Eddie playing the organ at Mass and making funny toasts at the reception. The brothers took turns dancing with their mother. When she walked out onto the floor on Eddie's arm, taking small steps in her long girdle, I thought, *He is a kind of prince.* That was my last good thought about him for a while, because we had a lot more of the Signature Cocktail and then a fight on the way home, as I'm sure a lot of people do, shut in cars after the odd brevity and letdown of the ceremony and then all the waiting in line and the tense, antique presenting of this person to that one, and the pouring and toasting and clapping, and the mothers with eyes red and smudged because, they said, they were so happy.

Two people agree to lock themselves in together, in defiance of reason and the Dissolutions column, and we celebrate it every time. I said something to that effect. Eddie said his brother's new wife, far from being stupefied, as I had suggested, by the ornate event she herself had planned in every detail, was simply a girl who knew how to be happy. "Is that right?" I said. "How?" He thought it was just another question like the ones I had asked about the Mass. Why did we clap after they kissed? Did people always clap in church? In movies I had never seen such a thing. Why didn't we kneel? Weren't you supposed to kneel, in the Catholic Church? Where were the statues and the candles? Why was marriage a sacrament?

THE SECOND PHASE BEGAN WHEN the narrow space of my apartment—a place I had chosen for its tight shelter—had made room for his piano and skis and kayak. If I woke up at night, I would see his two bikes, the front wheel of the city one facing its horns in on us from the balcony like a rained-on, aggrieved animal, and he, awake or asleep, would have moved onto my side of the bed, against my back. In the hot room his body steamed under the layers of covers he had to have.

Then he started taking my glasses off to look at me. I couldn't see him. He said, "I'm sorry, it's your eyes when you take off your glasses."

"Maybe I should get contacts."

"No, no, it's what I like. I like that sweet, bleary look."

"Shall I take off my shoes and get pregnant?" That's what I said, instead of saying I liked his eyes too, the black eyelashes that cast an openwork shadow when he played the piano or read under a lamp. I don't know why I did that. I don't know why I said one thing rather than the other, and kept trying to break something down in him, some resolute optimism, which had soothed me in the early weeks.

"OK, I won't do that any more."

"I can't see shit without my glasses."

"Are you trying to see shit?" Then, to be nicer or to get away from the table, he moved over to the piano and played a few bars of something.

"What's that?"

"Hovhaness. It's called 'Beloved, you looked into space.'"

That "Beloved" did it for a few days. Then he said something. He said despair was learned. Look at Shelley's problems—surely they had something to do with seeing John, our father, deal with things in the way he had, with his protracted mourning.

"Oh, for God's sake," I said. "*Protracted.* Quit talking to Karen."

If, Eddie said, he had had some struggles himself, he didn't intend to bring anybody down about them. What he wanted at this point was to ride his mountain bike or go hiking on weekends—by himself if I chose not to enjoy such things—and yes, maintain a good mood. Play music. Get married when the time came. Sure. Have children.

Children. Did he have any idea what that meant? *Children.* How *every minute of life*, children were in your power and you in theirs? How if you were no good at it, how if you disappeared—

"Let's say I wouldn't."

"Wouldn't what?"

"Disappear. Say I luck out and get a full life-span."

"There's no point. There's no point in arguing this."

"I'm not arguing, Jenny. Anybody see any kids here for me to run out on?" Finally he grinned, not so much at me as out the window at his bikes. He shook his head and said, "I've had some tough roommates, but we always worked it out, we always—"

"Go find them," I said. "Have a beer."

His expression didn't change, but he kept looking out the window. I said I was sorry, because his face, if I looked at it and forgot what he was saying, had that effect on me. I was sorry and I wasn't. I could see that we had fallen into a routine combat, but I wasn't sure which one of us I wanted to win.

When we finally decided he would move out, he came back every week to practice. It was too expensive to move the piano a second time. He came at the end of the school day, when I was still at work, but I could tell when he had been there because the radiators would be hissing. I could turn them down, I could turn them off if I wanted to. No more deadweight comforter on the bed, steamed windows, jokes from movies, trips to look at bigger places because our two incomes made one decent one and a piano could have its own room. No more schoolboy analysis of Shelley and me.

All this was in the second phase. It was in the first phase, right after he had moved in, that I was in Chicago to share with Shelley my good spirits, my change of fortune, my repudiation of doubt, and to meet Diana.

They had just bought a condo. If I had had to guess, I would have said Diana would be messy, but the place was spare and chastely neat. With the mirrors, the tall windows, the trees in pots, it had a sneaky luxury, somewhere between a good hotel and a chapel. It had an air of being held in readiness for something other than just sitting around. Some visit, not mine, some visitation. I thought of what Eddie would say about it. He would like it. He had not been raised by Karen; he saw nothing wrong with luxury. "Hey, a vet and a lawyer," he would say. "Why not?"

Right up to the day her law school loans came through, Diana had been poor. That's why she had Norfolk pines in the bay windows and hushed lithographs of winter branches on the walls: In the part of town she came from, all they had was tree of heaven, which grew in empty lots and stank. Every year, the school nurse sent notes home saying Diana came to school in shoes that were too small. Karen knew about the trees and the shoes from Shelley. Karen could always get things out of you. Karen said if they opened Diana's closet when they were showing me the place, I should not comment on the shoe racks.

I ran my hands over the slate coffee table and appreciated the view of Lincoln Park, the art, and Diana's law books high up, reachable by teak ladders on wheels. Diana climbed up one to show how convenient it was. I looked over at Shelley. She hadn't changed, she didn't notice where she was. She had given me a tour of the clinic where she worked, a cat clinic not far from their new place. She took a scrawny young cat with twitching ears out of its cage and the whole time we were walking around she carried it, confined in a towel because it was demented. A cat could be demented. It had been weaned too soon and had to be held in a firm grip and given something to suck. We had never had cats at home. What about the dogs by the side of the road?

"Good beer," I said when Diana handed me a bottle.

"Ale," she said, and winked at me. "*Blond.*"

I looked at the label. She took a long swig from hers. Her hair was the shiny flat blond of a Scrabble tile, though it wasn't clear whether that was a natural color because her groomed eyebrows were dark.

"Hey, don't flirt with Jenny," Shelley said.

Since then, Shelley had been home a couple of times, but I hadn't seen Diana again until they came for the wedding. Whenever there was a lull in the talk, she would go over and feel out three or four chords, standing up, in her listening-for-the-muse style—I tried to think of what Eddie would have called it. "We have to get a piano, it's time," she kept saying to Shelley as we sat around.

I was on my guard, but she got the story of our childhood out of me. Shelley said, "You already know all that."

"I just want to get the whole picture. You'd be a good witness, Jenny."

"You mean I'm easily led."

"I mean you answer. Not like Shelley."

"Shelley has dignity," I said. "So—now it's your turn."

But Diana was finished with our talk. She went out and stood on the balcony, where there were no bikes now, and came back stretching and yawning. "God, I just want to go back to bed. I do. I have to. There's no *sun* here. Isn't it supposed to be summer?"

They had my room; Shelley's eyes followed her as she closed the door. Into Shelley's face of stubborn reserve came a flush, a humble, all-but-witless half smile. She said, "She needs more sleep than some people." What was this? This was love? Was this what came about? This stupid, helpless smile?

We left early the next morning. Diana fell back to sleep as soon as we hit the freeway. She slept until the North Cascades Highway began its climb, when her eyes opened and she sat up and said, "OK, who *is* this woman? Jesus. She killed a bear."

"She didn't kill it," Shelley said. "Fish and Wildlife killed it."

"She tried to. She didn't do what he told her to. He told her to run. I mean, how do you know what you would do?" No one answered her. "So OK then, what would *you* do?"

"No idea," Shelley said. "What about you?"

"Well, I don't know! But Jesus, I don't think so. I mean, I identify, but I . . . no."

"I heard you were a girl of action," Shelley said.

"Yeah." Diana leaned around to me. "What about you, back there? You look wiped out." She rattled her nails with their arched moons against the compartment with Eddie's CDs. "It's that guy, isn't it. Poor thing." She made a pout of sympathy.

"Him or me?"

"You. What about you, would you do that for him?"

"Nope," I said.

"One person in a thousand would," Shelley said. "Maybe would have the presence of mind. Maybe. See out there? They call these the Alps of America."

Diana didn't look to either side: at a plunge into treetops on one and bare rock cut by a narrow waterfall on the other. After a bit she laughed and shook her finger at Shelley. "You would." She faced around again to me. "She would, wouldn't she. Your sister."

Shelley said, "No way."

"You would. You'd do it for me."

"Sure wish I could say that was true," Shelley said. "Think I'd be under the bed." We both laughed, but not Diana.

"Oh, oh, don't you think she would?" Diana went on in a kind of stern baby talk. "Don't you think so?"

"I just can't really say."

"Come on, you're her sister. You know how she is."

"She's pretty brave."

"She's that kind," said Diana, turning back to Shelley with satisfaction. "Yes you are." She put her feet in their glowing leather boots up on the dashboard. She was going to be too hot in those, on the east side of the mountains.

"You could bust a femur like that," said Shelley. "I took care of the dog from an airbag wreck."

"So it happened to a dog."

"It happened to a kid. The dog was in the back."

"You're always saying what can happen," said Diana. "Anything can happen. Let's just get that out of the way."

Shelley didn't answer, and after a while Diana took her feet down and went back to sleep. I thought of putting on "Fred the Cat." It was one of Eddie's favorite car CDs, another one by his favorite old guy Hovhaness. The dead cat goes up a mountain to heaven. Hovhaness was a celebrator of mountains. Eddie's plan for his own funeral was for somebody to play "Fred the Cat Flies Up to Heaven." I was in a mood to tell Shelley this and play the CD for her, but while Diana was asleep she drove in silence, over the two passes and down the other side, speeding a little on the curve of the Liberty Bell cirque, where the mountains, with their avalanche chutes and crusts of snow, swing back to show the dusty greens and the cream-and-tan stone and floating hawks of the valley.

WHEN HE WAS INTRODUCED TO Gerda, who had come back to Seattle to pack up the house she had locked three years before, our father was already familiar with the story. Soon after it happened he had heard it from Karen, who had had all those talks with our neighbor Lois. Later, news of it came from wild-animal vets in touch with wildlife people who had made a brief plea for the bear to be removed to a farther range. But hurt a second time, the animal was a worse threat than before, and local feeling said it had to be shot.

No reprieve for stopping in mid-attack. People had their theories as to why an animal not mortally wounded, not even gushing blood, leaving only a spray of drops on the river rock, would have quit like that. It was weak from hibernation. It didn't have the use of one arm. Bad teeth. Pain. Fate.

Yet it was not uncommon for that to happen, an animal to obey some impulse of its own, native to it, our father said, with his new willingness to expand on a subject. The same way no two people will do exactly the same thing. No, he had never treated a bear, but he had done a lot of reading since meeting Gerda. Often a bear just took off, ran for cover. A bear had been a cub. A bear had racked up experiences. About bears he wouldn't use the words *good* and *bad*. He explained this to me in the no-such-thing way he had explained *satanic* when we were little. No devil. No hell.

Then . . . no heaven?

No. No, probably not.

All this about the bear was between the two of us. I knew he would never say any of it to Gerda. He was willing to admit that she had in fact met the wrong bear, the one most mercilessly wrong. Although if you started to think about it, it might have been the hour of the day putting them all at the river that was wrong, or the hour of another day the fall before, when a hunter had shot the bear in the shoulder and when it rose on its hind legs blown off half its paw, or the hour when the sun warmed and woke the bear in its den. If it had a den. Dad said they didn't always have one. But: time. Time being the villain. Some aspect of time. Some cruel aspect.

"What does that get you?" Eddie would say.

Wait. If everything—and not only living things—carried inside it its particle of time. And if no two particles were in concurrence or accord. They could be, but they didn't have to be. They might be in some violent magnetic opposition. Two of these bits of time might be like nuclear fuel rods, not meant to touch. Needing cooling water between them. But no one, ever, knowing this.

"Then . . . ?" Eddie would say. Every *if* had to have its *then.*

The three-inch claws had mauled Gerda in one stroke, but with her the sinking in of incisors never got started, the grinding done with the molars, according to our father, that turns of itself into something unstoppable. Or seemingly unstoppable. For the bear dropped its head, wagged it, flung off blood, leaned onto one forepaw and then the other, and then, instead of launching itself at Gerda, wheeled around and shuffled away.

Bob was close to death. The husband. He had a little more than an hour left to live.

"He was ready to go," our father said, with the care his voice had when he said it about a dog. "He was that bad hurt."

THE PINES HAD A FIRE pit, encircled by a little Stonehenge of log benches and stumps. We were welcome to sit in the circle if we wanted to but not to cook in the pit, or on the old iron charcoal grill next to it, because there was a burn ban. Nearby were two picnic tables; the Burneys would bring out the food.

The wedding was a package. The Burneys, who owned The Pines and specialized in weddings, were providing the meals. We were responsible for the cake. It was one of those rum-filled, heavy, dozen-egg cakes that need an industrial mixer, but not having one, I had drunk the rest of the rum and beaten the batter by hand until my arm cramped and I had a relapse and called Eddie, and hung up on his voicemail. He had left the car for me without coming up; I could see it parked a little way down the street. He must have been on his way somewhere himself, to drop it off early like this, confident that I still had my key. Where was he going, not saying a word? Not even flipping a pebble at the window behind which we had been lying mere weeks before with our naked legs entwined.

The next day, the day Shelley and Diana were arriving, my friend Kitty came over with a pastry bag to help me. "Whoa, this thing is *pre-served*," she said, sniffing the cake and hoisting the weight of it on the foil-covered board. When it was thickly iced she splashed red food coloring into what was left and stuffed the bag full and fluted a messy border of roses. She licked her fingers and studied her work. "She won't mind. This is a woman who killed a bear."

"She didn't kill it." Because that was part of it, wasn't it? The giant exertion, the muscles afire with effort. A divided effort, to murder and save. The ax thrown down. And then life going on. People in the room with you talking. People offering you a ghostly respect.

I had to admit that I was afraid to meet Gerda, afraid she might be crazy.

"I don't think so," Kitty said. "Think of who we're talking about. Who would your father fall for? It would have to be someone special." But I was afraid our father might have said to himself, *Now or never.* He might not have seen, in the time they had spent together, that the word *survivor*, by which we mean one who has more or less made a comeback, might not describe the woman who had lived through this event. *Special*, *survivor*: more of those words. She could be crazy. Even a normal death could affect your mind indefinitely.

Mrs. Burney had a thin face and slender, careful hands, one of them walking its fingers up the banister beside her as she led the way. Each of her statements had two parts, which she uttered as one, to soften the fact that they were warnings. "This is the bath, watch the hot tap in all the baths." We had already seen my room. Since I was alone I didn't have a cabin; instead I had a room downstairs in the main house just big enough to hold the four-poster heaped with pillows. Mrs. Burney apologized because the dresser was in the closet. I said, "No, this is just right."

Diana winked at me and said to Mrs. Burney, "She lived under the table as a kid."

Mrs. Burney let us look into the bridal suite, where a pink dress hung in a plastic bag. Our father and Gerda had arrived the day before; they were off on a little hike, said Mrs. Burney with an affirming smile. "You people," Diana said to Shelley. I hate hiking, but I almost wanted to defend the practice. Work, or aimless play—did not the hike put both to shame? No getting around the fact that the genie of it had touched to life a holy order all over the trails of our state, all over the Northwest. Shelley was in the order. Our father was, on a rare Saturday when he didn't work. Eddie was, I was not. Still, I didn't feel I was in Diana's category.

They had already rehearsed the ceremony, Mrs. Burney said. "Or rather, they went over the vows," she said, glancing at us to see if we were anti-ceremony. She and her husband were Presbyterians, she said, but she had been ordained a minister of the Universal Life Church. "Oh, you have to be. We came out here in the sixties and that's what people wanted, and now they want it again." As she closed the door to their room with her soft alertness, I wondered what had happened in between. At any rate you could tell that she was used to people occupying the honeymoon suite before the wedding.

Mrs. Burney watched as we lifted the cake, in its splotchy collar of roses, out of the box. "We aren't exactly pastry chefs," I said.

"It's lovely. See if we can slide it back onto the board so it won't—"

She made a delicate adjustment with the heels of her hands and quickly flashed a spatula to remodel the side where the sun had hit the icing in the car.

"My husband had a fall, watch the porch steps."

With one wrist in a splint, holding a beer in his finger and thumb, Mr. Burney sat in front of the TV in a little den off the kitchen. He kept waving to us with splint and beer as we admired Mrs. Burney's elaborate trays for the next day and the pies she had made for the weekend, and as we unwrapped flowers and greenery and stood them in her vases.

She filled the vases with water and turned politely to her husband, who had received some signal to switch off the TV and join us. He was not a fat man, but he had on a too-small polo shirt and he wore his belt low, under the belly. He had a gray sixties ponytail and a mustache that dangled at the corners of the theatrical smile he had assumed as he was tipping himself out of the recliner. "Why don't you show them where the tables . . . Oh, careful—" She steadied the vases as he braced himself against the counter.

"Pardon," he said, tipping an imaginary hat.

AN AFTERNOON WIND HAD KICKED up. Mr. Burney, breathing hard in the heat, sat on a log bench answering Diana's questions about forest fires. You could see how she would go about taking a deposition. Burney was giving up all he knew: lightning strikes, fires that ran underground along tree roots and exploded upward, fires that chased herds and leapt rivers.

"Anything can happen," Shelley said.

"You got it." Mr. Burney threw his arms out, sloshing beer at the trees. As a fire precaution, they had been limbed thirty feet up; all around us they stood like huge table legs. Put a wind like this with fire, he said, and sayonara to inn and cabins, not to mention thousands of acres of the national forest that surrounded us where we sat.

The wind, loud in the branches, was bashing the wooden seat of a long-roped swing against the tree trunk. "That'll let up," Mr. Burney said as it whipped our jeans and swept ashes onto the stone lip of the fire pit. You could see the big trunks of the Ponderosas rocking. "That'll let up, no problem," he repeated, as if we might want our money back. "Don't you worry, we'll have that ash out of there. Can't have any smudges on the bridesmaids."

"It's OK, we forgot to bring bridesmaids," said Diana. She went back to her questions, and while she ticked them off, swinging her crossed leg and stroking the air with her long fingers, Shelley watched for minutes, chewing on a piece of grass, like somebody using binoculars on an animal as it roamed. Mr. Burney had spent himself. Every so often the hand holding the bottle would tip as if he had gone to sleep, and Diana would have to repeat her question. Finally she said, "So I mean, if all this stuff has to be done, limbing and burn-banning and smoke jumping and all the rest of it so we'll be safe, why are we out here?"

Shelley said, "Maybe we should leave this earth."

Mr. Burney pulled one of his gray eyebrows down. "Dear lady," he said to Diana, "this was her parents' place. But," he added, "the kids went for it in a big way, in those days. Get 'em up in the tree house and you wouldn't see 'em for days."

"Tree house?" said Diana.

"Look there. Left of the end cabin. Look up. High." And there it was, a neat structure with a slanted roof, on a platform.

"Holy shit," Diana said. "That's high."

Shelley said, "How about when the tree sways?"

"You hold on. Sure. But we got cables up there, we got shocks. Auto shocks. The problem was snow. First one, the roof fell in. So we made it a lean-to. My son came up with that."

"How did you get it up there? Can people go up?"

"Can if they get a ladder truck in here."

"How did you get up and down?"

"Had us a rope ladder. She said it had to come down. A guest'll get on a ladder every time. We had a groom go up there and call for help. No way would he do what he was told. We had to have our boy go up. The little fella. Coulda walked a sheep through a wolf pack. Went up after the guy and brought him down."

"No kidding. I bet Shelley could get up there. She does that stuff. Don't deny it, you do. Well, I guess I'll have to settle for the swing. Now, save my place." She patted the log by Mr. Burney. "Bet you climbed up and hung the swing too, didn't you."

"That'll swing a mile. Many's a kid jumped out and banged himself up, till she"—he waved his splint at the house—"tells me I have to take that down too. But I never did it."

Then for a few minutes we just sat there in the noise of the wind. "Shelley was just reading me about that sound," Diana called from the swing. "There's a tree book in the cabin."

"Her dad was your serious bookworm," said Mr. Burney. "Like her."

The loudness of the wind, as if a bellowing crowd were massing out of sight, was giving me a feeling that was part exhilaration and part the wish to go indoors. This would be the sound that Eddie talked about, of casual threat. Eddie kept track of sounds. He said an eagle sounded like a mouse, not a kingly bird. A bear foraging sounded like a larger, more appalling pig. As for wind, he saw himself as some sort of apostle of it, though not someone who would let it intimidate him. The birds could vanish, the deer bed down, Eddie would stay out in the wind for the joy of it. I argued with him. I know I was always arguing. Let it have its own joy. Who was he to stand up to wind?

Outdoor people. My theory was—here he would back away with his hands up—no, really, they weren't really outdoors, these hikers and climbers, these mountain bikers with their gripper tires. They made it all a kind of indoors. They went into the elements as if there were a two-way friendship out there. Even Shelley forgot her suspicions and talked about birdcalls and the moon. When what was out there was wind, with its purpose that could not be gauged. Wildfire. No friendship. A bear was out there.

Without our noticing, it had gone completely quiet. Mr. Burney reversed course on the dangers of the place. "Here comes Bob now. I told him, we got the tents, you come out here with the little guys, put 'em in a sleeping bag and see if they don't have a time. We used to be out here with our guys. We had three."

I should have asked where the three were now, but I was still thinking, *Bob?* Bob was the husband. The dead husband.

But he meant Bobby, Gerda's son. She had two; Bobby had flown in from the Midwest with his family, and Glen from Florida with his. The men—they were boys, really—were coming down the path from the cabins without their wives. Both of them stopped at the rope swing.

In no time Glen was confiding to Diana that he had had to put this part of the country behind him. It was ruined for him, the Northwest. Was it, Diana wanted to know, maybe a little creepy to be back? It was, and he wasn't sure why his mother had picked this particular bed-and-breakfast, when she had never been here either. It was nowhere near the other place, but it was *out here.*

"Hey, it's a nice place," Bobby said. "We always camped on the east side. Just look around you. That's why they'd bring us over here. Look at those trees."

"Incredible trees," said Diana, raising her eyes with their suggestion that things around her might be extensions of herself.

Bobby said, "See that thick bark." The bark on the pines had a pattern of segmented creatures swimming over each other to reach the top of the tree. "Smell it. Vanilla. There's nothing like that Ponderosa smell."

"Mm, I see what you mean," said Diana. "More like caramel."

"Yeah, we hiked, we camped," Glen resumed. "We rock-climbed, we orienteered. You name it. They made us go hunting, for Christ's sake. Our dad—"

"That's the dumbest thing I ever heard," said Bobby, socking his brother on the arm. "We wanted to go hunting."

"I've never camped," Diana said, pumping the swing. "My feeling about camping is that I would passionately hate it."

"Come on, I'm pretty sure you wouldn't," said Bobby. Neither brother seemed to know where to locate Diana in the family. She was swinging with her legs out in front of her. She scuffed her boot heels in the dirt and leaned back with her hair hanging. The brothers on either side, not quite arguing, did not push the swing but slapped at the rope when it passed them.

Shelley spoke up from the bench. "You wouldn't hate camping."

"I really want to crawl into a three-foot space and lie down."

"When you crawl out in the morning, it's just the world and you."

"I need more than that."

We heard loud whoops, and Bobby's two little boys came running down from the cabins, with his wife, Cindy, behind them, and Becca, short and stocky as a child herself, with a child's dusky tan, carrying her baby in one of those car seats with handles. "They wouldn't go down for their nap," Cindy said tiredly but without irritation. "Maybe that means they'll go to bed early." She was my age or younger, somewhere in her twenties, and Becca, as she herself had told Diana, was only twenty-two. Gerda's sons had both married young, just as she had. I wondered how Cindy summoned her weary patience. I wondered how it would feel to have assembled human beings out of your own cells. The way Becca swung the car seat it could have held the groceries. Eddie would have liked that. It wasn't as if no one had ever made the decision to have kids before. You should just do it. Get on with it, without worrying about the giant entry port you had just carved into yourself and a succession of others, for all the possible griefs.

When I looked into the car seat a blue stare leapt out like a shock from a carpet. "Well!" I said. "Who are you?"

"This is Justin," said Becca solemnly, like a child introducing a doll that you will have to pretend is real. "Justin, this is your aunt-to-be. She can hold you if she wants to, after you eat." As I bent over him the blue eyes narrowed, went out of focus, caressed me powerfully when they refocused, fixing me in some world without excuses or even reasons for what anybody might do. *Shall I hold you?* I asked them, because it seemed the power was his, he could just as easily pull me into the car seat with him.

Diana came over and looked in. She pulled back in the same dizzy way. "Wow. How old?" she said.

"Four months," said Becca. "Exactly a year and a half ago I gave up smoking so we could have him."

"Worth it, I bet," Diana said.

"It was worth everything you have in this world," Becca said with a dead calm as if she were reading from a brochure. "Turn around," she read on. She meant Glen; he turned and she pulled a folded rubber pad out of his hip pocket and sighing briskly, spread it on the pine needles. Glen hoisted the baby over onto the pad, knelt, and unsnapped him. A sharp sweet stench went up. After a bit Glen said, "This is cornstarch I'm powdering with," like a cook on TV. "The talcum they used on us, on our generation, was a poison. Went straight to the lung."

I had a vision of legions of us moving slowly, powdered white, poisoned. "And then they wouldn't let us have cigarettes in middle school," Becca mused, with the first sign that she could smile.

"Damn!" said Diana.

Glen said, "Becca, that is not a joke." She had her shirt open, show-ing a butterfly tattoo above the nursing bra, and she was reaching for the baby, but Glen held him back from her for a minute before handing him over. Becca began to nurse him in silence, as if language were being pulled out of her. Glen absorbed a tabulating look from Diana, and sat down.

Suddenly I felt, on us all, the eye of the father. The dead man. Bob. What if Bob could see this scene, with his sons, his grandchildren. What were they doing here? What if he could see what was going to happen? That in the morning someone who had lived a life in which she had loved him enough to die for him was going to stand under the trees and get married. So that love—had it not been a singular thing after all? Was it, with the unthinking power it had let loose, somehow repeatable?

After a while the baby let go and started in with a noise, a tone like a distant vacuum cleaner. "He'll make that sound," Becca said, resum-ing her recitation. At that, Glen's jaw muscles relaxed and they gave each other that look that has to do with a baby and some secret pageant of which it is the cause and the effect. Soon the little boys were running back and forth, making competing piles of the broomlets the wind had sheared off the Ponderosas.

"You know, Gerda is a wonderful woman," Cindy said to me, quietly.

The older one, Robbie, stopped with his handfuls of pine needles. "Gerda is Grandma," he warned me solemnly. "She killed a bear."

"You'll see. We all love her to pieces. But you know, Jenny—I hope I can say this to you—she has had a lot happen to her. The guys too. I hope the past won't come up. I hope we won't get into that."

"I don't think we will. I'll be careful. I know what you mean." I had just met Cindy; I didn't think I could ask her if her mother-in-law was crazy.

"And so when is your aunt Karen going to get here?" Of course while Gerda was closing up the life she had begun in Indianapolis near Bobby and Cindy, instead of the one in Seattle she had been planning to leave behind before she met our father, Karen had gotten to know Cindy. On the phone. "Yeah," Cindy said, "if she couldn't get Gerda, she'd call me. One afternoon we talked for an hour. She's something, isn't she? I just love her." I could imagine Cindy's afternoon on the phone with Karen. "And I can't wait to meet your daddy. I know he's such a gentleman."

I had one of those realizations you get when somebody makes a comment in passing, that our father was, indeed, a gentleman. When an owner brought in a matted old beast on its last legs, I know my father had comfort to lend, sometimes for an hour or more, waiting for the person to be ready before giving any sign that the agreed-upon syringe of release and departure lay on a tray in the next room. *He wouldn't have wanted a life where he couldn't run. This was a cat that couldn't have been subjected to daily needles.* And so, did that mean he understood someone who had killed an animal? Or not killed it, but fought it with the intent to kill? And did he ask himself these questions, or did he just finally meet somebody after all these years? And who was this woman? Did they all in fact love her, as Cindy said? Or was something about her blemished, touched with animal breath? I knew about that. Bears ate carrion: their lips slopped, baring the gum; their tongues lolled. They were not proud, lofty animals. The males would kill and eat a cub. "And I love your sister," Cindy added. "Aren't these cabins sweet?"

The cabins were knotty pine, with a sink in the bedroom and a row of faded books on the dresser. Every cabin had its books, and behind Mr. Burney's chair in the den were shelves of them, dim and formal, representing some farther-back life than the paperbacks in the parlor for the guests. A tall pump organ with fern stands on either side of it spoke of that life, into which Mr. Burney seemed to have stumbled from a later time but still not the present.

The cabins had tin showers and wall hooks instead of closets, but in the main house there were tied-back curtains, doilies under the lamps, and chocolates on the pillow. "Who would have their honeymoon in a bed-and-breakfast?" Diana had whispered loudly on the stairs. "I mean, young couples."

AS THE AFTERNOON WORE ON, Mr. Burney grew more unsteady on his feet. He had lugged out a cooler of beer and flung a tablecloth over a stump for the wine bottles. Shelley helped him with a case of soda water, and I went in to get the glasses while he veered off to the swing, where Diana was pushing the little boys and listening to their fathers.

Mr. Burney stood by for a while, rocking with the pines, and then he stomped over and yanked the cooler open. "Folks, what are you waiting for? Let's get started here." He made his way back to the swing, and with a formal concentration opened two bottles and presented one to Diana. Glen was explaining something to her, counting his points on his fingers, and without taking her eyes off his face she accepted the beer with a little wave. Mr. Burney raised his splint. "Hear, hear! Drink up! To matrimony!"

Then we all got off the stumps and joined in, except Becca. "She's nursing," Glen reminded Mr. Burney. "Anything she drinks, he drinks."

"Hey, look who we've got here!" cried Burney. And there they were, coming out of the woods, our father and Gerda.

I saw them swinging hands. Then she fell behind him, coming down the log steps at the trailhead. I could see a head of white hair and a hot-pink shirt. We all got up from our tree stumps and cheered as they came shyly across the pine needles.

Gerda didn't have an especially forceful grip when she shook your hand. She didn't look like someone who would hunt or climb rocks or even work out. Her hair was a solid glossy white and reached her shoulders, and her wide face had pink young skin just crisscrossed with lines at the eyes, which were blue and childishly clear. I felt them touch me, though. You could see she had been through something.

"Here she is," our father said, his face stretched tight with excitement under his new crew cut. He had a smile like somebody coming deafened out of a rock concert. No one knew who should be introduced first, so with his hand on Gerda's waist he started with us.

All she said was our names, turning to him with a look of confirmation as if the bearer of the name were all she could have hoped. She took Shelley's hand a second time and repeated her name. I felt her hand tremble when she came back to me a second time. "The little one," she said. Her eyes were the blue of her baby grandson's, with some of the same drag on you.

So this was Gerda. "Can't I just hug you?" Diana said, cocking her head. Then we all hugged Gerda and each other, and the sons shook our father's hand and the daughters-in-law hugged him and the first part was over.

In the middle of it all, Karen and Uncle Cal pulled in. Karen ran down from the car calling, "Oh, look at us, late to a wedding." She and Gerda hugged, held each other at arm's length, hugged again. "Oh, this is a happy day. Tomorrow I mean. Oh, you've cut off your hair. But it looks great."

"I thought it was time," Gerda said with a laugh. "You should have seen it," she said to Diana. "I hadn't cut it in three years. I had it in one of those braids." Of course she would pick Diana, whose straight hair swung so neatly at the neck. So Gerda did talk, she laughed. Like all women, she explained a haircut.

Our father had said she was small, but she was not small. She filled out the pink shirt and she was taller than I was. Her legs, wide at the thigh in stretch jeans, were almost as long as Diana's. The legs looked like they belonged to someone who would go shopping and buy herself an expensive bathing suit. Dad could not stop smiling. "So here she is, Jenny," he said again, when I took him into the kitchen to see the cake. Was it all right for the groom to see it? Mrs. Burney thought so.

"She's wonderful," I told him. "How long was her hair before?" What kind of a question was that?

"I don't know," he said, bewildered. He really didn't know.

"Hi, baby," she whispered when he came back. Very soft on the *b*'s, as if a tall man with a receding hairline really were a baby. She took his hand. It was then that I saw she was beautiful. It had escaped me until that moment.

I wondered if everybody else had known it right away. Who was seeing her for the first time? Only the three of us, Shelley and Diana and I. Two were her sons, of course, used to her—though Glen had stood apart, seeming to sulk, and made her come away from the rest of us to take him in her arms.

It wasn't the kind of beauty that effectively discourages the ones who behold it, not the pure or absolute, perfect-jawline kind. Whatever it was, it had spurred Mr. Burney to place himself between her and the group reconfiguring itself around her, in order to make sure she took her seat on the best-sanded bench so she would not get splinters. But she got up again and with no permission from Becca gathered the baby out of the car seat into her arms.

Becca sighed. "This is when you want a cigarette. When you can relax and somebody else has him. Not just anybody," she added, to Glen.

"I don't blame you," said Gerda. The baby's gaze, so electric and yet magically sedated with un-knowledge, roved over us. He closed his eyes as she held him to her face and inhaled against him. Maybe I had wondered how long her hair had been because in fact, I now saw, she looked like a woman who could ride by naked and a cruel tax would be lifted.

"Can we maybe just try to forget cigarettes?" Glen said in a high, despairing voice.

"*She* used to smoke too," Becca said, speaking to Diana. "Gerda. We would sneak off together."

"Oh yeah?" said Diana.

"I guess I've done everything bad," said Gerda.

I looked at my father. He looked back from under his eyelids, like a man lying in the pool on his back.

"Like what?" said Diana.

Gerda shook her head and leaned forward with her eyes closed to sip from the glass of wine our father was holding for her.

"IMAGINE IF THERE WERE A mousetrap big enough for a person," Karen said. She had found a mousetrap under the bed in their cabin. "Just imagine how you would feel if an iron bar snapped down on you!" So there must have been a mouse in it.

"Karen, you will never change," said Uncle Cal, looking around for somebody in our family who would know that he took pride in this fact. Karen was talking to the four-year-old, Robbie. We had eaten everything, including a watermelon and two of Mrs. Burney's coconut custard pies, and we were lurching between the tables stuffing paper plates into trash bags. Except for the two mothers, we were all a little drunk, some more than others. Bobby, for one, had stretched himself out on the pine needles.

"But there would never be a mousetrap that big," said Cindy. She took the smaller boy by the hand.

"Uh-*huh*," said Robbie, walking backwards away from his mother as he sucked custard off his fingers.

"Uh-*huh*," the little one repeated, breaking loose.

"Come on, fellas," said Cindy. "Let's get back on the swing."

"I want to see what kind of a mousetrap," said Robbie.

"I do, I want to see it," said his little brother. "What *is* it?"

"No, you are not going to see a mousetrap."

"I want Grandma."

"She's not going to take you to see the mousetrap."

"Where is she?"

"She's coming back out in a minute."

"I'm going up to Grandma's room. She said I could."

"I'll take them," Diana said, getting up, but Gerda was already coming down the path.

We had finished toasting some time before, and we had finished hearing the long story of how our father and Gerda had met at Karen's table and Cal had known that night not just what Karen and Lois had figured out in the afternoon, that they must meet, but that they would marry. Yes. Cal could have sworn to that before dessert. "It's true he predicts things," Karen said. "He predicted Bobby Kennedy's assassination. But seriously, no, it's almost always good," she said, raising her glass unsteadily to Cal. The sons had made little speeches, Bobby's filled with jokes and Glen's with quotations.

Diana wanted Gerda and Dad to tell what went through their minds at the first sight of each other. "I thought . . . I can't really say what my first thought was," our father said, and blushed, and we all laughed at that. The jokes about the shotgun wedding had petered out gradually as we looked at them.

Gerda said, "I thought, *He's good.* Oh, and of course I thought so many other things. Over the evening. Everything just had to sink in."

He agreed with that.

Mosquitoes had begun to whine. Becca held out her darkly tanned arm and said they never bit her. Glen, with his short-sleeved shirt and pale skin—the skin of his father?—was their chosen prey, and after much slapping had gone to put on another shirt as Mrs. Burney was bringing out dessert. She wore an apron stenciled MARRIED FOR HER PIES. She had lingered as we cut and ate them, trying to get Mr. Burney to go in with her. He had remained outside the whole time, hauling an archway made of varnished branches from the shed and securing it at the base with rocks and pegs.

"I'm so sorry about the mousetrap," Mrs. Burney said. "Usually there's no need, because there's an owl. Well, we'll be going in. You have your celebration."

"Why don't you sit with us and have some of this lovely wine?" Karen said.

"No, no, we'll leave you with the family."

"Well, just for a minute," said Mr. Burney.

"Tomorrow is a big day," said his wife.

"I'm going to see the mousetrap," said Robbie.

"Three blind mice," said the little one.

Karen looked up. "Did you ever notice they ran *after* the farmer's wife, not away from her? After she cut off their tails with the carving knife?"

"We won't get into that," Cindy said.

"Wait, listen to this, anyway," Diana said. "I want to read something. Shelley found this great book in the cabin."

"They're in all the cabins," Mr. Burney said. "Lifetime supply."

"Just listen to this while I can see to read," Diana said. "'If you have been long away from the sound of the Western Yellow Pine'—that's the Ponderosa, Shelley says—'you may, when at last you hear it again, close your eyes and simply listen, with what deep satisfaction you cannot explain, to the whispered plain-song of this elemental congregation.'"

"Ah," said Gerda and Dad together.

"I don't see how you can call that a whisper," said Glen. Drink had rendered him morose. But I was glad to think of the trees as a congregation, instead of pillars weighing tons, swaying overhead.

"*Plain-song*," Bobby corrected his brother from the ground, keeping his eyes shut.

"What do you think?" Diana asked Gerda, closing the book with a flourish.

Gerda said, "I don't know. I don't know how I thought I could live anywhere else but in the Northwest. I don't know about anything. I don't know how anything that happened, happened."

"We do love these trees," said Mrs. Burney dreamily into the silence that gathered as we considered all that had happened.

"We should be like trees," Karen sang out in a boozy voice. "Know who said that? Thoreau said that. Separate individuals. Individualism!

He should see us. Look at this war. Look at our trash. Look what we do to the earth."

After some thought, Gerda said soberly, "The earth is our mother," as if she had never heard of the sixties, and all their precepts that were now comedy, and perhaps she had not, married and a mother at eighteen. "All I know," she said, turning to Dad, "is that I met you."

"To matrimony!" Mr. Burney stumbled in Gerda's direction, glancing off the tree trunk as Mrs. Burney leaned forward to catch the bottle from his hand.

"Diana tells me we have two veterinarians," she began, already pouring for Gerda. Gerda knew how to drink. She kept it up with no perceptible effect. Maybe she was like Eddie's brother's bride, who just knew how to be happy. "And one works with cats?" Mrs. Burney pressed on as her husband settled into a squat. "We love cats. But oh, dear, we can't keep one here. We did have a little cat, Mitzi . . . Coyotes. And then we've had bears."

"I almost thought Eddie would show up," I said as the word *bears* hung in the air. "Because he likes Dad so much and he would have loved to meet you, Gerda."

"How would he get here? You have his car," Karen said. "She broke up with Eddie," she added to Gerda.

"I'm sorry to hear that," Gerda said, and the eyes touched me again with their almost musical sorrow and benevolence. I could see how my father might have been hypnotized into thinking there was a heaven after all. "But nothing's written in stone," she added.

"No indeed," said Dad. I noticed Gerda didn't encourage him when he spoke, the way the rest of us did. She had sat down and leaned on him. Some of the toasts had been long, and made him blush and even bend over in a kind of pain at the things being said of him. Every once in a while she had laid her hand on the small of his back, the way he had done with her during the introductions. He smiled. I saw that he had withdrawn even deeper into his happiness than he had into his unhappiness, now broken in on and honorably banished.

Was that smile the proof that nothing up to now had really been meant as we had taken it, Shelley and I? Could we have said to wasteful memory, or in my case lack of memory, "The deal is off," could we have taken a giant floating stride across the chasm of what was only, after all, the disappearance of one person?

"I guess that settles it about the t-e-n-t," Cindy said to Bobby, who had fallen asleep on the ground with his mouth open. "Animals." Bobby sat up and looked around.

"What about animals?" said Robbie. "Where?"

"Oh, we're quite safe here." Mrs. Burney stood up and went over to where Mr. Burney was sitting with his back propped against a tree. "Let's go back, your show is on," she said.

"Guess I better go in," he said. "Better do that. Leave the ladies alone."

"Goodness, Garvin," she said. It was hard to see how he was going to get up, and he didn't. After a minute she made a little steeple of her hands and said, "Well, everybody, just enjoy yourselves. You just—enjoy the evening and the stars." We all looked up, and the sky was spread with stars where none had shown themselves minutes before.

"Wait," said Mr. Burney, putting his elbows to the tree trunk and finding the muscles that would take him to a standing position. But he wasn't leaving. "For it is customary. On the night before the nuptials. That I say a few words." He threw his head back and surveyed the sky, as Mrs. Burney, in a kind of languor, took a backward step and then another.

"It is," she said. "He does."

"I know she had you in there for her little talk. And I would hope, I would *hope*, that you listened. Because she knows what she's talking about. That's a fact. But let me tell you—here—" He leaned close to our father, got his balance, and said in a stage whisper, "Don't worry!" He clapped our father on the back. "See, *getting along*? Don't sweat that. First place. It's not her you're dealing with, my good friend. It's not him, fair lady. Nope. It's life. You may not know, or like she'll tell me when we get inside, maybe you do know: *life*—is a thing—all to itself." Here Mrs. Burney fished in her apron pocket and handed him a paper napkin. He mopped his neck and flourished the splint. "I won't say—what I could say—about *that*."

Other than me, only his wife and Gerda had their eyes on him; everybody else was looking at the place where the campfire would have been if there had been one.

"Just get ahold, oh, you already did it, you're way ahead of me, get that little hand in yours and say, 'Hey! I'm gonna hold on.' Whoever it is on the other end. Some mean stuff is gonna come your way. Even at your stage of the game. So what you do is, you hang on. 'Know what I'm saying?' as our son used to say. That's what you do."

"He means love," said Mrs. Burney.

"Rose, Rose, I said what I mean. Would you say"—he bowed to Gerda—"I said what I mean?"

"I'd say so," said Gerda. "But Rose is right."

"I would not argue. Rose is right. We can agree on that. Some would say that I, on the other hand, could be wrong. Where, you may ask, did he get his information?" Here I think Mrs. Burney could have stopped him, but she spoke not a word. "Experience, that's where. We lost a kid. That, I will not go into. But. Gone." He tried to snap the fingers of the splinted hand. "The best kid, the best of the lot."

"There's no best," said Mrs. Burney without conviction.

"Rose, Rose. So, ladies, gentlemen, keep the faith. Drink up. Tomorrow you will attend the nuptial vows of this fine pair."

"Hear, hear," said Diana, knocking back her wine.

"I'M SORRY," I SAID, "BUT what is up with her?" Shelley and I were in her cabin, talking in the dark. Diana had been gone for an hour.

"Jen, for God's sake. She does that. She goes out. She runs around." Shelley had her eyes shut to keep the room from spinning. "She's *promiscuous*." She said it the way a mother says of a kid, "He's active."

"But—"

"That's the way she is."

"I see, she doesn't mean anything by it."

"Not that. It's just something to know about her."

"All right," I said. Shelley was possessive. This I did remember. For years, in the evenings when we came home from Karen's, she would make our father sit by her on the couch.

"She doesn't lie," Shelley offered.

"What's so great about that?"

"Wait, I better stand up. Better lean." She went over to the wall. "You didn't notice this before?"

"OK," I said when she opened her eyes again, "but it's Gerda she's coming on to. Her—her stepmother-in-law-to-be."

"Yeah."

"Right. But it makes me mad. How can she be a feminist?" I sounded like Karen.

"You're kidding."

"No."

"A feminist? Not interested. No interest. *Nada.*"

"I see."

"Look, her father was in jail. Her mother was an orderly in Cook County Hospital. Sold pills, messed herself up."

"I do see."

"So Diana was in foster care, she was in group homes. The rest of the kids in the family are all still doing that stuff. And she's out there doing . . . a lot of what she does is pro bono. She's a good person, Jenny. See, she's just . . ." She slumped against the wall, squinting at nothing.

I wished I could get up and play her "Beloved, you looked into space." But this was the way she used to be about the ladder and the gorilla, far from any remedy of mine.

"Oh God. Those things are streaming. Those holes." She meant the knotty pine. "Whoa. They're going sideways. Fast. I hope I'm not going to throw up."

"I don't think you will. How much did you drink anyway?"

"Too much for the drug." She would always have to take something. I knew that, but I would forget. "Did everybody go to bed?"

"Not the Burneys, not Karen. They're in the parlor. Karen and Mrs. Burney are still at it. Stories. Burney's passed out in his chair. That was him playing the organ. Could you believe that? Did you hear?"

"Sorta. The high notes carry. That vox humana."

Mr. Burney had sat down at the carved organ—actually Mrs. Burney had prompted him, though warning him about using his thumb, and we had steeled ourselves to listen—and pumped it full of sighs. This was around midnight, some time before Gerda and Diana went out to walk off the wine under the stars. He ran up and down the keyboard into "Come Rain or Come Shine," and threw in a line or two of the lyrics with his stage smile. Then he stopped and asked for requests. Gerda whispered to my father and he nodded. They wanted "Memories Are Made of This."

To my surprise, Mr. Burney was like Eddie: he could play anything, even without the use of his thumb. Of course he was going to croon this particular song in the voice of Dean Martin, but he couldn't completely obscure the organ, which ascended during the "sweet-sweet" passages into a high delicate region of its own. All the music of the sixties that had belonged to them, people the age of our dad and Gerda—all those songs, and this was what they asked for, as if the time of their own youth had passed beyond use, the time of my mother and Karen cross-legged on the floor with their guitars, singing "It's All Over Now, Baby Blue" and "What Have They Done to the Rain."

Mr. Burney at the organ was like one of those collarless dogs you see in the city, panting and loping on an errand of its own. I wished Eddie could have been there to hear him, slouched over the keyboard and pumping away with his feet. And indeed the next day, with an amp set up on the porch, Mr. Burney would play Mendelssohn just as well as Eddie could have played it, for Gerda walking down the path in her pink dress with a son on either side.

"I don't know where Dad is now, maybe out looking for the bride," I said to Shelley. "Are you going to have a fight?"

"You can't fight with her. She gets enraged and then she cries. She'll cry all night. It clears her head." She gave me the helpless smile.

"Clears her conscience."

"The next day she's OK, normal. Here she comes."

"Shelley?"

"Yeah."

"Hey, don't get any ideas. Don't go up there."

"Where?"

"The tree house. Or anything. Anything to impress her."

Shelley knew how to climb without a harness. But she answered me, "Ha-ha."

GERDA PULLED HER HUSBAND, WHO weighed a hundred and eighty pounds, out of the shallows of the river where he had rolled. His clothes were soaked and heavy. She could feel a pulse in his neck. She took off her shirt and tried to wrap the open shoulder. One sleeve of the shirt she took off was torn but she thought the blood was his. On the other side of him she found the artery under the dangling arm, crammed her rolled-up vest tight against it. Propping him with a rock under his shoulders she fixed the arm tight to the vest and bound the whole mess to his chest with fishing line. She pulled him a few yards by his collar, and then, afraid of choking him, she ran to the cabin for the sleeping bag, got his legs in and worked it up under his back, picked up the other arm from the rocks and stuffed it in, and pulled the bag up the hill to the car. By stages she got him onto the floor in the back. How that was done she couldn't describe to Diana. Some way. She started the car and drove nine miles to town on a dirt road. How fast? Fast. She knew at a certain point that he had died. A girl on a bike directed her to a clinic, which was closed, and then the girl, who had realized it was a Sunday and followed on her bike, yelled how to get to the doctor's house. She saw the girl glance down at the blood on the car. The girl rode up onto the sidewalk and streaked away. She had the doctor out of his house when Gerda got there, a big old man coming down the steps with the Sunday funnies in his hand. He performed CPR. His wife ran out with his bag and stood with Gerda, who was wearing only a bra with her bloody jeans. The bike girl stood with them. The doctor pretended to do things to stanch the bleeding that had already stopped, and after a short time he got to his feet and began tending to Gerda's arm.

All of this Gerda told Diana because Diana asked.

So of course Diana asked about the bear. The bear's eyes had no whites. They did not seem to be open very wide. The heat coming off the head and neck had a smell—no, there was nothing to compare it to. The broken teeth dripped a foamy red spit. The nose, the nose was the worst, two holes like toilet plungers. Yes, she could remember. She could remember everything. The whole time, she kept talking at the top of her voice to the lump on the ground. Of what? Of love.

Where did a marriage like this begin? This Diana failed to ask. What was the source of it, what made it get under way and continue and become a mighty thing?

At one point, at the car but not in it, he woke up. He was far gone, not in his right mind. It was hard to understand him. He said he wanted something salty. Could she give him something salty.

No one else, Gerda said, no one other than our father, had ever asked her about any of these things. People would tell her they had read it in the paper, but that was it. Even her sons didn't ask. People cared, of course they did. But they didn't think she wanted to talk about it, and they were right, she didn't. Yet she did. She had to admit it. She wanted to. She didn't want to join a group or anything like that. In a group, her friends told her, she would be safe. That's where it would be safe for her to talk. Both daughters-in-law said that. They said her sons were each attending a group, just dealing secondhand with the whole thing, their father in the jaws of a bear.

It was as if, Gerda said, as if . . . as if, if she were to talk in the wrong place, she would be in danger. Or somebody would. People let her know this without saying so. For a long time she felt as if she were up in a plane, at the controls, circling and circling. Bob was gone, the one who would have helped her land.

Then she met our father. Land.

And here she was pouring it all out again to Diana. "This isn't like me," she told Diana. It was the wine. It was night, trees, wind. John's wonderful family. No, she didn't cry, she just stood there in the dark with Diana, who had run out of questions. Diana's impulse was to put her arms around Gerda, but one of the things Gerda had said was that for a long time everybody did that when they saw her, everybody. People wanted to, as if for luck. That's when she first laughed, weakly, because Diana, who had done exactly that, said, "You must have felt like you should open a booth."

"That made her laugh." Diana was talking to Shelley, who at a careful walk had crossed the room to the little sink. "And oh my God you should see her arm."

"She showed you."

"Her shoulder and arm. Like a fork went down a cucumber."

Shelley had turned on the tap in the little sink. The pipes gurgled and the tap spat until she turned it off.

"I should go," I said. I wanted to tell Diana to be careful what she said to Shelley. Shelley was not just anybody, a person you could tease and torment.

"Anyway," Diana said, "after what she went through describing the whole thing, it would have been like trying to hug somebody who had just come out of an operation."

"People do that with their dogs," Shelley said.

In the end Gerda said, "But don't worry, I won't do this, you won't have to say, 'Quick, hide, here she comes, don't let her get started.'" They began to laugh, both of them drunk, and laughed and stumbled as they walked back. Gerda asked Diana to forgive her for spilling out the whole thing like that, every bit of it. Diana said she was honored.

Diana said, "Shelley, I just happen to have been the right person for Gerda on this particular night. When she's leaving her old life behind. People tell me things," she added with a look at me.

"They do," Shelley agreed.

"It's not like I pump them."

"No," Shelley said.

I started to say something like maybe it was easier for Gerda to talk now that she had our father, now that the padlock was off the story, but Diana went on. "OK, so how come I bring that out in people?" She was throwing things out of her suitcase into the little rattling drawers, and it was true, tears shone in her eyes. "Maybe because I talk to them. Maybe because I don't just sit there staring into space. It's not like I go looking for these people."

"No evidence for that," said Shelley.

Diana stopped unpacking and they faced each other.

"Goddammit," Diana said.

"Well, good night," I said. "See you in the morning."

" 'Night," Shelley said.

I climbed into the tall bed. I wished Eddie were there. I thought about what the chances were that he would find some transportation and get there. The room was hot, and I threw off the fat comforter that he would have rolled himself up in not caring that it was August.

How weak love was, dying of the weight of the covers if you let it. How weak it was at its birth. Eyelashes, hands on a piano. Could these become my father's mourning, Gerda's ax?

The wind had come up again; pine cones were banging on the tin roof and rolling off. I sat and looked out the window, which was so close

I could have leaned my head on the glass. I could see Shelley and Diana's cabin. The light was already out. I could see the tree house. I had imagined Shelley climbing up there drunk and desperate. But I was wrong; she had not done that. It could be Diana had not meant, after all, to dare her to do it.

Mr. and Mrs. Burney were out there. She was winding greenery onto the arch, he was shoveling ashes into a bucket. She still had on the apron, and it was flying up. She hunched over, and I thought she was sinking her face in her hands because of his day of drunken gallantries and the harsh way he had spoken to her, when she was guilty only of trying to extract a kind of perfection from the given materials, for our sakes. For the sake of a wedding, of all things. But she was only pushing the hair out of her eyes and calling some question to him, while he leaned on the spade a little distance away, facing the trees.

From

Search Party: Stories of Rescue (2013)

The Finding

This is how my new life came about.

It started with symptoms I thought might be neurological. As a nurse, I was alert to a new unfamiliarity in the way things looked, as if I kept finding myself on the wrong street, or as if I were traveling abroad. The stores of what was ordinary enough to be ignorable seemed to be shrinking. Sometimes I seemed to inhabit my body the way you stand on a foot that has been asleep.

It may be that the organs attempt, in a language we do not know, to give us tidings of their dim world. Or with secret promptings they may impel us to ends of their own.

I had never visited this practice before, but I had worked in the same hospital with the neurologist long ago. He had been someone I knew to say hello to, a well-liked man, a good doctor, married, though without children and said to be unlucky in his home life.

On the morning of my appointment I got up and looked out at the rain. Water was materializing on the windowsill, filmy and soundless. It was the first of December, so I put on a red sweater over my uniform. I took a bus from work in the afternoon, and in the neurologist's waiting room, which was empty, I sat up straight to give the nurse the understanding that I was not demoralized by the winter rains of our city, the slow or the steady, or the short daylight. I was not a depressed woman drawing myself up to the radiator of a doctor's attention. If anything, I was unnaturally cheerful. I wanted to seize whole tortes from cabinets in the bakery, bottles of wine from under people's arms, and sofas out of window displays that I had no room for in my small house.

In the clinic there was no one in sight except the short young girl with a triangular face at the desk behind the glass, who had slid me a clipboard of forms with her bitten fingernails. When she saw me looking at her half-inch-long hair she turned away and touched it with her fingers. Well, hair is that short! I thought. Where have I been?

After a few minutes she looked up sharply and said, "Just go through the door. He's there. Room Three."

From the hallway came a heavy sigh, a groan actually, just before the doctor knocked. Then his voice, very deep—I remembered the voice—sounded from the door. "My nurse is not here," he said. "In a moment Angelique will come in so that I can examine you." He was fifty or so now, with big pale flap ears, and neatly dressed, tall but not erect. He had the stoop of a person with a bad back, and the eyes in folds that I recalled from seeing him in the hospital years ago. Now that I was older I knew these were drinker's eyes. "My nurse called and said she would not be in. She quit. No notice. There are no charts set out, as you see. No X-rays. She simply quit." He appeared only half able to think, like a man who has been up all night.

"I am a nurse," I said, waiting for him to recognize me, although I had been younger and prettier at the time I worked in that hospital.

"I see that," he said, scanning the clipboard.

"I used to work down the hall from you at the university," I said, pointing to my name on the form, and then to my employer's name, to let him know I was not in search of a job.

"Is that so?" he said.

Angelique opened the door without knocking. "What if the phone rings while I'm in here?" she demanded, putting her foot in the wastebasket to stomp down its contents.

"We might empty that," the doctor said, avoiding her gaze. She ignored him. Hey there! I signaled him with an older-generation smile. Better establish some authority with this girl!

She did get down in front of the examining table and grapple on her knees with a step, which she yanked out for me to mount. I settled myself on the padded table surrounded with metal trees holding instruments. "If you're not going to have her *disrobe*," said Angelique, "I don't need to be here, do I?" and she went out, shutting the door firmly behind her.

The man looked blankly at the ophthalmoscope in his hand. Finally he switched it on and began to peer at my retinas, changing his angle minutely again and again, and breathing as if his belt were too tight. After a while he said, "I am going to have to dilate your eyes. I have not been brought up to date on your problems." He glanced at my forms. "You are a new patient. And you were not referred."

"No," I said. "I came straight to you."

"Headache," he said wearily.

"No," I said. I described my symptoms while he put drops in my eyes. After a while he hunched over them again. At length I submitted half blind to all the tests with pin and hammer, of reflex, balance, strength, and mentation, naming the year, the city where we lived, the president. It was at the mention of the president that our eyes met. This was some years ago. I could tell we felt the same despairing way about the man. "I am going to ask you to have an MRI. There is only one real finding, and it may be nothing. But we will take a look." He stood up and pressed his wide waist, stifling a deep, trembling yawn.

"I agree," I said. It was not like me not to ask what the finding was.

"Are you planning to stay?" he asked Angelique rather cautiously as we passed her cubicle.

"I have to study my Spanish. You don't remember, but my exam is tonight, so there's no point in going home. So I'll close up!" She swiveled the chair so her back was to us.

"Well, then. I will leave now," he said, "to pick up some things. Good night."

It was dusk, but the sun had come out, producing that low-lying light that seems to be coming from below rather than above. The air was full of water. You could hear water slipping over the edges of the grates in the parking lot. On the steps he said, "Now I remember you. Urology."

"Cardiology," I said.

"Well, I have business to attend to." He smiled unpleasantly, as if I had detained him. "My wife, soon to be my ex-wife, has my dog. I am going to get her. The dog." He searched his pockets.

"Where does your wife live?" I said.

"Where indeed. In *her* house by the lake."

"I wonder if you could give me a ride. I can't see. I do have a car, but I came on the bus. I ride the bus when I want to think."

"Well, if you have left off thinking for the day," he said, opening the door of his car. He performed a tight turn to get out of the parking lot, with the tires splashing.

I did not get out at the corner where I could have walked home; I had decided not to. Instead I asked him about the dog. This worked a change in him; his face lit up with malice. He began to talk. His wife was bent, it seemed, on punishing faults in himself that he did not name, and would not give him his dog, even though she disliked dogs and had not the slightest notion how to take care of them. She might have changed the locks to keep him out. She thought he wanted to get into the house and make off with things he had bought for her, when in fact he was perfectly happy to have left everything behind and didn't care even to go near the house again, except for the dog. The dog was his. His deep voice had become a snarl; he shook his shoulders and said, "Where exactly may I drop you off?"

I said, "Oh, we've passed the place." He had been talking, growling, for blocks. "I might as well go with you to pick up the dog, and get out on the way back."

He replied with his groaning sigh.

The house was hidden from the street by a dense laurel hedge. It was dark now but not raining, and if you turned back at the top of the steep walk you saw there was a dropoff with the dark lake spread out below, so unexpected it could have sprung right out of a rock.

A weightless feeling comes over me anyway at the sight of water viewed from high up on land. Looking at it, I felt a certainty that I was not sick, I was well. Instead of the sensation of being subtly awry, I had the feeling I was in the midst of a normal life.

But now I was very hungry. This looked like the sort of house where fruit would be set out in a bowl from which one could help oneself.

The locks had not been changed after all. In the front hall there was no bowl of fruit but a crystal dish of sourballs. I stopped to take a cherry one, and he grimly swept the whole lot into his pocket. I unwrapped mine and dropped the paper on the floor. He offered no apologies for the size of the house or the fussy luxury of its furnishings, but made straight for the kitchen in the back.

Sure enough, there was a dog, asleep in the shut-up kitchen without even a rug. It was a damaged version of a collie dog, thin, with an awful coat, and it scrambled up guiltily when we opened the kitchen door, like an old man pretending he hadn't been asleep in his chair. The dog had a smell, a putrid steam, which came up and surrounded us. When it began an agonized wagging and scooting towards him, he fell to his knees.

He knelt and pardoned the dog's appearance and smell, and used a voice to convince it that it was something besides these things, something an animal might not suspect itself to be. And he picked it up. It should have weighed too much for that, but it didn't. Without speaking, he indicated the keys he had put down on the counter. I locked the door behind us, and he lugged the dog down the steps and through the hedge, eased it into the back seat, and got in with it. I thought he was going to get back out, but he kept stroking and soothing the dog, which was panting unhealthily.

I had the keys. I got into the driver's seat. Nothing happened, so I started the car. I said, "You can't take a dog like that into a downtown hotel, now can you." He didn't answer, he was in a reverie petting the awful-smelling dog, like a schoolboy with his thoughts in his hands. In the rearview mirror I could see them both with their eyes shut.

"So if I took him to my house," I said after a while, "you would have to come every day to take care of him."

"Her. She'll die without me. Look how sick she is now. Good dog. Good dog." He sat for blocks stroking the dog as the fumes from its coat rose and banked in the car.

"In that case you would have to come with her," I said finally. I had seen the girl tell him what to do. I had seen the whole thing. I pushed all the buttons in the fancy armrest to open the windows. By now it was dark and cold, and the cold air, still wet, whirled in the car. The dog raised its nose to sniff.

He said, "I would have to get my things."

I turned to go downtown, where the hotel was. After a time he said, "Some of my things are at the office. I shuttle back and forth." So I doubled back. When he got out of the car the dog shut its eyes again, hopelessly. We hurried in. Angelique was alone, tilted back in the chair in her cubicle, studying her Spanish book. She had her shoes off, and there was a run in her tights.

"Well, look who's here," she said in a lonely voice. "I heard you in the hall. I hoped it was you and not a rapist." I looked down at her. For all her rudeness she was a hopeful girl, thinly dressed below the funny hair, and ill-fed. With some care she could be the daughter I never had.

The Magic Pebble

The flight to Lourdes was open to the whole archdiocese. Huge wide-body, full. I was in the middle of Coach in a row of five, in the middle seat.

All right, I'll make the best of it. I have my little Sony, I'll turn it on when they say we can and talk to two people, and that will be the program: me, the dressed-up old fellow on my left, and the woman on my right with a nun in charge of stuffing her bag into the overhead bin and getting the seat belt out from under her. At first I thought the woman was blind, but she was just slow, in a daze. The nun has a broad pink face, heavily and dramatically wrinkled considering its resigned expression.

I have become aware of resignation in others. By the time you reach the third chemo, one of the things you notice is that the people around you accept death, your death. It happened with my radio show; during my last sick leave, friends from the station kept telling me how well the show was doing on reruns, how I didn't need to feel I had to hurry back to it.

I'm back, though. Now I can ask for anything. My boss, Charlie, always did give me free rein, but the station manager has taken to sending me complimentary memos not unlike greeting cards. To the manager's way of thinking, according to Charlie, my illness drops a fringed scarf over the rummage-sale nature of the show, lends it a dimly glowing aura of the endangered, the soon-to-be-archival: items veined and burnished and distressed now, like fake antiques, by my attention. As for me, I have finished with the disappearance of the tiger and the frog from the earth, and with the university hospital where patients were secretly injected with plutonium. Away with reproach. On to *Inventions and Patents! The Sightings of the Ark! Birds in History!*

If you write a noun, any noun, on a piece of paper and slap it down on Charlie's desk, he grins, the radio snaps on in his mind. He remembers *satellite* new on everyone's lips. He is happy with his throwback job; he's a gray-haired, loping man who could easily have a beer with the campus agitator he was thirty years ago; he has his own tattered copy of the Port Huron Statement. He remembers *pacification*, newborn *fluorocarbon*, reborn *terrorist*. He charts the passage of world figures in the press, from *madman* to *strongman* to *leader*. "I'm beyond all that. I've given up," I tell Charlie.

"OK," he says.

"I'm going for the fun factual or the seriously miraculous."

"OK."

This trip I am taking springs directly out of *The Song of Bernadette*.

By the time we made our high school graduation retreat, the decline in vocations was serious and the hopeful Sisters were showing this movie. How beautiful and good the curious tapered face of Jennifer Jones was, so sad-mouthed, in that movie. Even so, we snickered at her dull wits, her inability to speak up for herself when she was the one, after all, to whom Our Lady had stepped out of rock, clothed in white and a blue beyond blue, with yellow roses on her feet—as we seniors of Holy Names knew despite the black and white of the movie. No human: a statue come to life, shining with unearthly glamour, melting with bridal politeness. An invisible power filled the air, but the girl could not stretch out her hands to determine the source of it. Much was offered, but touch remained in the realm of the unpermitted.

"From the remotest times, out of child sacrifice to water, out of rain-making and ceremonial cleansing, from sacred well, holy pool, fountain in oak tree—the *spring* has been thought to possess a miraculous power."

For music, maybe somebody blowing into a bottle.

"Unorthodox"—or maybe I should say *orthodox*—"as such a trip seemed when it first occurred to me at the end of chemo, I saw it as something that would perhaps . . ." *Perhaps* is a little clothespin not really sturdy enough, I'm afraid, for the vast wet sheet of the possible that I have to hang from it. Halfway through, I'll break in with passages from novels, pro and con. "That world of hallucinated believers," Zola called Lourdes—which won't be my position; I won't presume to judge. At the station they'll say, "This was her best show, she left her shtick at home, she was honest for a change." Because they know I'm always feigning interest. Even when it's one of my causes, in which I have the most intense interest privately, I slip into this broad-minded radio-interest. Whereas the mark of real interest would be silence, like that preserved by my boss, Charlie, at my bedside. "Saline infusion," I'll read him, "followed by the nitrogen *mustard* . . ." He'll wrinkle his forehead, squint, and then I'll laugh and he'll laugh. I can tell he would like to do a show on chemo.

My husband, with his inborn, unfailing sense of the thing to say to a person in chemo with tufts of her former self in her hands, says irritably, "What's so funny all the time? He's got a crush on you. Charlie. I'm serious, he does."

This trip to Lourdes is the second trip I've taken since then. First we went—the three of us, my husband and I and our son—to Lake Powell.

The hospital doors sighed open, and my little boy wheeled me across the rubber divide to the car all packed and waiting. "Southward ho!" my husband said as I waved up to the smoked glass of Oncology. My son was marching stiff-necked with the thrill of missing a week of kindergarten and Rafe. For him, kindergarten has been embodied from the start in the narrow-headed little boy with the buzz cut who glared at him from the next chair. Some of the mothers say the haircut was a practical measure. Rafe's own mother was afraid to wash his hair. She is his stepmother, actually, and she can't stand him, it is said. All she wanted was the father. I don't want to think about this. Stepmothers.

Rafe, a name breathed every night at our dinner table: one of those children who start school already old in the ways of power. After difficulties in another kindergarten, he came to St. Joseph's three days into the first week. Not a bully, exactly. His crimes were against property, a dogged wrecking of the bright room, or his part of it, the part where he lurked like a rook—the border, the lanes between respectful groups.

"Rafe," my son ventures, "cut the cat's ear with scissors," looking away in case our faces confirm his suspicions about the place where he lives his days.

At the hospital there was a party for the two of us who had completed our treatment. We were all saying goodbye at the nursing station when a cart rolled down the hall, with an ice swan on a bed of ferns. "From your sweeties!" the nurses chorused, calling the husbands out of hiding in the railed bathroom where so recently my roommate Tracey and I had been sliding down the wall in a sweat.

"She thought you meant *Charlie*," my husband grumbled to the nurses, who had been making much of his jealousy of my boss.

This was the end of chemo for both Tracey and me—whatever happened after this, chemo was, as they said, no longer an option. The swan was in honor of the *Birds in History* show I had finished taping just before I came in. The nurses ate the delicacies and we all admired the magnificent glistening bird being trundled up and down by Tracey's twins, three-year-olds who got their fingers and tongues stuck on the ice while my son watched.

My husband had gone to a lot of trouble to find a maker of ice swans. It wasn't just a shape—the feathers were etched in perfectly; the eye was an elongated, half-closed Buddha-eye, sleepy and benevolent; and the beak had a little nostril. It was a pleasure to see this life-size, realistic bird, after all the angels. Angel cards and angel calendars and angel balloons festooned the whole hospital. When people look back, these huge broody men-women will be the macrame of this period, says Charlie. "Looks like the millennium in here," he says, batting a string of them out of the way. "Never, never will we do a show on angels." Of course there have been requests. He found me Nabokov's story in which a huge moulting angel, all brown fur and steaming chicken-flesh, flies through a window and crashes in a hotel room. To mark its place he stuck in a card showing an angel on a rotisserie. "Like rattlesnake," the man with the baster is saying.

Tracey was way ahead of me in the chemo protocol, and that is not good unless you are getting well. When we met we lifted up our gowns and compared our scars. There are good scars and bad scars: hers was bad, formed of shiny blebs as if a red-hot choke chain had been slung at her chest and fused with the skin. Her disease was bilateral and had reached her bones; she had lost her body fat and was down to membranes and big fruit bat eyes, a praying, drifting, cloud-woman of the New Age, whose palm was always blossoming open to show me a pink crystal, a vial of aromatic oil, a spirit stone. She was twenty-seven; everybody loved her and her bearded husband and her curly-headed twins, who burst out of the elevator every afternoon and campaigned down our ward scattering action figures and jouncing the vials on trolleys.

The same height at five as the twins were at three, and rashy, tongue-tied, thin: that was our son, a daydreamer, quietly keyed up at finding himself present at their adventures.

I used to dream our son would fall off something, lose a limb, choke, drown. He had yet to let go of the pool edge and swim. Tracey comforted me; she guessed before I said so that the terror of the coming swimming lesson caused his afternoon vomiting. Of course I never told him of what kept befalling him in my dreams, but the psychiatric nurse would say he knew. This woman knew better than to give me *Love, Medicine & Miracles* to read, but she did give me a book I couldn't stand, *The Problem of Pain*. Tracey didn't mind her, but the ones I liked brought us *It* and *Pet Sematary* from the nurses' station. "That Tracey is a living doll," my favorite one would say whenever Tracey had been lifted onto the gurney and taken away.

For a while I thought of doing a program on living dolls. "Think of consciousness," Tracey would pant when she came back, joggled by the burrowing twins so that she had to hold up her arms on the IV boards—she had declined the portacath—"as a cupboard. All you know and feel is in there!" With Tracey, knowing and feeling had the nature of a bestowal, on the order of musical ability. "But you don't know what else is in there! What I did yesterday"—she showed the twins with a roll of her shoulders—"was I got up onto a different shelf. And I know"—she smiled—"I was still way down low!"

There is a tribe that bestows the name Sky on a woman who gives birth to twins. She is a blessing to all; her twins are thought to influence the weather.

"Don't forget," Tracey said as she hugged me from her wheelchair. That could have been about the cupboard of consciousness; or it could have been about the Hopi kachina she gave me, Pour-Water-Woman, who waters the heads of children to make them grow; or she could have meant the Chinese grocery where she had her fortifying teas made up.

From our bulletin board with all the angel cards, her husband unpinned only his snapshot of the real Tracey, wearing feather earrings on her trip to blessed ground in Arizona, long-haired and wide-hipped in a pueblo doorway. Shyly he parted the tissue paper to show me his present: the pale pink boa that would float out behind Tracey as her chair skidded to the elevator with a twin pumping on either side.

I had thought I wanted to see what it was like to get behind the wheel again, but we agreed I would conserve the energy. Down I-5 we flew, towards Utah.

In all the preparations, we had done something inexcusable: we had forgotten about Lake Powell. My fault; I am supposed to be on top of such things. It's just the kind of program I used to do: environmentocide, the intentional flooding of a proud and ancient desert canyon.

We forgot everything, we only knew we were driving south to get on a houseboat and drift for a few days in the sun. Heal. That's what the ad said, in *Sunset*. "*Sunset*," my husband said one day in the hospital, absently picking it up in his despair, "the magazine of the radiology waiting room."

I had a mental picture of a houseboat—something between a raft and a gondola, with a deck chair on it, brushing along the reeds. You could pluck a desert bloom with your lazy fingers as you went, in my preview, as you covered over the nasty record of the last year until it was completely crosshatched—the way we used to do segues on TV—obliterated by the new scene of desert sunshine, fish in hazel water, eagles, canyon swifts. It is swifts who are said to sleep in flight, so high in the vault of heaven that if they fall they will have time to wake up. "How would anyone know?" Charlie said.

Charlie found the poem that opened the show: "On a Bird Singing in Its Sleep." *A bird half wakened in the lunar noon / Sang halfway through its little inborn tune.* This bird of Frost's had "the inspiration to desist" when it was fully awake, and that was what Charlie liked, "the inspiration to desist."

The program became a favorite at the station and went into two parts, though I haven't heard how it came out with all the twitters and caws and screeches Charlie dug up, helping me because I don't even like birds.

We began with ancient Rome and the priest-augurs. "Augury was the reading of events in the behavior of birds. In their cloudy retreats, the augurs . . ." and so on; we painted them in, hunkering, shy, receptive men, self-trusting as prophets must be, watching the sky. Later I read that half the augury was accomplished on birds heading left instead of right when they scratched in the dirt.

In the course of this show, which had started out with endangered birds as its subject, in particular the little spotted owl of our own woods, we branched out, seduced by the oddness of birds, their dependable, vestigial peculiarity, no more in the reputation for cursing ships and causing headaches (if they weave a hair from your head into their nests) than in any number of real behaviors that must have made for puzzling prophecies: gaping and dancing and chaperoning and adoption and fratricide. We left these subjects to TV, though we interviewed an ornithologist. We'll hear from bird watchers, the kind of call we get after every show no matter how humbly I introduce myself as a dilettante. The auspices are never good when we get into people's hobbies. *Auspice* means "bird observation."

Lake Powell. The "lake" is a vast system of canyons into which river water has been forced by damming: a huge, walled kingdom of rock and sand, first seen by the colonizers in 1776, when two lost Franciscans— Franciscans!—ate their pack horses while exploring it for Spain. The walls of Padres Butte, above the now-submerged Crossing of the Fathers, gaze somberly down upon your water flea, your "houseboat." This is a camper on pontoons, if a camper responded to your steering late by so many seconds and wide by so many degrees.

Off the main gorge with its massive buttes are an endless number of subsidiary canyons, into which you can "cruise" to "explore," each with its own coves and caverns, and its chimney or arch that you are supposed to look for, sticking up out of the water like the stone arm or leg of its own drowned spirit, not the primary canyon-spirit but some underling, some kitchen girl buried with the pharaoh.

Once all of this arid land was underwater anyway, argued the dammers, who were just people like so many now, "like all of us, perhaps," I'll say if I do the show, people with no inspiration to desist. It was an ocean: sea creatures are embedded in its red walls.

Tour boats the size of ocean liners are afloat on this map of water, these hundreds of miles of "waterway," between the walls of rock with you and your houseboat. One of them meets you, passes, heaves at you a continent of wake. You smack into the wake if you have not swerved into position to "step" your craft across it, as the sheet of instructions says to. Inside or underneath your boat something slides, cracks, makes the noise of a spade pounding. The aft floor with just a railing around it dips under. The rented sleeping bags roll in inches of water.

Imagine you are weak and hairless. You have a taste in your mouth—oh, a diluted chlorine vapor—and a little hole in your chest like a gas cap for receiving liquids through a hose, and strip-mined patches on your arms where the skin leached chemicals from a puncture. You are an *entity* now. Your husband does not know this, though when your child looks at you, you feel him suspecting it. You have a tape recorder with you, of all things, to record impressions of this vacation for use in a program!

In a bracket on the bow, the two of them have installed a little flag they bought in the souvenir shop. All at once you hear the cloth beating, beating. The water is a blackening green. The wind—the wind has kicked up a bit: that's what your husband says, planting his feet wide apart on the deck. Your son is in his arms, thin legs dangling, turning the wheel, but now he sets him down. Waves erupt against the sheer walls and toss the whole channel up like water in a tub.

You must have known, and he too—he must have known when he looked up at the disorganized, silently colliding masses of cloud pouring into each other through downspouts and funnels. Now they are coursing heavily west. The water looks exactly like the writhing sea as you once filmed it for a story called "Tender: The Peacetime Navy," safe on a submarine tender in the Pacific.

You are not too disoriented to see that this is not—it is not—in the brochure. To your own surprise and disgust, you begin your weak hospital whine. Your husband laughs, with a note of uncertainty that only you can hear, and he and your little chortling son agree to confine you to your quarters so that you will not get in the way of the nautical affairs.

Now the wind seems to have scented something on the floor of the canyon that it once casually uprooted but now cannot reach. As it vacuums furiously along the water the sun goes out, the little hoofbeats of the flag speed up. Your son looks up quickly with his nostrils flared, like an animal. The temperature falls. "The mercury plummeted," you would say, if you could get off the bolted-down bench where you are curled and find the recorder. "The barometer bottomed out so fast our ears popped."

Your husband has given up wrestling the bizarre delayed steering against the wind and has finally run at dusk, disobeying a red buoy, deep into one of the branches of a side canyon and up onto a sandbar. "How will we find our way back?" you whispered when he wrenched the craft into the first wide turn. "Honey . . . ," he said, opening his palm to show a compass.

Some time ago, he and your son went over the side and down the ladder and waded onto the beach, where hordes of a dry thorny weed pulled loose by the wind are blowing at a furious rate against their legs. They are in the matching red bathing suits bought for this trip. Long ago in all of your minds there was, incredibly, the idea of going swimming. In a transparent inlet, the two of you demonstrating to your son how it is that lazy circles with the arms easily hold the body up in water.

No one swims here in March. You would have known that if you had been thinking, any of you.

They must make a wide *V* with the ropes and plant the two anchors in the sand, but they can't get it done. The stern of the flat, ungainly vehicle is tossing and dragging too heavily. The engine has stalled twice. "Bring her in if she breaks free!" Could he have yelled that? Each time they stomp one anchor into the sand, the other pulls loose, causing the boat to rear back like a horse on one rein.

It is so dark, the air so full of cold flying sand, that you can hardly see them. You can see your son's white running legs and his arms bent like hospital straws, sticking out of the life preserver that is mandatory for children every minute they spend on this lake. You can't hear them, though once the wind brings you his voice over the sound of your chattering teeth, piping thinly to his father about the stinging weed. He is not crying, though. You are crying.

What are you afraid of? What could possibly frighten you now?

The boat is going to tear loose and spin out of the cove to dash itself to splinters on the red walls of the canyon. Man and boy will be left on this fragment of surviving desert, actually the flank of one of the lower mountains of rock, where the temperature plunges at night in this month, March.

No one told you not to come to this place in March. No one told you not ever, ever to come. You should have known that. Only now do you begin to see it, and only an edge of it, beyond the reach of your trained curiosity, your facts and film and tape—and not just you, *anyone*, anyone who would even listen to you, any tourist of knowledge: *It*, the water-carved, the sheer-walled, ancient grounds, now defiled, of the unpermitted.

In the morning you will be dead, washing along the canyon floor with the Cretaceous sharks and the cacti, your frantic spirit seeking to drag another houseboat off its course into this tiny canyon to rescue your husband and son. One may come, or one may not. There are ninety-six canyons.

I HAVE HAIR NOW, VERY short, chic. With a lot of makeup on, I am charming again. Going up and down the aisles I could get twenty good stories if I wanted to, but we like to say three are better than twenty. A good half of the passengers are caretakers, like the nun in our aisle—one of many on this flight I'm sure, though few others display the little headband scarf, and the suit of a vaguely official off-blue—who guards the woman to my right. The nun's liver-spotted, wedding-ringed hand lies ever on the sick woman's coat sleeve.

I came alone. All this has made my husband tired, willing to stay home with our son, who is not allowed to leave kindergarten. His teacher, Ms. Lemoine, put her foot down: your son has had his special houseboat trip; he must have stability now. He must be provided with structure, continuity. These are the wicks around which candles will form to light his way. Those are not her words; she said, "Let us take care of everything, Mom." Only three of us are *Mom* to her, the mothers of her favorites. Ms. Lemoine is young, right out of school herself, and a convert; she had two dozen five-year-olds making the sign of the cross and droning the tunes of the St. Louis Jesuits before they could trace their hands. Not that we aren't secretly grateful that she has her clear favorites: the weak ones.

We're in the air. We're going by night, over the Pole to Paris. "The Eiffel Tower!" says a little wraith in front of us to her mother.

"Would you consider letting me interview you?" I ask the old man on my left.

"I'll certainly consider it." He winks. He got on late, climbing over the woman on that aisle who had already begun to pray with her eyes closed or else gone to sleep. "Pardon me, pardon me, ladies—!" He bowed to her and then to the rest of us, and smacked his crutches one at a time into the hands of the flight attendant, a slight young man with large ears, who looked familiar to me.

The old man has more hair in his white eyebrows than on his lean crinkled head, and he's done up in sharp pleats, heavy cotton, silk. Wingtips. One of those prosperous old guys who genuflect like Fred Astaire. He's ready without any urging and has no idea that despite his promising Chicago accent, on tape he will prove to be what we call a boulder. Boulders are usually men—though a woman can be one—who have sunk into position in themselves, and can never be jostled loose by an interviewer. You may circle and pester them all day, you may scratch your questions on them, they will not budge. They may have sought to be interviewed and looked forward to it, but it turns out they can't explain, they don't intend to.

What is more, the problem with his hip is not intrinsic, not a disease; it is the result of an accident. Someone caused it—kids who knocked him down and robbed him in front of his hotel on a cruise to Mexico. All this he gives out in short puffs of speech with no full stops. "Hip"—prods under jacket—"pinned twice: replaced the thing: won't heal." I catch a whiff of cologne. This man would never say, "All of a sudden I was lying on my back looking up at the orange sun, and a voice was speaking, saying '*dolor*,' and the pain was shooting everywhere." On the other hand neither would he say, "I know it's not a matter of deserving or not deserving this, but I feel it has made me take a closer look at my life and I see that . . ." He has a Knights of Columbus monogram on his bag. Of Lourdes he has the businesslike expectation of an appointment to be kept by two. "Crutches: think I'll leave 'em?" he says, nudging me, sensing a doubter. "I hope so," I say. Perhaps there will be a cave-storeroom piled with crutches.

A man across the aisle has crossed his legs and poked out a stump with a sock on it. I don't believe one-breastedness produces in the viewer the immediate vicarious anguish of one-footedness. He licks his finger and flips the pages of the airline magazine. Of course that man isn't going to Lourdes to pray for a foot. At one time I would have said so, a while back, though that far back I would not have done a program on Lourdes. I would not have wanted to embarrass the good Virgin of my childhood or myself if, dazed with jet lag in the grotto, I heard myself ask for a miracle. But on the trip to Lake Powell I changed my mind. If you ask at all, why not for a miracle? Like the accidentals in music, the notes that are not in the key signature. It might not be the heaving water calmed, or anything so plain.

At Lake Powell we heard about a rabbit that fell out of the sky onto a tent, shook itself, and hopped away. People who had just come in from camping in the desert were telling us about it on the pier as we waited for our boats. An eagle dropped it, they reported. Who knows how many wonders befall animals. An animal would be more accepting, unable to marvel to begin with.

I thank the old man and turn to the woman on my right, the dazed woman. It seems she has been waiting; her cheeks are a hot veiny red. "No, excuse me, the gentleman—!" She leans forward to address him, not me. My boss calls this dating—as, "You let them date all through the show. You should have taken charge." "Sir—sir? Those boys who robbed you in Mexico were in the wrong. But what if your own son did something like that?"

The old man is not to be ruffled. He stops her with a commanding palm. "Pardon me: this calls for—" The flight attendant has just reached us, that smiling big-eared young man I feel sure I know. We all smile back at him. His face is one of those mysterious human sights that refresh you. After a moment I see what it is: I see he looks like Alfred E. Neuman, if you can imagine that face groomed and somehow *matured*. The old man, who should properly utilize the attendant in the other aisle, calls out, "The burgundy, if you please sir!" lifting a white eyebrow and holding up his fingers to indicate two. "And"—he rummages briskly—"the ladies." He is going to treat us.

"Wonderful," says the flight attendant—who must have been picked for this particular charter—in a pleased voice fresh as the celery he has ready in a glass of ice. "Sharon," he calls, "I'll take care of the gentleman here. Ladies? Red or white?" And this choice seems, as he offers it, such a pleasant one, so emblematic of all we have to choose from in life, that we sigh one after another, "Red."

The woman won't wait. "My son was responsible for a terrible crime!" On her sleeve the nun's hand begins to pat. I'm ready; I know the way people will sometimes talk when the tape is running, the formal and even pious language they will summon up. *Was responsible.* Like *orthodox*, it means the same as its opposite. He *was responsible* for it.

"He needed money for speedballs." Ah! Voice of brown permanent, glasses, little parish-council face, saying *speedballs.* "He was high. Very high. We don't even know what it means, the rest of us."

Who says we don't? I've had enough Percodan to hurt somebody for fun. Sure. If the nurse with the wrong books had come in at just the right moment, when that octane was flowing in, who says I wouldn't have drawn my knees up and let fly with both heels at her soft stomach?

I'll do a voiceover on the pause where we let down our trays for plastic glasses and wine, and screw open the little snapping lids. Maybe I will. Let the voice fade into the background noise and come back up farther down the line.

"He didn't know what he was doing. People died. A young couple."

That's enough. I don't want to be told. I don't want the rumors of earth up here, I've left its cities behind, I'm flying to Lourdes. At my most earthbound I don't do crime stories.

"I'm just—I'm just about—because my son—" She groans, loudly enough to make people turn around. "This young couple—and he came through the window. And there, there, there—!" Her hands make that up-held gesture from paintings of the martyrs.

We fill our glasses. The old man keeps sipping and nodding, as if what the woman has said comes as no surprise to him, merely confirms his own experience. The nun is shaking her head. Seeing the woman's distress, and the recorder, the attendant has paused to listen, turning his big semitransparent ear to us.

"So"—she draws a deep breath—"he did that. He did." She squashes the paper-covered pillow to her face and scrubs the skin with it. Then she jams the pillow against her belly and doubles over with another sound, this one harsh, explosive, and absolutely abandoned, more a belch than a groan, a noise a cow or a horse might make in the barn.

I brought this on, with my little mike. I thought she was going to stick with *responsible*. It's my fault. After a minute I say, "I'm sorry, and I see what you mean about those kids in Mexico. I have a son. I'm sorry."

"Nossir, Mama's right there!" The old man hastens to set me straight. "Selling trinkets! We're nothing but tourists to them! American tourists! Parents put 'em up to it." Forgetting, because he is old, everything the woman has been saying about her son.

She doesn't look at him, but her companion does, with a wondering distaste. A deep surprising rumble, the voice this Sister produces at last. "I believe that's a popular myth about crime in poor countries."

The woman has pulled herself erect and allowed the cushion to be slipped behind her, and she rolls her head on it. "You have a son." She's talking to me. "Let me tell you something. *If you see drugs, you take him to the hospital.*" Each time she says *you*, she points at me, right up near my collarbone. I am sure she was once a woman who would never have pointed. "You *make* them lock him in. If they won't, *you don't leave.* Oh God. No wonder I'm in an institution."

"You're not, you're in Martha House." The nun glares across the thrashing woman at me.

"You *make* them. You don't let them tell you, 'Go home.' *You* tell *them.* Or you'll never, never . . . You'll be like me. I can't read a book any more. I can't pray the rosary! I can't drive a car."

All together we drink, as if there has been a toast.

"Never mind that, why not tell them a bit about your son," the growl-voice says calmly, with no sentiment at all. "He liked to read, didn't he? He was good at drawing." She's setting up a known routine; she speaks as though the woman's son, long dead, can show himself decently as a child.

"There was a fairy tale he liked," the woman begins obediently, her forehead smoothing out with that look that goes with the repeated, the taken-out-and-unfolded, the *engraved* stories. "A little pig found a marble that turned him into a rock—"

"*Sylvester and the Magic Pebble!*" But I stop myself; this is no time for yelling out, "That's not a fairy tale, everyone knows that book!" Instead I say quietly, "It was actually a donkey."

"Are you sure?" she says dreamily. "Well, this—donkey's parents went out to look for him. They looked everywhere and years and years went by . . ."

I know this story. I have read it to my son, regretting that it is not one of his favorites. It's a book parents read aloud at night with tears in their eyes.

Staring in front of me at the seatback, where there is a phone, I am lost for a minute in missing my son at bedtime, unmoved though he has always been by the boy turned into a rock and, worse, by the parents—who are somehow *old* in the illustrations—as they search and search. Unmoved by any of it. The despair of it. The hopeless decision the parents make one spring day to go on a picnic.

Unmoved. It is good that he is so. A sign, a small sign, of strength. I say to myself, *There's a phone right here, I can call him.*

The woman's son had another reaction altogether. "Every time I would read it, he would *hum*. He couldn't stand to hear it! You see? This was a boy they said was heartless. Heartless they said, at the trial. He'd put his hands over his ears and hum the whole time the pig was a rock."

"And then he's released!" I say. Uh-oh. The nun has a repertoire of black looks. She thinks I mean the son. The woman knows, though. Surely she remembers the ecstatic ending of this story. She must remember that. I remind her, I urge her on: "They spread the tablecloth on him! They find the pebble and put it on him by chance while he's wishing!"

"Never was he heartless," she replies in a dry, tearless whisper.

"No, no," the nun, who seems blessed with no skill but patting with her hand, concludes the matter with a last scowl at me.

I can't do anything with this anyway, I'll have to start all over again in another direction, when we get to Lourdes. The woman squeezes her eyes tightly shut when I thank her, and weakly waves me away as she lets her head fall on the nun's shoulder.

I switch off the recorder and lean back. There in the seatback in front of me—the sight of it filling me with an almost intolerable desire to wake my son up so that he can speak to me—is the phone.

I didn't want to think, on this trip. It's as simple as that. But it's too late. My mind, steered by force away from my son's sleeping form in the dark bedroom where my husband must have finished reading to him hours ago, wanders and fidgets over his routines, and alights on his school. *I can't stand his teacher.* I say this to myself with deep, poisonous pleasure, up here in the sky. Not just because of her "Mom," her "Let us take care of everything." She's the only teacher, so who is this *us*? The living? The little Flores boy, this snub-nosed young woman says with an apologetic grimace, just *pollutes the classroom.* That's her word, *pollutes.* I wonder if she would say it on tape.

It's Rafe, the boy my son is afraid of, of course. Ms. Lemoine is recommending that he be steered to a more suitable school, where there are other children with a similar learning style.

"That's *Rafe,*" my son says with pride, indicating with his shoulder, afraid to point at him. No one plays near Rafe. He kicks over the Lego buildings, pees in the sandpile. Of course he does. Tortures the cat saved from the pound to show the kindergarten birth.

He is heading for major trouble. He's heading for the pound himself.

Under the shadow hairline the little beast-face. Poor little devil. An idea rises in me rather grandly and stupidly, unsure it has been untied, like a hot air balloon. One of those large ideas that sometimes exert a force on you in an airplane. Ah. No. Not at all what it says in *The Problem of Pain*! It says, if I remember, that the pain of animals, their tearing each other to ribbons, their *dying*, does not figure into the equation. But if anything is left out . . . if pain . . . or rather evil, if they are not the same thing . . . if anything is left out . . . But it's no use. As fast as it came to me, the whole contraption bobs and drifts away. I can't get it back.

FIRST THERE WAS THE HEAD appearing, coming up the ladder. My husband carrying something under his arm like a bedroll. Bringing it up from the dark beach.

It was our son. The sight copied itself on the way to me, coming by degrees as if I were blinking. This is the way the lightning of reason blinks through the mind, too swift, too hot for one steady cut. He was dead, drowned, and I would soon be dead! With an awful thrill, I inhaled the cold green air and held it. In a rigor of pity for my husband, I dragged my eyes to his. But he knew our son was not dead.

A sound echoed out over the wind. I reached up. My boy was ice cold, wet, laughing. "I went swimming! I got my head wet! Dad didn't, but I did!" He shook his wet hair onto me. I reached up. His cold skin sanded my palms as he planted his freezing kiss on me. "I swam!"

In the middle of the night the boat yawed, bumped—what were these intermittent thuds coming from the underside of it, like a huge stymied heartbeat?—and strained at the ropes. We were all three frozen in the wet sleeping bags. Miraculously, two had gone to sleep.

I did not notice right away that the wind had stopped and that I was hearing the water lap against the hollow pontoons with a chop-licking sound. I had pulled way back, up into the night, and was looking down at a walled ocean with tiny rocking huts sheltered in every inlet.

I unfolded my sour limbs and got up unsteadily, my bare soles squishing on the indoor-outdoor carpet, to rummage for the tape recorder. In the dark I whispered the date to it. I was ready to continue, but nothing came to me. I sat there, sliding against the wall and slumping forward, back and forth, with the boat's movements. I sat there for a long time, maybe an hour.

It was then I received the augury. I saw birds, four of them, long-billed shorebirds of a tawny pink color, and transparent, like tinted cellophane. A foamy tide ran in and out around their feet. One, slender and high-stepping, stretched its neck and flapped its wings. All of this with no sound. That one was young and was, I knew as you do in dreams, my son. About the others—the adult ones, the *three* adult ones—something could not be put into words at all, but I knew it. That I passed over, in the dream.

So my son would make it through adolescence, into a long-legged, proud stage. He would get that far.

Off to one side and above the beautiful, backlit sandy reach on which these birds were stepping, hovered, or actually sat in midair—its wings were folded—an owl. It was smaller than a spotted owl. It did not really have the implacable eyes of owls, but half-closed, rather sleepy, childish eyes. Words came from it. I saw, or read, or almost heard them, words of the deepest comfort. Not the words themselves, but a hum, a bird-signification, some note at a very low frequency was sent to my ears and meant . . . I don't know what it meant.

I knew at the time, but I lost it when I woke up. I felt wonderful. I was at home. I thought, *I'll call Tracey, she'll love this,* and I did, but she had died. Then I really woke up, and saw that I was on the houseboat.

It was palest morning. Not a single bird. Orange-tinted boas of cloud were lying on nothing, above the water and halfway up the stone chimneys. All around us the air had a faint tremble and a taste, like air in a room where the TV has blown out. The thorny weeds had exhausted themselves against a shelf of rock, the sky was a swept-clean floor.

THE SISTER SIGHS. SHE IS too old, older than the old man, she has worn herself out in Martha House, cleaning up after sick, messy, dislocated women with somber grievances. The old man is even now—accepting no rebuff, squinting out of one eye in the quickly achieved tipsiness of age—making an effort to bring things to a satisfactory conclusion. "Now, sacrifice . . . Now, the Blessed Mother . . ." I know this old man; he is a lordly old midwestern tithing Catholic of a disappearing kind, apt to fall into teasing reference to saints and sacraments on the golf course or at the dinner table. He's the type, with his expensive shoes, his *if you please,* to have some right-wing justification for capital punishment in the back of his mind, that he's too chicken to mention openly to the mother of a criminal son.

On the other hand, he could be simply comparing the confused grieving woman to the Blessed Mother.

I don't know. There's no way to know.

I won't ask anybody anything for the rest of the flight. Why do I have to? I don't have to. I'm going to make a telephone call, and then I'll rest. I'll go to sleep.

We bank sharply, perhaps avoiding something, some unimaginable night-sky traffic, and for a time I can see the crescent moon gliding from window to window as the plane slowly rights itself.

Someday my son's kindergarten class will laugh at the elephantine maneuvers of jets. They will have their own wonders, as I have lived to see the day when a telephone call can be made from an airplane.

In India the face you see immediately after looking at the new moon . . . Is this the new moon or the old? I have forgotten how to tell. How few I have actually stored, of these alchemical facts! If the face you see is the face of a good man, it will bring you luck the whole year. Don't look down on luck, bedraggled though it may be when you pull it up out of the jumble and see it is yours, all tangled with planets, clouds, wind, inventions, dolls, pebbles, birds going left or right.

The face of a good man. Oh, where is the flight attendant with his tender smile? But it's too late, I've glanced at the old man, who has gained no satisfaction from the Sister and is opening his third burgundy. All right. So be it.

I excuse myself in a businesslike way and pull my card through the slot. I know the number. I have something to say to that young woman, my boy's teacher, advocate of stability, of security, that she is. Take back what you said. *Pollutes* is a serious word at St. Joseph's School. You can't expel that boy, the Flores boy! His name is Rafe. You have a lot to learn.

No one answers at the school, because it is night.

Please leave a message. I will. I'll leave a message.

Not so long ago the answering machine belonged to very few. All that was required was the assembly of separate inventions to call it into existence, and already it is giving place to something else. Soon, if you are not there, there will be a hologram of yourself to deliver your messages, simple enough for a child to operate, and even if he stretches his hands right through it, it will not go away.

The Llamas

Ann told her friends she was nowhere. What was ahead? She didn't love her boyfriend. He accused her of not liking him but he thought the love part could survive that. He didn't like her, either, even though they maintained a truce over their differing views of the world. Ann's had always been that where the world was not cruel, it was treacherous, even though many advantages surrounded and secured her, including a job several rungs above his in the same company. His view was that the world didn't matter if you were having a good time.

When Casey Clare's brother died, Ann had to attend the funeral because she was Casey's boss. She felt the obligation even though Casey had been her assistant for only a few months. Todd, her boyfriend, said the obligations she felt were imaginary half the time and did nothing but add random pressure to her crowded life. Her friends said the same thing. They didn't press the point that she often shirked these responsibilities after getting herself into a state about them. But she had said she would go to Casey's brother's funeral, and she did.

As an assistant—Ann had known it within a week of hiring her—Casey was not working out. She could spend half a morning being reassured and primed by Ann to get down to jobs that weren't all that complicated or taxing. Every day she presented herself anew with her blunt inquiries into Ann's affairs, and then a rundown of things seen and done between close of business the day before and the reopening of the office doors. Ann had to sit turned away from her computer at an awkward angle, looking up at Casey with an expression of commiseration, gradually picturing how it would be to lean over the in-basket and slap the girl into action. Girl—Casey was thirty-three, two years older than Ann. But her big smiling face and her packed lunch and her blouses a little too tight, as if she had just grown those breasts, made Ann think of an overgrown schoolgirl turned loose in the workplace and fending for herself. Or not entirely for herself: Casey did have a large family, a whole phone book of relatives advising, making demands, dropping in with food, all comically devoted to each other. Not to mention the dozens from her church who prayed at the unconscious brother's bedside.

He was in the university hospital. Every day Casey urged Ann to visit him, as if the problem Ann had was simply getting up the nerve. Casey said, "Yeah, why not this Sunday? Just stop by, come up to the floor. After you get done with the vigil." She knew Ann attended the Green Lake peace vigil—not that far from the hospital—any Sunday that she could make it. She had done that since before the beginning of the war in Iraq.

"Come on," Todd said. "Let's get out of town."

"The vigil is all I do, and I have to do it or I'll go crazy."

"That's crazy," he said. He didn't go out of town without her; he didn't have the focus to plan a trip and get in the car all by himself and stay with it, and she didn't say it but that was why he wasn't getting anywhere in his job.

The peace vigil: that was no problem for Casey. God wasn't on either side, how could he be? Almost every day Casey had a question about God for Ann, and not trying to smoke her out as an atheist either, but simply assuming that the matter of what God would think or do would interest anybody. "I mean, you wonder," Casey would say. September 11, war, and the accident that had befallen Randy—an angel to all who knew him, a fireman, minding his own business and raising llamas. "You wonder how these things can happen." Ann would agree, clicking her nails on the keyboard as she appeared to give thought to the conundrum. Eventually Casey would go sighing back to her desk, where she would pick up the phone and call whoever was sitting with Randy in the ICU. She herself began and ended each day with a visit to the hospital where he had been lying in a coma since before she started working for Ann.

"I admire that about her," Ann said to Todd, who was telling her that if she couldn't face firing Casey she ought to get her transferred out of the office right that minute, before she wormed her way in any further. Ann thought about that and because it raised the question of exactly where, at work, her obligations lay, she said, "I think she'll get down to work when her brother gets out of the hospital." But the day after they had that talk, Randy Clare sank deeper and died of his injuries.

HALF THE PEOPLE WHO HAD arrived from the funeral were standing in the rain, mud oozing into their shoes. They were smoking, drinking wine from plastic cups, and watching two llamas.

They had trooped out of the house where the wake was going on—or not wake, reception, or whatever the church the Clares belonged to called such a gathering—off the sagging porch, and down the path, really a pair of ruts, to see Randy's much-loved pets. Two wet animals as tall as camels stood by the fence. One of them, head high, had apparently walked as far forward on its front legs as the back legs, stationary in the mud, would allow. The other stood with its four feet—pads with toenails were not hooves, were they?—close together. That one was almost tipping over, like a tied bouquet. Then the stretched-out one raised a delicate bony leg and then another, and stepped a few paces away from its mate—if it was a mate—and the mate sprang loose and planted its feet on a wider base in the mud.

Ann said, "Does it seem to you like they're posing?" All the while a soaking rain fell on their thick wormy-looking coats and on the long faces both supercilious and gentle. One of the women said, "Those poor things aren't rainproof like sheep, did you know that?" and people answered her, as they had not answered Ann. Some of them knew that piece of information and some didn't.

The eyes of the llamas were glazed and gentle. But the heads were poised atop those haughty necks. A face came vaguely to mind, someone looking around with a sad hauteur. Who? An actor. Somebody gay.

The woman, an older woman with a smoker's voice, knew something about llamas, though no one, she said, could hold a candle to Randy Clare on the subject. Randy had explained to her, as he would to anyone with an interest, the spitting behavior of llamas. Llamas spat when they were annoyed, and what they spat was chewed grass, a kind of grass slop brought up from the gut and carrying the smell of that region.

"See the pile of dung over there? That's their bathroom. They all use it. They don't just go any old place."

A wet dog trotted up and crouched, head down, licking its lips and yawning with eagerness as it peered under the fence. Ann thought it might suddenly slip under and give chase, but it did not.

Even so, the two heads of the llamas swung around and the big, dark wet eyes rested on the dog and then moved back to the group at the fence. Certainly there was some emotion there, in those eyes. Did the llamas know they were bereaved?

"All right," Casey said. "You've seen 'em. Bootsy and Baby. His darlings, except for Baby isn't so darling. Let's get back inside and get dry and get drunk."

They waded back to the house. Nobody said anything about caked shoes and muddy pants legs, though the women fussed with their dripping, flat hair. They piled their wet raincoats onto a top-loading freezer in a room off the kitchen just big enough to hold it and leave space to pass through the back door. "Deer meat?" Ann asked Casey, indicating the freezer, proud of herself for recalling that Casey and her brothers hunted deer. "No way, not now," Casey said, closing herself into a tiny bathroom off the kitchen. "Donna's catering stuff," she yelled from inside. One of the sisters had her own business; she had done the rolled meats and the trays of vegetables and dips in the dining room, and the laurel leaves on the tablecloth, which were actually sober and pretty, Ann thought, with white candles at either end.

Around Casey's desk, and now at the copier too, the sagas of her sister Donna's business could be heard any day: the crushed cake boxes, the tiny refrigerators some people made her manage with, the cucumbers leaching dye from beets.

At the table sat the not-very-old mother, wearing big tinted glasses. Three of her grown children had lived in this small house with her. Two now. Why didn't they leave home? "You're all together, that says so much about your family," Ann said to Casey through the bathroom wall, hearing the sugary tone in her own voice.

"There were seven of us." Casey came out waving her hands behind her and saying, "Don't go in there just yet." Her eyes were extraordinarily red; they looked the way Ann's had long ago, in college, on weekends when she smoked too much weed. It occurred to her that that might be what Casey had been doing in the bathroom. "Rocky and I are the last ones, and who knows when we'll get kicked out."

"Watch yourself," the mother called out from her chair in the dining room, pointing with the cigarette, taking a deep draw, and coughing with her mouth closed.

Casey grabbed a framed photograph from among the cakes and pies on the shelf of the cutaway window to the kitchen, and held it out to Ann. "This is him. Randy." The picture was of a very young man with a florid, heavy, smiling face. He had the fireman's neat mustache.

Half the city fire department was in the house. They had all driven to and from the cemetery in a caravan with little flags flying from their windows, though Randy had died not in the line of duty but as a result of a freak crash on a secondary road in the eastern part of the state, where he had gone in his truck to pick up a variety of hay the llamas liked to eat.

The firemen all seemed to belong to the same church the Clares did, or to be familiar with its terms. *Prayer partner.* Ann heard that one twice as she moved from one spot to another with her wine. She was on her third full cup. "Randy Clare. Casey Clare," Todd had said. "Shouldn't they be Catholics?"

The rambling service, with its speakers standing up for the mike to be passed their way and its sudden calls to prayer, had had an air of unfinality to it, like a wedding where the vows had been written by the bride and groom when they had had a few too many. In the huge, carpeted sanctuary, light poured through skylights onto a botanical garden. The music for the funeral was piped in, but sound equipment hung from the ceiling, along with banners and American flags, and the plants rose in tiers to a bandstand with keyboards and a drum set.

Years ago, Casey told her, the founder of the church had gone around the state preaching against war. That was in the eighties when there was no war going on. He was a young man and he was preaching against nuclear war. Being attacked on our own soil had washed all that stuff out the window. This afternoon in the hot, crowded house Ann had heard several restatements of this position, from people steaming, as she was, in their damp clothes. The firemen seemed to scent her politics—whatever her politics actually were.

She poured herself more wine. There was ample wine. The massed bottles were positively Irish. Ann's own heritage was Irish. That was why she had to be careful, as Todd would have reminded her if he had been there.

As far as she could tell, there was no one in the crowd with whom to be ironic. She had to answer, "I'm sorry," when a broad-chested man blocked her way and said, "Casey tells me that's your car with the NO WAR sign. Well, I sure wish there was no war, too. And not only that, ma'am, you're gonna need a winch to get you out, where you parked." She had felt the car settle into mud. There had seemed nowhere else, by the time she got there. She gave a shamed, appeasing laugh. Fortunately Casey appeared and said, "Sam, you leave her alone. That's my boss."

"I know that. That's why I'm talking to her. I'm making a good impression."

"This is my big brother, Sam," Casey said, flashing her red eyes. "Come in here, I'll show you Randy and Rocky's room," she went on, taking Ann's free hand and pulling her. By the laden table Ann pulled up short and set down her cup to refill it. She had come, she had done her duty, but she had to protect herself. Casey kept hold of Ann's hand and held her own cup out to be filled too. "You haven't actually met Mom," she said. "This is my boss, Ann," she called to her mother across the table, waving Ann's hand at her. Her mother was talking to several people sitting up close to her chair or bending around her, but at the sound of her daughter's voice she looked up and smiled, wreathing her forehead with the smoke she was blowing straight upward into her own nose, away from the faces of her listeners.

"How do you do?" she said. Behind her frames her eyes were the same blue as Casey's, though their red seemed more like that of normal weeping.

"I'm so sorry," Ann crooned to her across the laurel leaves. "I'm just . . . I'm so sorry."

"Oh," said Casey's mother, waving her fingers through the smoke, "we all are. Did you know Randy?" It rushed into Ann's mind that it was Vincent Price. The llamas. Their expression. Vincent Price.

"No, but I feel as if I did. I've heard so much about him from Casey."

"Randy," said the mother. "Randy was the one."

"He was," the group around her said in unison.

"Donna, you get Ann something to eat," the mother said, and a blonder version of Casey stood up and began forking sliced meats onto a plate. "Kendra, honey, would you just get me a little more coffee. Right there, the decaf. That's something you could do for me. Donna, you don't need to make her sick."

"I get to decide," Donna said, winking at Ann and kissing the top of her mother's head. She added baby carrots and cherry tomatoes and leaned her big breasts across the table to hand the plate to Ann. She fluffed out one of the little napkins and handed that over too.

"Oh, thank you," Ann said, immediately starting to eat. She wiped her mouth. Her impulse was to go around and seize the winking, sensible, food-providing Donna with a hug of sympathy, but Donna had already sat down again beside her mother.

"Come," Casey said. She was leading Ann by the edge of her full plate. "You need anything else?"

"No," said Ann, eating as she followed, popping a log of rolled-up ham into her mouth and glancing up insolently at the firemen they were bumping into. They had to let her pass, with Casey in the lead. She sank against the doorframe, once they were in Randy's room. But of course it wasn't only Randy's; there were twin beds in the dim, close room. The other brother, Rocky, was in the service. He had been at the bedside as much as he could be, but then he had been flown somewhere he couldn't get back from in time for the funeral. "He'll never get over it," Casey said. "Not being here." He was stationed at McChord, getting his training in something to do with cargo aircraft. Something Casey kept saying the name of, day after day.

Todd would say she had let herself be lured into this room where Casey had the advantage and would talk her ear off and somehow get something out of her that she would be responsible for remembering when they got to work on Monday. Not only that, she had drunk too much, too fast, and she wasn't used to it because of her regimen of abstaining except on weekends. She wobbled off the door. Her limbs were heavy. "Oh, Casey. I ate too fast and I've had too much to drink." Now she'd done it. This would be something they had between them, on Monday.

"So?" Casey said.

"I think I should just go outside. The cold air's good."

"Go ahead," Casey said, sitting down on the bed.

"Are you all right?"

"I'll never be all right," Casey said, swilling her own wine. "But I think of all the people who've had someone die."

"That's true," Ann said, letting her eyes fall shut.

"My father died, but I was too young. I didn't have to really go through that. The older ones did. Mom did."

"My father died," Ann said in self-defense, looking into the dark red-brown of her own lids until that too began to swarm and she had to open her eyes. That was better.

"I know," Casey said. "I know that." Ann could remember getting up abruptly and leaving for the ladies' room at the office, after Casey had somehow tapped into the story of her father. "You were ten, I was six," Casey said. "I wasn't the youngest, Donna was. Well. What can you do." She lay back on the bed with the cup in her hand. "Oops, spilled. I hoped you'd come today. And Jesus told me that you would."

Ann had stayed close to the door, but she couldn't turn tail and make her way to the sanctuary of the little bathroom, she couldn't just leave Casey lying there. She said, "Your brother. Tell me about him."

"Nothing to tell," said Casey. But she drew a long, sobbing breath of preparation.

"Oh," Ann said. "I don't feel well. I'm sorry."

"You could lie down," said Casey, without moving.

"I think I need to get outdoors into the air. I'll just be a minute." The crowd from the dining room had filled the hall, so that she would have to push even to get out of the room. "Uh-oh," she said. "Do you have—is there a wastebasket?"

"Here, just hang your head out," Casey said, rolling off the bed and yanking the window open. Ann got there and fell to her knees, thrust her head out into the cold air, and let it hang down over the cracked, mossy sill. "Or you can climb all the way out," Casey said. "That's how we used to always do it." She pushed the window up all the way. "There's no drop. It's low. Just put your leg over. Oops, yeah, it's sorta rotted out. There."

Ann climbed out the window, threw up a small amount, and felt immediately better. The rain had stopped and the flower bed gave out a powerful earthen smell. The dirt was wet and black but not mud. Leaving footprints in it, she stepped carefully over the tips of crocuses and the puddle of chewed meats she had left. "I'm sorry," she said to Casey, who was kneeling at the window just as Ann had been a moment before, except that now Casey was praying. She had her face raised to the sky, her hands on the windowsill with the palms turned up, and her eyes closed.

"Well, hello there," said a man's voice. It was Sam, the brother, out in the yard. He saw his sister in the window and said no more until she opened her eyes. "Hmm," Sam said. "Case, you're stoned. And your boss . . . I wonder if she might be a little smashed."

"I am not," said Ann. "Or if I am, I am."

Casey hoisted herself through the window and fell out onto the dirt and the crocuses. She held out her arms like a child. "I was asking Jesus to come and be with us."

"He's in there with Mom," said Sam, picking her up.

"I'll go back in and sit with her," Casey said. "We were just getting some fresh air. Oh, I wish this whole thing was for something else. Oh, if only Randy was here." Sam did not answer but took a bandana out of his pocket and with uncommon tenderness, Ann thought, wiped his sister's smeared arms.

"I'll change, I'll get this off, don't worry," Casey said. "Now, on Monday, this won't have happened. I won't have fell out the window. Fallen."

"And I won't have barfed," said Ann, surprising herself.

"Don't worry," said Sam. "You're not the first."

"Everybody does it. Not only that, everybody falls out the window," Ann said. Ordinarily she could find a note of bored flirtatiousness at parties and get through a whole evening on it. But this wasn't exactly a party, and how could she talk to him in that or any other way? For one thing she would have to brush her teeth. She'd go straight to the little bathroom—would there be toothpaste she could put on her finger?

It was no longer raining but it was getting dark. How to get out of there. There was no way she could drive, even if she could get her car out of the mud and around the other parked cars. Casey was pulling on her, hanging from her arm for balance, using the wet grass to scrape the soil off her shoes.

"Seen Randy's llamas?" Sam said.

"I did. They're something."

"See the baby?"

"No, I did not." She was forming her words with care. "See a *baby*."

"The cria. The baby llama."

"No. No baby. Not when I was out there."

"She's in the barn. Born Saturday. Day Randy died. Shoot, what he woulda given. We told him, but—"

"He heard us," said Casey. "The nurse said they hear."

"Maybe," Sam said. His eyes on Ann said he knew her skepticism about that, about everything. "Come on, Boss, have a look."

"I'm . . . I think I should just go in and sit down."

"You'll be fine." He looked her over. "The walk will help. Come on, Casey."

"Except you think Mom needs me?"

"Nope. Donna's in there."

THE BABY LLAMA LAY ON a bed of straw in the dark little barn. Its forelegs were tucked under its . . . was it *chest*? *Breast*? Nothing so softly narrow could support either name, with a thin column rising from it, pale as mist, to hold a flower. On either side of the flower glowed a giant infant's eye, in an aged, creased lid. Ann caught her breath as a bottomless innocent darkness took her in. The petals of the forehead narrowed to a small black rose. The nostrils flinched. Did it smell her? Its coat was white, spotted with a pale brown, and it wore a little canvas jacket.

"You can sit down if you need to," Casey said. "Straw's clean."

"Better not," Sam said. "Hey, Case," he said, grabbing Casey's arm as she got ready to plunk herself down. "Come on. Stand up."

Ann said, "Why isn't the mother in here with it?"

"That's Baby. She wants to think about it. She's not real sure about her baby. We're feeding this little girl. Every couple hours since Saturday. She got her colostrum from the vet."

"Randy would have a fit," Casey said. "I'm glad he can't see how Baby's acting."

"If he was here, who knows. Everything would be different," Sam said. "Baby was hand-raised herself," he explained to Ann. "That makes them cantankerous."

"Could I . . . Does it mind if we touch it?"

"Her. No, that's not the problem, she doesn't mind. See, she wants to nurse off you."

"Off your finger," Casey said.

The baby did seem to be feeling for Ann's hanging fingers with its divided lip.

"But no, don't pet her," Sam said. "All we do is feed her. It's them she has to be with, not us. She does fine with her daddy, and there's still a chance with the mom. Whatever, it's them she has to pattern after. Too much is going on, when you're this size. You can get so turned around you don't grow up right."

Ann felt like crying. Her mother came into her mind, the still, listening look she would get on her face when Ann was mean, in middle school and high school and even after that, and the unanswerable thing she would say every time, "You used to be such a happy child." And before that, her father and his cancer and his long-drawn-out unfriendly death. *Oh, no, don't let me get started,* she thought as she began to cry. Neither of the others noticed for a minute, and then Casey saw and moved to circle her shoulders with an arm and pull her off-balance again. Casey began to cry too, while Sam simply looked away and shook his head. He was not the crying type, Ann could tell. At least the tears had a cleansing effect on her mouth and throat, if she had to kiss him. This barn. The rain, the mud. Llamas. Firemen. She was going to have to stay the night. She wanted to. It would be like running away with the circus. They would put her in that little room, Randy's room. The hell with Todd. The hell with her car in the mud and her life. It was llamas she loved.

The Stabbed Boy

The summer of the stabbing he attended Vacation Bible School. Who took him there, along with his sister, who did not survive? His teacher, Mrs. Rao, from the Methodist church where the Bible School was held. How did she know them? Had anyone in his family ever been to a service there? That was for his biographers to answer.

His sister was in a class down the hall, with the kids who were already in school and reading. She was seven years old, he was five.

Because there was polio then, on the first day the teacher handed out a note for them to take home, and after that each kid came with a thermos or a jar of his or her own juice. For him, Mrs. Rao brought a clean glass and poured out juice from her own thermos. She did it for his sister too, because he and his sister were her helpers and the three of them got there early. Sometimes she used the time to play the piano, always telling the two of them that it was out of tune. He came to think he could hear what she meant.

One day Mrs. Rao took him upstairs into the ladies' restroom—past the open doors of the still room of wooden rows, for which he did not have the word *sanctuary*—and combed his hair with a little water. Another day she washed his hands. In their workbooks they were doing Put On the Full Armor of God, which he would find later to be words of the Apostle Paul, about whom he would write a poem when he was in his fifties. They were pasting silver and gold breastplates and helmets on an outline of a man with bulges in his arms and legs. "A giant," he said. Then and afterwards he spoke in bursts of one or two words. "No face."

"It's a silhouette," said Mrs. Rao.

Silhouette. It sounded like a bird, not a giant. He had been careful not to get paste on his hands, but she washed them anyway, leaving him with a clear memory of gray water with bubbles in it going down the drain of the church sink.

Now that he is famous, he sometimes brings up Mrs. Rao in interviews. His story is not known, it is not in his poems, he's in L.A. now, and in his adult life and travels has never even met anyone familiar with the small once-industrial city in the Midwest where he was born. So it is not unusual for him to be asked about his youth, urged to recall something that might have set him on his path as a poet. One of these interviews in which he gave credit to Mrs. Rao's attention, her eyes, piano, black hair in a sort of coil—for this hairdo he had yet to find a word—resulted in the phone call that led to his third marriage.

"Oh my goodness, it is you! It's Lisa! I was Lisa Rao. Lisa! The Raos' daughter! I'm visiting my daughter here in town and I just had to call you up. You're right there in the phone book!" He had a little speech for deflecting this kind of admirer. But what a coincidence! She was sitting at the breakfast table and just happened to open the entertainment section of her daughter's paper and there was the interview, and there, her mother's name! "I was in Vacation Bible School with you! I can see you now, that little plaid shirt you had on every day!" Tactless reminder, and what could have possessed him, that he invited her to meet him for a drink? He must have seen her as coming at him straight out of a church basement in Michigan, from a table of paste and scissors, a woman who would say grace before drinking her juice and never come upon the life-altering taste of alcohol.

He wouldn't have recognized Lisa Rao, or seen in her any of the Indian reds and golds and graces he had added to her mother over the years, but in the bar she walked right up to him. He had chosen the place to send her on her way, a dark bar with hunched permanent occupants and a smell of beer in the floorboards. Quickly she drank two rum and Cokes. Like him, she had had two marriages. She said Frank, her favorite, had died three years ago and while they had had their rough years, there were things she missed a great deal. She suggested he come to the motel where she was staying. Her daughter had too many children to allow for a guest room. He went with her, and nothing came of it because, although her way of lowering her eyes in the grip of her own imaginings had not escaped him in the dark bar, she was much too old for him, his own age. But they met again the next day, and over time and with her persistent phone calls and visits to L.A., they became friends, and finally he married her. It was his one good marriage. She cleaned up his house and banned his drinking friends in favor of a private rite for occasions ending in the bedroom.

His sober friends were relieved that it wasn't one of his students this time, but they compared her to Nora Joyce: she was uneducated, crudely outspoken, and bossy, while he, the poet, as a result of what they called "the damage," was a ruin. Under the charter of long friendship they listed his traits: could someone like her have any idea what it meant to join forces with this most embittered, tense, infantile, drunken, paranoid, alienated, critical, silent, secretive, and easily hurt of men?

Of course Lisa knew that first night that there would be scars on him, all over the chest and ribs where his mother had stabbed with his father's Buck knife, in search of the heart. "What an awful thing to do to a little boy," Lisa said in a practical voice. Her finger rubbing with no awe on the fat seams of scar on his naked torso made them seem a simple thing, almost something that might be discovered under the clothes of any man, just one more in a tangle of ugly things in the past that a decent person could only shake her head at. "Ah. And your poor sister, who didn't have your luck." His luck!

That night in bed, as if he were any old friend, she reminisced. "We lived not all that far away, but I couldn't come over to the trailer park, not even for trick-or-treat. None of us kids could. We were the Asian kids, so proper. I always wanted to. You-all had that little house thing, at the gate. We called it the witch's house, even before that happened. My mom went, she went right in there because she knew you kids were in there. She wanted you out of there. She talked to your mom. She said your mom should be in a hospital."

His father had been the manager of the trailer park until he ran off.

Thereafter, by virtue of living in the gatehouse instead of the trailers, his mother was the manager, but she never did any of the things his father had done or went outside or answered the phone. People stuck notes in a hole in the screen, left broken fans and sink pipes by their step, and torn-out stove burners and bags of garbage. Their own stove was black with the overflow of things his sister tried to cook.

He was not in kindergarten because you had to have the shots. His sister was in second grade and had the shots; his father had seen to that, Mrs. Rao told him, giving him a choice: a father running off, ducking into the woods behind the propane tanks, or a father taking his sister for her shots. Some things allowed this choice of what to remember.

When he went back to Michigan with Lisa, the first thing she did was take him to see her mother in the nursing home.

At the sight of Mrs. Rao he stopped in the door. He would not have known her, any more than he had recognized a five-year-old girl in Lisa. "It's Robbie, Mama, Robbie Forney," Lisa said. Mrs. Rao lay on her side and did not speak, though she was awake and breathing quietly, her eyes open and looking at him. The first lines of a poem came to him. There was no way to hug someone lying in bed, and he was not a man who would try that, although now he sometimes found himself wrapped in the heavy arms of Lisa without knowing how he got there. He was a famous man, but once he was her husband it was all the same to her whether he was a known poet or nobody.

He stared at a cup of water with a bendable straw on Mrs. Rao's nightstand. Feeling shaky doing without his drink, he picked up a plastic fork in cellophane and scratched at his wrist. "Robbie's a professor now," Lisa said. She didn't say *poet*. To him she said, "You can call her Mama, or Gloria. Call her Gloria. I guess Mama could be anybody, but Gloria is her. Take that chair."

He sat down. "Mrs. Rao," he said, very low.

Mrs. Rao might be ninety-seven and lying there with white hair, but she had the same big eyes in smooth, heavy lids. She looked back at him. The irises had gone a lighter brown. Far down in them was a table with scissors and paste, and his sister sitting on Mrs. Rao's lap, having her fingernails cut with a pair of round-tipped scissors. His sister had laid out the scissors herself, each on top of the armor man from the Teacher's

Workbook, while he chose the locations for the big jars of paste and the flat sticks they used to get it out. He would have no children, so for the rest of his life he would not recover the smell of the paste.

Mrs. Rao lifted his sister's thin, long hair from her neck and drew it up in a ponytail. "Like mine," said Mrs. Rao, whose hair gleamed with comb lines and bars of light that traveled up and down the black, offering the eye a quiet for which there was not a word. His sister got down and went off to her own classroom. This was not the last day of her life, a day hidden even from his poems because there were no words for it, the day of who and why. This was a hot summer day in the first week of Vacation Bible School. He remained at the table, carefully tearing from their perforations in the Teacher's Workbook a set of pages containing breastplates and helmets and metal shields for the front of the legs: a page per child, enough for each one's silhouette to have on the full armor of God.

Later or Never

On the days Lawrence could walk, Cam sat with him in the old grade school. His house had a ramp, but there were days when he could do stairs, and they would negotiate the seams and curbs of two blocks of sidewalk and the school's railed steps in order to drink coffee at a table in the entrance hall.

In place of the children who had worn the edge off the marble steps in two troughs, the high-ceilinged classrooms now held shops and restaurants. Sometimes those old children could be seen standing up close to photographs hung in the corridors, pointing themselves out, prim or devilish at their desks. "See those holes? Those are inkwells," they would be saying with a hopeless pride, to kids who must be their grandchildren. Great-grandchildren. Cam thought the kids in the pictures looked like orphans. Dressed up, dark around the eyes, staring with grins and scowls into a time in which the classroom, the teacher, and they themselves in their bunched-up plaid shirts and bloused dresses did not exist. Yet there they were behind glass, jittering in rows like kids anywhere, waiting to be let out the doors and onto the buses lined up in one of the pictures on their bicycle-sized tires.

"Did they all wear white?" Cam wanted to know. "The girls?"

"Little brides," said Lawrence, tipping back his head. "Brides of knowledge." He raised one of his eyebrows at her.

"So how did you keep clean if you went to school in a white dress?"

"Clean wasn't so big then."

Cam didn't say, "How do you know?" After all, she asked these questions. And Lawrence had an interest in many subjects far afield of his own, which was French literature of some time period.

He was squinting out the open doors at the hedge that bounded the parking lot. He spoke a line in French. "A poem," he explained.

"Yeah," she said. She could have said, "I mean, look at your face. *French poem.*"

"The blue sky. The blue sky is God, the only difference being that it exists. The hedge, the sun over there? All in a poem." This seemed to please and agitate him at the same time. She hoped he would not recite the poem.

The hedge was seething with tiny birds. His eyes were giving out on him, but he always noticed the same things she did; like her, he was always on the lookout for something. Something sudden but expected.

For Lawrence, she could see later, the thing watched for would have been more specific than it was for her: some change in the course of what was happening to him. He had the kind of MS in which the body rapidly divorced the brain. She knew about it from a quarter on disabilities; it was the worst form, but there was a chance of reversal. She told him that. She should have known that instead of arguing he would bring in his poet. His poet was Mallarmé, the subject of his book, the one he had published as opposed to the two rubber-banded stacks of paper in liquor-store boxes in the closet.

"Chance, yes," he said. "Not *a* chance. A throw of the dice never will abolish chance. *Le hasard. LE hasard.*"

She knew *hasard*; she had a string of French words now. She knew when he was quoting; she knew when it was his poet because of the way he held up both weakened hands like a conductor, two fingertips of the right just meeting the thumb.

His book had received one review, and she knew the name of the person who had written it. Lindenbaum. "He did say it wasn't a biography, but, by *Jesús*"—he always pronounced it the Spanish way and then apologized because Cam was Catholic—"the man knew his Mallarmé."

"If it wasn't a biography, what was it?" At one time she had expected he would give her a copy of it, but he never did. She knew where the cop-ies were, in another box in the closet.

"*Une vie.*"

They had both seen the birds swoop in, dozens of them, and make themselves invisible in the hedge, so it seemed to be shifting of its own accord. "God of the weak," Lawrence whispered. "God of the little birds, protect them now." To Cam's mother, the way he looked saying this would have been proof he was crazy. But Cam knew these prayers of his. He liked to put his palms together and roll up his eyes. It was something he did when they were watching the news. "O God, we ask that you turn the general, as he testifieth before the Congress, to stone. Also the at-taché with the briefcase."

"Fob," he was explaining. "The prayer for the birds. Fob, who wrote about animal life."

"Fob," she said obediently.

"F-a-b-r-e. He's saying a prayer that the owl won't *snatch* the bird." With his better hand he made a snatching motion. "*Snatch* the mouse. Fabre doesn't hold it against the owl, even as he describes how it's done. Every chew. Except, of course, an owl does *not* chew. He swallows. Vom-its out the little bones et cetera."

"Whatever it is, somebody's gonna know all about it," Cam said. "And then tell you."

"You're right." He said it warmly, turning to face her. He liked exas-peration. He was a child that way, always goading somebody, a teacher or a mother. She knew that.

"There's that face," he said, something his mother also said to Cam on occasion. "That baby look," he said. "Know how a baby, certain kind of baby, won't smile at you? That baby will . . . she'll drink your blood before she'll smile at you. You could turn inside out, and she would just look. And you know she thinks you're already inside out, you're so ugly and frightening and you smell."

"I don't think that."

"To a baby, we smell like zoo animals. To a baby." His face emptied, the way it often did when he remembered something not connected to a book, and he turned away, so she was able to do a mental drawing of his profile. His skin was sweaty and drained of blood, almost the gray of a pearl. A freshwater pearl, like her grandmother's present. When she was in her cap and gown her grandmother had fastened the strand for her. It barely met around her neck. It burst the same night, when she went off to drink beer with Ray Malala. Ray had been her friend since St. Benedict's, the new fat boy in third grade, because both their fathers had died. By high school Ray was a DJ everybody wanted at parties, and a football player. Being Samoan was a plus by then. He got her the place as the team water girl. The guys liked her, but they didn't get around to going out with her. Ray, on the other hand, had acquired a fair amount of experience over the years. "All right, listen, Cami," he told her when he took her home after graduation, "don't you be doing no more stuff like that right now. Hear me? I'll tell your brother. Here's your beads."

A freshwater pearl had dents, though, and Lawrence's face, familiar to her eye and her mind's eye, was uncommonly smooth, except for one crease between the eyebrows. No one would read his age in the features, which, despite the cheeks rounded by prednisone, reminded her of the smooth, heavy-lidded face of Rose of Lima. He had the same look of secret pride and refusal. The picture of Rose in her first communion book, *Our Saints and How They Lived*, was of a statue. The tapered plaster fingers didn't even have knuckles; this was Rose before she dipped her hands in lime so as to scar them. Cam's communion-class drawing of the face of Rose, sleepy and secretive under a crown of roses, had stayed on the refrigerator until it curled around the magnets. For weeks after her father's funeral she would check it for a miracle. Rose of Lima's miracles were not listed in *Our Saints*, though she had performed them or caused them to happen or she wouldn't be a saint and, as not only Dominicans but Jesuits too had sworn, more angel than human. Even then, Cam knew herself to be half pretending to expect, and finally faking the expectation, that Rose's lowered eyes might open. If they had, it would have meant her father had arrived in heaven, if there was a heaven.

In time, like her brothers, she had a list of reasons not to go to Mass. Then she heard her mother start the car and drive off alone because of having a husband who was dead and kids who wouldn't go with her to Mass, and that ruined the hour anyway. Years of Sundays. By the middle of high school she was doing better with her mother, but she discovered she had let God dry out like a plant.

•

ONLY A CERTAIN KIND OF person, the kind you could be pretty sure would not pass by, would pause to figure out Lawrence's looks. "There's something the matter with that guy. He could be fifteen and look forty or he could be forty and look fifteen. And that girl with him. Fat." Though Cam knew she was not fat, so why put the word in the mind of an observer? She was tall and solid but with large bones and a body mass index within the OK range—she knew that from her nutrition course. Not so big, in the eyes of some people. Pacific Islanders. That, she knew from Ray Malala. Columnar, Lawrence's mother said. He often told her what his mother said, which was a way of taking her side against his mother. And in fact Lawrence was thirty-nine, so the observer's second impression would have been the right one.

His mother's name was Daisy. Cam knew it was a name his mother had given herself, the way she had given him the name Orion and left it up to him if he wanted to change it in high school. He named himself after T. E. Lawrence. Cam must have seen the movie? Peter O'Toole? Cam defended herself. Where would she have seen that?

"Of course I changed my mind, about Lawrence. But it was too late."

Daisy was a small, pretty woman who must, since she had had Lawrence in her teens, be in her fifties. Cam listened for any mention of the parents who must have been around, and had some feeling about what was going on, when their daughter was pregnant with Lawrence. She could imagine her own mother's reaction. She could see her face. And her father's, if he had been there—no way he would have let a boy who got his daughter pregnant dodge his responsibilities.

A designer, Daisy called herself. Her garden pieces in glass and cement and her elaborate stone figures mortared into walls cost a fortune and were featured in magazines. Cam admired them when Lawrence showed her photographs. The bulky figures were not exactly people. They were Daisy's idea of myth, Lawrence said.

Daisy wore eye makeup, and leather pants with high heels, and did not look like someone with the muscles to work in stone or cement. Drawings. That's what she said the figures were. They gave the effect of being trapped in the walls looking for a way out, but in a lazy, drugged way, like bears in a zoo. At the same time, their stone faces or muzzles or whatever they were, raised from the background and pointed skyward, wore half smiles, "to make rich people feel at ease," Lawrence said.

"They're sculptures," Cam said with the confidence he expected of her where art was concerned.

"Reliefs," Lawrence said. His mother wouldn't use the word *sculpture* because that would land her in the hell, she said, of galleries. People with MFAs writing up wall cards.

"Did she want to be a sculptor?"

"Of course," he said.

Daisy was a drinker, Lawrence said—as if that excused her from all the responsibilities she left to others—but she worked in her studio all day first. The idea had wandered into Cam's head that Daisy might lead her into the presence of a white-haired couple on a yacht, holding martini glasses, who would say, "You must have a scholarship to"—what was a famous art school?—"right away."

Often Daisy took men along on her travels, but she had no fear of going off on her own in pursuit of ideas for her designs, into deserts and ruins and villages where the women mixed bowls of paint and dipped their fingers and printed symbols onto the mud of their houses. She made friends with these faraway artists; she preferred them to people near at hand—like her son, Cam thought—and wrote them letters, without the least proof, Lawrence said, that they could read English.

Daisy had a lot of travel coming up in the fall, and before she embarked on it she fired the other two shift nurses, both RNs, who took care of Lawrence, and hired Cam, who had no real degree, to live in. There was every reason to do this, Daisy said. Each nurse had had her own way of tormenting him. The older one, Iris, had her own physical complaints—her back prevented her from using the lunge belt to get him onto his feet on a bad day—and talked all day on her cell phone. The other one, Sharon, teased him, sampled his wines, and used his computer. Sharon wore tight jeans and tanks and used a tanning bed; Cam saw the bend from the waist for something dropped, and the backward arch when sitting, for something out of reach. According to Daisy, Sharon had not bothered to remove her browsing history from Lawrence's computer, showing that she had looked him up and done a search for his ex-wife with the different last name, and even his child. He had a son.

There were no pictures of the son. Daisy never said the word *grandson*.

When Cam revealed to Daisy that her mother feared gossip because Cam was moving into a house with a man, Daisy grinned and said, "The poor dear."

At least I have a family, Cam thought. *My mother doesn't make me live with some slave so she can leave the country. I go see my grandmother. My parents were married.*

"Your *mom* called me," Daisy said early on, when Lawrence still had Iris and Sharon and they were seeing how Cam worked out on an eight-hour shift. That's all that was legal, eight hours. But Daisy didn't care what was legal. "Your *mom* called just to make sure everything was OK. She calls you Cami! Cami with an *i*?"

It was Daisy who had written the ad: "Mature, cultured companion for invalid. Medical credentials."

HE BORES HER UNTIL SHE has to yawn and stretch, until she almost says "I'm not one of your students," but something in him so unsuspicious, so ignorant in proportion to his knowledge that it's almost a kind of sweetness, stops her and lets her stand it. Not that he would notice whether she could stand it or not. Though at times his eyes will pass quickly over her like a flashlight. When she wore a plaid shirt of her brother's, he said, "Don't wear that."

He has dropped his head back so he seems to be scanning the heavy school light fixtures strung on cables. She knows he is trying to fill his chest with air.

Just before he got sick—so even Daisy can't claim that was her reason—his wife divorced him to marry someone else. Moved three thousand miles away, taking their son. Cam pictured a little boy having Lawrence's wide, greenish cloudy eyes, with a permanent crease between the brows, staring hopelessly and knowingly over his shoulder as a woman dragged him away. A blonde in glasses. Cam knew that much. She knew because the wife wasn't the forbidden subject; from the beginning he had talked about her, a woman who couldn't see a foot in front of her, and ran in marathons, and made him go to parties he hated. A woman with long blond hair her students mentioned in their critiques because she played with it while she lectured. But a woman who lectured, a woman with a PhD. When Lawrence spoke of her it was the same as when he spoke of his mother. Women. Women who existed to torment or exhaust you until you simply—simply—simply—here he conducted with his hands—*put them out of your mind*. Cam listened in the understanding that this was a race to which she did not belong and for which she did not have to answer.

But how old was he—five? ten?—the son looking back as he was dragged away?

HER DRAWING, WHEN HE LOOKED at it, did not surprise Lawrence. She saw that. He had expected it.

Later her mother expressed the opinion that the drawing should have been entered in a contest before she ever let it out of her hands. "A contest. For one drawing," Cam said. "Right. I didn't want it anyways."

Lawrence would have let her know about it with an eyebrow if she said *anyways*. Or *somewheres* or *lost for words* or *on accident*.

Now he had seen three of her drawings. "Don't show these to my mother," he said. "She'll make suggestions." Cam didn't tell him Daisy had one of them, the one of him. It was the one he had let her do while he was in the chair by the window, why not, it was what he did all day, though, by *Jesús*, there ought to be a skull on the windowsill. He could sit forever looking out the window. Not only *now*, he said irritably. Not just this particular summer quarter when he was not teaching—as if he would teach again in the fall. Looking out the window was an occupation for all seasons. "Sickly spring, lucid winter, et cetera."

She didn't tell him she had met twice with Daisy, once for coffee while she was still working the morning shift, and once right before she moved in. The second time was in an old hotel, by the fireplace, for wine and what Daisy called snacks—perfect little dollhouse dinners on plates thinner than the heavy napkins. They had finished two bottles and ordered a third. Daisy did most of the drinking, but Cam kept up her end. She was underage, but nobody asked her. She didn't look it, with her size and the kind of face she had, "not so much scowling as . . . solemn," Daisy said, as if she had come to respect Cam's choice of face.

In the early hours of this occasion Cam had laughed a good deal more than she usually did because Daisy knew how to be funny about herself and her art and her son, exactly the same way he made fun of her, showing no pity. "Where were we? Lord no, no more Pinot. Take it away! I admit he didn't have the best example, growing up. *But*—he appealed to women. That is something that *cannot be helped*." She filled her glass and Cam's. "*She* ran off with a bore from the business school. Of course there were plenty left to comfort him. Coming around. For a while."

The telephone rang all day. He answered it or he didn't, depending on his mood. Cam could have told Daisy that. No one, man or woman, came.

At some point in the evening, Cam was drunk for the second time in her life, and knew it, and gave in to the impulse to flop over her canvas bag and pull out the drawing she had made of Lawrence. Daisy looked at it in silence and then she tried to stand up. She had some trouble getting out of the deep chair because she had already met somebody else for a drink before this. "You hold this, I don't want it on the wet table." Then she was gone a long time, fifteen minutes. Finally Cam followed her to the ladies' room. You could suffer a clot or a hemorrhage at any age; Daisy could be sprawled under the door of the booth.

There was Daisy, at the big softly lit mirror with her eyes shut. She had a mascara wand out, lying open among crumpled tissues. "I can't find the top," she said in a hopeless voice, losing her balance. Cam picked it up off the floor. "Where did you put that?" Daisy rasped, when Cam was in the booth.

"I just gave it to you."

"I mean that picture."

"In my bag."

"Don't show me things like that, oh, no, no, no," she said when she joined Cam at the table some time later. "Sign it." She never asked if the drawing was for her, she just took it. After Cam had signed it Daisy sat with her eyes shut. Cam decided to order two more plates of the miniature crab cakes with caramelized onion, even though it was Daisy's treat. She beckoned the waiter over. She felt Daisy had put things in her hands.

They would talk on the phone, they would make lists in his kitchen, but this was the only evening she and Daisy ever spent together, socially.

THE BOOKSTORE IN THE OLD schoolhouse was gone. Taped boxes filled the space where bookshelves and display tables had stood the week before.

This upset him, but he pulled himself together. "Good thing I brought my own," he said. He had sent her back into the house to get it, the scuffed little *Symbolistes*, from the pile on his bed that she knew to leave when she pulled the covers up.

It was early afternoon, shadow just leaking from under the cars in the parking lot. A group of girls came up the school steps, laughing and talking on their phones, slapping the marble with their flip-flops. She recognized them; they were from her high school. At the top they wheeled and set off down the hall, one of them showing a roll of skin above her cutoffs. That one had been in her art class. Cam had liked her; she liked people her own size and bigger, liked to think of them standing in front of a mirror seeing if they could pinch the number of inches of belly that meant fat.

She leaned, as if a current from them had swept her. She couldn't tell if they had seen her. She was two years ahead of them, or at least of the one she knew from art class. Out in the world. Despite the C's on her transcript, she had finished her CNA at the community college in a year. Once she was certified, it was easy to find a job with a home health agency. Probably just speaking English, Daisy said later, got her that job. For two months she had cut thick toenails and helped old men take showers. Not many agreed to it, and half of those who did would not let her into the bathroom, and every so often one of them who did, sitting on the shower chair with water streaming off him and calling her "a big gal" or "a doll," would ask her for something she had to pretend not to understand. She changed their loose gray jockeys or pajama bottoms or long johns, or reported on the fact that there was nothing to change them into, and sometimes, though as a home health aide she was not supposed to do what either a nurse or a housekeeping aide would do, opened the bathroom door on messes that would throw her schedule off for hours.

Then she saw the ad for Lawrence. She quit the agency the day after Daisy interviewed her. The salary was more than either her mother or her brother in the service made. To everything she said, Daisy's reply was, "Mmm, yes, so, mm-hmm . . ." The next day Daisy called her on her cell while she was trying to talk her way into a huge old guy's apartment while he blocked the door with his belly—never mind finding soap in the cat-smelling dark behind him and getting somebody his size into a shower stall. Daisy said, "I think we can work this." As if it were a scheme between the two of them.

Nothing about *mature* or *cultured*. Cam hadn't even met the invalid. Why was his mother hiring her when he was a grown man, a college professor? Because his mother had the money. And he didn't want to do it, so why should he? That was how Daisy saw it, and apparently Lawrence too.

"He's just like me," Daisy said. "He was."

IF HE IS IN THE bathroom, Cam doesn't go into the hall because she doesn't want him to think she is listening. If there is cleaning up to do, she does it later. Sharon told her she would need to get in there, and showed her the 409 under the sink, stored in small jars because the jug is too heavy for him to lift. The time is not far off when she will have to rinse him off, bathe him. Touch the knobs of spine she can see under his shirt.

This was part of the routine for the other nurses. Sharon made sure Cam was informed about his "endowment," as she called it. But with Cam, for some reason, he is back to shutting the door. He even locks it. It's an old door, with a sticking lock. He doesn't realize that with his hands the way they are he could get shut in there. Things like that happen. People get trapped. In her week of training at the agency they learned how to take a door off the hinges. She has already made sure the hinges aren't painted over.

Daisy put in a big open shower with bars, but he has to seat himself on the chair, and Cam can hear him stumble and knock it against the tile or knock it all the way over and have to take his time scraping it into position.

In the garage, draped in a tablecloth, sits a wheelchair more expensive than a car. Daisy will have to sell it on eBay unused. In a crowded hall rented for the memorial—who are all these men and women Cam has never seen, saying they have lost him?—Daisy will say, "There's that face," and having never touched Cam before, close in on her with a hug that knocks the breath out of her. And there, the blond wife, with a husband trailing after her, and there a tall sullen boy of about eight, with no crease between his eyes but unmistakably thin and careful and watchful, there at last the son.

ALL AT ONCE THE TINY birds burst out of the hedge like spray out of a nozzle. His eyes widen, meet hers. Clearly he saw it, whatever he says about his vision. No one but the two of them saw it, she feels sure. "Ah," he says. She waits; always he has to put words to what goes on. He begins. "Once, anything could fly." Is he more cautious than usual? "Of old, that is, anything could be depicted with wings. Even snakes. The Egyptians, the Phoenicians, the Judeans . . ." He pauses, looks into his cold coffee.

The girls from her high school come by, going the other way. This time they all give a wrist-wave—so they did see her before, and identified her and talked about her.

The one she knows says, "How's it going?"

"Good. What's up at school?" Then she remembers they must have just graduated.

"Good," they sing out, and give the wave again.

Lawrence sits up straighter while this goes on, because girls are near, but he doesn't really notice them. He has no idea Cam knows anyone, anywhere, except him. He is concentrating. "One and all, they esteemed a winged cobra," he goes on. "And the winged snake, remember, in . . . in . . ."

Cam says, "Yeah, that guy."

"In Herodotus." He smiles. Then she can tell by the way he chews on his lip and says, "He saw the wingbones," that he is tired and they will have to get going. Waiting for him to let her take part of his weight so he can stand up will take a while. Half the time in public he leaves the walker collapsed. Sometimes, even walking, he'll carry it for as long as he can and then have her carry it.

Wait. He is not quite ready to stand. "Last night I was at a party having one of those conversations where you're buried up to your neck and people are going to step on your head." She knows he means a dream; he wasn't at a party, he was in his study looking out the black window and she was in the living room watching TV.

He recites in French. She stretches, gives up on holding her face in what her grandmother says a woman should never part with, a pleasant expression. A willing expression, as if French matters. *"Biting the warm earth where the lilacs grow,"* he says, just barely lifting all ten fingers.

"That would be you-know-who," she answers. Then she's sorry because the tone of exasperation that normally pleases him has caught him off guard.

After a while he says, "I'll show you something." He has made a decision. "Let's see the book. The book, the book."

"Sorry." She gets it out of her bag and gives it to him. The way he takes it, carefully in one hand, makes her think of her mother handing the missal across her to her father at Mass. Her father parted the halves of his coat, felt his chest as he always did, and sank onto the kneeler. Was he taking the right medications? A weight of shame for all of them in her family settles on her. When he sat in his chair at home, did she, Cam, bring him anything? She bows her head. She says to Lawrence, "I don't think my father had any books."

"Never mind." The flashlight look. "As Molière tells us, reading goes ill with the married state."

"The married state." He likes it when she simply repeats his words. "See this?"

She shrugs; it's in French.

"With his times," he reads to her, bending close to the page and following his finger, "the poet should not involve himself. Da da da . . . Here it is: he should work mysteriously with regard to later or never." He holds up his hands and spreads them triumphantly. "Ah! With regard to later or never."

She shrugs again, to hide the yawn.

"That's not what I want you to see." He is feeling among the pages with his stalled fingers. Finally he comes to an illustration, covered with a sheet of onionskin. "Here we have," he says, beginning to smooth the cover sheet like somebody stroking a kitten. Finally he lifts it by a corner. "Here we have. Ah."

She studies the painting of a man. It must be a painting, though it is in black and white.

"There. Manet. Manet painted him. Everyone painted him. Sadness incarnate. You see?"

She nods.

"Having a salon of *symbolistes* did not protect him. He was a bourgeois like everybody else. He lost his little son Anatole. This picture," he adds, "was painted before that happened."

To him, that was logical. She could understand that. She understood everything he said. The order in which things happened might be nothing, when you thought about it. Your life was there, like your fingerprint, inescapable. Why not? Each year filling with what belonged to it and to you, and flushing away what was going to turn out not to be yours. A disease could seem to come out of nowhere. A job, a person. Not out of nowhere. Yours. It was all lined up like the school buses. Rose of Lima had foreseen the day of her own death.

He closed the book and leaned over to put it in her bag, resting his forehead on the table as he did it and for a second or two after. That was a first.

He prepared to stand up. They looked at each other in their shared life. Everything was familiar. It was all coming to pass as if they were reliving it, what they would do now or later or never.

Two years later she would be a wife, her husband not someone she met after Lawrence had died, but a man she had known since grade school. A friend of her brother's, a friend of Ray Malala's. She would go on drawing, but nothing would come of it. She would never, with all her children, be as married as this.

Who Is He That Will Harm You?

I heard what you said to your girlfriend."

"Why do you say that, *girlfriend*?" She looked up, stretched out on the couch with the Sunday paper, into his frown. "I mean, I don't say *girl*friends. A friend's a friend, right?"

"I heard what you said. You said what you'd put in an ad."

"What?"

"What you'd *advertise*. You were on the phone."

"I'm not following. So now—*what*?"

"You said, 'Slim with big breasts and fat toes.'"

"Oh my God. We were talking about our bodies. Jeez."

"I heard."

She put the newspaper over her face. "It was Teresa from school. Saying what she would put in one of those ads in *The Stranger*."

"What about you? Did you put an ad in?"

"Yeah, right. I totally did. I'm looking for a guy with a—"

Something happened. When she opened her eyes she was lying on her back with things on her. Papers. She was under a low roof. Half under. Table. Couch. Glass thing dangling. Lamp. She funneled through time, and found her name. She was Mary Ann. Her head hurt. Down the room a blurred man stood with his legs apart.

Earthquake? She lay there in the prickling of details that weren't really thought. Her mind was joined to her body in a combination of exhaustion and alertness. She couldn't tell if there was silence or she was deaf. At length she heard her own voice produce the sound, if not the words, of a question. No answer. Her mind tried to sleep, but she kept her eyes open, thinking with a slowness like moving in a bath.

Dennis. She knew him. Dennis.

Her tongue was sore. Seizure. But pain . . . her head . . . huge . . . a word for it . . .

She was in medical school. There.

Dennis. Not helping her. She let her breath out. "You."

"I what?"

"Hurt," she said, drawing up her knees. She could move. She could produce words, she was seeing double, but she had her speech centers. "You." She raised a finger off the floorboard. Where was the other hand? On an arm twisted back along her head. "You. Get. Out."

At that, he took one broad step, grabbed the lamp, and hurled it. The cord whipped after it; somewhere glass shattered. She rolled her eyes up, seeing the underside of his jaw and thinking—and at the same time noticing that she was thinking—strategically. She had her second realization, and with it a knowledge of what the word *realization* meant. He was panting. It might not be over.

There on a level with her were his feet. In socks, if he kicked. "Oh God," she said. Her voice surprised her, a normal groan as if she were telling him how much reading she had to do.

"Oh God," he responded, but he had backed away, he had sat down. That was good. Not on the couch, on the rocking chair, and he was rocking it, of all things, so hard it ground on the wood floor. If she shut one eye, she could get two flushed, small, handsome faces condensed into one.

How long was she out? She was starting to give a history. She had speech, she was speaking reasonably, and the person listening in the ER would be somebody she knew. A nurse would be best.

The phone rang, with a muted sound. "There's your call, there's Mom," Dennis said in a mincing voice, or was that her imagination? Did she have her imagination?

Her finger kept softly touching the leg of the coffee table. I hit a table. Marble, from Goodwill. Iceberg. We call it the iceberg. So she had her mind. The brain works to repair itself, just like blood, which wants to clot. It doesn't want out into hair.

"Is there more to this?" the nurse would say, or maybe just "OK, cut the crap. What happened?"

He did it.

She started over. Maybe he hit me with a lamp. I don't know. I don't remember. I don't remember getting up this morning. What day is it? What time is it?

What a comfort it would be, if a nurse were to say, "Three o'clock." The day would be half over. They would have figured everything out.

Why was there no question of tears?

She turned her head and vomited, an act requiring no effort on her part. The phone was ringing again. So, Sunday. Her mother called on Sunday.

How was she going to get to the ER?

Now she saw in his face something she had not learned about in her years of learning everything rapidly and well. But she detached herself from the sight and went limp as he shoved the iceberg, toppling her books, and dropped to the floor half beside and half on top of her, tearing newspaper out from between them. I wonder if I'll beg, she thought. No, this was something else. He had started to cry. He sobbed, banging the floor with his fist. Would someone come? "Don't you know you can't talk like that? Big tits and fat toes? Don't you know that?" She could barely hear him. He weighed her down, her head pounded. I think maybe he killed me, she told the nurse.

AFTER A COUPLE OF YEARS she never referred to it. People did not encourage that, as anyone back from an illness or a travel ordeal, her father said, or even from travel without an ordeal, will tell you. He was explaining not to Mary Ann, but to her mother, to soothe her mother and give her some rest from talking.

People who had known Mary Ann when she was in medical school knew of the episode; that's what they called it, as she did herself. What else to call it? She had not been murdered.

•

WHEN THEY MOVED HER OUT of the ICU she had her own window. Across the street stood a big tree where there was a bird the size of a goose or an owl, even bigger, too heavy for the limb it sat on. No, no, not a bird, merely leaves, the giant leaves of the tulip poplar: her mother brought one up to her room to prove it. There was no bird as big as the shape she was seeing. But a bulky green bird with a half-open beak sat there day after day, neck craned to peer into her room. The nurse she liked fixed her pillows and said to her mother, "Must've escaped from the zoo."

"I'm sorry!" her mother said, almost in tears with the leaf in her hand.

"I don't care," Mary Ann said. "Let it sit there."

"Oh, it's worrying you," her mother said. "It's making you uneasy."

"No."

HER FRIENDS PUT ALL HIS things in two boxes to be picked up. They glanced through a scrapbook Teresa found wrapped in a lab coat at the back of a drawer. Drawings, dozens of clippings about random subjects, photos of Mary Ann cut up and pasted into collages. His name, Dennis Vose, written hundreds of times. Somebody came to collect the boxes. Her parents were in touch with his lawyer—he had a lawyer!—and through the lawyer he had turned over the key to her apartment. He could have given somebody else a copy, her mother said. "One of his henchmen?" her father said from the big hospital chair. They were both professors, but her mother had taken an indefinite leave of absence from the English Department. Her pacing, her bringing up things from books, her fury of analysis, always broken at its height by tears, did not bother Mary Ann as much as it bothered her father, who sat with his hand over his eyes beside Mary Ann's bed with its rails and gears.

FROM THE BATHROOM OF THE new apartment she could hear Teresa on the kitchen phone. "Yeah. Yeah. Yeah. But . . . Yeah, but how do we convey to her . . ."

Teresa was staying with her until her mother could get there. She had passed her Activities of Daily Living—they wouldn't discharge you until you had mastered those—but she was going to have to have somebody for a while anyway. That was fine, but she was not going to leave Seattle and go to Portland to be with her parents. Nothing and nobody was going to make her leave her physical therapist, Nolan. On her last day in inpatient rehab, the PTs clapped while she was having the tantrum about Nolan. People with some aphasia, they told her—"some" was what everybody said she had, and it would resolve, most or all of it—would almost always find they could curse.

Nolan had to call her mother to explain that some patients developed a dependency on a particular therapist. He said that as an outpatient Mary Ann would have somebody new but he would go on working with her himself as long as she wanted.

"You're a lucky girl," the nurses had told her when she was first sitting up and listening to what was said to her. "Medical students get the royal treatment." "Pretty ones. No kidding, they have a special saw they use on them." "Don't listen to her. Seriously, you should have seen these guys taking care of you."

Every resident who came in went over the whole thing with her. The nurses' account was shorter and had blood and mess in it. From when she arrived in the ER still pretty much herself and talking, downhill fast. Intracranial pressure. When that went high enough a team came in and sawed into the skull and lifted a section of it off, to be frozen and put back on later. In a case like hers, where the piece of bone turned out not to be sterile, they used plastic. A piece of plastic, said one resident, as expensive as a car. A used car, Nolan said when she got to him. He made her half-dozen procedures sound like a science project she herself had undertaken, well meant but half crazy.

Bone or plastic, the piece was held in place with snowflakes.

Snowflakes. The snowflake, the surgeons explained in their careful, tiring way, was a little half-inch plate that fixed the piece back into the skull with screws. The plates got their name from the spokes sticking out from them, into which tiny screws were sunk. "Think of a dance floor in your skull," Nolan said, "outlined with spangles."

Teresa said Mary Ann would be playing tennis again soon, and they would be running their morning miles, but Nolan made no mention of that. Nolan never spoke of a possible improvement until it got close. *Milestone* was a not word he used. But Mary Ann was getting around, growing her hair, starting to read. Doorknobs and shoelaces gave her trouble, and forks, and stepping out of reach of the hug Teresa wanted to give her first thing in the morning when she wandered into the kitchen in her bathrobe.

"You know, your sweet little fat guy Nolan says we can go ahead and talk about anything that comes up," Teresa said, pouring her coffee and Mary Ann's milk. Mary Ann no longer liked the taste of coffee.

"Why are you looking at me?"

"I'm just looking at you. You're looking at me too, babe."

"Am I different?"

"Well, you've had a little work done. A little makeover."

Mary Ann didn't laugh, because a laugh had to be assembled from scratch. Once she had laughed at everything. They all said so. You could tell where Mary Ann was sitting in a lecture hall. "I don't mean looks," she said to Teresa.

"Neither do I," Teresa said.

"MARY ANN, HE YANKED YOU by the arm, hard. I saw him. And then the time you were dancing at the sink. He spun you around. You snapped your fingers. You thought he was doing some flamenco thing. You thought he was going to dance with you."

"I did," said Mary Ann, not making it a question.

"He pushed you. He was furious. I know this. *You told me.* He said, 'People can see in.'"

"They could, too," Mary Ann said. The big windows of the apartment where she had lived eight months before came back to her clearly, with plants on the sills. Were these plants she had now the same ones?

"You talked about getting a cat." Teresa seemed to have a drill, a list she worked from, of things that were normal and things that were not normal. Mary Ann saw that the list was scrambled but could not be sure where Teresa came down on some of the items. "He kept going to see his family in Canada. You liked the same music. Music was a big thing to him. You knew him three months. He said he was studying for the GREs. You didn't say you had lived with guys before. He is, I admit, an incredibly good-looking guy. You told your mom, 'He's the best-looking man I ever saw.' You told your mom everything."

"I did."

In his backpack he had kept a pill container, and when she clicked open the compartments for the days, they were all empty. She didn't know which of Teresa's lists this would go on. Sometimes a thing that seemed in his favor, such as the fact that he had cried and played "Come As You Are" all day the day they heard Kurt Cobain was dead, were on the wrong list.

Teresa picked her up from PT so often she was getting to know Nolan. "That Nolan," Teresa said. "He used to be a wild child, know that?"

"What do you mean?"

"He went here as an undergrad and then he trained here. Said he used to live down at the Blue Moon."

Mary Ann didn't ask what the Blue Moon was.

"He was a drummer of all things! He drummed with some band."

How did Teresa know that?

"What a little sweetie," Teresa said.

SMELLS. DETERGENT, FOR INSTANCE. THAT smell contained the time she said, "Jesus you waste a lot of electricity." Dennis worked out every day in the fitness room in their building, and after he showered he put in a wash. He didn't mix his laundry with hers but went down to the basement machines by himself and came back with a small folded pile. When she said that, he stood there with his back to her, holding the laundry against his chest. She put her arms around him from the back and she could feel the heartbeat shaking his body. Gradually it slowed down.

"How come you don't criticize me? How come you don't get mad?" she said. "Like when I swear. I know it bothers you."

"You know it but you do it," he said without turning around. "Is that the idea?"

AFTER A YEAR HER MOTHER was the only one who talked about it. Only her mother craved an exact tally of what had been altered or erased, and searched for it in photograph albums, in Mary Ann's old transcripts and letters of acceptance.

He had pleaded guilty. Something was wrong with him, so he was in a private institution. Where? It didn't matter where. Wherever it was, he could not get out. Her mother assured her of this until her father said, "Gail, that's not something Mary's worried about."

She didn't worry. Even later when her mother was in bed dying, Mary Ann was not worrying. Her worry centers were gone, Nolan said. He wished his were.

"You need snowflakes," she told him.

FOR A WHILE HER FRIENDS would remind her of things, explain things, question and prompt her. Reason with her. They liked to tell her stories of herself, how she had drunk beer half the night and aced the anatomy exam, how when they got their grades she had climbed onto the iceberg and danced.

After a while she saw less of them because more than a year had gone by and they were in their clinical rotations. "It breaks my heart," her mother said. "Where are they? Where's Teresa?"

"She's at her apartment," Mary Ann replied. She was the logical one now.

"The only person you see anything of is Nolan."

"I see the doctor. The OT. I see those people downstairs. I see you and Dad."

"I wonder if Nolan knows who you really are," her mother said in her new voice of thin argument.

Mary Ann didn't argue any more, with her mother or anyone, the energy for it having left her. It was to Nolan, now, that she told everything.

"She means who *she* thinks you are," Nolan said. "She can't help it." Nolan understood everybody. He had to. Once the doctors were finished, he took over. In serious rehab, with the Hoyer lifts and the parallel bars, you saw it all. "We get the guy who makes the winning touchdown at three o'clock and at six o'clock he gets hit by a bus. Whoever thinks they're somebody, they're right: some body." Nolan didn't interfere with their pride, but he didn't throw compliments around either, just eased gradually into his system: moving the limb in question or getting squared away with the non-limb. Not looking back. Not forward either, any distance into what might or might not be achieved. Just right in front of you.

They were not allowed to skip a session, but they could feel free to yell at the top of their lungs; they could curse, weep, soil themselves for spite. Nolan said it was a pity the doctors didn't get to see what some of these patients had in them, the pain they volunteered for, the feats they were capable of.

Mary Ann saw the doctors step inside the gym in their hard shoes to make suggestions. When Nolan was the one who knew. There was mind and there was body, and on the washed-out road between them, he waited for her every day. At their wedding he said, "I know two things: what bad luck is, and what good luck is."

SHE HELD HER BABY, TOUCHED his ear. Tory. Sometimes her love for him sent a shudder through her so strong it woke him up if she was holding him. All things fell to one side or the other of a line like a tennis net: safe or unsafe.

"Your mother was just the same when you were a little one," her father said. For her mother had died.

Now whenever she read about a man who had run over his girlfriend or gone after his wife and kids with a shotgun, she checked the name, she read to the end, she turned on the news. This was a few years before you could track people down on a computer. It couldn't be him, though; he was in a hospital, probably in Canada. He was Canadian.

"He put that accent on," her father said on one of his visits, with a deep sigh. "He wasn't Canadian." She saw that her father—and if her father, then others as well—had information she did not have. "Dennis Vose . . . ," her father began.

"It's snowing!" she said from the window.

"It's not going to stick." For a minute she was in two lives, so clearly did she hear her mother. The wet snow trickled down the pane and she had the unwelcome thought of her mother as she had been long ago, when she was still an English professor and had ideas about everything, including the weather, art, poems, the health of children, what to wear, what made people believe in a God, and how her friends wished they had a child like Mary Ann, whom she had decided, on first looking into her eyes, burning with infant wisdom, would be named after George Eliot.

"Not for the looks," her father would always add.

The baby woke up crying. He gave her a wild look, and when she picked him up he shivered as if she had found him lying out in the snow instead of in his crib. Already, after so few months of life, it seemed a baby could be visited by dreams. "I'll always, always come," she told him.

WHEN HE WAS OLD ENOUGH, they told him she had hurt her head and there was a plate in it for protection. With fingers infinitely gentle, he liked to tap and rub her scalp, exploring for the snowflakes. Of course he didn't know what had happened to require them. She didn't want her son to think of such a thing, her warmhearted, dreamy little boy with his spontaneous songs. Nothing prepared you for motherhood, for the tide that knocked what was left of any other life right off the shelf, while you waded around it and sloshed it out of your way, with your child held close, held above it, above all things.

"I WAS A DRUMMER," NOLAN said. "That meant you had to drink like crazy but not lose the beat. For me it was one or the other, so I went back to school." He was talking to her father, who had perked up as he always did when Nolan was around. They had driven down from Seattle to give him some exercises for his arthritis. He liked talking to Nolan, sitting at the breakfast table with Tory on his lap. "I had a physiology professor tell me why not forget the whole thing, join the navy," Nolan said.

"What? What?" her father said in an old man's loud voice that made Tory turn to look up at his face. "You could have taught *him* something."

"Hope I won't have to," Nolan said.

SHE HAD A DIFFERENT HANDWRITING. Strong smells gave her a headache. She had no blue clothes any more. She prayed. Not to God. But when she was waiting for her son at the preschool door she prayed steadily. Not because she was anxious. "Don't worry," the aides were always saying. She was not worried, she was praying him back to her. While the other mothers talked by their cars, when the high syllables of the last song rang out behind the shut door, the prayer intensified until it was answered.

SHE AND TORY, WHOSE SHOTS were behind him, were watching the clinic fish steer in and out of a pearly castle when suddenly the woman who had come out of one of the doors behind the receptionist turned into

Teresa. She was heavy, with blond hair instead of brown, and a stethoscope around her neck. She looked up. "Oh my God," she said, steadying herself with a hand on the receptionist's shoulder. "Mary Ann!" She ran out into the waiting room and hugged Mary Ann as if she had been searching everywhere for her.

"And this, this beautiful child is yours? Your little boy?" said Teresa, squatting down in front of Tory with her hands out in a way that said to Mary Ann that she might clutch him.

"He's shy," Mary Ann said.

"I'm not shy," he said.

"Oh my God. Mary Ann! Come into the back, come into my office so we can talk. I don't have a patient right now. Are you waiting . . . Who are you waiting to see?"

"Dr. Cooley. We saw her. We're just waiting for a prescription."

"I'll tell her I've stolen you. Oh, this is unbelievable. I'm just here on a locum, I don't even work here. Oh my God. How many years is it? And how old are you, little buddy? I bet you're . . . five."

"I'm five," he said.

Mary Ann couldn't pin down when Teresa must have graduated and gone away, so she said, "I haven't seen you in a long time."

"Nine years? Ten? Is he your only one?"

As if there could be another. As if this love could be repeated. Mary Ann nodded.

"I have three," said Teresa as if to apologize. "I married Alex."

"Alex . . ."

"You remember Alex."

"Oh, yeah. Yeah, I do, I think."

"We went to Chicago for our residencies, and then he did a fellowship year," said Teresa, leading the way into an examining room, "and then we lived in Chicago again, so I sort of don't know what happened to anybody. Sit right up on that stool, sweetie." Tory had already climbed up and sat, swinging his legs. "Mary Ann, Mary Ann. So. How are you?"

"I'm fine."

"So-o . . . tell me."

"Tell you?"

"All about you."

"Oh, OK. Well, remember Nolan?"

"Of course I remember *Nolan*."

"We got married."

"You got married." Teresa did the thing with her hands again that made Mary Ann think she might be going to grab her. "And had this beautiful child."

"I didn't get pregnant for a long time, but then I did."

"Yes, you did. I can't believe this. I can't believe I'm seeing you. And your son!"

"We live here," Mary Ann explained, to settle her down. "Nolan's at the same place. The hospital."

"Where's my Spiderman?" Tory whispered to her.

"Everybody just scattered!" Teresa went on. "We just came back and I've hardly seen anybody from the old days. Well, anyhow, I'm a pediatrician. Can you believe it? Who would have thought? Did you think I'd be an old married lady in Peds? Remember when I was going to put an ad in *The Stranger*?"

"Here he is," said Mary Ann, handing Tory Spiderman from her purse.

"That's all I thought about in those days. I know I went out a lot, but I didn't have the boyfriends, like you did." Teresa smacked herself on the forehead. "Did I really say that?"

"What, about boyfriends? I guess so, I guess I did. My mom kept pictures of me with some of them."

"Your mom! How is she?"

"She died."

"Oh, I'm so sorry. I'm sorry to hear that. Was she ill?"

"She just . . . got worse and worse." A vague shame came over Mary Ann. She didn't know what her mother had actually died of. Her heart bent in on itself: her mother had never seen Tory.

"What a shame," said Teresa. "Things were hard for her. Did she live to know about Dennis?"

"About Dennis?"

"That he died?"

"Dennis? He died?"

"Oh dear. He did. He died quite a while ago."

"Did he get out? What happened to him?" She saw Dennis walking out the door of the institution and being hit by a bus.

"Oh dear," Teresa said again.

"It's all right," Mary Ann assured her.

"Well, I'll be in trouble with somebody for this. He jumped off a roof." Teresa said this in a whisper. She made a steeple of her hands and turned to Tory. "But this wonderful boy! And—Nolan! Why don't you run in here after your appointment so we can really catch up."

"We already had our appointment. Why did he?"

"Good lord." Teresa sat down. "What do you know about Dennis?"

"I don't know, I guess nothing."

"He was in and out of those places for years. I have a little patient like that right now that I'm referring to the Vose Center." Teresa took some glasses out of her lab coat pocket and put them on to look at Mary Ann. "You know about the center? For when the whole thing starts in childhood. No? I've had to be in touch with them a couple of times. The *Vose family.*" For that she put on a little accent. "A big deal. Oh, Mary Ann." Teresa got up and threw her arms around Mary Ann and hugged her as if she would never see her again. "Oh, I hope I haven't made things harder."

"Things aren't hard," Mary Ann said when she got loose.

ALL THIS SHE EXPLAINED TO Nolan on the phone, after she took Tory to school. She was trying to get used to the all-day kindergarten. She told Nolan what had happened to Dennis Vose. There was a silence, and then Nolan said, "I have to say that I knew that."

"You didn't tell me."

"I didn't. I'm sorry," he said. "Do you think that was the same thing as a lie?"

"No," she said. He tried to tell the truth, but he couldn't always do it. You couldn't if somebody asked you at work, for instance, if their scars made them ugly.

A SHORT FAT WOMAN IN an orange smock answered the door, eating a candy bar out of the wrapper.

"Carolyn," a voice called from deep inside. "Will you see if that's our visitor? Use the viewer." But the woman had already said "Come in."

Mary Ann stood still. There, past the French doors opening onto a long room with urns of flowers on stands, was the marble table. The iceberg. With the rest of what was in the room in pink and white and gold, it became a piece of whatever that kind of furniture was called.

Not from Goodwill. From this house.

"AM I SPEAKING TO MARY Ann Kemp? This is Mrs. Vose." This voice, a flat voice with pauses and little slurps as if the person were eating, was asking her to visit the Voses in their home. Where did they live? In The Dales. North of the city on the Sound.

They wanted her to come that same day. "I can't get out there unless there's a bus," Mary Ann said to the voice. "I just drive around here. Just in the area."

"We'll send a car," said Mrs. Vose.

She called Nolan again, and he said she should go if she wanted to. He had heard of The Dales. He didn't think she needed to have him with her. He would pick Tory up from kindergarten and take him back to work with him, where he could have a good time on the rings in the gym.

"But I always pick him up," Mary Ann said. "I'm always there."

"Just today," Nolan said. "Let these people say they're sorry."

"Sorry?"

"Sorry they didn't tell you. Sorry they didn't give you a heads-up back then that their son was from someplace else all right, but it sure wasn't Canada."

So she called back. The car Mrs. Vose sent was a pickup truck, driven by an old man. He said he was coming off his shift at the gatehouse. After he said he did some driving for the Voses because they didn't get out in a car much since the stroke, he was content to drive without having a conversation with her. On the freeway, The Dales wasn't that far after all. The man smoked with the window open, and at the end of one cigarette he slowed at a gatehouse and saluted the face in it, and then after some hills and circling around they turned into a driveway. "Thank you very much," Mary Ann said, but she couldn't remember his name. He didn't get out of the truck. "I live down the road," he said, gesturing at some woods in the distance. "Four o'clock, I'll be back." She wondered if she should have had money to give him.

"This is Carolyn, our daughter-in-law. Dennis's wife. Come with us, Carolyn," Mrs. Vose said. She was old and walked with an aluminum cane. She lifted it and for a minute Mary Ann thought she was going to give Carolyn's legs a tap with it to get her going. Carolyn had finished her candy bar and Mrs. Vose took the wrapper from her and put it in the pocket of her dress.

Mary Ann got the smell of a cat. Not strong, but there. She liked cats and looked around for one. She and Carolyn sat on the couch, the Voses in wing chairs covered in pale green stripes and roses. Mr. Vose was a heavy man who wheezed when he moved, sucking in the flushed rounds of his cheeks. Another old woman came very slowly and sideways into the room. She set down a big tray of tea things on the iceberg, and they didn't introduce her, so Mary Ann saw that she was the maid.

The mother, who had a small, childish, lined face—a perfectly shaped face Mary Ann had seen before—poured unsteadily from the big teapot, and right away she said, while she was stirring, "We're told Dennis was happy when he was with you."

For just a minute her heart had gone out to Mrs. Vose because she had trouble with her speech and had to keep wiping her mouth with a handkerchief. When she said this about happiness the father glanced at Carolyn.

Mary Ann said, "I don't know." You didn't have happiness or unhappiness as a memory. You had specific things like your face in the steam and suddenly behind you in the mirror another face. A certain kind of music being on all the time. "I don't know," she said again. She had something she was going to say, though. "In your twenties"—here she was quoting her mother—"you're having fun. You aren't ready, you aren't ready for . . ." For what?

"Dennis was not in his twenties. He was thirty-five years old at the time," his mother said.

"Thirty-five," Mary Ann said. A year older than she was now, the boy crying in front of the TV because Kurt Cobain was dead.

"This is a picture of his wedding," Mrs. Vose said, taking a photograph out of her pocket along with the candy wrapper, which she shook off her fingers onto the rug. "He married Carolyn while they were there." Carolyn did not seem to have to be included in the talk.

In the picture a fattish couple stood in front of a cake, smiling—Mary Ann would have said idiotically, but she knew, now, never to use such a word.

"He always wanted marriage and a family," his mother said. "From an early age. That was all he wanted in life."

"Well, Dorothy, we knew that was unlikely," said the father.

In Mrs. Vose's way of speaking, halting but irritable, Mary Ann began to feel some threat, as if some crude or ugly word might come up the middle of what she was saying. Carolyn seemed to be dozing rather than listening, except occasionally her head would snap up and she would look at the father with a dog's mild anxiety.

Coming up the freeway beside the man in the truck, Mary Ann had decided to tell the Voses that she had loved their son. Now she saw that the word *love* could not be trusted on all occasions. And in reality, she loved only her own son. Oh, she loved Nolan, or liked him more than anyone else. But her son . . . her little boy: for him, for him, something had been turned on and even after it filled her it never stopped, there was always room for more of it. So she was not after all going to use the word about anybody else.

"Actually the center has been around since the twenties," Mr. Vose said. His bleary, helpless gaze seemed not to match his words. He seemed to want her to know something. Was it that they were sorry? "Later we came in with some backing in Dennis's memory, and they renamed it."

"That was where Dennis lived?"

"From time to time, in the early years, yes, he did stay there."

"He developed schizophrenia," said the mother, training her eyes, wide in the rings of old skin, on Mary Ann.

The father wheezed even attempting something as simple as taking off his glasses and rubbing his eyes. "Usually that type of thing won't show up until the teens. But in his case it was a little earlier."

"He would never have hurt anybody. Something would have to provoke him," said Mrs. Vose, taking her cane and stamping it twice into the rug, which sent up dust. "Something."

"Dorothy," her husband said.

"You're alive," Mrs. Vose continued, to Mary Ann.

"Dorothy."

Another woman, not as old as Mrs. Vose and the maid, came to the door, took a look at Mrs. Vose and another at Carolyn, and went away.

"Somebody just told me," Mary Ann said. "About Dennis. I didn't know about that."

"About what?" said his mother.

"That he ended his life." Those were the words suggested by Nolan. "Teresa told me. My friend from medical school."

"Of course I know who told you," said Mrs. Vose, fussily swatting the air. "She called us to let us know, last week I believe it was."

"This morning," said Mr. Vose.

"I haven't seen her in a long time," said Mary Ann. "I'm not sure how long, but I did see her today when I took my son to the doctor."

"You have a son."

"I do. I have a little boy, Tory. He's five."

Mrs. Vose was wiping her mouth. "Five," she said through the handkerchief.

SHE HAD LEARNED TO TYPE with both hands, but she was typing with one finger, to keep an arm around Tory. Sometimes he hit the key for her. "V," she told him. "O." He loved the alphabet; he had known the letters since he was three. Not just to say them: he could read. He could use the computer.

There were pages on Dennis Vose, benefactor of the Vose Center, with his wife, Dorothy Suttler Vose.

The Vose Center. The webpage had a picture of a campus, and another of a smiling, attractive child. The child stood still among trees; the nurse behind him had on a white uniform. Nurses didn't wear white uniforms any more; they wore ugly print tops and white pants, or scrub suits. Mary Ann knew hospitals. In the cafeteria of the one where she had lived, she still met Nolan for lunch. She still ran into people in the halls who had known her at different times. When they spoke of those times they did so in certain ways, depending on which time it was they were recalling. She recognized the ways; they didn't mention the episode, but they all knew more about a period in her own life than she did. They cared more. She had her snowflakes.

At any rate, she knew people didn't wear what the nurse in the picture had on. They didn't wear what Dorothy Vose had had on that afternoon either, a navy-blue dress from some dim time, with big chipped buttons and a pocket where you put a picture of your son's wedding.

If they had invited her in order to say they were sorry, they had forgotten to do it. By the end of the hour Mrs. Vose had lost track of things, and seemed to think Mary Ann had come to bring them something. Several times she inquired as to how Mary Ann was going to get home. When the deep chimes of the doorbell sounded they all sat up straight in relief, except Carolyn, slumped against the cushions. "Her medication," Mr. Vose said softly to Mary Ann. He wheezed on the way to the door, where Mrs. Vose said, "Where is your coat?" and Mary Ann said, "I don't have one—it's summer," and Mrs. Vose said, "Oh, at this time of day my mind wanders so."

Mary Ann got into the truck. The man had the windows down to let the cigarette smoke out, so she leaned her head out to call a goodbye. Mrs. Vose was ducking and twisting her shoulders, trying to keep her husband from guiding her back into the house. Because her mind wandered. If you lost your son you would search, you would have promised to, your mind would not rest.

IT WAS LATE AND THEY sat in the kitchen listening to music while she told Nolan about the cane and the wedding picture and Carolyn. She told him about the iceberg. "But I doubt if they sit there," she said. "In that room. I bet they go someplace else in the house. Where the cat is."

They had the CD player turned low so as not to wake Tory. At the end of a hard day Nolan still put on Nirvana. At work he liked music on, and when you were his patient he would play whatever you wanted, as loud or soft as you wanted. When she was in rehab, Mary Ann had not been able to choose. So Nolan said a select few of his people liked to do their PT to Nirvana, which did them good and did him good. Because of the groan. Any song by Nirvana had the groan, he said. The howl. "Things are far gone, but yet a song is being sung about them," he said. "And not only that, a little bird told me Nirvana is your favorite."

That made her jump. She saw the tree with the green bird. Things like that would happen to her then, even though she quickly knew what he meant, knew he meant a person had told him and it was Teresa.

That was early in rehab, when she first knew him. Even then, he didn't say *"was* your favorite." He put on certain songs and waited to see whether she liked them. Not whether she remembered them. Whether she liked them. "Sort of," she said. "Sort of not."

"You know something about you? You don't pretend," he told her, his first praise.

She finished telling him everything, and then they just sat there listening. After a while he said she wouldn't want to know how much beer he and his friends in PT school had put away to the tune of "Come As You Are." But you didn't have to like a song for it to take you back. Music she had once loved, he said, might make her want to go back to a time before he and she knew each other, let alone were married. She said no, it didn't do that.

Tory was on the stairs. *"Come S.U.R.,"* he sang in his high voice.

"OK, man, come on down," Nolan said, and he came into the kitchen in his Nemo pajamas and stood near Nolan's chair. He put a hand on the leg Nolan was keeping time with. Finally he said, "Why did the man jump off the roof?"

"Well, my guess," Nolan said, "would be it must have been Spider-man." He looked at Mary Ann to see if she thought that was a lie.

From

Criminals: Love Stories (2016)

Bride of the Black Duck

O if I am to have so much, let me have more!

—WALT WHITMAN

It was my husband, not me, who had the binoculars and the bird books. He closed his heavy Audubon on his chest and died with a finger marking a page. The nurse moved the book, so I don't know which bird his eyes saw last. I didn't want to look at them. I never wanted to know all about birds. What Walt Whitman told us in poems, of his little canary greater than books, his frigate bird that "rested on the sky": that was enough. His gray-brown thrush. His mocking-bird. Not symbols but animals with souls, like himself. One his sad brother.

My husband would have been glad when the black duck appeared, glad to see me take an interest in it. In the first months, I would hear his voice in the house. "Take an interest!" "Go ahead and cry, I'm honored. Cry, but not all day." "Go to the doctor." "Just give the bird books to the library." He had loved birds, put time and thought into them, but they were a hobby. He would not have stayed up at night worrying about a particular one. Yet if you were to do that, he was a man who would have tried to console you.

The year he died, the year the duck appeared, I got involved with a family in the neighborhood, the Lesages.

Raya, the mother, would not settle for anything halfhearted once you crossed into her house and she into yours. That was a troth. People were always breaking it, though. Half the friends she had made had lost patience with her drinking and her high-handed, possessive affection. Of a defector she would say, "I don't know what it is, I've known her forever, she's someone I love."

"That's probably it," her son would say. He could say it kindly.

The one I would have wanted when I was young was her son, for his beauty. He, Randy, was a twenty-one-year-old boy with a perfect good nature—the only good-natured one in the family. It was hard to say how an ordinary liking for people could have sprung up in that family. But Randy would single you out, invite you. "Connie, come upstairs. You can see my stuffed animals! Mom kept them all." He would take the stairs two at a time: to him you were not somebody having to grab the banister and catch up. In his old room, stuffed animals by the dozen were flopped on the comforter and sitting up on the shelves. Looking out of the black eyes at us was Time itself. I lost my breath. Did I have sons in their fifties, living in cities of their own? Where had I put the donkey, the elephant without ears? Quickly Randy gave me his arm.

Randy was a sharer; he stood ready to share your moment of panic. He had long-lashed blue eyes, a child's eyes. He could disarm and flatter you with a beautiful, intimate, predatory smile, for along with his sweetness went a streak of something less than cruelty but more than mischief.

He lived with his lover, Hans. Hans was in his forties, a fit, handsome, unsmiling man with hair cut so close you could see the curl only as a silver ripple. "You're going to love Hans," Raya said, and she was right. I would love him for his resemblance to my husband, in his austerity, his ardent, unshareable, preoccupying interests, but would he love me? I didn't say that of course. At this age we are thought to have left off longing to be anyone's favorite, while coming ourselves into a manageable and harmless general fondness, as for books we finally have time to read.

"I know he's a lot older than Randy," Raya went on, "but I think of it this way: Randy's safe there. He's safe with Hans."

Hans was a professor of anthropology and had a name in his field;

he was Hans Klaas, author of books about the peoples of the inland and coastal Northwest. Once he knew you he would let fall facts about them here and there, in his withdrawn but precise way. What happened to these people to eradicate all they lived to do was too serious for conversation. You had to go out onto the balcony of his condo in winter and stand in the cold rain at night, hold the wet railing with him in a stiff homage to the lost. You had to look down at the Sound, cross out the freighters and tugs, the ferries with their lights, and place on the black waters one high-prowed dugout canoe as long as a semi.

Hans never touched on the subjects Randy chattered about away from him—the two-spirit, once known as *berdache*, who dressed and lived as the opposite sex, or the "manly-hearted woman." "Don't ask him about that stuff," Randy said. "No no no."

That first night, on being told that I had taught English and even written a book in my younger days, Hans said "Indeed!" The cold smile he gave me was the opposite of Randy's.

"It's about Walt Whitman," Randy said. "I'm halfway." People are always halfway through your book. Zeno was right; they will never reach the end. I'm thankful not to have written another. "It's good!" Randy added.

"I would have assumed no less," said Hans. That was our meeting. It didn't matter; we would be friends. A midnight would come when, overcoming his hatred of the phone, he would call me and say lightly, "You don't happen to remember where Randy's class was meeting, do you, dear?"

Randy was attending the community college, where he could get night classes, though moving in with Hans had taken him far from the campus and the cruising areas of Capitol Hill.

The rooms were huge, spare. There was an elaborate sound system, and once Hans knew I was losing my hearing he would invite me over to listen with the volume up. He planned carefully so as not to do this when his neighbors were at home. The music open on the rack of the piano was the Diabelli Variations, but he had an intention tremor that had put a stop to his playing. "He won't shake hands," Randy told me in the elevator, the first night. With someone my age, however, politeness compelled Hans to offer the hand with its slow tremble.

"I'm his only friend," Randy said in the elevator going down. "People come over because of his cooking. I'm the one who talks to them. If they touch the piano, they can't come back. I tell him he's just like my mother—he doesn't like anybody." This he said with some pride.

"They both love you."

"Oh, love." Randy waved his hand.

The strength of Hans's feeling for Randy was such that when you were in the room with them the air felt close, as in a dedicated enclosure like an ICU or an indoor pool. He wanted Randy home; he disapproved of his day job as a transporter at the hospital. "I couldn't possibly quit. The nurses bring me cookies!"

"Ah," I said. "But now half the nurses are guys. And the doctors are women." This I had noticed in my recent stay in the hospital, but what made me say it?

"Guys can make cookies now, it's the law. Hans makes the best macaroons."

THE DAY I MET THE Lesages I was halfway through my cardio circuit with the pedometer when I heard shouts coming from one of the big houses. I didn't know who lived there. Even without my hearing aids I could hear the words. *Never! Never! Liar!* A man and a woman. It was ten in the morning, an hour when most people are not home to scream and weep, but safe in the office or school. A third voice, young and shrill, joined in. I had stopped walking anyway, short of breath and lightheaded, but I listened until a silence fell and one of them opened the door and let the dog out. The dog was a golden retriever, so I put out my hand as he—or as it turned out, she—tore down the steps and ran at me. She was whining rather than barking. She bit me on the hand. After the bite she hung her head, curled her tail under and retreated. A tall woman stepped onto the porch. "What are you doing here?" she said. Her face was white.

"I'm walking," I said. "Your dog bit me."

"You're trespassing."

"I'm standing on the sidewalk."

"You're spying."

"I am not. I'm having a heart attack." I squatted down to rest my palms on the sidewalk, which tilted and became a gray slope. A phrase

I had read came into my mind: desert of sidewalk. Something from the paper, about a suburb. *Desert of sidewalk*, I said to myself as I got down on my side. I reclined like Whitman. I felt I could begin on a poem.

"Oh God! Nathan! Call 911! Morgan bit her! Jesus, she's having a heart attack!" The woman ran back into the house, where, as she would tell it later, her stepdaughter stopped crying to say, "And if you say *Jesus* in my presence one more time, I will call the police," and she, Raya, the stepmother with two DUIs, in therapy for failing this girl, Caitlin, and all the other members of her family, screamed, "Do that, they'll love it, they'll lock you up and shock your little shit brain. Jesus! Jesus! Jesus!" This Raya was to confess, and many worse things screamed, in the ten-year marriage, at this praying girl entrusted to her as a daughter. "But I love her!" And she did, faithful as Caitlin was at that time to a group of kids who stood passing out leaflets about the Rapture. "Convicted Christian! Convicted! That's the word they use!"

Meanwhile a man had crouched and rolled me onto my back. He had his arm under my neck and he was cramming an aspirin past my teeth. "Chew it." I swallowed and whispered, "You're a doctor I bet."

"I am," he said with that proud sternness they have. Of course he was, as my husband had been, along with the owners of a good number of these houses. He picked up my bitten hand, looked at the toothmarks. He must have been thinking, *They put a dog down for this.*

"For God's sake, Nathan, start CPR!"

"She's breathing, Raya, and she has a pulse." The aid car pulled up.

The next day was the first of our friendship. I was going to have a bypass in an hour. The Lesages walked into the CCU holding hands. "I'm so sorry I said you were trespassing," Raya said, starting to cry as she raised my hand with the IV in it and kissed my fingers and her own. "Oh, if you'll just believe me."

"About what?"

"Just please believe that Morgan is a gentle dog. She was worked up. She can't take screaming. She starts racing back and forth, up and down the stairs . . . Oh Jesus, what's wrong with me?"

To this her husband had no answer, but while we were waiting they filled me in: Nathan was an orthopedist, and this was the hospital where he admitted. They had a son, Randy, who had a part-time job there; Raya volunteered there. "Actually it's community service. Court-ordered. My real work is at home," Raya said. "Destruction and repair."

From the CCU you go in your own bed instead of a gurney. Everybody said hello to Nathan as I was rolled along half hearing—now my hearing aids were out—and looking up at the soundproof tiles. I thought of his shouts the day before. What if the OR techs putting on their soft booties had heard him? What if a patient knew the surgeon had been at home screaming "Because you're a bitch!" before gentle hands gowned him in the OR?

They both walked me all the way to the elevator, where the doors opened for my bed and Raya laid her hand on her heart.

AT THE BUS SHELTER NEAR my house we have a round lily pond with turtles and ducks. That's the kind of neighborhood it is. At least there's a bus. The people waiting at the river-rock shelter, with its shake roof and benches and pleasantly leaf-strewn floor, carry briefcases.

Across the way is a low ivy-covered church whose bells clang out a hymn at noon. "Joyful, Joyful, We Adore Thee," a hymn I sang as a child. "Wellspring of the joy of living, ocean depth of happy rest!" The bells are so out of tune that the newspaper ran a letter of complaint. It said you should not do that to Beethoven, and who would disagree? In deference to a life of such mad certainty and exaltation, re-erupting out of every misery, you must not play the music except perfectly. That's what Hans would say, did say. The tragedy of Beethoven's life went far beyond the deafness. No one would love him, let alone marry him. Were his last words really "The comedy is over," in Latin? I wish I had asked Hans. He would have known.

You must start right now memorizing music, Hans advised me. Where my hearing was concerned he was almost tender.

I know without needing to hear it that ducks quack to each other in little snaps, sotto voce. It's an intimate voice, not looking for a response from anything but a duck.

The dog walker goes by with six dogs, who do not bother the ducks or fight among themselves or even cross leashes, no matter that they did not choose each other. He lets them off the leash in the empty parking lot of the church, where there's a fence and they're safe to play like children. Before she moved away with Nathan and Caitlin, the dog Morgan, who bit me, was sometimes among them. She would recognize me, but quickly look away.

All spring, nannies and a few mothers come to the pond wheeling the new giant strollers, bringing toddlers to feed the ducks. They squat with their bags of crumbs, unconcerned about avian viruses or anything else disorderly or malign, like the SUV that jumped the curb and landed in the middle of the pond among the lily pads. It was nighttime and no one was hurt, not even a duck. These are calm wide streets where you might buy a house and move in imagining you had reached a kind of resolution.

Yet things happen here. In this long year an old man's wife died under suspicious circumstances, drowned in the bathtub. The same day, their son disappeared. The old man was cleared; the son was the person of interest—over forty and back living at home. He was odd, of course. That's what was being said. Odd to do that, come home at his age as if you had given up, and yet dye your hair black and wear the haircut of a Beatle. Odd to go mad like that—if he did go mad—and commit such a crime for the sake of the old man, his father, yet never to have walked with him as he went around the block every day stamping his cane or eventually his walker and sometimes having to be steered back by a neighbor.

I would see the old man, but I didn't know he was searching for his house. He didn't know I had a husband who had died. I would look the other way so he wouldn't see tears on my face. Maybe he had them on his too. One day he was standing under a tree looking up with an awful concentration and I almost said, "Are you a birder?" The wife stared balefully out from the newsprint. The article said she had been in the habit of beating him with his own cane, a revelation forced on him when the investigators made him take off his shirt.

The ducks hide their eggs on little islands in the pond or among the bushes and tree roots on the banks. In the spring they swim forth, each pulling a filmy banner of puffs. One mother could have as many as ten or twelve ducklings. The line grows shorter; one spring will not leave her so many. The males swim along behind, or fly off together in a rush, and once the ducklings have grown too big to get entirely under the fluffed-out feathers of the mother, too big to be crow or raccoon bait, all of them sun together and groom their feathers on the banks of the little pond.

One day the black duck and his mate appeared among the mallards. They joined the flock, although without any friendliness, and stayed on. They were not wild ducks; someone must have left them there. Such ducks exist in a city—pets, or pedigreed animals from gardens with water features. "Ornamentals." Unlike the mallards, who rise up as one and disappear over the rooftops, these birds do not fly. They are runner ducks, I found when I looked them up, though I never saw them run.

The black pair stood apart, bigger than the mallards. At times the male would lower his head and snake his neck at them. They weren't interested in his mate, but he could not seem to help it. Soon after their arrival, the female was hit by a car. No one from the neighborhood would hit a duck. Even the buses come to a stop so the ducks can parade to the big lawns across the street. But people from elsewhere don't know, they just barrel through. They killed the black duck's mate. I didn't see it; the city park people told me.

The duck went into an ugly mourning. He interrupted the shaking of his torso and stabbing at his breast only to snake his head at any duck who came near him, male or female. The green-shining black of his feathers went dull.

I got out my husband's books, trying to see what the future might hold for such an animal. I started a sheet in one of his notepads: "Interbreeding: wild w/ domestic. More males—'oversupply.' Female offspring of hybridization often infertile, take on male plumage. ???"

AFTER NATHAN LEFT RAYA AND went to live with his girlfriend, Randy would sometimes spend the weekend with his mother, and when he did that he would meet me at the park bench to watch the ducks. Sometimes he would have a friend with him.

The black duck would not come to our bench with the others. He didn't have a look to spare for our kind, so occupied was he with tearing at his body in a ritual to which the others paid no heed. He drove his beak into his breastbone or rooted in his wings, or spread his flat tail and worked it up and down in spasms as if to rid his body of it.

"Poor baby, he needs a new wife." This was one of the boys Randy brought with him. He and Randy were in a poetry class together. It was the second time I had met this particular one, Reed, who wanted to be a poet. He was the only one who accompanied Randy more than once on these weekends. Randy had given him my book about Whitman and he was halfway through.

"I don't think they can have more than one wife," Randy said. "I think it's all over for them after one."

"Can't we find him a bride?" Reed persisted.

That's when I said, "'Out of the Cradle Endlessly Rocking.' Do you know that poem? Stay here. I'll get it."

"Oh, you don't need to go all the way home," Randy said.

"I want to see it," Reed said.

"Her house is blocks away."

"Please," Reed said, turning to him.

When I got back with the book, they took turns reading to themselves. The off-key bells started in, and Reed looked up and laughed, but when he got to the end of the poem he sat in silence. He asked if he could read it aloud. I wasn't sure about that, because he had laughed, and there we were at the duck pond after all, with the toddlers. But he read gravely. He was studying acting as well as poetry. Randy said so before he started. Not everyone can read this poem, with its terrible sincerity, the extremes of its romantic lament and final ecstasy. All these things amuse some readers, some students in particular as I remember. From a bird in a nest the poem moves skyward and seaward to the immeasurable—and, to Whitman, relieving—subject of death.

"Loved! loved! loved! loved! loved!" That's the chant of the remembering bird in his nest close to the ocean. There the narrator listens to him and to the sound of the waves, which at first, before the sea makes clear its true word, comes to his ears as "Soothe! soothe! soothe!"

The mate called to, coaxed, beseeched, never comes. The true mate is death, and that is the word from the sea. "Death, Death, Death, Death, Death," the boy read. When he had finished, even the toddlers were watching him, dribbling crumbs from their bags. Finally he turned, and he and Randy looked into each other's eyes.

By Sunday evening of these weekends, whatever boy Randy had

brought with him would be gone and Hans would come to dinner at Raya's and he and Randy would go back home together.

A FEW WEEKS AFTER NATHAN left to be with his girlfriend, he came to get his daughter and the dog. All that time Caitlin had been living in a new peace with Raya. Nathan said to me, "I know how it looks, I know what Raya's told you, but this time I've got it right. But, Connie, I want you to watch over Raya, because she's capable of anything. Anything."

I had been spending time with Raya as she gathered his things and Caitlin's into boxes, saying nothing against either of them for the first time since I had known her. A trance of mildness had come over her. Caitlin too was as she had never been, free of accusation, packing up her room without stopping to pray. "Capable of anything," I said. "Like what?"

"OK, fine," Nathan said. "Fine. So we all are."

It wasn't Raya who was capable of anything, or Randy with his secrets and the strange absence, in one so amorous and kind, of what we use the words *a heart* to mean. It wasn't Nathan, who stayed behind when his girlfriend vanished into California. It wasn't Caitlin, who, within a week of going with her father, had taken his car and driven without a license back to Raya's. It wasn't the dog Morgan, who had consorted with strange dogs in obedience to a stranger, and once in her life given in to the longing to bite. It wasn't even the black duck, who stayed behind alone when the mallards deserted the pond, lost his feathers, and did not know his bride when she came.

It was Hans. Caitlin was at my door, ringing the bell and banging. "Connie, Connie!" When I opened the door she sagged into my arms. "Can you come? Come. Hans died."

Died is better than *is dead*. *Died* is a word for an act; it contains a bit of time, it contains for the briefest moment the idea that the person can somehow go back on it. When the doctor told me about my husband, I asked her, "Are you sure?" "Yes, he has died."

Hans jumped off the balcony where we had stood when he cleared the Sound of ships to show me the great canoe.

Before he jumped, he tried to strangle Randy, but in the middle of the attempt, he let go. He gave up. He walked to the balcony doors—we do know he walked, maybe resuming his stiff manner on the way, so Randy didn't know to hold him back—and drew them apart.

As a witness to the act, Randy got into the crowded elevator with the police and descended to the sidewalk. Desert of sidewalk. "I witness the corpse with its dabbled hair." That's Whitman. What Randy said, we don't know. The police had no trouble getting him to admit to the struggle between himself and Hans, and the questioning satisfied them. They photographed the bruises on his neck, measured the distance from bedroom to balcony and the height of the rail.

Raya told me several times about a thumbprint the size of a tablespoon on Randy's trachea, the whole neck purple where Hans's unmatched hands had grasped and released before he jumped. She got into describing it again the day I went over to say bon voyage. "Don't think I'm excusing my son for driving that poor man mad," she said. I was afraid she was going to say something like "We all loved Hans," but she did not.

"Oh God, speaking of the mad, Nathan's already threatening to join us in Mexico," she said. She and Caitlin were going. Caitlin had the suitcases out on the sidewalk ready for the airport van. "Here's where I met you," Raya said, pointing to the spot on the pavement. "And Connie, look at this." Around her neck she had a gold chain with a six-month AA medallion on it, from Caitlin. "Yeah, check out the 'Recovery Gifts' site," Caitlin said. She was going down to join a group of Catholic students who were building an orphanage. Raya was going to visit a famous well nearby, where people came with bottles and the farmer let them pump the curative waters. "I want to be a different person. Daria says that's possible for me." Daria was the social worker assigned her by the court. "Oh, Connie. How I long for things to just simply somehow someday be normal."

When we say *normal* I think we must mean *good*. Is that right? How widely Whitman opened his eyes, his arms, to find death normal.

My own feeling is that we never change. Not by choice, not on purpose. I didn't say that to Raya. For one thing I had just been noticing the new attitude in her daughter now that she was sixteen. "This will be good. She can just drink the water or pour it on herself or whatever," Caitlin told me, getting into the front seat of the van with the driver. "Take care, Connie."

Raya opened her window in the back. "Oh, I'm leaving you here all by yourself."

"I'm fine," I said. Because she wanted to be the only friend you had, you didn't say to Raya that there were people who would look in on you, or that you didn't care whether they did or not, because you didn't want the helpful, oh, never, never. For yourself, you wanted the ones who would not answer, the obsessed, the ardent, the lost.

As for Randy, in the summer he was driving across the country with Reed. They were going to explore Long Island, called by the native peoples Paumanok, where Walt Whitman heard the sea speak to a bird to console it.

His Rank

Knox had a favorite bar, because of the bartender, a woman he was preparing to get to know. It was on a block where the university ran up against a changing neighborhood, close enough to the campus to bring in the grounds crew and campus security. It was small and dark, with nothing except neon beer signs in the window to set it apart from the outbuildings of the university.

The bartender had hair cut as close as Obama's. Her eyes were so large they took time to complete a blink. When Knox first started coming in they had had a happy hour menu; now a guy in the back washing glasses would make you a plate of nachos, but that was it. The bartender was on her own, no servers.

Knox decided *beautiful* was a word thrown around—he had employed it a good deal himself—when it should be reserved for examples of indifferent power like that in the curve of the bartender's eyelids as she worked the taps. When she gave you your beer she looked straight at you, and that was like being wanded at the airport. Even if you were white, the eyes could say you were a man. Then something nice with the lips though not a smile. Then the luxurious blink, as if you, and the whole arrangement—time of day, frosted glass, work, play, men, women—had made her sleepy. Yes, he was going to make his move.

•

HIS FEET WERE STIFF FROM being hooked over a rung of the high wooden stool by the window. He had been sitting for an hour breaking up with his girlfriend, who kept saying, "It's because I gained the weight."

"That has nothing to do with it."

"I weigh more than you do. You think I'll get that big." In a booth two hefty women in the black uniforms of campus security were sharing a plate of nachos. "Right back." She stumbled getting down off the stool; she couldn't hold her beer.

A man held the front door open and allowed a pit bull to precede him into the room. Big guy, already spotted by Knox in the crosswalk with his dog, with a funny look on his face that made Knox say casually to himself, *Don't come in here, dude.* The man had on a green tank, though it was not really warm enough for that, and he was handsome in a flaring way Knox had to admit made him uneasy even in some sports figures.

"Dog can't come in here," said the bartender.

"She can't, huh?" The man advanced into the room with the dog, snubbed up tight on the leash so its front paws had to scrabble for the floor.

"You tie him up." The bartender stretched out her whole arm and pointed her long finger.

"Bus stop. Can't tie this kind of a dog up in a bus stop."

"What you want to come in here for?" said the bartender, not unkindly, filling a schooner and setting it on the empty bar. "This that new dog? He nice?"

"She." The dog sat, facing the table of the two guards eating nachos. "You did it," the man said to the bartender. The way he said it made the dog look up and emit a growl. "You goddamn married him."

"I did. Last Friday. I said I was."

"You did it. OK. All right. Where is he?"

"He can't sit around in here. He's at work."

"He knew you were with me."

"I wasn't with you, baby."

The man reached in his pants and pulled out a gun, small as a phone.

People set down their drinks in the quiet. He scanned the room with the gun, like a flashlight. The bathroom door opened and Knox's girlfriend came out. Knox held perfectly still, praying the man's attention onto her. But one of those girl guards was sure to pull a weapon. Everybody in the place was going to get shot. He, Knox, was going to die.

Somehow, his girlfriend took in the situation. Moving slowly, she sank into the booth with the two women. One of them put a fat arm around her. The other one had a walkie-talkie.

"Don't nobody go on your cell or nothing," said the bartender. "This is Jerome. I know Jerome."

"You think you know me." He pointed the gun at her.

"Come on, Jerome. Don't do that. You don't want to do that." And she came out from behind the bar and put her hand up in front of the little stump of gun. She took hold of the barrel with two long fingers and a thumb as if it were a straw she was going to drop into a drink. "Come on, now." She raised the flap and went behind the bar. Jerome got up on a stool, and instead of putting the gun out of sight the bartender laid it down on the bar. *Jesus God, are you kidding me?* Knox screamed in his head.

"Sit," Jerome said to the dog. Then he put his forehead down on the bar and his shoulders began to shake. "Baby boy," the bartender said, spreading her fingers, with the gold ring on one, around his head and holding it while he shook.

At one table a man got to his feet. "Hey, don't you forget the check," the bartender called. Then Knox's girlfriend stood up, hugged the big security guard, and started across the room to Knox. Her face shone with tears. He stared at her outstretched arms. So people loved, even many of them, and his rank among them was not high.

Astride

There was an incident, the summer I worked in the Pentagon. My supervisor vanished.

That summer I didn't know any better than to take the job offered me. I knew nothing. My father worked in the Commerce Department and raised a few Angus in Virginia, in that wide grass circle, not then covered with suburbs, that poured civil servants and in summer their college-age children into the offices of the government. I remember the commute. In the morning you would pass combines and dairy herds and girls up early schooling horses in the wet grass. I was newly appreciative of the green beauty of my state, the Old Dominion, because I had come back to it after being away at college for the first time.

I took a typing test and not long afterwards walked up the steps of the Pentagon. I did that. I have no excuse.

One morning towards the end of that summer my supervisor's door was standing wide open when I arrived, and all that was left of him was the straight-backed wooden chair he had brought from home. He never came back. He had a high security clearance, though that was downplayed because the official reason given for his disappearance was thwarted passion.

This was early in the sixties, in the days before anyone came to levitate the Pentagon. Certainly no one had attacked it. Its enchantment was internal and impervious. Whatever else has changed since then, I know the vast building must still be filled, despite the throngs inside it, with the same cathedral air, of hushed, guarded, exquisite knowledge. No photograph really shows it as the massive thing it is, a stone wheel covered with portholes, an inhabited wheel, spun down into Virginia swampland and fallen on its side, to be cordoned and protected forever.

It was a city, with sloping ramp-avenues leading to a vast city square of shops and restaurants, the Concourse. The Concourse had the feeling of a great hotel as well as that of a department store. Dignitaries were led along it, parades marched through it, shoppers crowded the aisles of pottery and books. Other countries may give their generals villas, but surely they are outdone by this bazaar of flowers and souvenirs and cosmetics, of pastries, crystal, and the scented wood of carvings, available to everyone, right in the heart of the fort.

In the seventeen miles of corridor, which radiated in spokes and revolved in concentric rings, pedestrians flowed aside for motorized carts carrying men with brooms and buckets, or sometimes tanned young lieutenants in summer uniform, calmly steering little vehicles among the civilians on foot. Little boys saluted them. There were crowds of children there, headdresses, saris floating. Regular tours came through from schools and embassies.

It was never clear which individuals were not important. Always disputable. A janitor could be going through the wastebaskets on the orders of a foreign government.

Underneath the building was an enormous depot with the green-and-white buses of Washington and the red buses of Virginia, and even Greyhounds, pulling up to dozens of stations and surging away with echoes and grinding of gears. In the late afternoon I descended a numbered stairway to get the bus to Commerce, where I would meet my father, whose day was longer than mine. Hundreds waited with me on hot platforms with puddles steaming where the air conditioning dripped. In the gloom you looked through open hangars to the white air of Virginia. The buses shimmered one last time as their backs crossed into the shade. Blue exhaust, islands of pink gum on the concrete, at every station people just down from the Concourse with their bags and packages.

Anything could have been carried into or out of DOD, as we called it, the Department of Defense.

What really happened to my boss, Mr. Orlenko, was that he was accused of a security violation. All of us knew we stood to lose our clearances, even our jobs, if we failed to take every precaution with classified material. But we knew, too, how unlikely it was that our little errors would hurt us; we knew we were innocent.

From the secretaries—"Mr. Orlenko, what a pain!"—we knew he had a wife still in shock from the DP camp after years in this country. He was Ukrainian. He hated the Soviet Union with a devotion of hatred. At the mention of Khrushchev his heavy-lidded eyes would grow sinister. From his window he would scout the wide parking lots as if he could see the hammer and sickle creeping in a liquid Disney shadow across them. He hated the president, whose inauguration was still fresh in everybody's mind, mine in particular because of the raising of a *poet* to the dais, white-haired Frost, pure as his name—nobody then knew of meanness in a poet—the poet I had studied all the spring before, in my freshman year.

I was a clerk-typist. Somebody read through records and newspapers every day looking for certain references, then gave the marked passages to the typists to type into lists for Mr. Orlenko, who was able to enter each item into lists of his own.

Mr. Orlenko was an analyst. Subjects he analyzed were apt to be already classified and to move up to a higher classification because they had been worked on by him. His desk was a haystack of legal pads and folders stamped SECRET, and like all the other offices, his had its safe, that is, a filing cabinet—in his case two of them—with a combination lock and a steel rod dropped through the drawer handles and padlocked.

The theme of our summer was National Security.

The theme covered everything from the aims of the Soviet Union to our own missteps and oversights. At that time, one-use carbon ribbons preserved everything we typed in a readable form; although the letters jumped and skittered unevenly along the tape, a spy could unfurl the ribbon and read your whole document. Of course the college students with summer jobs were the poorest at remembering to take out their ribbons and lock them up at the end of the day.

Considering that we were there not to help them but to spring into jobs above their heads at a later stage, the real-life secretaries were lenient about our carelessness and indeed about everything, including the job of proofreading what we typed. "You passed the typing, hmm?" Typing was the major part of the test we had taken to rule out nepotism in our placement.

That summer, no matter what we actually did at our desks, we were called interns, and we heard lectures in one of the small, dark, deep-chaired auditoriums to be found in the building, like chapels, though there were actual chapels as well, filled in wartime, we heard, with praying employees. At any rate, men spoke to us in a comfortable chamber, gray-blue, soundproofed because some of the movies shown there were about ordnance, or materiel. We all liked the word materi*el*, and liked to throw it into conversations. "But did you have any materi*el* on you?" The movies were presented as entertainment, as none of the interns that summer was an engineering student who might go into materiel. We were an unpromising group; most of us were English majors, displaying volumes of poetry or existential novels on our desks. The girls typed; the boys shadowed a deputy assistant for the summer. No history majors, only one in political science. The light went down and a blue glow stole out from a recess above the paneling. A silver cone crossed the screen to the music from *Exodus*.

During the showing of the films, we looked around and picked out people to have coffee with afterwards. Romances began.

One stood out, flourished, for the first few weeks of the summer: Holly, a senior, tall and blond, and Alex, younger than she was, but from Yale. He was the one majoring in political science. They were the two glamorous ones. Holly, for Hollis, was graceful and southern in a way that those of us who lived in the grass circle outside Washington were not. She had made her debut, and gone to school in Paris. Her family was an old Carolina one, we heard, her father a general.

With every explosion on the screen, Holly covered her eyes, and finally she looked between her fingers and said, "Doesn't matter *who's* doing it, I can't stand it." The boy from Yale looked over irritably, but when he saw the blond hair hanging down he moved a seat and sat forward to talk to her, putting his body between her and the screen.

Holly's loose shifts, in shades of blue and lilac, were the style of that year. On most of us these were a neutral fashion, but on her they had a slipping, mussed air: they weren't ironed, or the armholes were big on her thin arms, or a button was missing just where the sharp shadow went down between the surprising breasts she had. "All I want to know is where somebody thin *got* those," one of the secretaries said, once they knew her.

Alex was tall too, with a shaven, silken, lean-cheeked face. Their eyes fell naturally on each other. Day after day Holly brought a little more of her dreamy attention to bear on the blue eyes behind his glasses, the tanned fingers firm on his manila folder or his book, forefinger marking the place.

"Alex is going into politics," Holly told me. He had finished his freshman year at Yale, whose elevation above her college in Lynchburg was of no moment to her. He too was rich, we learned. His father managed a company making aircraft components.

Alex was always being called away from whatever he was doing and introduced to visitors by his supervisor, who was said to know more than anyone else in Washington about the missile gap. But when Holly walked by the door he would leave the friendly important men and rush to lean his arm on Holly's in one of the little stand-up coffee bars.

Soon they were walking out to the parking lot and she was folding her legs into his MG after work, and telling me about the horse shows they went to on weekends so his family could get to know her.

I have never seen work done with the feverishness with which it was done in the Pentagon. People say bureaucracy, make-work, nothing gets done, et cetera. But vast projects are undertaken, brought to the verge of completion, redesigned completely, completed, canceled. Thousands upon thousands work late into the night, day after day, sweating and smoking, or they did then, coughing, drumming their fingers. Hundreds come in every few days while they are on vacation, just to keep up.

Mr. Orlenko was one of those workhorses. By the time we knocked on his door he would have been reading for hours, standing up, massaging his back, a bulky man in a white shirt and a tie with a silver clip, with dark hair going gray. He would lower himself onto the straight-backed chair he had brought from home, where he would write in longhand for hours more without stopping.

He would stand too close to us and order us, in his accent at once haughty and intimate, to type his tables of figures with their crossed sevens and curled nines. Few men typed at that time. Mr. Orlenko wrote with a fountain pen, making a lacework of corrections, holes rubbed and stuck through the paper where he used a typewriter eraser with a stiff brush. "Why not *pencil*?" we all groaned. With this pen he also doodled trees, all over his DOD blotter and in the margins of the legal pads he wrote on, and then scribbled them out.

He never took sick leave or even his full two weeks of vacation, despite the wife. There were children, but they were thought to be grown. Nevertheless the secretaries acted them out, saying, "*Da*, Papa!" and banging their heels together. His fingers were a deep saffron, and the thumb too, because he curved it under and petted the end of his Camel while he was thinking. Above his heavy, carved features flew thick black eyebrows.

From his thick, brushed hair came a breath of nutmeg when he bent over your desk. He was very clean, and that—not all that common in those from his part of the world, the secretaries said—was because of the DP camp. He would shake out a white handkerchief and hold it as he worked. He kept a drawer of them, ironed, according to the secretaries. His wife ironed the shirts he wore, of which the garment bag on the door, they said, held extras for when he worked overnight. He never appeared tired, and he kept his erect posture, arrogant and foreign. When a secretary had checked our lists and we took them in to him, his eyes meeting ours never lost their intense warning, though a moment before he would have been squinting into one of his folders with a kind of tenderness.

"You know, I'm intrigued by Mr. Orlenko," Holly said one day. "He seems like such an interesting man." We made fun of her accent, the way she said *intrigged*, and *mayan* for man, though indeed Mr. Orlenko was from another time. "So European," she said. "He *works* so hard. The *N* is for *Nazar*, did you know that? Nazar. Nazar Orlenko."

Often when there is a gruff temperament in the office, the gentler ones will find something touching in it, I did learn that. They will cosset a man who chews Maalox and slaps his blotter and bangs his telephone receiver. In the Pentagon we saw women attentive as mothers towards some bitter GS-9 who had to park in the farthest lot and walk in, and be spurned by the younger secretaries. But Mr. Orlenko did not have one of those office mothers, and in fact had nobody except his never-seen wife, for whom the accepted word was *pitiful*. Nobody until Holly in her freedom—as Frost tells us the lovely shall be choosers—chose him.

In Frost's poem, the lovely woman is punished. When he wrote "The Lovely Shall Be Choosers," Frost was living in a world in which there was an audience presumed to believe, however mistakenly, that beauty conquered all. It may be the Kennedys didn't know the poem and really thought the lovely were choosers and that was that. We'll never know. Maybe they were not concerned with Frost's zeal to show them the bitter lot of beauty, or with anything except "The Gift Outright," in which there is the line about "many deeds of war" being the deed to the country.

The three of us, Holly and Alex and I, were traveling the outer ring of the Pentagon on our lunch hour, talking about Alex's future. He was going to run for office as a Democrat. He would start locally. The Secretary of Defense was coming towards us, surrounded by men with cameras on their shoulders and strings of spiral cord looped around them, and he was laughing, not exactly heartily but not with the craven note, either, of a man who would live to write a book about how bitterly mistaken he was in this period. He was not much further along than the interns, it turned out. He, too, had a lot to learn. "Hello, Alex," he said.

"Is that somebody?" said Holly.

"That was the Secretary of Defense," said Alex in despair.

"No, really?" Holly said. "Why don't we have one of those chocolate milkshakes instead of coffee." In the Center Court she sat down on a bench while Alex went to buy the famous double chocolate milkshakes of the Pentagon concessionaire. Pressing my hand, Holly said, "I have something I want to tell you. It'll surprise you, I bet. It's a little bit bad, now." I said, "Tell me." But Alex was already handing her milkshake over her shoulder from behind us. "Well, we'll talk later, hear? I *need* to. Alex, now you brought me—this can't be double chocolate, is it? Well! I remember it as so very delicious the last time."

A FEW DAYS AFTER SHE told me, I knocked on Mr. Orlenko's door. After a second he said harshly, "Come in." None of us sat down in that office, but Holly was sitting in the chair in which Mr. Orlenko seated his superiors, with their strange deference to him. She sat with legs crossed, in her lilac shift and the rope sandals she had started wearing to make her less tall, frowning, as if she had not been fervently talking to me in the bathroom half an hour before while she ran cold water on her wrists. Ordinarily Mr. Orlenko liked me; he explained my tasks to me with that exaggerated foreign intentness and then stood back satisfied to see me read what he had written. But he looked at me now as if I could be loathed as thoroughly as Khrushchev. I thought in surprise, almost in fear: *Holly told him. She told him she told me.* And I looked back at him as innocently as I could.

They both lit cigarettes as I recited my message and held out my document. "Put it with the rest!" he said with a jerk of his arm, hitting his *t*'s hard and striking his knuckles with the cigarette on the side of the safe. He tore off his glasses and massaged the black eyebrows.

Then I saw them in the hall of war paintings. This was a still, wide gallery of a corridor, with tall doors bearing teak plaques. Hundreds of paintings. Cannon, trenches, foot soldiers of the Spanish-American War, the battle of the *Monitor* and the *Merrimack*. Torn sketches taken from the pockets of the dead. Orlenko was stiff-armed and wore his sinister look, Holly was the one leaning and pleading. I saw her put her hand out and hook her long fingers with their oval nails in his belt, and then rudely, no longer pleading but with force, pull him against her.

That was what I saw. But a secretary who dared to open Orlenko's door when he didn't answer her knock saw more, and the story raced out, a spark along a fuse. The thing that lit it was this particular secretary's choice of the word *astride*. Astride. Without that word the story might have died away. Somebody else repeated it. "She was right there, astride him in the chair." "Astride *of* him" were the actual words. Of course that was something you could not help picturing. Her long legs, her blond, hanging hair, his arrogant face thrown back, the chair.

No longer did Holly pause outside Alex's office and lead him off alone under the eyes of his supervisor. "Come *with* me," she would say to me. "Alex will chase after me if you don't." She no longer liked to be sent around the miles of corridor with documents; she liked to stay in our hallway, smoking dreamily in the ladies' room, drifting to Orlenko's door. She would knock a music of three knocks and then one, soft yet urgent, and lead him away. She concealed nothing; she liked to smile into everybody's eyes in a blinded way.

Orlenko began to take a lunch hour. His phone would ring, and at the nearby desks we could hear his chair scrape back, his terrible sighs, his scrabbling in the drawer for his Camels. Then he would come out, close his door, and go.

Alex would come up out of his chair and be at the door of his tiny office—he had been given an office—if he saw me walking with Holly. He would start right in signaling me to leave him alone with her, but Holly always said to me, "Come on, you promised." Holly walked ahead of him while he whipped his thigh with the manila folder. Then he began to hiss at her. "Why, Holly? Why?"

LATE IN THE SUMMER WE were sitting in the Center Court where the paved walks wound in and out of tended rosebushes. There were traveling clouds, an intense four o'clock sun in the hedges of arborvitae planted in half circles around the stone benches. Someone tended them. Someone worked to keep aphids off the roses, as had been decreed by the landscape designers for this building, the Pentagon.

None of this was mystery, to me. "Leave something to learn later." That's what Frost said.

Holly was not sitting up straight. Her hair was tied back with a scarf as if to expose her two pimples and the darkened skin under her eyes. The scarf went halfway down her back, a relic of her stylishness. Alex couldn't take his eyes off it. Finally he took between his fingers the tiny rolled hem of silk he had been touching on the back of the bench.

"I don't know," Holly said, bending her head so that the scarf puffed off in his hand, "Oh God, I don't know. Nobody does!" and she jumped up, scattering the pigeons. "They don't know where he went!" With a sob, she covered her face. Because she was beautiful, everyone out on the sidewalk turned and looked at her.

I was sad for Alex, too, as he went after her with her scarf in his hand. Myself I see crossing the little garden, looking up at the inner walls of the building and seeing movement in the windows, a uniformed back, a flash of light off glasses, and half thinking to myself that this love triangle—all at once it was one, now that it was over—was more important than what the people in those offices were doing behind the windows. It was this that the books we carried around were about. Even if they pretended to be about war.

That was what I thought at eighteen, in the Center Court of the Pentagon, ready for some passion to overtake me as it had Holly, steeped in my right to it. I am haunted now by the thought that some page in that sheaf of papers, that endless list we ridiculed as we typed it, figured in the death of a little boy like my own, the one I would have in ten years when the war that did not even have a name that summer was dragging to its end. I can't remember. I can't remember a line I typed. There we all sat, typing. There we all stood, drinking our coffee and falling in love. What was I dreaming of as I typed so fast, the Selectric ball whirling the letters off my fingers? Did they land in someone's flesh?

At the center of that week was the safe: the failure of someone—Orlenko—to drop the rod down through the drawer handles and padlock it, his failure, one night, even to twirl the combination lock on the top drawer. Only by coincidence had the oversight been discovered and reported, by someone who stayed in the office even later than he.

"We are always at war," one of the National Security speakers told us. "Only sometimes we allow ourselves to forget that we are at war." Even so, the precautions were often forgotten; it happened to the summer interns all the time. In the morning you could hear the cry: "Oh no, here's my *ribbon* still in the *machine.*"

All Mr. Orlenko had to do was make an appearance before a security board and be reprimanded. But instead he vanished. Within a week it was given out that his departure was a breakdown of a private sort. In other corridors the talk was of a college girl, a beauty, who had lured the head of a division away from his immigrant family that had lived on potatoes for three years in a camp on an unpronounceable border. And then she wouldn't have him, of course. *Her* family stepped in. The father an officer. That was what was said.

Strangely enough—though for days Holly was away from her desk all day being interrogated somewhere in the building, along with her father, who had been called in from his base—in our corridor everyone shielded her. We pretended that it was all a matter of wild rumors having their origin in some other corridor. *People from—where he was from.*

They're paranoid. They'll bolt. The secretaries even included Holly in the talk, bringing her coffee and aspirin, soothing and pampering her.

"I GOT A LETTER." SHE drew me into the auditorium and pulled the doors shut. She felt for the switch of the blue light, so that I could read it. There was Orlenko's crested, beautiful script. "He's gone, he's hiding. No address. Even if I could write him a letter, I couldn't make him see it's *nothing*." She was biting her broken thumbnail. "Where can he go? He doesn't even have his family with him. He thinks he's running for his life, he doesn't know what *country* this is."

And what country is this? I could have said, but neither of us would have known.

"Terrible things happened to him in the war, you know. *Terrible* things." Her violet eyes went black. "But he never gave in. He drew pictures. His hero was a poet, a famous poet from there—oh, I'll get you the name—who drew pictures with a lump of coal when he was starving." That war was only twenty years in the past, but they were our years—we were eighteen and twenty-one—and we were both gazing into a history as uninvestigated as calculus. We knew the Allies and the Axis. We were majoring in literature.

"What else does he say?"

She looked away. "My 'beauty,' is what he says, made him careless." She held the envelope against her chest. I remember the crooked stamp and the elaborate capitals of her name: *Miss Hollis Baird*. It had been mailed right there in Washington. "He's not here any more, though. I know it. He doesn't trust anybody. Everybody over there hurt him, Russians, Germans, everybody. And *this* place, oh God, I hate this place. These *people* in here. They're the ones did it, up in Security, they're the ones *scared* him."

ALL THE REST OF THE summer Alex comforted her, listened, took her coffee, walked her up and down the corridors, stood with her while she cried in the hot parking lot, until we all went back to school. "I just told poor Alex goodbye," she said on the last day.

"She's going to marry him," the secretaries predicted. But she did not. She sees him now and then, just as she writes sometimes to me. She is the mother of three grown sons who attended the same private school as his two. I have read that she is a Washington hostess, though she has nothing to say in her letters about that.

For some reason she got back in touch with me, years after this. For a while, she said, she went a little wild. "God, I went through the whole thing. In San Francisco I tripped, I marched, I hung around the Dead. I told my daddy off." Looking back, she was glad of it all, except for what she had done that one summer, might have done, might have caused to happen—because we never knew what happened—to Nazar Orlenko. "Do you think there's a love of your life?" she wrote.

In the last picture I have, you can see she is heavier, though she stands behind the three tall sons. The arms are plump, the blond hair short. We have all changed, and any of us may change again, although Orlenko, strange sacrifice, will never come to her again in her beauty, nor a secret list extract itself from a torso, nor the Pentagon wheel back up into the sky.

Da Capo

Before the musicians walked on, we sat there with the sad but alert expression worn by concertgoers. All around us were the French braids, the waved white hair, the freckled scalps, the university beards. Our organs were crowded by all the food we had eaten, but we kept a disciplined stillness. Paul shifted his shoulder away from mine.

We had been fighting in the restaurant. We had to fight quietly because the place was small and the owner, who waited on the tables while her partner cooked, scented our fight and kept coming in close to offer us the special she had just written on the blackboard, the wine label to study, the food itself in several stages, the peppermill, and in a last sally the pastry tray. Eventually four other tables were occupied, but it was us she favored. We had to keep pausing for her in the midst of our eating and our fight, which should have become funny but did not, partly because of the woman's small tense face set forward at the jaw. She breathed audibly. She had some instinct like the one that makes our dog roll on dead seagulls at the beach. She even made us talk to her, and got out of us where we were going after dinner.

When she approached the last time with our change she said, "Chamber music on a summer night! Wish I had tickets myself." She winked, as if chamber music were something between us that other people might object to. "You still have plenty of time to park," she said, following us to the door. At first I thought she said *part*. But she was not the Sibyl, and she should have known how to be chilly with people who fight at dinner. She should have a remote, worldly air.

On the way over Paul drove not recklessly, as he sometimes does when we fight, but with a kind of hunched carefulness, a meagerness in his steering, as if motion would hurt him. His face was not swollen with anger, but tired. Fights like this, that leave you tired, are the worst kind.

I went back, in my mind, to the moment when our voices changed and that feeling came over me, of my head filling like a cup, to the ears, to the forehead, with daring and invention, and then brimming over with words. In the past there was joy in our fights, our blood rose against each other as chosen enemies, a pleasure could find its way into the shudders of insult and retraction. I was not tired the way he was, I could have gone on fighting.

His tiredness had to do with Sophie. A year ago Sophie had been determined to have him. Her determination had flagged, according to him, but she still hovered at the edge of things, did not pick up her bruised family and move away, kept up with her busy practice as a counselor.

Although Sophie has nothing more than an MA in psychology, and a job as a private counselor, she was the one brought in to give Paul's office a seminar on avoiding hierarchy in the workplace. After her presentation several of them took her down to the cafeteria for lunch, and she began to cry, because her cat had been put to sleep at the vet's that morning and she had not been there to say goodbye. Her crying, I am told, went beyond what might reasonably be passed over. Paul was the one who walked her to her car and questioned whether she should drive.

Think of that. Paul doesn't like women's tears, because of the many years of trying to stanch his mother's. Think of Sophie, always in tears, asking waiters for Kleenex, hunched over the ferry railing in the middle of the Sound, stumbling into elevators in her tear-fogged glasses, sobbing at the dentist's, lurching out of a movie in the middle.

Think of such a person trying to sort out the troubles someone is confiding to her.

I know about these things because Paul told me. He let them drop, so that I had to picture him at a movie in the afternoon. They did that. Both of them shirking jobs, watching for people they knew, wasting the only time they had. How could they do that? I was screaming at him. What movie did they see? Did they go to the grocery store? Did they put gas in the car? Did they pretend they were married?

Once I knew Sophie existed, he couldn't stop himself from speaking of her. He thought he was just letting out a few details to relieve the pressure. Crumbs I could follow to get him if he got too far. He came home once with a grubby shadow on his shirt where they had tried to rub off tears and mascara.

I know about this kind of abject love. About him, what he is like when you are going through it. He goes through it too; he is not a bystander.

A lover of music, Sophie could be on her way to this concert. We were all here in this same hall once before. He and I had the children with us. Karen, the younger of our girls, said to me, "Why do you look like that?" They never knew that Sophie had us in her sights and was leading us, like a sniper. Of course they knew nothing of Sophie and her red hair and her terrible cramps and her MA, even when their father talked to them on the phone from the hotels where he was staying with her, because he had to make sure we could reach him in a family emergency.

And what would she think if she knew she was not even mentioned in the fight we were having only a year later, in the hurt we were taking and giving? One of my friends said, "Try not to fight with him, just for a while." She saw the need for caution. But we would have had to change, and if that change could be made, why not the one he was contemplating?

The children had thrown a match to our quarrel while we were getting dressed. They came in from riding their bikes, sighing and scowling because I won't let them stay out on bikes at the end of the day, in rush hour.

In a study, out of some number of children—in the thousands, I think—asked at random times what they were thinking about, none mentioned an adult. Sometimes you think of things you have it in your power to do, that would force your children to think about you, the power you have to break into the room of childhood, which they think is locked against you. Anyway they were certainly not thinking about us, about our plan to go out, to face each other alone across a table and then sit in a darkened hall listening to music, and to reach underneath these things to lift out the buried excitement, distantly related to that of playing outside at dusk when we were their age, and try to keep it alive for an evening.

All three of them were getting ready to play Clue. Robbie had used up his time on video games for the day, and having renewed his haggling for more time, had angered Paul and lost his game privileges for the weekend. His face dark, he was lying on the floor in the girls' room, drumming his thumbs, while they spread out the Clue board with its obsolete miniature weapons and detective notepads.

Not far into the game they began to disagree. "Goddammit," said Robbie, ten years old. I was standing in the doorway and Jenny and Karen looked up at me. Robbie bowed his head over the board.

I don't want to have brought forth a family in which a ten-year-old says *goddammit*, not as a challenge but with adult bitterness.

Robbie is not in adolescence, but he is drawing near; he has the size—big feet, big joints, and squaring jaw—and the melancholy that prefigure it. Because of his birthday, he is with children a year younger than he is in school, and this summer he is perplexed at some of their interests. He tries to go back and retrieve his love for the action figures he put in a bag to give away. When you are that age, each year really is a closed system, a stage. Maybe throughout life each year is a stage that we are too distracted to recognize. "It's because she's forty-one." "Ah, forty-one." It might be that we would treat a year more respectfully if it were granted its own characteristics, even a name. There are not so many that we couldn't do that, greet each year at the birthday as, original as a snowflake, it descends with all the coming situations of mind and body sealed in it.

The year the alewives washed up on the Chicago beaches. Paul and I lived, new lovers, above a tavern in a neighborhood with shrines in the back yards, with the Virgin or St. Francis holding out their arms over little fountains. The people with yards and statues knew we were not married and, we felt, watched us. The smell of decomposing fish along the shore of Lake Michigan, the smell of the stockyards near our apartment—these not only did not repel us, though we indulged in rich complaint, they seemed to us to be the world in its real, as opposed to its fancied, glory. Our fights were the same thing: words as dark, stinging, and flavorful as the beer we drank.

What dispelled the glory of these fights, their predictable but mysterious descent, I do not know. By means of them, it was possible that year to descend into a dim red place of bodily pity and remorse, and desire to please, and pardon. A little room, a confessional.

The year I read half of Anna Karenina *on a plane,* leaving the country for the first time, thinking about the dullness of Levin and Kitty as a couple. The question was why people married so relentlessly, when it was the nature of love to take place outside of marriage. Over the cramped hours in the air, the stodgy Karenin made his increasingly pathetic appearances. There was something I didn't know, even though it was there in the book for me to read and I read it and thought I knew it. The most important thing: the thing Anna lost, dwarfing lost virtue and pride and even the love of Vronsky. Her son—her beloved Seryozha!

I read it but didn't know.

The year of Mr. Mead, holding *First-Year Algebra* in his hand as we all took a deep breath every time he turned, shoulder blades back, layered muscles showing in the Ban-Lon shirts his wife bought him, and wrote on the board. A full year of being unable to drag my attention from the way his wide back funneled smoothly down into his narrow, beltless pants. When he turned from the waist, it struck me that his sides moved the way a slab of modeling clay does when you begin to twist it. I went over and over this similarity. I was hardly any distance from scissors and glue and clay. One minute in braids, stiff with pride, carrying up my clay man to put on the teacher's tray to be fired, the next tall, slumping, sore in the breasts, mysteriously weakened. Mr. Mead.

And that obsession was only a shadow of the first one. Lately I wonder if it all goes back to the way you begin, and after that you love in that way, or go sleepwalking after something that evokes the luxury, fatality, sorrow, whatever the strong taste was, of that first one.

The year of the bad boy. The year I was eleven I liked the bad boy all year. Because of that boy, I am helpless in the hands of my son, who sometimes looks out with the same yellow-eyed look of a playing dog that would like to bite you, and barely restrains itself. A boy's look when he is finished with childhood and doesn't know it. That boy. *Boy.* A silly, jocular word for the mean, thin, graceful thing, the ghostlike thing.

He always had dark circles under his eyes, from having no bedtime, the teacher said. I waited for his high infuriated laugh after he stood in the corner while we read aloud, the sass he would mutter if she turned her back, the finger he would flick on the way back to his desk. "Class, it wasn't funny," she said when he was in the principal's office. He was a serious troublemaker. He did things we could not be told about.

He knew something about the way I felt. When he passed close by my desk so he could rattle his knuckles on it, I could smell the briny iron smell of the monkey bars on him, mingled with playground dust and a smell that was himself. I saw the unraveled hem of his T-shirt sleeve where his thin, hard arm emerged. Bruises all over it, lakes of bruise, disappearing onto hidden skin. Vague rumors about his father's meanness. We didn't have the word *abuse*.

For a while I thought the others were pretending indifference to the dark eyebrows drawn together, the bitter, grinning look that so afflicted me. But I was the one pretending, turning my back at recess, making the face the girls made when a teacher dragged him off the playground. *She likes him.* The girls knew. But I could not stand up for a passion. I denied him.

It was a passion, although we called it *liking*. All the girls did. *She likes him.* Nothing I have felt since then has ever put it in the shade.

THE CHILDREN GO BACK AND start over, and begin an elaborate plan to deprive Karen, the middle one, of the advantage she showed the last time. She chews her sandy hair casually. She takes part in the plan to handicap her, knowing she will win anyway. It is all established in the year each one of them is undergoing. Robbie will fare badly, thus he says *goddammit.*

I don't think in this actuarial way about the family for long. Soon the children have to go back to the beginning and start again because Robbie has used up his guesses early and he is crying. All three of them are oddly tenacious about Clue, as if they must expose a real misdeed. To the exacting oldest one's chagrin, her sister has put random objects on the board, a paper clip and a bottle cap, to replace the lost tiny pistol, the noose.

Then minutes later it happens again. They will not give in to Robbie's tears; he has made his mistakes and must play on without a chance to win. He cries loudly in his new way, with groans, the last—though he does not know it—that he may ever cry until somebody wrenches tears out of him when he is our age. Karen, the winning one, says something I can't hear. Her way is not to fight but to make observations about weaknesses in the others that they think are secret. Robbie hauls up on his elbow and hits her between the shoulders with his fist, hard. She knows I'm there in the doorway, so she does nothing. Robbie scrambles up, scattering the pieces, and begins slapping her on the head with the Clue board. The dog gets stiffly to his feet, points his nose down, and barks. The board tears down the middle.

At this, Paul begins to shout, "Stop it! Just stop it, goddammit!" All attention shifts off what is happening with the Clue game and onto his stamping approach. Robbie's eyes flash through his tears, and the girls shift their hips righteously in their pink bicycle shorts. "Stop it," Paul says from the doorway, in a lower voice. He looks at his hands, and turns and goes noisily downstairs, throwing an angry look back at me as if I have allowed the children to make him want to hit them.

He would never hit them. Fatherhood he accepts as a vocation. Something happened when he was a boy that required this of him. He may not be a natural husband, but fatherhood is a marked-off territory in his mind: there he will not be found wanting. He always preferred to stay home rather than hire a babysitter, and he doesn't have to pick one up now, because Jenny, the oldest, is almost fourteen. Downstairs the girls hug us loosely, waiting for us to be gone. I go back up to kiss my son. I have to kneel down because he's sprawled against the girls' dresser with his arms loose beside him. "Oh, well," he says, sniffing deeply and shakily. And he puts his head on my chest like a dog. Paul comes up, too. When I leave he squats down and talks to Robbie. I used to think Paul gave Robbie advice, but lately I have overheard snatches of their talks and I think it is more that he is begging Robbie not to be temperamental and violent and clumsy, as Paul was when he was a child, but to be happy.

Paul still calls home in the middle of the evening. But now that Jenny's old enough to babysit for other people, we think and say to each other, "They're safe, the family won't let anything happen to itself."

Of course, we know a story to undo that faith: a story from Sophie's household. Sophie's toddler fell out of a doorway with no steps, in the house they were remodeling. All the while Sophie was crying with Paul at the movies and on ferries, her husband was lugging planks in and out and cutting drywall and breathing sawdust to turn the house into one in which she could lean back on the couch in front of the sunburst window, spread out her red hair, curl her thin toes and be happy. The little one fell several feet, onto cement, while in the care of her teenage sister. She was a ball of solid flesh and was bruised but not badly hurt anywhere, it appeared. Later in the day her sister could not wake her, and took her back to the emergency room, where she was found to have bleeding in her head.

The blood formed not one clot but two, it was said. It was a bad case, days of alarm, confusion, and guilt at the hospital. Sophie was not at the meeting in Denver that she had left home the day before to attend, but in a lodge on the other side of the Cascades with Paul, and could not be found. Fortunately Paul, daily envisioning just such a thing, had left a telephone number. But snow fell; an accident closed the pass, and he was unable to rush Sophie down out of the mountains to the hospital where her child lay, and thus, while the unconscious two-year-old was being wheeled in and out and having her scans and being operated on for the clots, many things had to be known, and said, and suffered over, on the telephone. And I saw how it was then, for Sophie's husband, Stan, and their teenage daughter, and for Sophie herself, and even for Paul, now that Stan knew, and I felt myself banned from the circle of suffering because I had known for months and my own knowing had not shamed anybody or set in motion any such spreading sorrow.

In the tiny restaurant with its ceiling fan going and its front door open to the cool air of the street, I observed, "You're confusing the kids. Lately either you give in to everything or you're yelling. What about quiet discipline?"

He said, "Quiet discipline. Like you." That was how it began, harmlessly enough. But something had been there all week, coming and going, flickering. Then we tried to get in everything over an hour's meal, but a silent agreement over the last few weeks not to bring Sophie into it blocked us.

It always used to come back to weeping red-haired Sophie twenty blocks away, in her house with its side cut away and draped in blue plastic, who never wanted to hurt anybody. Indeed, after the baby's injury and long, stalled, only partial recovery, Sophie withdrew for months, more than half the year. Still, when spring came it was unusually warm, and under its loosening influence she was ready to sink back into desire and secrecy and tears. But Paul had had a chance to catch his breath, he was not quite ready, he was thinking it over.

It seemed possible to me that he was thinking he might have to stay the way he was, married. Bitter thoughts. When he was twelve, his own father left the family and married somebody else, and he was recalling that time of furious sorrow and hatred.

His father got married to a woman down the street whom they had all known. She was divorced, raising two sons whom Paul's father would later urge his own sons to think of as their brothers, during the brief visits he made. Those dwindled away in a year or two. The woman had pitch-black hair down to her shoulders and came out onto the sidewalk in her pink bunny-fur dressing gown carrying her garbage can. Fussing with the lid on the can, smoking. Paul always described her that way, on the sidewalk, inhaling. Long before they knew anything about their father's adventures, Paul and his real brothers had noted the hair, the pink fur. They had talked secretly about the woman.

As women did more frequently then, Paul's mother went on a downward slide. There were not many magazines telling wives in her position what their responsibilities were. She raved, she drank, she cornered the girl Paul took to the prom that year and wept in her arms.

Years later his father was passing through the town where Paul and I were in college, and he took Paul out to dinner. He boasted about the black-haired wife to his son. He said, "She's still a wild woman."

"Ugh," I said, when I heard that. Paul didn't tell me about it until after we were married.

Paul said, "I was through with it all by then."

"That's what you think," I said.

He thought for a minute. "If I had seen him a few years earlier and he had said that, I would have killed him."

But maybe now he was finally thinking about how his father felt. I didn't know how long this period of thinking could go on. Thinking and waiting. Nine people waiting.

•

THE CONCERT WAS PART OF a festival: four chamber works by different groups. Two-thirds of the way through the first one, during the pause after the Andante, Paul got up from his seat and crawled across me to get out. He was gone for the rest of the quartet and the two mazurkas. When the intermission began I threaded my way through the crowd in the lobby, but I couldn't see him. Finally I went up to a pair of student ushers, a boy and a girl who were laughing and pushing each other, and said, "Did you see a man come out and leave, at the beginning of the concert?" The boy looked down at me, a woman with glasses and lines at her mouth. "Lots of people go out," he said in a voice meant for the girl. She stepped in front of him and said, "A man did sit out here for a while. I don't know, he might have left."

In an alcove by the cloakroom I found him in a telephone booth. This was in the time before cell phones. He was not on the phone; he was sitting in the booth with the door closed. He was leaning back as if he were asleep. For a horrible moment I thought he had gone into the telephone booth and died.

Though I had made no sound, it was too late for me to leave because he had seen me. He stood up as if he had been getting ready to come out just at that moment. He wrestled with the door, trying to push it outward instead of pulling it towards him. I remembered something I had forgotten, how when the children were babies I sometimes thought, at a certain stage of tiredness, of climbing into the crib with them. I saw myself, the wife standing outside the booth, as another person, the one who would have come into the room if I had been in the crib and said, "What are you doing?" Someone proprietary and without impulses, a balding Karenin, a jailer. "*What are you doing?*"

I wanted to say I saw nothing peculiar about his being in the phone booth and I was not there to bring him back. But he got the door open and came out, shaking out the knees of his pants, and without a word pressed through the crowd with me to the refreshment table. I could have said, "Are they all right?" pretending I thought he was calling the children. Or I could have said, "You called her, I know." But I didn't want to, because of the question of whether I had driven him to it. Not what if I had, but what if I hadn't. What if I did not figure into it at all.

We had come for the Schubert trio that was last, after the intermission. About the thin slivers of torte and the half cup of coffee that went with them for six dollars, we did not make our habitual jokes. Pale now, he went off to the men's room. When he came back he was standing behind me for a while before I knew it. Then the lights dimmed and everyone surged back.

A woman in a pleated caftan with shoulder pads pushed by me so hard I hit the doorframe. I looked back to see if Paul had noticed, and I began to feel chilled and uncertain. He looked ill. Surely at dinner he had fought as fiercely as I, although I couldn't remember any of the things he had said.

We rustled, sat, settled, gazed at the stage. The musicians arrived looking fresh and combed as if they had just laid aside aprons, washed their hands, and come out ready to serve us something they had prepared backstage. We grew still, the musicians smoothed their music, signaled back and forth as they tuned. Silence. Silence. The trio began.

It was to hear this trio, the B-flat, that I had bought these tickets months before. In its Andante an almost untroubled devotion would be told again and again.

When life is dark I listen to Schubert. I have taken books about him out of the library to learn why this should be so. Reading them the first time, and even rereading them, I have had such a strong feeling of woe, and of responsibility, as he stepped along his path, that it was as if I were reading about my son. For Schubert, there was no untroubled devotion. No wife, no proud children. He was himself the twelfth child of a teacher and a cook. Just five lived. So, seven deaths, for the teacher and the cook who had Schubert to bring up. He grew to only about five feet, not tall enough for the compulsory military service. He was known by the nickname Mushroom. Some of the piano music he wrote was too difficult for him to play. He drank too much wine, could not earn a living. No wife. No children. Even so, he was able to chart a despair and longing that seem to me to belong to marriage, although it may be I'm confusing marriage with life.

Schubert finished this piece in his last year, before dying at thirty-one of typhus, typhoid fever, or syphilis, depending on the biography you accept. Thirty-one. The year was 1828, *the year of mysterious pain, fevers, of businesslike attempts at sales. The year of death in youth.*

Here we were, hearing his lost idiom and understanding it, as though one hundred sixty years had not chewed through the world leaving nothing Schubert would recognize, except maybe the three on the stage, two men and a woman, with the violin and the cello and the huge piano with BÖSENDORFER emblazoned on its mirrorlike black side. The young man is bent over the keys guiding it. The air of an important but not—for him—difficult test hangs over him.

I fell in love with Paul in a class. I saw him bent over his spiral notebook, with dark circles under his eyes. He was carefully writing, shielding the page. I watched for a while and saw that he was not taking notes but writing a letter, which I felt sure was to a woman, a girl, as we said then. I started to think about how she would feel if she stopped getting the letters. When he looked up he looked straight into my eyes. He looked familiar. He had the flashing sad eyes of someone else. A boy. He looked like the boy from my grade school.

For a long time I used to say to myself, *No one can distract us from each other. Either of us.* It was impossible that anyone else could offer more than we were offering each other, in the days of the alewives coming in on the waves of Lake Michigan.

I did something.

I called Sophie. We arranged to meet at a restaurant. I knew who to look for. I had seen her across the auditorium that night when Paul stiffened and I followed his eye. I knew she would get to the restaurant first because she was a therapist and would know that the seated person has the power. She was there, with a book, a novel. It was one of those novels that maintain the reputation of being for the serious reader while in fact everyone reads them. I wanted to say something crushing about it, for I had read it too, but I just said, "Are you liking it?" as I sat down.

"I do like it," she said, and she added, looking at me searchingly as though I might help her, "but it's taking me forever." Everyone complained proudly of the long climb of this awful book.

Was she pretty? No, but she had abundant red hair, and her eyes were large, and made up to highlight their blue-gray. Something about her did not look good. She had that skim-milk skin, blue under the eyes, that goes with the hair. She was not wearing her glasses. Things I had been afraid would come to me as I looked at her, physical things, did not. The need to be composed overrode any images.

"I don't know how to tell you how sorry I am," she said. Did this mean he had told her he was going to leave us? I didn't want to ask questions; that would make me the outsider. But I didn't want to let her ask questions; that would make me the patient.

"I know you are," I said.

"You must wonder what kind of person I am."

I knew this was a consideration of the utmost importance to her. "I have some idea. I assume this isn't your usual way."

"God. I would never have believed this could happen. Never. Never."

"But it did." We kept making these statements, one after another. Somebody was going to have to ask a question, or take a stand. The waitress came for our order, and Sophie complimented her on her earrings. I could see she was going through life like this, making everything a little better for this person or that.

"So tell me what kind of person you are," I said.

"Oh God. I'm . . . I'm . . ." She resisted the temptation to go on. Paul thought she was intelligent, and maybe he was right. Her face grew intent. She had on black pants and a discreet blue-gray turtleneck, with a big necklace of hand-painted beads lying between her breasts. I could picture her without the makeup and the jewelry, at home like anybody, with her family.

"Tell me about your house," I said.

She swallowed, and then she laughed. "Oh God. Why not. This is going to be a strange day. I knew you would be like this." This produced Paul, hovering as if she had passed her hand over a lamp, telling her all about me the way he told me about her. What would he say? *This is my wife's year of sadness, of strangeness. Of energy feeding out of ordinary life into her as it always has, but being turned into stasis, as if cries were being converted into print, or chords into notation, or dances into diagrams on the floor, and backwards from there into just thought, thought, thought, so that she, my wife,* says Paul, slapping his forehead with the realization of what has happened to me, *does not do anything this year.*

And she is not like that, not passive, he would say, I hope he would say. Not a victim.

"My house," she said, leaning forward and waving her hand through the vapor of Paul's image. She was actually going to say something about the remodeling, I thought. Fortunately she said only, "It has come to a stop since Jenny got hurt." It's the worst irony that we gave our daughters the same name, but at least I know the thing didn't get its start until after she had Jenny.

Now her Jenny has what they call deficits. Jenny is not going to grow up to do anything like what either of her parents does for a living. She is not going to do much more than the basic things. Sophie is worried about who marries the kind of women she will be. *"Mawwaige,"* I said when Paul told me this. We always liked to say it the way Peter Cook does in *The Princess Bride,* at the wedding of the maiden to the vile prince. Paul grimaced. "She means who will take care of Jenny," he said hoarsely. He takes responsibility for the fall out the door, the ruined brain. "Let's face it, you may have to provide her with a dowry," I said. I could say anything. He knew how I felt about what happened to a child. He knew I would not draw the line at hurting him, though, and would in fact try as hard as I could to make his feelings of wretchedness more intense, until he would have to come closer in—because he always had to talk everything over, the worst, the most unassimilable things—closer, to be comforted. He let it go.

Talking of her child, Sophie had momentarily let go of whatever held the proud tension in her skin, her thoroughbred look. She mottled and sagged. Her nose reddened and her eyes clouded, and she took her white hands off the table.

"Let's be done with all this. I want to make a bet with you."

"What is it?" Sophie said, raising her chin with a determination not to be surprised.

"I want to tell you about us. I don't want you to interpret what I'm saying. I just want you to see the two people, the five people, you wandered in on. And then, I'm not asking for anything. But I'll make a bet with you that you'll get out of it. Because something that has been set going and gone for years, that is on its own course, something like *this,* something *made*—" Here I ran out of breath.

Sophie knew not to be friendly now or to supply me with words. She looked sick. We paused to look at all the men and women in groups having lunch meetings, with their personal lives set aside.

"Why are you asking me this now? I haven't seen him, we haven't seen each other, it's been—"

"But that's not your choice, is it? I'm asking you now because of a thought I had last week. I thought, *I wish I could just shoot her, the way I could in a French movie. I did.* That's when I decided to call you." I said this in a rush, though quietly. I had gone into a pawnshop because somebody told me that was where you should get the guitar for your child's first lessons, because they all wanted to be rock stars and yours might not be serious about the guitar for long. While the man was showing me a very expensive guitar a musician had pawned, I looked down and saw in the display case, nestled among the ring trays, a small pearl-handled revolver.

"Are you threatening me?" Sophie was cool, though her skin was muddy.

"I just wanted to meet with you." That sounded so professional, as if we could share ideas for a project.

"All right. All right. Have you been so happy," she said slowly, "that you think telling me about it is going to change my feelings?"

"I don't know about your feelings," I said. "What does happiness have to do with it?" Of course she knew how we have fought all these years. I moved and she jumped. What if I had the little gun?

"I do want to hear," she said. "I'll listen."

"And don't listen as if you're going to counsel me," I said. "I'm not your patient."

She drew herself up. "When you're finished, do I get to tell you my side? My story?" she said. "I realize I am in the role of the bimbo who appeared in Paul's life and deflected the . . . the chariot of your marriage." She went rosy at this turn of phrase, with the excitement of speaking more sharply than she usually did. She was used to other people being the ones who got excited. "And furthermore," she said, breathing unevenly, "people fall in love with the, the *spouses*"—she expelled this word like a pit—"of their *best friends.* So they know all there is to know, and furthermore they like or they even love their friend, and in some cases

that doesn't make any difference at all to what has happened to them—
it's beyond their control." Her voice broke.

She's going to cry, I thought. *That's all right.* I kept still.

"You can't always control life," she said plaintively.

"No."

In the silence, she gasped. She gasped again and bent forward. "I'm having the most awful cramps," she said against her hands holding the table.

"I see you are." I felt a thrill of pleasure. Oh, I had heard about these cramps of hers. But she gave a groan.

"Oh God," she said. "I was afraid this would happen. All morning I was—" She pushed her chair back and got herself into a folded position, breasts against knees. She stayed like that and people looked over at us.

This is not really fair, I thought. *It's a way of taking over.* Though I did not doubt that she was in pain, because she had no embarrassment about the position she was sitting in. Now the people in the restaurant were going to some lengths not to watch us. The waitress with the earrings gave me a questioning look.

"Oh! Oh, no!"

"What?"

"Oh, no. I'm bleeding." She started to stand up and then crouched back onto her chair. "Oh, no. Oh, no. I can't stand up. I mean this—I'm hemorrhaging."

"Well, let's go to the ladies' room," I said, picking up her limp blue arm.

"I can't. Listen. This is not just my period. This is something else. This happened once before. There's blood thumping out of me. Oh God. I have to get to a hospital."

The waitress heard the word *thumping* and ran to the phone. People began pushing back their chairs and heading towards us.

When the aid car arrived, a woman wheeled in the gurney with a casual speed. The sight of her settled everyone down. She gave the rest of us in the room a small gesture that said to get out of the way. Sophie wept and grabbed the woman's hand on one side of the trolley and mine on the other. It was true, her chair had blood on it, though not a lot.

In the emergency room they gave her something that stopped the bleeding and made her silly. She lay holding my hand. She gave the doctor a weak wave of her other hand. "There's something so funny. This woman wanted to shoot me." Even in this condition she had her effect; the doctor stood there smiling down at her. "But you weren't going to, were you?" she said sweetly to me.

"No. I don't have a gun." The doctor gave me a stern look. "I would never buy a gun," I told him.

"I didn't think so," Sophie said. She craned her neck on the paper pillow and said to the doctor, "You look tired."

"But you never know," I said.

Sophie said, "I want to tell you something. Come here. I want to whisper." I bent down. "This is not a miscarriage," she said. "Don't think that. This is something else. I've had it happen before." I didn't answer. She pressed my hand.

I had never thought of that. I had never thought that could happen. That she and Paul could have a child. It had never, never before this, come into my mind.

I TOLD PAUL. I TOLD him the same day, about everything, the pawn-shop, the stupid book Sophie was reading, my plan to explain our life, the EMTs with the gurney and the shock pads. As I talked his face became slack and his eyes faraway. I told him how Sophie wanted to tell her side. How she had spoken of her children but not her husband. How a scene had come to me in the ambulance, in which Paul, summoned by her husband Stan for a talk, would not speak of me. The two of them would talk as if Paul had risen out of the sea and laid hold of Sophie. I told him how it all came to nothing with Sophie, nothing, because we had not even begun our talk when she did this. I said, "Why didn't I delay her rescue and just let her bleed to death? There was a moment when I might have pulled out the gun if I had had it." I didn't say what the moment was.

"I don't think so," Paul said.

"Women do that. You think I liked her!"

Paul didn't smile. He would not let me joke with him. He would not let Sophie come into the realm of things that were ours. Ordinarily I could have said, "Turn around, talk, goddammit. Don't stand there with your back to me thinking about when you can call her!" But the children came in from outside, not thinking about us.

LATE IN THE FIRST MOVEMENT the cello broke a string. It was a particular seventeenth-century cello, according to the program. Crack! The sound echoed in the hall as if the bridge on the cello had snapped, but it was just a string. The three limped to a stop, all grinning, not as in Schubert's time, when surely humiliation and ruin hovered lower, in greater readiness to descend on one, than they do now. The most awful things happen now, but no one will call it ruin.

The gallant cellist, who had a thin, humorous face and a little beard, left the stage to restring. The others got up and walked after him. Loud rumbling talk began in the hall. I had been in Schubert's world and I didn't want to come out. In the lapsed tension I had a desire to cry heartbrokenly. Paul had the armrest now and had propped his cheek on his fingers, hiding his face from me. "Are you crying?" I whispered very softly.

It would mean he knew, he had heard in the music, that he and Sophie had finished.

He dropped his hand and glared at me. He was not crying. That was not what he had heard in the music. "What?" he said haughtily.

I said aloud, "I meant about Sophie."

"I'm going to cry about Sophie at a concert?" he said, not so much angry as alert, now that her name had been mentioned.

It must be one of the strangest inklings afforded us in life to feel, momentarily, the coursing through the one we love of love for someone else. "It's the music," I said weakly. "It makes me want to cry about all of it, everything."

He said, "Everything. So you've been attacking me all night because of Sophie?"

"I haven't been attacking you," I said. "You always say that when we fight, so I'll think I'm a bitch and not fight."

"You are a bitch," he said. But he smiled. Our eyes met. He put his hand on the armrest as if he knew the sight of it, with its distended veins, would make me cover it with my own.

I didn't know whether he had talked to Sophie or not, and I didn't know how to find out. I didn't know what to do next. What would come next? I knew nothing, really. Nothing about how life could be conducted so that one did not have to go swimming with one arm like this, trying to hold on to someone in the current. It was not as if I were saving him. He wanted to swim away.

Many statements, rapid and theatrical, suggested themselves to me. They crowded up from the past, the kind of things I used to say when my beloved all through high school broke up with me to go out with girls who were new in school or girls his friends had broken up with. *Go see how you like her,* I would say. At the height of it there was half a year without him. *I thought I would die, at Christmas, when everyone was happy. I thought I was going to die, without you.*

The year I thought I would die, for love of that boy in high school, while somehow seeing at the same time a future in which he had utterly disappeared. In the vision—this was before I had decided against marriage—I was married to a man I can only describe as Paul.

EVERYONE IN THE CONCERT HALL seemed to be in a noisy, elated state. The cellist walked back onstage with his instrument held up and out like a puppy in disgrace. The applause that greeted him was a tremendous crowd-sound, with whistles and cheers. Everything about this entrance was filled, for all of us in the auditorium, with inexplicable happiness.

The musicians settled themselves, lifted their arms, and went back to the beginning.

During the music my mind cleared somewhat, though the past had not receded and indeed it came closer, summoned by certain passages. I thought about how, when I went to the county high school, where students from all the little towns converged in the eighth grade, I looked for the boy I had loved in grade school. The bad boy. I longed to see him, but he was not there. No one except the few who had gone to my grade school had ever heard of him, and it was hard to bring up his name and hear what they remembered of him.

For years I looked for him. If I denied him in school, I have kept faith with him since. Now that I have children I see that his condition was more serious than we thought. His stealing, setting fires. It may be that, just as our teachers said, he was headed for one of the jails that are the estate of such boys. Ruin. If he lived to be ruined. But something told me, when I was grown, that his father did not kill him, as I sometimes dreamed he had, and that he himself did not hurt anyone, that he was not in jail. That he went on and lived, found pleasures that no one refused him. Maybe his temper cooled, maybe he enlisted in the army—no, not Vietnam, no, he might have had a record that would have kept him out of the service. No, he lived. He straightened out, found his work. Or if he was the criminal they said he would be, a year came when he broke free, fought his way out of his earlier self, and in a face he saw one day, found me, the one who would love him forever.

You Would Be Good

The burglar was stoned when he cut his way in. It was snowing hard enough that he had the stuff in his eyelashes. Somewhere inside, where even if he scared her for a minute he could maybe get through to her, was his ex-girlfriend. The place had one of those doorbells with pipes on the wall like an organ, and he could hear the dim clangs. He kept pushing the button through ten pairs of them, but she didn't come to the door. He went back to the car, got the stuck trunk open, and found his glass cutter. Above the lock of one of the big double-hung bay windows of the living room he etched a curve. He knew she was in there, she had to be, she was housesitting. He pushed in the half-moon of glass, unlocked the window, shoved it up, and threw his leg over the sill. Before he got the other leg in, he had the sensation that told him a house was empty. He would get that, a quick shim in the gut that said, *OK get in, do your thing, get out.*

Then his left arm was tight in the jaws of a dog. Jesus. The dog. The burglar had been a high school athlete and still had his arm muscles, and he got hold of the collar and twisted.

The dog bulged its eyes, pawed, choked, and sagged to the floor, a big black dog with a dark lolling tongue. He couldn't remember the breed, but it was one of the biggest breeds, to go with the house. He knew the dog. That tongue.

She must have gone out for something. What time was it, anyway?

Everything was quiet, as if it were early in the morning, but maybe it was the no-car quiet of snow. The dog lay flat out on its side. The window let in the smell of snow.

When left by itself, the dog was supposed to be shut in the den so that it wouldn't dig its thick claws into various windowsills and slobber on the panes in its intense patrol for the family's return. They often forgot to shut it in, and had to punish it when they returned. Erin always left it loose in the house, and at those times, she said, it didn't claw the windowsills because she would be gone such a short time that its confidence would not desert it.

That's what she would do for a dog, reassure it, make its life easier. The rules didn't matter to her; she would let a dog up on the couch and into the bed. A small one like a pug, she'd let up on a dining room chair or hold on her lap while she ate. "Feel this," she'd say. "Here, feel the tension. He's so tense he's shaking. A dog shouldn't have to feel that way. They shouldn't leave this little guy. He can't get over it." A dog has ways to relieve tension, but if it is a good, trained dog, like the big one he had just choked to death, it is long past the callow relief of chewing furniture or leaving drops of urine where it alone will ever know they have dried in secret testimony to its anxiety and love. It must suffer unaided. She had taught him this.

He said, "Now he'll do this when they're here, get up on the table."

She said, "No, he won't, he knows them. It's them he loves, poor thing."

In the hall a scarf was dangling on the horn of a statue. These were the kind of people, world travelers, who would have in their front hall a wooden statue of a goat, bigger than the dog, a tall, thin goat with spiral horns, on a heavy base. Carved the way they do in Africa, so it spooked you more than a real one would have in a hallway.

She must have come early and gone back out for something because of the snow. She would have come in with her books and her ten days' worth of clothes, calling to the dog as it threw itself against the door of the den, and fed treats from her baggie into its big mouth, and let it stand up and plant its big paws on her chest, wagging and whining and squatting to keep the weight on its hind legs so as not to hurt her.

But instead of this, as he was to learn, she was lying on an ER gurney. Snow—expected as a mutant few inches at this time of year—had moved in over the city in a rolling bag of gray, and the bag had opened. There was a pileup on the freeway, and somewhere towards the middle of it two semis had crushed a couple of cars between them. A dozen drivers had arrived in this ER. She was the only one in a coma.

A year before this, she had been taking care of the house and dog while the owners were in Europe. In the huge oven of the eight-burner range she had roasted a chicken for him. They had eaten it on the terrace overlooking the lake, with their own white mountains in the distance, while the owners would be specks on skis on the same white above some pass in Bavaria. Then they would come down and visit cathedrals; some of the great ones were near the slopes.

On the terrace she had talked to him about the fact that he and she had both been raised Catholic. The effect on her was different, because of the big Irish family of girls she came from, with their understanding that any household not Catholic was abnormal, if forgivably so, while from the start there was no way he was going to get the good out of Catholic school, no way he was not going to hate it, being not only a boy but the kind of kid, unsupervised at home, who got in trouble every day.

They had used the owners' china and wineglasses, but spread a tablecloth she brought from her apartment for the occasion, because when she lifted a cloth from the linen pantry and shook out its heavy folds, it had occurred to her that if the wine left a stain she would have to send it to the cleaners. She couldn't afford that, and certainly he couldn't. His money went for things she knew about by then and was set against, things that were going to part them.

He looked to one side as he passed the dog, and when he was out in the snow he dragged the window down with a thud. He didn't take anything. He wasn't going to anyway because that wasn't the point; the point was seeing her. He had to get out of there before she got back and found the dog. There was no buyer anyway for the kind of stuff in the house, all the silver crap, the dark carvings and creepy woven hangings, the carpets too big to move. These people took their cameras and laptops with them. What he really needed was cash. In this house there would be no cash. He got into his car and drove, doing twenty-five in the snow so he would look careful and not attract attention to an old car in that neighborhood. The snow was coming down hard.

In the late afternoon her sister Briah called him. For a second he thought her voice on his cell was Erin's. He interrupted. He could explain. Briah said, "I'm with Erin in the hospital." She was calling him, she said, because she thought he would want to know. For a time he didn't really hear. A bubble formed in his mind, with scenes floating and intersecting like drops of oil. The thought he was having was that Erin must not have had a boyfriend since him, because he was the one Briah was calling. After all, Erin had not had somebody waiting at the time; she had simply gotten rid of him. She was right to. He was going downhill.

He had gone about as far as he could get, and now he was coming back up and he wanted her to know. He had known she was going to housesit; he kept up with a girl who knew her at school.

Briah was saying they didn't know if Erin would live or die. "I've got her key," she said between sobs. "I'm going over to feed the dog. I got in touch with those people. Their info's on her key. They're on a plane. I'm going before it gets so I can't make it on the hills."

"It's already that way," he said. "Got all-wheel drive? Or you won't make it now, down by the lake." He surprised himself by saying he would take her. He didn't have all-wheel drive and his tires were bald, but he was a good driver.

"You know what?" Briah said. "They're up there in the sky looking for somebody to housesit. They have a list and they're going down it. A list. Somebody to take Erin's place. Erin! Erin! They didn't even ask if I'd feed the dog. They said he could wait."

THERE WAS NO DOCTOR AROUND, and the ICU nurses wouldn't say, but when Briah went to the bathroom he asked them again and he could tell they believed Erin was in trouble. When Briah came back she had washed her face and had the key in her hand. The blue tag on it had Erin's looping *g*'s and *y*'s. He could hardly breathe. "This dog knows me," Briah said. "He'll let us in."

THE DOG IS NOT DEAD. It's standing in the hall by the goat statue, with one big paw on the scarf it must have pulled off the horn. Again, it does not bark. At the sight of Briah, who goes in first, it begins to wag its tail slowly. To him it seems a little wobbly as it comes forward, sniffing first Briah and then him, his feet and legs, in a careful way. If it connects him to anything bad, it doesn't show it. The big dogs aren't the bright ones, Erin has told him. Some of the little ones aren't either. Like people. But some are deeply wise. Those were her words.

He feels a jet of cold air pass his cheek, from the hole he cut in the window. Briah finds the dog food and fills the big dish, but the dog won't eat. It lies down heavily on a fine rug the people keep in the kitchen, a prayer rug, he knows from Erin. But when he sits down at the table it gets up and comes over and takes his forearm in its mouth. He sees that this is a form of greeting. The dog lets go and flops back on the prayer rug.

They let him out to pee in the snow and leave him loose in the house when they go back to the hospital. "He's a hospitable dog," says Briah, crying again. "He'll be nice to the list person."

She lets him sit with Erin by himself, and he goes over everything again with her. How desperate he has been, how he has the prospect of a job thanks to his parole officer. He is off the stuff and he thinks this time it's for good, his PO thinks so. All he had today was weed, and not all that much of that. He still owes people money. He's volunteering at the encampment where he lived for a while after she kicked him out. Doing better than he was then. This hospital where she is lying, remember, is the place he once worked as an orderly, when they were both at the community college. When he met her. He is going to put in an application here today in case the other deal falls through.

He tells her how deep the snow is. How he wondered what she'd do when she saw him in the living room. The two of them in one room. How quiet everything was. No one was ever around in the daytime, in that neighborhood, except gardeners in the summer. How he talked to them back then and they were all illegals with more problems than he had.

How sorry he is—no way to say this, sorry needing a punishment, sorry beyond any look she could send his way to let him off, if she opened her sticky eyes. How he had been wasted, even on such a small amount, and forgotten the dog's name, forgotten the dog entirely, thought it was attacking him.

If she had been there, nothing like that would have happened. If she had gone out in the snow to start her car ten minutes sooner, or later, a minute sooner, three seconds later, this impossible crushing would not have happened.

He thought she was ignoring the doorbell. He had to talk to her. Would she have called 911? Knowing how he felt about her? No. No. She couldn't answer because she had a tube down her throat. He thought he could see her eyeballs flick under the lids.

WHEN SHE DIED BRIAH STAYED with him in the waiting room while the nurses were unhooking and arranging everything so that the two of them could go in and sit there for as long as they wished. Briah told him she would call him when her parents got there and they figured out the funeral. She was wiping her eyes on the hem of her shirt because the Kleenex box was empty, but he was breaking down, and she must have known about the problems he had when things got seriously bad, how he would go every time, no matter what he had promised, and find what would help him. She knew because she hugged him and told him not to despair. She got down by him on the floor where he was sitting and told him hospital floors were not clean and gave him a lot of advice. She had seen how he was in the kitchen with that dog. She said the thing that would help him now would be to get a dog. It was true she felt that way because she and her sisters were dog people, had grown up in a dog family, where it was believed that you should have two dogs because to leave one dog alone in the house for longer than it took for Mass to be over was a cruelty born of ignorance, and now their parents were on a plane and who knows how they had managed the matter of the one old dog they had at home. Briah had dogs of her own, but Erin, like a priest who had forgone marriage, had taken other people's dogs as her obligation. Once you had a dog you had to stand up, you had to get up every day and feed it and take it out, you had to meet its eyes, you had to be its leader, it did not know you merely owned it, had found it somewhere, it thought it had found you, its leader, the confidence it felt would shock you, make you worthy, you would stand up, you would be good.

He could see that. He could see a big dog out with him somewhere in the open like a beach. No one else was there. It ran ahead low to the sand in a straight line until it was out of sight. "They always come back," Erin said.

Sleepover

Angie sat up. "Come in," she called, but no one came and there was no second knock. She got out of bed stiff from hard sleep and opened the door. A woman stood there in a purple bathrobe very like her own, long and quilted, with a satin collar. It was Cham. Cham, the housekeeper. Angie put her hand on the commotion in her chest. No need for it. She was in her daughter's house, in the guestroom. One of the guestrooms. Cham was here.

"Somebody here," said Cham. "Boy."

"Who is it?" Angie responded foolishly, reaching for her own robe. Hers was red, given her by Bill Diehl just before he got married, as a consolation. A size too big, owing to her loss of weight. Cham helped her with the inside-out sleeves, not even glancing at the arrow of scar where it sank cleanly down the neck of Angie's nightgown when she reached back for the armholes.

"Boy," Cham said again. "In there, with girls. One girl turn off al-ahm." *One girl. Not Erika, your granddaughter.* Cham's face gleamed with oil, and she had a purse in her hands. Would she keep a gun? In a special purse, for the nights she was alone with a child in this outsized house?

Would thirteen-year-olds at a slumber party let in someone they didn't know? A sleepover. "Don't say *slumber party*," her daughter Pat had warned her. "Or *pajama party*."

"We're in this together, Cham," Angie said. Cham's feet were bare, and a strong smell of nutmeg wafted to Angie, perhaps the oil Cham had on her face. *I don't see why she can't be friendly,* Angie thought, following her down the long hall like a child, but they had reached the great dim room and Cham was already turning without a word to leave her there.

The moon was high and the skylights spread four pools of gray light on the floor. At the far end of the room where candles were burning on the glass table, the girls huddled in a cloud of pillows and sleeping bags. Sniffing for marijuana, Angie got only nail-polish remover and candle wax. The couches with their rolled backs seemed more ponderous in the half dark, under the vaulted ceiling. A hushed laugh drifted in the room.

"Your grandma!" someone hissed.

Next to her granddaughter in the circle sat a blond boy.

ANGIE'S HEART ATTACK HAD BEEN written up in a medical journal. She was proof that women might have a reaction all their own to having their arteries blown open with balloons, or cut up and spliced. They might repay the most delicate and constructive of procedures with clots, wild rhythms, ugly infections, fevers. "Now, Patty, would you not give me that look," she said to her daughter on the first day of her visit. "Just remember, when you came down to see me I was using a toilet chair. I've come a long way. And what about you? If you get any thinner, you can live in that wall of yours."

Pat's wall was a block long, built high enough that no one on the curving boulevard to the lake could see a house behind it, even the roofline, let alone the lake below. Apparently no law said a city ought to be able to see its own lake. The wall was a foot thick and had its own miniature roof of slate tiles. Pat said nothing, but went on looking at her, and it was true that in the vast, smoky mirror over the fireplace, a wraith could be seen standing with Pat, nodding and pointing, instead of a solid woman with round arms and a good neck for sixty-seven.

Sometimes, Angie did not say to Pat, it seemed the blood pumped off during her bypass and fed oxygen for all those hours had run back into her carrying seeds of despair. But at least she had not lost her wits to the pump, as people her age frequently did. They woke up confused and stayed confused. Pumpheads, the doctors called them. Once it was clear it hadn't happened to her, her friend Terri had told her about pumpheads. Terri was an ICU nurse.

Angie was not a pumphead. Still, she had not really picked herself up and gone on. She was waiting to decide. Decide what? Pat would say. Pat had her own copy, from the Internet, of the article about Angie's case. Nothing would convince her that Angie understood it. Coronary artery bypass, or microchips, or the human genome: why should somebody like Angie try to catch up? Angie's territory was the past. But the past that clung to her was mixed up, for her daughter, with movies that had come out long afterwards, and dressed things up. *The Summer of Love* and *Woodstock*. It didn't matter to Pat that Angie had not been at Woodstock and had in fact been a pregnant woman in her thirties at that time, with a husband too sick some days to get out of bed.

Pat didn't remember her father, Rudy. Angie could supply her with dates: how she and Rudy had started in before there was any such thing as a hippie, crisscrossing the country in a van and signing people up to buy record albums that might or might not come out. How long she had been married and how tired she was by the time Woodstock came around, how hungry to go back to Oregon and live alone with her husband and, at last, their baby. Pat.

"OK, so a beatnik," Pat would say. And she didn't mean the real past, anyway, she meant the past-in-the-present. She meant Angie's shawls and posters, her friends who got arrested on picket lines. Her boyfriends, who might be younger, in their fifties, and wear those thin ponytails—or like Bill Diehl, fluffy blow-dries—and see no harm in accepting loans from a person like Angie who always had work.

EARLY IN THE COURSE OF the birthday party Angie had angled the big suede armchair to give her a good view of the girls. Just when she thought one face was perfect, another would come up from the tray of colored bottles—they were painting each other's toenails—and this one would be dreamier, longer-lashed, more perfect. Then fine red hair would fall across that face and another would look up, skin taut, full lips parted. That was her granddaughter Erika, getting up with the phone to her ear. Then a composed, high-cheeked face with shining bangs: that was Tamiko, who had come to the door in the company of her uniformed driver. Then another, fringed in unruly curls, a child's face, black-browed, heart-shaped.

I'm old! Angie thought, without any real opposition. *I don't envy beauty any more!*

The girls had on T-shirts in parakeet colors that bared the studs in their navels. "Our birthstones! Stick-ons!" they crowed, pulling them off to show Angie. "Except Erika's." Erika had a thin gold ring threaded through a real hole. They all wore ankle bracelets and multiple rings. With that high agonized laughter of theirs they kept falling on their sides on the rolled-up sleeping bags.

"Don't let them fool you—these girls are tough. They all do sports," Pat had told her. "Basketball, track. Wait till you see Erika run the four-hundred-meter. And the relay! See those legs?"

Angie thought of saying, *Long, all right. Eric's genes in action*, because of the important tone Pat gave the word *relay*, when it was just another form of tag, something you did at recess.

Or she might say to Pat, "Is she as smart as you were?" Angie saw Erika roughly once a year, she didn't have much to go on. Erika didn't seem to have the brains Pat had had in school.

"Erika's the leader," Pat went on patiently. "You'll see it. They all follow her like ants."

"Maybe because she's tall," Angie said. "The tallest ant." It must be that they considered Erika the prettiest, she decided. And their standard must be just this blondness and slenderness and height, and the air Erika had, patient but dissatisfied. Like a woman in a store trying on shoes, nothing unfriendly about her but nothing obliging either.

Angie watched the muscles slide in Erika's telephone arm as she moved away from the others, talking seriously. When the call ended she spiraled in one motion down onto her back, laughing and slinging the bag of cotton balls in the air so they rained down on the others. "Wait, wait—it's on my foot! Hey, Jessie just did my third coat!" The girl with the innocent, triangle face drew her black eyebrows together in a mock scowl. Then she too lay back with her arm over her eyes, gracefully waving the foot with the cotton ball stuck to the toes. She was a pretty little thing, more a little girl, perhaps, than the others. Watching her, watching all of them with their long waists, their pearly collarbones, was like being sung to, Angie thought. One of those songs in Gaelic or some old tongue. Rudy's material, sung at county fairs when he was first starting out. Ballads. Before the war heated up and all those lords and maids and cherry trees and narrow beds were put away, and the guitar took up a harsh line.

She could see him, in the full-sleeved shirt she had embroidered with birds and ivy, and in tiny script on the collar—it was when sewing machines first did that—his name, Rudy Rudeen.

Now the five girls were on their backs with their hair spread out on the rug, waving their legs, all talking at once. Erika was on the phone again. They had on that three-chord harmonizing stuff they listened to now. Boy bands. When the time came, Angie's job was to light fourteen candles on the cake and carry it in. She didn't see any presents. These girls might be beyond presents.

The armchair in the computer alcove was so big there was room for a small child on either side of her. And this was no alcove, really, it was an area as big as her own apartment, enclosed by plants and low bookshelves, with two computers and a copier and two fax machines on a counter of grainy stone. It was part of the same room where the girls were, but Angie was some distance away from them. The whole center of the house was laid out in an open design, with divisions suggested by slate inlays in the shining maple floor. You could lose your balance out there, as if you had wandered into a bullring.

Tropical plants in stone tubs marked the inlays at either end. Most of the lake-facing front of the house was glass, and four skylights poured light on the tall muscular plants and the area rugs and scattered islands of furniture.

This was a famously dark, rainy city, but in her daughter's house you would think you were out on the lake in some kind of a glass atrium. Maybe on a cruise ship, where you could unwrap yourself behind a palm and quickly slip out of sight in a warm pool. Angie had been on a cruise, to Mexico. Her daughter had sent her on it, along with Bill Diehl. "Why not take your pal Bill." That was what Pat called him the whole time he shared Angie's place. "The car salesman," she called him after he moved out and got married, although Bill didn't sell cars, he sold boats, a harder job, more uncertain.

Bill was sixty-some, a few years younger than Angie, but Angie's friend Terri, the one he married, had just hit her forties. Angie was the godmother of their baby girl. "Well, you remember Terri," Angie had said when she called Pat, after she sent Bill off in the U-Haul with his couch and his cat, "how pretty she is." She was half hoping Pat would offer up some female curse and half relieved that she did not. "And beauty is everything," Angie went on. She liked a conversation that would go from there, even an argument. She would have welcomed "Beauty is nothing!" or "Are you kidding? We're talking about sex!" so that she could reaffirm her hospital vow to keep clear of the negative and appreciate everything. "I'm not making excuses for Bill. It was one of those things."

"Right," said Pat. In the past she would have said to Angie, "What's with these men? Why is this the story of your life?" But by the time the godchild came along, Pat was no longer making painful or intimate remarks to her. "I don't know about my daughter these days," Angie said to Terri and Bill. Terri had placed the baby in Angie's arms and she brought its wide-eyed face close to hers. "What do you think? Think maybe aliens took my girl and sent a copy?" But what happened with Pat is a secret, she thought. A secret from me because I was the mother.

The metal stairs at either end of the huge room were like the companionways on a ship. Guests, if there were any guests, climbed up them to the second-floor wings, where they could settle into one of the balcony rooms, or the suite with its own kitchen, where Angie would have been staying on this visit except for the fact that her daughter had taken one look at her and said, "Wait, I'm going to put you in the little courtyard room down here. Rika, ask Cham to make up that bed."

Erika's bedroom was up the metal stairs. Angie had an idea it was something to see, but she had not yet had a look at it. She had tried to, going up hanging onto both rails. At the top a metal walkway ran the length of the great room, a sort of open-work bridge. When she got close to the top she turned and sat down to rest. She waved to Pat, who said, "Come down. Now. And hold on."

Pat said the previous owner, a man whose company had done business with hers, had hardly finished remodeling the house in this semi-industrial style when he retired and moved to Hawaii. He had left a full wine cellar behind. "Well, sure I will, I'll have a glass of wine," Angie said.

"Oh," said Pat. "Sure. I never think of it."

"Red wine is good for me. And you said he was going to live here all by himself?"

"Not for long," Pat said.

Angie had heard the stories about shirttail relatives who turned up in Seattle when the software fortunes were first being made. Right from the beginning Bill Diehl kept her up on those things. "Pat's going to break the bank up there. She's smart, she's in the right place at the right time," he said. Bill had no money of his own, but he could always sniff it when somebody else had it or was going to get it. "Some people get kinged," he said, "just like in checkers." He was a man of no resentment, and that was what Angie had loved. She had loved his gleeful accounts of sudden, undeserved windfalls, occasions of wild luck. In fact, when he and Terri realized they wanted to be married to each other, he told Angie this could almost be one of those, the first of his life.

Angie could not stand in the way of such a thing. "So what are you waiting for? She's the one for you," she said. "I know about that. I had that. There's only one."

Of course she did not believe this. If one, why not more than one? Fortunately Bill would not think of it in that way. His way had always been to skip over twenty-five years of Angie's history and treat her as a widow. Early on she had made the discovery of his serious gift for comfort, his knowing at what point to pour the wine down the sink and wipe a woman's tears with a clean handkerchief. He had bowed his head to the story of Rudy more than once. So let him see himself as an episode late in the day, for Angie, someone with whom she had joined forces for a couple of years, and shared one vacation, and a cat that gave birth in the closet. Though for his sake she had been at some pains to keep up the idea that their arrangement was a romance.

"We bonded over a stray cat," she would tell people. Bill was the cat lover, but they spent weeks united in the search for homes for the kittens. In the end the cat went with Bill, even though she had won Angie over in her solemn hunt for each of her given-away young.

"Why did the guy put these railings all over the place?" These were of a luminous metal and had a decorative, all-purpose look. Angie had taken hold of one herself a time or two. They were in all the downstairs bathrooms and ran along the first-floor walls.

"He had a fall. Rock-climbing. I'm going to take the rails out, but I haven't had time to hire anybody."

"What happened to him?"

"A chunk of the rockface fell on him. Crushed his legs."

"No. That's awful. Does he still have them? His legs?"

"He does. Lots of rehab. Listen, he's out of the wheelchair, he walks. Don't worry about him, he's a tough guy." Was Pat's voice bitter? Had the man been her lover? "He tried to take me over. My company."

"So you ended up with his house?"

Pat smiled. "I bought his house." In her head Angie heard what the old Pat would have said to her. *It amazes me the way you're always ready to sympathize with some guy. It could be anybody. Somebody's always hurting these poor men. The guy fell. He went to rehab. He moved. End of story.*

PAT DID NOT GIVE ANGIE a tour; she didn't boast of anything in the house, or the garden with its tall fountain, blown out wide some days like a sheet on the line. While Pat was at work Angie gave herself a tour. She sat on the rim of the fountain by herself. *I'm not kidding, I wouldn't trade with you.*

Oh, because I'm not a good-time girl like my mom?

You're not the only one, Patty, who's had more than one life.

They didn't say these things any more. Why was Pat lost to her?

When Pat came home the first day Angie said the high ceilings made the place echo, but Pat had her yell to prove it, and there was no echo, only her shout.

Pat had not indulged herself, beyond Erika's school and this house. She didn't travel except to meetings, and she didn't buy cars or wear good clothes. She didn't join a health club. In Oregon, Angie lived among people who were barely making it, who swore by health clubs. But Pat ran. Her legs showed knots of muscle and her hips were narrow from the miles she ran, as if she were training for Erika's relay.

After she ran and showered, Pat came out and flopped down with her feet up on the coffee table. This was the best time of day to approach her, sitting around the huge table, a metal ring on tube legs holding up a four-inch-thick slab of clouded, pocked glass. You had to be careful where you put a drink down on it because the glass had hills and valleys. "I bet this thing cost you," Angie said the first day, not sure about swinging her own feet out and raising them to the level where they could be propped. Anyway, the table might be for Pat's feet.

"Do you like it?" Pat said. She never took offense or acted like she didn't care for Angie's meaning, as she once had; she never argued any more. She was above argument.

"Yeah, I sorta do. It's weird, but it appeals to me."

"Weird," her daughter said with a dreamy expression.

Angie knew this expression. "I know, honeybaby," she said. "I know it's art."

"Well, a sculptor did it." Angie wondered if the sculptor was someone Pat knew. Other than the wheelchair man, Pat hadn't mentioned anyone she knew. If the phone rang, it was for Erika; Pat didn't even look up. "I know about that," Angie might have said. "I was blank that way after your father died." But as far as she knew, nobody had died.

"By the way, you don't have to do the wash," Pat said. "Cham will do the wash."

"I just put a few things in. I like having something to do."

"Right, well, maybe you'd do something for me. Rika's birthday. Fourteen." As if Angie didn't know, didn't have presents in her suitcase. She wasn't sure about them, though. She knew to stay a little ahead of the game, but she could see that Erika had suddenly taken a step. Mention of her previous interests would bring a vague, regretful smile.

"I'll be here for her actual birthday, but then Friday I have to go to Palo Alto, and the party's that night. If I change it, half the girls can't come. You have to get these things on the calendar. I can hire a party coordinator, but Erika won't like that."

"A party coordinator? Are you kidding? You asked me, I'm doing it."

Cham would be in the house, of course. The girls couldn't put anything over on Cham, a woman who had run into a burning grade school. You could see scars on Cham's neck and jaw and only guess about the rest of her, always covered up. She had hidden in a sow's pen, swum through sewage, to get out of Cambodia. Angie knew that. Somewhere back in the dark of that period was a family, children Cham had had, the ones who had been in the grade school. A complicated story of who had gotten out of the country. None of the children. Cham was alone here, suspicious of everyone but Pat. Cousins were here in the city but there was a problem with them; they thought Cham had cursed some relative. She had been with Pat for years now, arriving with a double name that Pat had shortened.

Cham would be right there, in her bare feet and khaki pants, keeping an eye on everything. But it would be better if Angie met the girls at the door. And you had to be careful with sleepovers. Sometimes boys this age came around. How they got there Pat didn't know, since none of them drove yet; they were kids. They would come in twos and threes, with cameras or flashlights or masks, after the parents were asleep, and not do anything, just occupy themselves in stealth and heckling and making the girls hysterical enough, as these skinny prepubescent boys could somehow do, to burst out with confessions to their own parents the next day.

Sometimes drugs turned up, of course. Nothing big so far, knock on wood. And some of the parents had a high enough profile that they had to worry about their children for security reasons. Guard them. One of the party guests was in that category, with her own bodyguard. Or custody disputes, same thing.

"Some of them know boys from . . . I don't know, a previous school, or camp, or even church. Or community service. They have to do community service, through the school."

"Well, good for them," said Angie. She knew Pat expected it of her. "What do I do if they show up?" She pictured a string of boys sneaking up the bank from the lake, past the fountain, with knives in their teeth.

"Send them home. Say you'll call their parents. But you won't have to, they can't even get in the gate. Oh, now you're going to worry. Hey, even if they cook something up, they're pretty much a joke to these particular girls. At this age the boys are way behind the girls. This group has a lot to keep them busy. The boys they see in school—they're so-and-so's son, but these girls know they're twerps. Erika does. She's like me," Pat added, and it was true. But not in the way Pat meant it, not the way Pat had been at her age, full of tears and threats and some display in her walk, Angie thought, some sad teasing, some heat coming off her that might have been called slutty before they all, Angie and her friends, knew *slut* was a patriarchal term.

Angie remembered sitting around on the floor with the women she had lived with when Pat was little, women considerably younger than she was, leaning on radiators as they nursed their babies. Every once in a while they dropped a new term into the middle of their sleepy talk, like cloves into the stew. Their subject might be the commodification of breasts. But they would slip back, they would sigh over Angie's little daughter's rounded beauty, her awareness of her limbs and body as she bathed and danced and fastened her barrettes, her languorous, sweet manner with their boyfriends. But smart, too. Very smart. Competitive. Up in the high percentiles when she got to school, skipping second grade. So there was some connection, after all, between that little girl and the Pat of today.

And no father. A father who was gone, dead.

Pat had no memory of Rudy. So she said. None. She had seen the pictures, heard the tapes. When she got to be seven or eight she didn't want to go with Angie to the cemetery where Rudy was buried, but once, later, she let her boyfriend, Eric, take her. The Grave of the Unknown Rock Star, she called it. No, she wasn't especially curious beyond that.

Pat didn't have Angie's problems with pregnancy; she could have had ten babies. But she had only Erika. Rika, now: Erika had renamed herself, just as Pat had. *Pat* was not Pat's real name, of course. Her name was Parvati. Angie was not going to apologize for that. She and Rudy were back in Oregon; it was 1969 and they had moved into a double-wide just before the home birth—trailer birth, Pat called it—with Mount Hood visible above the pines. Parvati. Daughter of the mountain.

IN YOUR THIRTIES, IN THOSE days, you thought time was running out. Angie had been pregnant four times. "I'm staying put this time. I'm going to have this one if I have to stay in bed the whole time. You do whatever you want. Go on. Go with them!"

This was after she had scattered the carload of girls who followed the band. She got up from the bed and routed them out of the motel parking lot where they were beating tambourines on their hips. Pregnant, Angie was a terror. *Get out of here! Leave us alone!*

There were always pretty girls around, in droopy long dresses, with cracked heels and no makeup. But they weren't the ones she had to worry about. She had to think for a minute, remembering. Those two who had traveled with them, and had some right to be there, those were the ones—Mariah? Mara. "Mara, meaning bitter," the girl would introduce herself, twisting her ripe lips. She sang with the band, and had crying fits on the road requiring Rudy's presence in the room she shared with her friend with the made-up name. Sky. Mara and Sky. Names Angie had imagined were written on her skin, dug into her palms. And she had forgotten! Or almost forgotten. She was old.

But she hardly ever felt old. On the contrary, she had been old then. They were old, she and Rudy, for what they were doing, the company Rudy liked to keep. They were on the far edge. All around them were kids. Rudy was tired of the band and they were tired of him. During his guitar solos they liked to wander around the stage talking and drinking. He wasn't all that well because he was careless with his insulin. When he went to the free clinic for his cough the nurse told him to quit smoking but she said it was the diabetes that was going to get him if he wasn't careful.

Rudy was trying to quit smoking. He did quit. He got a job. The baby was born and then the changes came of their own accord for several years, and then the diabetes went out of control again and this time his kidneys failed and then his heart, and he died.

"I wish he could see this house," Angie said. They were having breakfast on the terrace, on the second day.

"Who?" Pat said patiently.

"Your father."

"Why is that?"

"Oh . . ." Angie took off her glasses to wipe off the fine spray from the fountain. Why? Why this wish to get the attention of the dead, force them to marvel at some exceptional thing? As if the sight of the living themselves, fighting and sleeping with each other and crawling through sewage, would not be enough to shake the husks of the poor emptied-out dead. "It would . . . mean something to him." But what, exactly? She felt a flash of conspiracy, the arrival of an undermining opinion, cool as the spray on her cheek: Rudy would laugh at this house. "Well, he didn't have money in his pocket till near the end. You know"—she turned to Erika—"when my dad hired him, he was out on his own. Hitched all the way from West Virginia to the Oregon coast. The reason he came at all was to play music at the carnival—we had a timber carnival in town. He was thin as the neck of his guitar. That kind of diabetics aren't fat. He had to give himself shots, and my mother was a goner when she saw that, that and the smoking. She was going to put a stop to that, and feed him up. But he was a grown-up sixteen." The quality of Erika's listening changed. "He went right to work in the yard. The lumberyard. You could be a man at that age, back then, if you had to."

"Don't tell her that," Pat said.

"We ran off together a year later. I was a bit older."

"She's heard all that."

Erika said, "I have not and I don't remember."

Angie pried the picture of Rudy out of her wallet. She looked into the green eyes until the restlessness showed itself, as if the eyes would look away from hers if they could, and then she handed the picture to Erika. "We had to come back, though, we didn't have a penny. I knew my parents would take us right back. Poor things, they wanted grandchildren. But they never lived to see any, did they."

"No, they didn't," Pat agreed, looking at her watch.

"I'm not going to have kids," Erika said.

"Is that right?" Angie said. "So Rudy put in ten years at the yard with my dad. He was good at it. Then the strangest thing—folk music came in, overnight, and we packed up. We thought it was now or never, it was his chance. Oh, we roved around the country. It was before anybody ever heard of hippies. I just followed along. That's the way things were then."

"Not any more," Pat said. "Nowadays girls don't tag along after some guy they married, do they, Erika? Rika."

"Whatever," Erika said.

"Come here," said Angie. "I want to kiss the birthday girl." She was never sure Erika would come, but she did, she leaned across the table holding out her smooth cheek smelling of apricots.

"It's a whole different ball game," Pat said.

PAT'S BOYFRIEND ERIC PLAYED BASKETBALL. In their senior year the whole state knew Eric. He had the longest leg bones Angie had ever seen, and the biggest joints; he had a long neck with a prominent Adam's apple, and the fact that he was not, at first glance, a handsome boy didn't bother the rows of girls at the tournaments, chanting and holding up cut-out letters of his name.

Angie loved Eric. She would be the last to find fault with a boy who noticed whatever you had left that was feminine. But she knew that politeness of his, that warm look of attention. She knew a ladies' man. *Don't cling*, she warned Pat silently.

Pat had lipstick on and her curly hair fell down over her shoulders. Women were getting permanents for just that soft look. But Pat was not exactly soft, even then. She and Eric were going down the porch steps, lugging the metal sides of a bedframe. Eric had to prop them so they stuck out the back window of the car, too big for the trunk, where Pat had crammed most of the books from Angie's house. "You don't read, Mom." She hugged Angie to her. "Say me goodbye," she crooned, as she had as a toddler when Angie left for work.

"But I'll see you in a month," said Angie in sudden fright. She already had the time off, to be there when the baby was born. Pat was eight months pregnant, but she was going to college. The state university had offered her money. Only one of them could go, to start with. "He'll support me and then I'll support him," Pat said, and that was what they did, after a fashion.

Eric shut the trunk and came back up the steps. "I'll take care of her," he said, putting his arm around Angie.

But Eric wouldn't be like Rudy—Angie was willing to bet on that— always making that wide circle back to home, because down deep Eric wasn't forsaken, and making up for it, the way Rudy had been. He didn't have Rudy's sadness, his need. He wasn't going to stay in a sporting goods store in Eugene for long, losing his chance to play basketball while he put Pat through college.

Angie was wrong, Eric did stay. He stayed faithfully, taking care of Pat. But the thing that happened to Pat was under way, by then. Pat didn't cling at all, she did the opposite. She wouldn't set a date to marry Eric, and then she wouldn't marry him. She floated away, lighter all the time, quicker, smarter. In no time she was someone whose job paid a sum she wouldn't tell either one of them. Then she was someone who talked on the phone with her feet on the table and said, "All we need is the space and three hundred thousand dollars."

Eric turned out not to want anything for himself, except Erika. When Pat took her away to Seattle, Eric surprised everybody by not going to school on the money she offered him. He took off for Alaska.

From the first, he stayed in touch with Angie. He wrote that he had a job on a fishing boat. Every winter he appeared, tall and windburned, in her doorway. He had girlfriends but he didn't marry them. He didn't change. Angie decided he was one of those men pledged, with no loss of manhood, to his high school self. "I'm ready for this sunshine," he would say, hugging her. "Saw my little girl on the way down. She's about ready to do a summer up with me." He had been saying this about Erika for years.

ERIKA JUMPED TO HER FEET. It was the fastest Angie had seen her move. The others were still in their jeans, but Erika had put on a white cotton nightgown with ribbons trailing from the neck.

"Hello," Angie said lightly, crossing the room. She didn't exactly swoop in, she was slow at this time of night. "And who have we here?"

Smoothly the boy got to his feet, while Erika cried "Grandma!" in a stagey voice. "This is Jonah."

"Jonah," said Angie, holding out her hand. The boy shook with his left hand because he had a cast on his right arm. He smiled, a smile devoid of excitement or fear. A small boy, thin, shorter than Erika, with hair peroxided white-blond and dark eyes puffy on the upper lids. Small, flattish nose, deeply curved mouth, surprisingly adult. He looked familiar to Angie. She said, "Have I met you?" At that some of the girls choked with laughter.

"I don't think so."

"Well, Jonah, I'm afraid you'll have to go. I didn't see your name on the guest list." She didn't like the sound of that after she said it.

"OK," the boy said. Standing up alone in the ring of girls, he went on smiling steadily. His face was like a chunk of carved and sanded pine. The swollen eyes made her think of Bill Diehl. That was it. Bill's came from alcohol.

The boy didn't say he was sorry or make a move to leave; he looked at Erika, who was playing with the ribbons at her neck. He was waiting for her to say she had turned the alarm off and let him in. Angie knew that. But Erika was not going to say it. "Bye, Jonah," Erika said, waving her fingers. She made a little kiss in the air.

When the boy moved, Angie followed in her trailing robe. "Where do you live?" she demanded.

"He lives—" Behind her somebody covered the speaker's mouth.

"Near here," he said, facing her at the door with a mild defiance and ringing the hanging pipe-chimes of the doorbell with his knuckles. His eyes in their full lids suddenly flashed at her, like a dog's when you try to take something away from it.

"Can you get home?" Angie said. "It's after one."

"Sure."

"Do you need a ride?" she persisted. "Should I call anybody?"

"No!" the girls cried. "You'll get him in trouble!"

Cham was back. Close behind them, she gave a hiss, a dog-shooing noise, whereupon the boy slipped through the door and was absolutely gone.

With a dark look over her shoulder at the girls, Cham punched the keys of the alarm. She had the purse with her again.

"What's in your bag?" Angie said. She couldn't help it.

"Luck," said Cham. Angie pictured dried roots, a nutmeg, something sewn into a cloth. Cham opened the purse, let Angie look, and quickly snapped it shut. There was a rock inside.

"Stop it, Rika!" The girls were play-slapping each other.

Angie said, "Well, I think that's that, Cham. I think we can get back to bed." To the girls she said, "Don't think this is any surprise to me. I had a daughter, you know."

At this they crowded around her, touched her arms, flirted with her, eager to have their say. "He would have been in big trouble if you called his house." "He would get it. His father—" "Not his father, dummy." "His foster father—whatever, he's crazy." "His foster mom's pretty bad, too."

"Well, did you consider that when you invited him?"

"Invited him!" They all mimed shock.

"You invited him, Erika," Angie said. "You called him. I saw you on the phone."

"He just came," Erika said, quickly sullen.

"You might think about him out there at this hour, trying to get a bus if there is such a thing in this neighborhood." They nodded solemnly, all but Erika. "How old is he?" Angie had a sudden feeling the boy might be in his twenties.

"Fif-teen," one of them said, drawing it out. The dreamy-faced redhead, Jessica. "Fifteen? I think? Right, Rika?" They all smiled and swayed. So they were all in love with Erika's boyfriend.

"He is not," said Tamiko. "He's older."

"He's sixteen." Erika folded her arms and recited in a patient singsong, "He's not from here, he's from Alaska, the caseworker took him away from his father, they always do that, they don't understand his people, he missed school so he's a grade behind."

"Only a grade," Angie said.

"He's smart," Erika said with the pride of possession.

"You can see that," Angie said. Erika's fingers with their light blue polished nails lay on the skin of her folded arms without pressing. *I bet you don't usually get caught*, Angie thought. *I bet you get away with a lot.* "So now, go to sleep, girls. Get down in those bags. Otherwise I'll have to stick you in bedrooms and you'll never find each other. Anybody need a pillow?"

Crawling on their knees over the sleeping bags, they grabbed their pillows and began to thump each other with them. "Hey, quit it, I give up!" Then quickly with their ringed fingers they smoothed the pillows and held them up for Angie's inspection, subdued now, a devout little group. Tamiko hugged her two pillows and laid her head on them. They all copied her. That was the one Pat had referred to, the one with a bodyguard. Tamiko. Her driver had taken off his hat and handed Tamiko's two pillows to Angie with a bow.

WHEN ANGIE WOKE AGAIN IT was just her three o'clock habit. Wide awake this time and knowing where she was, she found the bathroom without turning on the light, and sat getting her breath. Along the rail under her hand were nicks and scratches where the poor fellow must have backed and tipped his wheelchair getting on and off the toilet. "Don't worry about him, he's tough." So Pat had said. The girls, too: "These girls are tough." And Angie: "You'll do fine, you're tough." And it was true, Angie had done fine. All the same, if everyone was tough, then no one was heartless. When she came out she stopped at the window and parted the half-open vertical blinds with a finger, to look at the fountain. She could see its plume drop straight now with no wind. The moon still cast full light. She saw the blond boy, leaning forward—was he crying?—with his forehead buried in the tangled clematis on the wall that half enclosed the courtyard.

There was someone else. Someone he was leaning on, against the vines. Arms unwound from his back. The girl pushed him away from her, just enough to get a gulp of air, and then she stretched herself out against the wall and drew him back. She was smaller than he was, hidden by his body. It was not Erika.

Angie could feel, along the front of her own body, the straining and pressing of the two small frames. The boy had made an effort to get the cast out from between them and had it propped against the wall over the girl's head so that they could lie together upright in the vines. Finally he stepped away, shook himself like a dog, and faced forward, leaning back heavily on the wall and fitting his shoulder to hers.

It was the little girl Meghan, with the flower face and black curls.

Now the boy threw his head back and Angie could just hear his voice, a faraway moan. The girl answered, slowly but with an up-note, a question. Gradually, without looking at him, she made some quiet argument to him, and twined her arm in his, taking his hand. With their backs against the wall, holding hands, they turned their heads slowly to face each other. It was as if the kissing had been forced on them, and now for a minute they were free of it. They could have been on a stage, holding hands, about to open their mouths and begin a duet. Something unaccompanied, lyrical, medieval, with pain as its subject . . . pain and secrecy. Secrecy enclosed them.

So maybe it was not Tamiko, but this one, who required a bodyguard. If that was so, they would have to plan around it. They would have to figure it in, they would know all about how to pretend, how to see that suspicion fell on someone else. On Erika.

The boy let her drag him against her chest and back to her mouth. She had him around the rib cage as if she might lift him off his feet. His knee was between her legs. Of course. Of course. That was how it went. Angie could feel her own pulse, keeping the same old heavy beat of curiosity and objectless longing.

Then she saw Erika. She was standing on the balcony of her own room, above the wing that was Cham's, looking down into the little courtyard. Angie saw her white face, her blond hair falling forward, and followed her gaze down to the embrace against the wall. No, there was no argument, no way to refute what was going on. When she looked back, Erika was gone.

Angie turned from the window. Was she out of sight in the dark of the room? She wanted to get back into bed, into Pat's soft sheets. But she would have to take charge, the boy Jonah would have to leave. At least the girls should all be in the house, wherever the boy was. She didn't like the thought of Erika up on the balcony. In the tantrum years, the years of the forming will, she had taken care of Erika—never a child to be shielded, pitied. And what could Angie say, if she went now and found her? *Don't let it hurt you?* For a long time she stood by the bed. Finally she pulled the red robe back on, tied it, and softly opened the door. Cham was standing a few feet away. "Same thing again," Cham said. "Girls get up."

"Are you familiar with this scenario?" Angie whispered. "Is this what happens? What's the story?"

Cham said doggedly, "Girls get up. Erika and one girl."

"I mean, are we supposed to take action?"

"This boy is not for birthday. Not for girls."

"Well then, I'll see what I can do." She swept past Cham down the hall, and counted the girls in sleeping bags. Erika was one of the four.

At that moment the house exploded in blaring sound. Angie tripped and almost fell. Her hands found the rail, but that drove the buzz up her arms. As it poured in on her, the girls clambered up, screaming. Cham was running flatfooted to the door. She peered through the hole and stepped back, making a violent crisscross motion with her hands at Angie to show—what? "Stop it! Turn it off!" Angie shouted.

"Girl," Cham said, raising her voice angrily. "She try to open. So—" She pointed at the top of the door. A metal plate had dropped two inches to block it.

"So let her in!"

The girls had their pillows over their heads, all except Erika, who yelled, "Turn it off! Turn it off or the cops will come!"

"Oh, no, the cops!" The girls' heads came up. "Jonah! Rika, Jonah's not here, is he?"

"Cham!" Angie shook her by the arm. "Turn the alarm off this minute and open the door. We don't need the police here. It's Meghan!"

"A man," said Cham. "A man is here."

Angie pulled Cham away from the peephole and looked. First she saw the weeping girl, then a badge, held like a playing card between two fingers. Behind it a short, heavyset man stood grinning, moving the badge aside to show himself, then bringing it into view again. "For God's sake, Cham, it's her—employee! OK! It's all right," she yelled through the thick door. Cham was finally punching in the code.

When the alarm stopped, the house seemed to sag like a parachute. Angie shot the bolt back and the man turned the knob, passed Meghan neatly in before him, and stuck out his hand. "Kirby Wells. With her dad's firm." He had thick brown hair combed steeply back from a creased forehead. He gave a short man's bow, leaning into the handshake as if from a height, and then he flicked the badge into his right hand and offered it to Angie. "If you don't mind—gotta catch up with somebody."

"I do mind," Angie said, taking care to stand still and give way to no fluttering, elderly gesture. "Who?"

"Little guy out there. Party crasher."

Angie smoothed the robe and raised her chin, gathering herself, like Katharine Hepburn. "Oh, dear, you don't mean Jonah? He is an invited guest."

"Excuse me, ma'am, but this young lady has a few restrictions on her."

"Ah. But this young man wouldn't be one of them," Angie said.

"Wrong. Watchit there." Angie had backed onto her hem. "Sorry, ma'am, but that's not the case. This kid is a menace." Meghan looked straight ahead, her swollen mouth clamped shut, paying no attention to the three girls rocked back on their heels among the pillows, or to Erika, who had crawled down into her sleeping bag and hidden herself. "So like I said, I'm sorry," the man said, "but the kid's going back."

"Back where?"

"Juvie. Sorry about that."

Angie thought he actually was sorry, sorry that she, his opponent, was silly and old. He wasn't all that young himself, the hair might be dyed. Above his muscled neck he had a low-slung face, engaged in some inner calculation, at once gloomy and self-satisfied. Gauging his own supply of whatever it was that kept men going at his age. "Why, I'm surprised to hear you say that," she said. She was getting into her role, not so much Katharine Hepburn now as any old woman invested—self-invested—with a secret authority that could turn dire. "His family are friends of my daughter's."

The man positively spluttered. "No! No, ma'am!" He rubbed his big short-fingered hands together, then jammed them into his pants pockets. "Nossir. These girls are shitting you. Excuse me. This kid's a problem from way back. I can guarantee you, your daughter does not know this family." Wells turned his lower lip out in a cartoon face of disgust.

"I know them myself," Angie said in the dowager voice. "There's no telling who another person is acquainted with." Though looking at Kirby Wells she was in the process of guessing a whole life for him. "Now, I don't know where you're stationed tonight, but I bet it would be all right for you to go off duty now. Please tell Meghan's father we had no idea he felt this way. I certainly never got any such information from her mother."

"Mother don't have a thing to say about it," Wells said. "He's got a court order."

"Now, Mr. Wells. I promise you I'll watch Meghan. I'll be right here where I've been all evening. Well, actually it's morning, isn't it? How about a cup of coffee? Cham . . . ? And do you have a partner out there?" Cham gave her a baleful look and did not move.

The man's hands in his pockets were balled into fists. He took them out and shook them. "I'm a one-man operation," he said. "Tell you what I need, and that's a restroom."

Angie sighed. "That way and down the hall. All the way down, on the left." It was over. She felt mildly winded, as if she had been gripping the ropes of a swing.

But it was not entirely over. The door chimes rang out, echoed, rang again. Angie put her eye to the hole again. Two policemen stood there, with the boy Jonah between them. They had hold of him by the elbows, loosely enough that he was unwrapping a stick of gum.

Angie opened the door. Her high spirits drained away as the two men nodded soberly to her, creaking in the straps of their holsters and radios. But the taller one said in a friendly way, "I think we maybe have us a cat burglar. Is this what set off your alarm? Says he knows you."

"*This*," Angie said, "is a friend of ours. Jonah, what are you doing outside at this time of night? And who called the police?"

"Your alarm went off, ma'am. We respond to that. The company gets the call and a few minutes later"—he showed his watch—"we get the call." He was speaking to her a little more slowly and loudly than necessary. He was young but bald, and the other one had a buzz cut that showed his scalp. Both of them had the attractive neat police mustache.

Angie took a breath. "I'm sorry, Officer," she began. "I'm Angela Rudeen. This is Jonah, and Meghan, and over there are my granddaughter Erika and her friends Brianne, Tamiko, and Jessica"—she spread the names out with their mild distracting power—"having a slumber party. It's Erika's birthday. If they've been in and out, I'm to blame. I can't tell you how sorry I am about the alarm. But it is a birthday party. Fourteen," she added.

The tall one said, "These false alarms—they'll get you a big fine. If this is your first one, you're in for a shock."

"Oh, it is," Angie said.

The shorter one said, "We get them all the time. The dog sets it off, the maid sets it off." He glanced at Cham's bare feet. "They call us, we come out. Pretty soon, no police response for anybody. I'm just letting you know, ma'am."

By this time they had let go of the boy's arms and he had begun to smile and crack his gum. *Don't do that*, Angie thought. *Don't smile. They're ready to go. They'll leave if you stay still.*

Of course he was smiling for the benefit of Meghan, who was haughtily pushing the stuck curls off her face. She had been shooting looks at him from under her black brows, one after another like rivets, and he was replying with a message of his invulnerability. Her smile in return was radiant, if radiance could be secretive and not wholly benign. She put her shoulders back and her breasts up, and Angie saw that for all her slightness she was not a little girl at all.

Far away the bathroom door opened. Kirby Wells was coming.

"Well, here comes Mr. Wells!" Angie cried as he came striding on his short legs. "Mr. Wells ran over when he heard the alarm."

"Well, looka here," said Wells. His face was deep red, as if he had had trouble in the bathroom. "Hey, you got him."

"Please," Angie said. "I was just explaining the situation to Mr. Wells," she added.

"The situation is, here we have the man himself, Mr. Smartboy," Wells said.

"And Mr. Motherfucker," the boy said with his smile.

"That's enough!" Angie said. But she sagged at the knees and the tall policeman's hand shot out for her elbow. "And Mr. Wells—! But let's sit down, why don't we," she said. The door was flanked by granite benches, where no one ever sat. Angie was the only one who did so now, and as the boy took a gliding step in the direction of the open door Wells grabbed his good arm so fast it spun him in his tracks. What struck Angie in that second was how ferocious a small thing like that could be, not at all like people throwing each other around on TV. It was as if a sharp gas had been released into the room. They all breathed it. Both policemen stepped forward.

"That's assault," the boy said, shielding his narrow chest with the cast in a way that would have brought tears to Angie's eyes if he had not, the next minute, grinned around at all of them. *OK, my friend*, she thought, *you can take care of yourself.* This was a boy who was aware of his effect. He must get by on it, the pang stirred up in others by that combination of looks—for of course the girls had chosen him for what only now struck Angie as his beauty—and the suggestion of a misery, some error he was set on compounding.

"What's so funny?" Wells demanded. "You. What's so funny?"

"Oh, dear," Angie said. "Mr. Wells is trying to help, I'm sure, but really, at this point I'd be happier if he'd just—maybe he'll listen to you."

The tall policeman looked at her and at Wells in turn. His eyes swept the room. "Having fun, girls?" he called. "Whose birthday?"

"Hers," they all said, pointing to Erika in her sleeping bag.

"Looks like she's sleeping through it," he said. The radio on his belt gave off static and then a voice, numbers, an address. "And we've got your guest here, Mrs.—?"

"Rudeen," Angie said. "Yes, you do."

"Uh-huh. We apprehend a guest from time to time."

The younger policeman got up close to the boy and spoke to him. "Buddy, you might be a guest, you might be whatever, but you need to clean up your mouth."

"Rudeen?" said Kirby Wells. "Any relation to Rudy Rudeen?"

"My husband," said Angie.

"Uh-huh. Well, things seem to be under control here," the tall one put in easily. "Don't you think so, Frank? I think we can all just get back to business. And you're a neighbor, Mr. Wells?"

"I'm security personnel for Mr. Nicholas Pappas," Wells said, rocking back and flapping his trousers from the pockets. "I keep an eye on the safety situation of his daughter. Yeah, I'd say things are under control."

This satisfied the tall one. "Do you want to file a complaint?" he asked Wells.

"Wait a minute," Angie said. "Mr. Wells is in my house. My alarm went off. Wouldn't I be the one to file a complaint?"

"All we'd need is, we'd need to run a few checks, maybe get your boss on the phone. And if not," the policeman went on comfortably, to Wells, "you may as well call it a night." His radio blurted again.

"No complaint," Wells said. "I'm outta here. Whoa. Rudy Rudeen."

"Uh-huh. And, ma'am, you might want to shut down your borders. The gate. Gate's wide open. You can go ahead and shut it when we leave. Give it two minutes." He stepped aside so that Wells could precede him through the door.

"Well, yes, I will. Thanks again, all of you." Angie stayed sitting down, to conserve her energy. "Thank you, Mr. Wells. Good night. Seriously, don't worry."

The moon had swung to the rear of the house, and from the bench she could see long, pale washboard clouds. Cham shut the heavy door. "All right, now," Angie said after a minute. "Girls, get back in bed. Meghan, go to bed. Wait, Jonah. I don't know what I'm going to do with you."

"OK, see this?" Meghan had come to life. "See his arm? Wanna know who broke it? Ray. His quote-unquote father. And look." With a rough sweep, almost a blow, she pushed the boy's nylon soccer shirt up. Across his chest ran what looked like a purple tattoo but proved to be a band of raw skin with scabs clustered along it. "That's rope burn."

At that the boy sat down beside Angie, shaking his head modestly as if Meghan were listing his accomplishments.

So Angie had been wrong again, wrong in thinking such a boy could take care of himself. And once she had been so unfoolable. She leaned back against the slate wall. Pumphead. "You'll have to stay until morning," she said to Jonah, keeping her eyes closed, "and then I don't know."

"Just take this off!" said Meghan, plucking at the neck of the boy's shirt. "It's pulling the scabs. See? Oh! See? They tie him up, they break his arm, and now he'll get killed."

A loud, strangled sob burst from Erika's sleeping bag.

"Oh, yeah, Rika! Yeah, hear that? How do you like that? You got him over here. You turned the alarm back on. You got him into this." Meghan's lips had gone white, and she bared her small sparkling teeth as if she might sink them into Erika.

"That may be, Meghan," Angie said, "but she was a little bit duped, if I'm not mistaken. And I can guarantee you, he won't be killed. He'll stay right here until we're sure." Sure of what? What could they manage for this boy? And Pat was getting back at noon. But she, Angie, was the mother. She was not afraid of Pat. "And now, and I mean this, you're all going back to bed."

As Cham stood ready to push the buttons on the panel there was a knock on the door. "Hold it!" Angie got herself off the bench before Cham could take any action. "Great, now we have the police force again." But when she opened the door, it was Wells.

"I'm back," he said, walking straight in. "I'm thinking, wait a minute, you don't wanna leave the fox in with the chickens." At the same time he held his hands up to indicate some possible compromise. But Jonah had already ducked into a dive against the man's belly. "God—damn!" Wells hollered, catching at the bench but going down, sitting hard on his haunch and ankle with one leg out. Angie heard the bent knee crack. From the floor he grabbed Jonah's pants leg, and yanked until the boy fell on top of him. They began to roll absurdly to and fro on the flagstones, rocking one of the stone tubs with their feet so the tree in it gracefully dropped a leaf. The boy's body arched as he strained to get his knees under Wells and throw him off. He didn't have to; Wells toppled heavily of his own accord. What kind of bodyguard was he?

This all took place rather slowly, giving Angie time to think how stupid, ugly, and yet coordinated it was. As Wells rolled on top of Jonah and pinned him, she had time to see the man's sweaty scalp, the white in his part where the brown had grown out. She saw the back of his hand, a dry old thing crawling with fat veins, as he got a grip on the floor. He had on a wedding ring. His head swung low between his shoulders.

Suddenly Meghan was in the middle of it. "Dammit, Kirby! I told you!" She had him by the hair, wrenching his head up. "I told you! I told you, stay outta my life!" The cords in her neck were standing out like tree roots, and it seemed to Angie, who let out a yell, that this was a girl who might not stop before she broke a man's neck. "Christ!" Wells had a hand up, flapping at the girl or protecting his head, and she had bitten the hand. It was then that Cham charged, in her purple robe, driving Meghan off with an elbow, not to spare Wells at all but to slug him with the purse. She hit him in the spare tire towards the back, where the kidneys were. "Cham, for God's sake!" Angie snatched the purse out of her hands. The boy rolled free, and Wells let himself down onto the floor with a groan.

Meghan got Jonah by the cast. "Get outta here!" she hissed, dragging him. "Don't go home! He's nuts—he'll go to your house, he'll get Ray up. Get outta here!"

"Oh no he won't." Wells hung from the bench by one arm. "I quit." The voice came out of his belly. He brought his watch in front of his face. "I'm nuts? You're a bunch of maniacs. As of now—three fifty-five a.m.—I quit."

WELLS KNEW THE MUSIC OF Rudy Rudeen. "The man had a voice," he said. He knew because of course he played the guitar. At least half the men Angie ever ran into played the guitar, Bill Diehl being the exception.

In the eighties Wells had played with two bands nobody ever heard of. The good one, he said with the picky, musician's air familiar to Angie, was modeled on the E Street Band. He considered that he had been pretty good himself, but too old by the time he got good enough. And not in the big leagues, like Rudy. Not with those stubby fingers, she thought. She did not correct him and say, "Actually it was the minor leagues."

"I'll tell you, it was drugs messed me up for a while there. In the service you could get anything you wanted. But hey, Rudy Rudeen."

Angie gave a deep sigh, tried to place the accent. "Are you from West Virginia?"

"Close. Ohio. Crost the river from Wheeling."

"What are you doing out here?"

"Mountains," he said. "My brother-in-law's out here." Not *my sister*. It was funny who people had. Cham and Pat, for instance, had each other. This man had his brother-in-law. Angie had Bill and Terri, to bring CDs with them on the night before her surgery and play her "Take Another Little Piece of My Heart." Angie had a baby goddaughter, their child. She had Eric, almost a son.

"I've got a son-in-law I feel that way about," she said, though Eric was not her son-in-law and Wells hadn't said how he felt about his brother-in-law. "Your sister's husband, or your wife's brother?"

"Ex-wife's brother." He saw her look at his ring. "This keeps the ladies off."

This could be a joke or one of those unlikely truths. "Anyway, I wasn't going to faint," Angie said. "I got dizzy. I get that if I stand up too fast."

"You stay where you are," Wells said, with some authority.

ANGIE LAY ON THE COUCH with her legs bundled in the red robe and the shawl Terri had crocheted for her. She pinched her cold legs, and drank the hot coffee she had made for herself and Wells. While she was pouring it in the half dark of the kitchen, Cham had come in and stood there without switching on the bank of overhead lights, wringing her hands and talking under her breath. She had her khaki pants on and there were streaks, sweat or tears, in the oil on her face. When she saw Angie she jumped and stopped her mouth with her fist. "Oh, Cham, I'm sorry—" Angie began, but Cham stepped back from her and waved at the coffeemaker, saying from behind her fingers, "I, I will do it."

"No, no, please, you get some sleep," Angie said. "Believe me, I won't. I really won't let anything else happen. I mean it, Cham. I'm sorry." Cham rubbed at the streaks on her face. At the doorway she threw Angie a squinting look. "OK. So. You. You will watch. OK. OK."

The candles were burning low on the glass table, but the sleeping bags were gone; Angie had banished the girls to Erika's room. "Let them fight it out," she said to Wells. "Hey, you, go to sleep." Across the room in the business alcove Jonah was playing a computer game, his face flickering blue.

When he didn't answer, Wells got to his feet. "Did you hear the lady?"

"Yes, *sir*," Jonah called back. "I'm going to sleep, *sir*."

After a minute Angie said, "You know, women won't let you go after a kid."

"Some will," Wells said.

"I'm sorry Cham got into it. Sorry she hit you. I didn't see that coming. But Cham had children." Angie had a vision of Cham running into flames, while soldiers went about some awful business. "Cham lost everything." She tried to think of some reparation that could be made when someone had lost everything. There was nothing. After all the marching and chanting from that war, there was nothing. What must they look like, all of them, to Cham? And she had worried that Cham didn't like her. Didn't like her. "Cham lost everything," she said again. "But she still takes care of her skin. She oils her face every night in when she goes to bed. That's a good sign."

"Got herself an altar in there, just like back home in Saigon. Incense sticks, oranges, the whole works."

"Except not Saigon. She's Cambodian. You're telling me you went into her room?"

"I opened a couple doors. Went by the john the first time. This place is a hotel." Clearly he had figured out it wasn't Angie's place. "Lucky she can't swing, no arm on her. Anyway, the kid went after me, if you noticed. I let him off. I'm not going to beat up on a kid. I'll keep 'em away from Her Highness, though, I'll do my job. These kids can smell money."

"I don't think it's money he's after. And you just quit your job."

"If I had it after tonight. But you'd be surprised. Pappas knows the score. He's onto that little gal. Last time she run off, she went clear to Bellingham on the bus. Met this fella there and they went to the doctor, if you know what I mean."

"Ah," Angie said.

"I know stuff he don't want to know, her dad. He can forget about watching that one. He's running the company, but she's running the show."

"They grow up," Angie said sagely.

"Thirteen, fourteen—everything works. All systems go." He sat forward. "Uh-oh."

Angie followed his eyes. Erika was on the metal bridge and she was naked. With her arms outstretched and hands flat against the air she was treading slowly backwards, holding the frieze of girls who followed her at bay. Meghan came first, soothing her—"Come on now, Rika, come on"—but Erika was climbing onto the metal banister. When she got herself positioned she hooked her ankles and rocked.

Kirby Wells had the shawl whipped from Angie's legs and Jonah was out in the open staring up, knees bent, curved lips caught under his teeth as if he were going to shoot a basket. *Ha!* Angie thought, kicking to get her legs off the couch. *See that? You'll find out! It's way more complicated than you think, with your fists and your kisses.*

"You don' know!" Erika croaked. "How do *you* know? We were too going to Alaska! I was going. We were gonna see the Northern Lights!" She righted herself, grasped the rail with both hands. "I wanna, I wanna go!" She teetered on the rail. "We were too going!"

Angie got to the stairs, but Wells was already at the top. With a heave, the way lumbermen threw bagged sawdust, he had Erika off the rail.

"My dad!" Erika howled. "He's in Alaska! Get off me! And Jonah's! He's there. His real dad! *You* don' know! Tell 'em, Jonah! *Jonah!*"

Tamiko, holding her own cheeks in her hands like a flowerpot, leaned over the rail and raised her melodious voice. "Grandmother! Grandmother! She took pills!"

"What pills?" Wells had Erika wound tight in the shawl. "Spell it!"

"X-a-n-a-x. Two pills! From her mom's room! And—she drank wine, a lot of wine," Tamiko quavered as an afterthought. "It spilled all over her nightgown."

"How many pills? Get 'em!" With a knot of tassels, Wells doubled Erika over in the shawl while he stuck what looked like his whole forearm into her mouth. Obediently she retched, groaned, and vomited a stream that dropped in pink flags through the grate. Wells shook off his fingers and plunged them back in. "We got pills in this mess?" he snarled down to Angie. "Don't just stand there. Look."

"I don't see . . ."

"Get down and look. Two pills? Is that it?" He shook Erika, who flopped against him. "Answer me! That's all?"

"Tha'ss—all." Erika came to herself enough to hide her face in his jacket.

Tamiko was back with the pill bottle. "Here it is! I know it was two, I swear, I saw."

"Thanks. You're good, you can apply for my job." He called down to Angie, "She's all right, better than she looks. Two of those won't slow you down much. It's the wine." Another girl began to retch. "That's nothing. Copycat. They've all had a few too many, though, the little turkeys. Except this one here, the smart one." Tamiko stepped back, offended. "Don't worry," Wells called to Angie, "I did a couple years on the rescue squad."

Angie held on to the metal. Where was Cham? But Cham was shut away in the room with the altar. Cham had taken her at her word. *I won't let anything happen*, she had said. She wouldn't let Cham down; she would clean up the mess before Cham got a look at it. Then she thought, *Pat's going to try to get the whole story out of me. All of it.* Then she thought, *If my heart stops now, I'll get my chest ripped open by Kirby Wells of the rescue squad.*

"CAN'T TELL YOU WHAT-ALL I shook outta kids," Wells said sleepily.

The girls were up. It was too late to go back to bed; it was frank morning, and they were taking showers. Three of them were going back and forth along the walkway in a special, created quiet, carrying soft piles of enough towels for twenty bathers, coming down to get lotions out of their bags to offer Erika, who was showering for the second time. Meghan they softly cajoled through a closed door. "OK, here's the thing: you two have to make up. She will if you will."

A feeling of aloneness came over Angie, like the silence when a vacuum cleaner is turned off. Her legs were cold. The room, too, felt cold, and bare as the hall of a castle. One of the old castles. Not the newer ones, as she had seen for herself in Europe, taking the tour Pat had sent her on before Bill Diehl, but the small ruins, maybe from the middle ages—she had not held on to her brochures—that stood in the middle of nowhere with thick broken walls. The ones where women must have lived, with children if they were lucky, and few arrivals. Each one a kind of king-dom. A kingdom without a king, no matter how they gazed from the roof and waited, most of the time. The men would be out raiding.

Not any more, Pat would say.

Angie leaned back. "Did you ever hear the term *pumphead*?" she asked Wells.

"Nope. Something to do with a bong?"

"Ha. It refers to somebody who was on the heart pump."

He was trying unsuccessfully to stick on the Band-Aid she had brought for his bitten hand. "You," he said. Glancing into the open neck of her robe, he zipped his thumb down his chest.

"Give me that," Angie said. "Better see somebody for that. She broke the skin."

"You're a bossy lady."

"No, I'm not, actually."

"Lucky she got this one—see? Not my chord hand."

Funny how chord, the word *chord*, still went through Angie. She didn't listen to music. Her records slumped on the shelf; she had never even bought a CD. She had turned her back on music, outsmarting the traps laid by the past. Doing this gave her a stubborn satisfaction, a feel-ing of concealment, as if from a hiding place she could see people from those crowded days of travel and music and sleeping together but they could not see her.

Up and down the rungs went the girls' bare springing feet, their rings on the metal rails making a cross between a rasp and a chime. They took care not to wake Jonah, who sprawled on the couch in the computer alcove, flat morning light on his smooth ribs and tiny nipples and scabs, although they had peered at him long enough to memorize his openmouthed, frowning, half-slain condition and relay it to the two upstairs. They smelled of shampoo; they had pulled their hair back into rubber bands; their eyes shone.

Angie's eyelids were sore and she let them droop. She was not going to offer explanations to Pat. And Cham wouldn't either, she felt sure. There was Pat's Xanax, after all. The Xanax had to be absorbing some-thing. Cham must know about that. Maybe Cham looked after Pat that way, kept things from her, mothered her. Even though Pat had a mother.

It was her father who had gone staggering away from her with his arm hooked over Angie's shoulders. "We'll be back," Angie had called to the neighbor, who hoisted the child up and made her wave. But Angie had come back alone.

The boy would still be in the house when Pat got home. That, Angie would let Erika account for. Erika would know what to leave out. She might not have any notion, anyway—if she had any memory of it—of what had possessed her to parade like that with her clothes off. Or maybe she would. Maybe Erika had worked out, already, that although it might appear otherwise, some things might never be hers. Or they might come to her not by any right but only by being gambled for up to her limit. More power to her, if she did. More power to her. *Only don't give up,* Angie thought. *Don't give up. I saw you.* And indeed, before she thought of a fall onto stone floor, or of pills, or that she was the one in charge of a granddaughter, all she had seen was a girl on a bridge, tall and naked and beautiful.

One night on the deck of the cruise ship, with Bill Diehl seasick below, she had felt a pause like that, at the wakeless speed the ship maintained in a narrow bay. She had been watching the sky turn a bold, calm purple with the steep land outlined against it. She remembered the rail growing warm in her hands as the color in the sky deepened. Not for years had she been in this state, but she knew it right away. It wasn't weakness or age. It was something first made known to her at the timber carnival when she was a girl.

The thin new boy. The boy stubbed out his cigarette carefully to save it, and picked up his guitar, while she sat on cedar logs beside a bonfire and looked at him, suspended. And then . . . and then hardly any time later the doctor came in and told her the boy, now a man with caved-in cheeks, unconscious on a hospital bed, might or might not go on living.

She had been looking at Rudy's face, with its parched, invalid's beauty, all day. It was time to go to the neighbor's and pick up the baby—they called their little girl the baby, though she was four years old—but Angie just sat there rocking back and forth in the chair. The last time Rudy's eyes had opened they had stuck open for several minutes. Fever had burned off their expression. Her feeling was not even happiness at the news that he might not die, he might live. It was pure rocking, like a kitten swung in a cat's teeth. It was not conditional. He didn't live. It was in this sensation, and her surrender when it came, she thought, watching Kirby Wells as he began to snore, that she knew the girl who had sat on the logs was herself. She knew the girl, and the girl knew her. The boy sat down. His guitar gave out a bass, private note as he propped it. The girl went on looking into the fire and into her life, the life on the way to her. Lives, she knew now. A relay of lives. But the one who caught up with her was herself, passing on the same heart every time.

Novel of Rose

This would be the novel of Rose. First, two stone houses on adjacent hills, in the long pause after the war when everyone in Virginia was raising children. Five chimneys between them. Seven children, four parents, two dogs, the same cat seen in the grass and moving from window to window in both houses, old walnut trees dropping black fruit, locust trees in the fencerows, with groundhog tunnels in their roots. Innumerable empty shells of the real locust, the insect, a wheat-spun-to-glass color, clinging to bark and fencepost one particular year, the year Varden first unsparingly, despairingly loved Rose.

Anne and Sarah—the Montgomery girls. Their younger brothers Roger, known as Mont, and Varden. At the time Rose's family arrived, Varden Montgomery was seven.

Will, David, Rose. Two boys and a rose. The Chestons. Rose, also seven, was an Indian, a Tamil the Chestons said, though as she grew everybody saw that at the same time she was so dark, she looked like Mary Cheston. She had the same gravelly voice her brothers had from their mother, as well. The Chestons had gone away to India and stayed years. They had gone with two children and come back with three. The novel of Rose would go into the trouble a Virginia grade school made about her color.

James Cheston was a doctor but not a rich one. With money from Mary Cheston's family they bought the house next to the Montgomerys, out of shouting distance but always seen as an offspring of the big old Montgomery place. In actuality it had been the original barn, a stone structure on the lower hill, accumulating dignity because of its years in county memory, and the time and labor that had gone into its conversion—the carving out of windows, for one thing, in stone walls two feet thick. And then it was a house, an immediate landmark, facing half away from the main house onto vistas of its own.

By the time the Chestons bought it, the house itself was old, and grown shabby inside, with a remnant of rat society, descendants of the barn-raiders of the century before, still holding certain passages in the walls.

Seven children pounded up the steep front steps and landed against the screen door, where, if they yelled a password in time, they were safe. The screen hung ruined. If it was a Saturday and James Cheston was not out on a house call, he would speak quietly to the winner, who when she reappeared—for Rose, though the youngest, was the fastest—would tear unredeemed down the steps into the pack and down the hill.

At that time their ages ranged from seven to eleven, and for a year or two the older girls, Anne and Sarah Montgomery, played as wildly as any of them, wearing necklaces of locust shells they never would have touched had not Rose been the one who strung them.

They always played on the Chestons' hill. The Chestons were the newcomers, but they held the power. Partly because of their foreignness, their greater indifference to risk, but more the result of their deep voices, they prevailed over the Montgomerys. Their courage, passed to each one like an allowance from the father, who after fighting in the war had gone into the hills of India to fight malaria, led them into proud dangers. It was nothing to them to climb out onto roofs and use the chimneys as base, squeeze into laundry chutes, excavate groundhog holes to make caves, creep up on the neighbor's bull, play on tractors parked out of sight of either house. Their innocence, another gift of the father, kept them from cruelty, from the clever reprisals Mont Montgomery was known for at school. As it was, Mont gave up some of his own ambitions in order to be with the Chestons, though to his sisters he made fun of the

Hindi patois they could chatter in their odd deep voices. "Abela-babela," the Montgomerys, except Varden, called it. In time Will Cheston, oldest of the boys, held them all in a willing servitude. His rule developed without any intention on his part, because like his father he was half shy when not outdoors, where his daring carried him away.

The other factor in the ascendancy of the Chestons was Rose.

Like her mother and father, Rose had a sweet nature to go with her beauty. At the thought of her, of something she had said, Varden would stumble as easily as at the sight of her, streaking downhill with the dogs to the fort in the locust trees. She always beat him. Her speed and relentlessness in a race gave way to appeasement and little gifts—dandelions and violets out of the grass—for him. But she gave them to the others, too.

When Anne Montgomery faded into her teens, she tried to get her sister Sarah and Rose indoors and upstairs, where on one occasion Rose was induced to have her heavy hair put up in bobby pins.

By then Varden Montgomery was far gone. He hung in the doorway when the dampened hair was being rolled into black coins. The effort to make any movement casual set his face in a spasm. Now he was ten, with no foreknowledge that his voice would not change until he was fourteen. In his bed at night he tried to pitch it to the low enchanting hoarseness of the Cheston boys, and Rose, Rose too—all of them had the mother's soft growl. Varden loved the mother too, Mary Cheston, who seemed to know his feelings and even to expect them, who gave off a faint scent his mother said was curry powder, and whose eyebrows tapered like Rose's, though not so dark, in long arches his mother told his sister Anne not to attempt on herself with an eyebrow pencil.

Now Anne wore lipstick and kept to her room reading *Silver Screen* with the cat in her lap, though she sat by the open window and looked out when they were running. Now they were six, four boys and two girls. The fort was a castle in India. The boys and Sarah were defenders of the perimeter, Rose the queen.

In the novel of Rose, this would be the childhood in which some secret was embedded, to be unraveled in later life and serve as evidence that things proceed from a cause.

Varden Montgomery's love twisted his insides, he thrashed in his sheets to get at the root of it. A kiss, his shut lips on the open laughing ones of Rose, burned his inexpert mind at Scout campfires. Eventually he would surprise himself with success in sports, reach high school, Yale, and so on, and practice law like his father and his brother Mont, though milder than either in a courtroom. He would marry and have two children.

Before his marriage he bought out his siblings to own the house where they had grown up and where the dog and cat were buried, and at his insistence the Chestons' dog. He did not live there, and in time he let it go and had a rough likeness of it built elsewhere out of lighter materials.

It was long before this that Will Cheston, seated at the dinner table, saw a tear drip from his father's jaw.

Mary Cheston went back to India, taking Rose.

Sarah Montgomery got a Fulbright to India and found Rose. The two of them came back and lived years together in New York. In the novel, these years would have the figure of a dance, a kind of reel. Rose would dance first with Sarah and then with others, and then, keeping to the nature of dance, with a final partner entering from the dark of the scenery.

Will Cheston died in Vietnam. Varden's children never knew their aunt Sarah, who stayed in New York, pursuing Rose for many years. Rose slowed her speed. A still point was coming. Resolution. The novel must end in a satisfaction of sorts. The ones that follow instead a logic of their own succumb to it and end in the ground.

In India, Mary Cheston is speaking of her dead son Will to someone who listens with his hands clasped. The younger son, named David, the other brother of Rose: did everyone forget him, what happened to him, and so on. The novel would have gone into this. Though the novel might not linger over the house in India as it did the ones in Virginia, in the novel we would see the man. He would be in some contrast to the soldier's mustache and doctor's kindness of James Cheston. What could he be like, to exceed these things? The novel would have told us. We will never know.

Criminals

The time came for Jean to meet Michael's friends. Like his house-mates, the friends, two women and a man, were his own age, a dozen years younger than Jean, who was forty, something she knew was not going to matter to them because they were easygoing about everything, while Jean kept coming back to the fact that she had been a girl of thirteen when somebody was weighing the newborn Michael, the size of a kitten as his mother always told him, on the little scale for preemies.

She sat half awake at Michael's picnic table in the sun, waiting for his friends to arrive. Dozens of tiny birds had swooped into the forsythia and made it blink with bits of gray. They were the minute, restless bushtits she had once watched in her own yard in summer, at a time when she had paid attention to birds and looked them up in guides, a time when she had had interests.

The table occupied a clearing in the yard, under a gnarled cherry tree with a net over it. Mylar balloons printed with owl's eyes flew from strings tied to the net, and higher up, wired onto the gutters of the house, sat two large real-looking plastic owls. All of this was to protect Michael's cherries. The yard was full of lumber and sawhorses because he was re-modeling and had just finished ripping out the back steps, so going in and out of the house they had to use a ramp.

The three friends came through the gate, threw down their packs, and shook her hand. Before she knew it that part was over and they had opened beers from the cooler and straddled the picnic benches. They cut into Michael's bread and soon they were all, all but Jean, talking lazily in the sun. They were complaining about music. They didn't know all the songs the way they had even a few years ago, when there was a song for each of their occasions, each of their moods.

They seemed little more than children. Yet one of them—Jean could not remember which one—worked in the DA's office with Michael.

The conversation turned to song titles and Jean heard herself enter it. "I used to wonder why there's no song called 'I'm Pregnant.' A happy song."

There was a moment and then it caught. "A girl song! Or how about 'I've Got My Period,'" said one of the women, the one with the shining, light brown braid. Lisa. She had swung her long leg over the bench and begun tearing wedges of bread off the loaf Michael had made, spreading cream cheese and cherry jam, talking with her mouth full. "Well, that's an important occasion. And for some of us it was a real cause for celebration. When it first came, I mean. And then of course many times afterwards," she added, licking her fingers, "so I guess the song would be ambiguous. Michael, your jam is incredible."

"It's the cherries," said Michael. They all gazed up at the protected tree. "Starlings. They'd get 'em all." Everything you do, Jean thought, all this shoring up of house and yard every weekend, making jam, growing zucchini for God's sake, all of it is orderly. It's all planned, it's careful, you write it down in those notebooks of yours. What for? Is it important? Why be so careful and ceremonious? Of course it was because he was a lawyer—or did he say "attorney," the way people his age liked to? Why be a lawyer at all at his age, and in the prosecutor's office, when it didn't suit him—surely when he had children he would not be good at punishing them—why try to do it, or any of the complicated, futile projects he engaged in, if not out of pride masquerading as modesty and simplicity? And yet he seemed modest, simple, kind.

By a silent agreement they did not have to work at any conventional understanding of each other, they had bypassed that. If they were seriously interested in each other, and it was not clear that they were, it was in some other way.

"But why not 'I'm Pregnant'?" Jean persisted, realizing as she said it that it sounded like an effort to turn things in her own direction. Neither of the women at the picnic table had yet been pregnant, as far as she knew. Or no children, anyway. No marriages. No deaths.

"Yeah," said Lisa thoughtfully. "Maybe a reggae. Hmm. There's 'Having Your Baby.'"

"That's different."

"What about the poor pregnant teenager?" said Steve. Already Jean didn't care for Steve because of his frequent soft, confident laughter, and her suspicion that he was the other prosecutor. "'I'm Pregnant' would be like 'Oh God what am I gonna do now?' It's kids that songs are for now, they don't write them for us." He ended with the soft laugh.

"Country songs, they do." Jean looked up because this was said by Michael.

"For you, maybe." Steve slapped Michael on the plaid flannel of his small, hard shoulder.

Michael had persuaded Jean to spend a weekend with him, then another. They did not sleep together. Why was he pursuing her? The question made her queasy. I am, she said to herself, like a can of something in the back of the refrigerator: web and mold. But not mold, because I'm not alive. You don't know that though, she thought, eyeing Michael, so you can't be blamed. Or if you said "dead," it would be a metaphor.

The sun was high. It was afternoon on Sunday, on his mowed grass with the neatly stacked lumber, netted tree, tomato plants and trellised peas, picnic table, all encircled by the high cedar fence he had built, with a row of hollyhocks growing up against it. In the spaces between forsythia bushes he had planted the tall flowers, soft, worn-looking blossoms with furred leaves. That was what he liked, that suggestion, in the countrified pink flowers, that nothing in the tiny field inside the fence had to do with what was outside it—the freeway they could hear gusting close by, the courtroom a few miles down it where he went in his gray suits. But Jean didn't want to be in a little field. She was waiting for the friends to go so she could say goodbye to Michael in some acceptable but abbreviated way and get back to her own unmowed, flowerless yard, her house. Her house! Her heart gave a throb of appetite and fear.

"Maybe you should move," Michael had said. At that time he hardly knew her, her friends pointed out. But he hadn't said, as those friends of hers, friends now half forgotten, had said, "What's in that house for you?"

She couldn't tell them, but she had told Michael. *His soul.* His soul is there. It hasn't gone, not yet. I can't leave. I don't like to be away this long, a whole weekend.

"OK, Jean," was all Michael would say to her wild look. Pity. She recognized his talent for graceful pity. A person could cry in the rather sharp hollow of his neck and shoulder, certainly; she had done so. But she would not again. Tears were not what they had been on that occasion. Tears had reverted that one time to their old purpose of cleansing and relief. Usually they were more like vomiting, they worked on the muscles, and now the few times they came, mostly in the car, she felt afterwards as if she had fallen down the stairs.

"Have you considered seeing somebody?" This he threw out lightly, while he was making the bed. She had been standing at the new window the whole time he was putting the room in order because he was going to give his friends a tour of the house. She had picked up her things, there was no reason not to stand there a little longer and lean her head on the glass.

"Who, a counselor, a grief counselor?" She stopped him with her palms on his chest.

"Oh, right, I'm talking wellness." In the morning, climbing the hill in silence after he made her get out of bed and put on clothes and walk around the lake with him, they had seen it, the bumper sticker: VISUAL-IZE WELLNESS. Jean was out of shape and couldn't get her breath. The three-mile walk, the steep grade were nothing to Michael, a five-mile run barely raised a sweat, but when he walked with her he always stopped to give her a rest. This time he leaned on the car with the bumper sticker and screwed up his face. "I'm visualizing. I think I'm getting it." He opened his eyes. "I'm not going to say what it is, though. Each person has to see Wellness for him or herself."

He never came closer than she wanted. Now he was letting her stand at the window in his bedroom. If she wanted to she could stand there all day without moving, just looking out and smelling the wood; he would not interfere. He merely said, "I would not make suggestions to a person unless"—he paused—"I really wanted her to be in OK shape so I could use her and cast her aside without any qualms. Because she's older. And us young guys don't have any conscience yet. That comes when you're forty."

"Well, maybe it does. And conscience is going to keep us together?"

"Oh, you want to keep together?"

"Oh, Michael." She did like using his name. It had been the name of her son's best friend. Was still his name. Michael. She could hear it being called down the stairwell in a voice. Out the window in a voice. *Hey! Michael!* "They'll be here and you won't have any lunch ready," she told him.

"I'm not giving them anything except bread. Bread with accompaniments." But he had made the bread. There were men like this in Seattle, still.

In the mornings his room was filled with dusty sunbeams, and when she lay trying not to wake up all the way she could feel sawdust in the sheets. Though he did not have to, Michael shared the house, like most people on his street, in his part of town just across the freeway from the university. Several houses on his street were starting to receive new roofs and paint and to have their deep porches, which had been converted to front bedrooms, opened back up. He was taking part in all this, happily but with a certain fixedness, as if he had to invent the methods of renovation.

His housemates were away bicycling for the weekend. She had stood beside him to wave them off yesterday morning, with their bikes locked in frames on top of their van, two kids even younger than he, in those shiny black skintight pants everybody wore now to bike in, with small helmets and goggles, and tight mesh sleeveless T-shirts. They had shown her their slim packs of dried food. "Well, have fun," they said together, and smiled at the couple on the porch being left alone in the house, new lovers, seemingly. They were sincere, wishing Michael well, the one with his coppery beard and the other blond and open-faced. They were so direct, like Michael, that looking into their eyes Jean thought, I must stop lying all the time and just tell the truth, just say . . . nothing. That is the truth. Nothing nothing nothing nothing nothing.

Why do I pretend to be nice? she thought, shaking their strong hands. I had friends of my own and they let me be. Why am I standing here with friends of his, as if I were nobody? Because I'm nobody, she replied to herself, nobody and nothing. But she didn't mean it. She was something. Something high up and loosely put together, like a cliff nest of debris and bones and shed, hollow feathers.

Why would he have put his arms around a person like that when the car broke down?

They had met when her car stopped on the freeway. It was late at night, raining, after she finally went to see a movie. Her first in seven months. Coming out into the parking lot in the rain she could not have said what movie had played, but her head was aching with chagrin at all the color, the woman's careless babbling, the foolishness, the man's inconsequentiality, the failure of anyone to account for the emotions being enacted. Children are born because of characters like you, she thought, born and made to live and made to go through whatever happens to them because you—*you*— With a pounding in her head she drove onto the freeway.

The timing belt, Michael said later. The car just sank to a stop. She was a good driver, she had time to realize what was happening, change lanes, steer onto the narrow shoulder against the wall of the on-ramp, all before it came to a stop, like a top spinning its last and falling on its side. The rain droned on, the windshield wipers had not stopped. Of all the possible passers down the freeway at midnight—the murderer, the guy strung out on drugs who would force her to let him into her house, where he would torture her—the man who walked into the red of her taillights with his arms out from his body to show no ill intent was Michael.

He came into her rearview mirror as a shape, outlined in rain by his own headlights.

While she was explaining, she let him get into the car out of the rain, because he was short. I'm taller, she thought, probably stronger. He can't hurt me. Though when she sagged against him she felt the muscles, like small sandbags.

His pleasantness in response to her tight voice explaining that she had never had any car trouble brought on one of the bad episodes. She cried for fifteen minutes. My son is dead! she said repeatedly, shouting almost, in the shut car. He was ten years old! Ten! And he, turned in his seat facing her with his arm on the dashboard, had drawn a black 10 with his finger on the fogged windshield. There was traffic, cars passing so close they shook hers with a *whump*. So this is hysteria, she thought.

It was exactly like being drunk, the impossible load of wrath coming up from somewhere, the operatic gestures with hands on slimy face. And I, she whispered coldly, raising her head, when she got herself stopped, I was at the wheel.

Did he say, What happened? No, he must have said very little, but mysteriously conveyed his nonresistance to being told. Finally he put his arms around her. He was a hard, small man like a jockey. She accepted his offer of coffee at the International House of Pancakes.

On down the freeway to the University District he drove in his loud van, where in the dashboard lights she saw a pointed face with something impassive in it, abstracted, despite all the drama of her crying, which still seemed to echo around them. She looked into the back. No seats. Rope, boards, a gasoline can. He could tie me up and set fire to me, she thought, or lug me down the bank to the lake and roll me in. She looked again. No, there were bags of tied newspapers, bags of flattened cans. Recycling. Not a killer.

He said, "Don't worry, I'm not a killer."

She entered the House of Pancakes furtively, surprising even herself with the sight of her face, gnarled like a mop, in the dark glass of the door. But it didn't matter, because, blessedly, nothing mattered. It was the first time in months that these disfiguring tears had soothed her. She was released from all matters, in the steaming room with its brown-and-orange blinds half down like weary eyelids over the rivers of drips on the windows.

They sat down. He did not say anything sympathetic but explained again what he thought had happened to the car. Then he went to call the police, and later when she reached for the check he covered her hand with his.

"What is with you?" she heard herself say. "Are you a pervert?"

"Am I what?" he said softly, as if asking their joined hands.

"I mean, do you like suffering middle-aged hags?"

"Some," he said with a dignified smile.

TWO OF HIS FRIENDS WERE lawyers, Jean knew that, but most of them had nothing to do with his work; he had friends all over the city who sought him out. Why? Because of his unusual good nature? She ought to listen to the friends, look them in the eye, stop making statements. Of course he had told them about her, and they were prepared to like her. The fresh-faced Lisa, like a diligent little girl, was trying to appreciate everything she said from the perspective Lisa assumed her to have, of a bereaved person.

The sun shone, the birds in the weedy forsythia along the fence had begun a liquid chatter. This was a Sunday afternoon in life. And she was here. Whereas he, her son . . . had become a soul. The soul did not follow her when she went out, but stayed where it was. Where? If anyone tried to pin her down, she could not say. But somewhere in the house. It might be in search of her, because on a Sunday, until recently, she had always been there. Looking for her, in its trapped, groggy, spirit way, in its insistent delaying in the world of things, each move it made for her sake, each wrench out of stillness having, she knew, pain in it beyond anything his years could have prepared him for. She saw it, his soul, not as vapor or smoke, not ghost, but more like something pulled in strands through an underwater lattice, a net, and the strands trying to reunite, and unable to, and pulsing, pulsing to her, through the element that held them back.

She must go home. It was that feeling, still familiar all these years after his babyhood, of a period of time like a length of rope, which, when you got to the end of it, pulled you. You had to be back in that one room, reach into the crib and draw up to you the bounty, the bounty of his requirements.

But she was here in a sunny back yard, with people treating her in a friendly way. She had no wish to know them. Yet no saving antipathy was coming to her, of the sort that had yanked her out of her seat at concerts when she first tried to listen to music—how was it she had never realized she hated the jerking, sanctimonious concentration of chamber musicians?—and driven her to slam herself into booths where she had her rite of pressing herself against the wall and fixing her eyes on a white toilet until it became an unknown thing, a circle in a dark haze. She thought of her ex-husband at those times with sincere feeling, hating everyone but him. He too might be somewhere hiding in a booth.

But now, this much later, she was denied the ecstatic ill will that had been hers, like a dance she had made up. It failed her. Without that fury in her she had to sit and talk like a normal person, like anybody.

The chuckling Steve and the other woman, the dark-haired one whose name she had forgotten, had fallen silent after Lisa said in a thrilled voice, "Listen, the birds!" The dark woman closed her eyes and threw back her head. They didn't care that the tiny gray birds had just been chased away by starlings, or that the starlings produced a song like the opening and shutting of scissors.

"So how's your book coming?" Michael said to Steve. That jolted her. This silly boy, writing a book?

"It's getting there. It will actually appear on earth next March." Steve turned to Jean with his little idling-motor laugh, and laid his hand on his chest. "My firstborn," he said, and as her being, her whole scalded being leapt in the air, she saw his eyes cloud and his smooth skin darken to the forehead with fright at having said that to her. *Firstborn*. She shut her lips and detached her eyes from his—even his lids had gone red—with a smile she knew was bizarre, humble.

Lisa said, "Oh my God, congratulations!" Jean got her breath and re-met Steve's half-shut eyes. She was willing to speak, but nothing came. Lisa said, "Now, it's about the jails . . . ?"

"About the parole system. How disorganized it is. Nothing having the desired effect. And . . . and so on and so on, all my deep thoughts on the subject. My master's thesis. Expanded."

"Well, you should know these things," Lisa said sweetly.

"Maybe," said the other woman. "But it all boils down to somebody's whim, who gets out and who doesn't."

"That's his point," said Lisa.

"You guys, you DAs, I don't know," the other woman said sleepily. "Bet you would have been public defenders in the eighties." Jean looked at her for the first time, thinking maybe she and Steve were lovers, and at the same time, for reasons she could not pin down, feeling sure all of a sudden that the girl beside her, Lisa, had been Michael's lover. Buttering bread with the same detached expression, the dark woman addressed herself to Jean. "His thesis won a prize, when it came out as an article."

Jean fixed an expression on her own face of readiness to hear about the parole system. Finally, when no one else took charge, Steve leaned over and said to her, "I'm a parole officer. Juvenile."

"He's a cop," the woman said. So the lawyer was Lisa.

Maybe Jean could bring up Michael's remodeling. What .., what was involved in stenciling a wood floor? But she could not find the energy to ask, and she turned to Michael and let him put his firm, small hand on hers. This softened the atmosphere, and the four friends resumed the conversation, excusing her from it.

After a long time, during which she fell by degrees into a familiar unthinking state, Michael said, "Listen, we'll have to call it a day. Jean has to get back."

"I do," she said. "I'm sorry. I should have gone sooner. But don't you leave, Michael, I'm fine. Please stay, don't leave your guests."

"Guests." Steve started up his laugh.

Michael said, "You don't have your car here." Lisa and the other woman and Steve stood up, as obliging as the housemates. Even now giving Jean latitude to be remote, or perhaps rude: Was it rude to call them guests? Customs changed between generations. Things became funny. Things became stupid that had been normal. Her son had taught her that.

"But come in for a minute and see the upstairs. And take a look at this sander," Michael said. "It's a tractor." Steve and the dark woman stood up—she settled against him while she pulled her shoes on, so they were a couple—and followed Michael up the ramp into the house. Lisa stayed behind.

Lisa said, "I guess you must not like to drive now."

Personal. This girl, Jean felt it, had definitely been involved with Michael, and now she was his friend, a switch people he knew seemed to make without a lot of fuss. Now she wanted to be friendly and personal with Jean, cross the distance between the old girlfriend and the new, as well as the established chasm between the afflicted and the unscathed. Although Jean knew, she knew now, that people would always surprise you, most of them would have gone through something or other and not be intact themselves. It was a mistake to think the average person had absorbed no great blow, just because of smiles, the pushing of grocery carts, the driving of cars, remarriage. It was always a surprise, terrible, not kind, that this thing happened, this growth of membrane over a raw opening, and that the membrane thickened, the rawness grew more and

more opaque, and slowly vanished, so that you couldn't tell by looking that a membrane was there, and then it really was not there, it was
the skin itself, and the person would be proud of that. "It was bad for a
while," the person would say. "You think it will never end."

All right. Suppose you ceased to judge what you had done, your speed
and steering, your being on the road at all, with your son strapped beside
you in the hopeless indenture of childhood, unable to say don't take me,
not tonight, don't take me. Suppose you began to see it as something
unavoidable. He with ten years' life in him and no more. Yourself giving
birth, at his birth, to this night in which he is to be hurt unto death.

No, it must not sink into the thread of some hellish tapestry woven
in aged, excusing greens and blacks. No, there must be repayment.

Yes. It must never end.

She knew she did not want to hear whatever it was Lisa might want
to reveal about her own misfortunes. "I never liked driving," she told the
girl curtly.

Michael had told them the details, she knew. It was a story they
might have read in the papers. Jean knew people here and there might
mention it even now, whether they had ever heard of her and her son or
the other victims or not, especially on the peninsula where it happened,
where some evil destiny had laid down a road, as if a road could simply
be mined out of dark forest, and be traveled, black with rain, by week-
enders driving to trailheads and campgrounds, forgetting the road was
the den of machines of such weight, such speed—logging trucks with
their tall prongs up when they were going in empty and down when they
were coming out loaded with logs the circumference of their tires. And
so it was not farfetched that a logging truck should appear on a curve,
sliding sideways, drifting, with the illusion of slowness, on broad wings
of spray, and lose its load. Hit its air brakes hard enough to heave the top
logs off and torpedo the oncoming cars. The farfetched thing was that
some few should open their eyes in the wet, black New World of the next
minute: the truck driver, a teenager from a full station wagon. Jean.

Lisa began, "I only mention it because—"

"It's all right," Jean said, looking up and beginning the rueful smile
that said the past, for all its confounding injury, was the past. "Michael
has helped." You had to soothe people. It was the opposite of the popular

idea that people did not want to remind you or to be reminded them-selves: they did want to talk to you, touch you as Lisa was doing now, hand on her arm, and thereby touch the thing that had happened to you.

"I know you've done a lot for him. But nothing seems to convince him. He won't accept comfort. I guess that's it. I don't mean to butt in, but I'm so worried about him."

"About Michael?"

"He's leading such a hopeless life."

Michael came out onto the ramp. "Lisa, they're going to leave with-out you."

"I'm coming," Lisa said. She scooped jam onto her bread and turned. "Goodbye, Jean. I hope . . . we'll talk again, I hope."

When Michael came back, Jean considered him, his lean face with the symmetrical features that should have been handsome. But something was not in them. After a while she said slowly, "Tell me about your life."

"My life. Great. What did Lisa say?"

"She said you're leading such a hopeless life."

"Oh, she did? A hopeless life."

"I don't think it's fair, if that's true, that you haven't said anything about the hopelessness of your life."

"Wait a second. Do I look hopeless?"

"Don't just blow it off."

He studied her. "She means my past," he said, and shrugged.

"All right."

"So I don't have to tell you."

"No, you don't."

He put his hand on the table beside hers so his fingernails fit into the grooves of the wood. "I killed my father."

Jean did not move, but after a while she said, "I thought you said you weren't a killer."

"I am, though. So what do you think of me now?"

"Did you murder him?"

"Ah. She's quick. She asks the question."

"That must mean no."

"I didn't murder him, if you mean first-degree murder. Premedita-tion. Or second-degree murder. Intent. No. I killed him, though."

"I wish you would just say what happened."

"It's a story I prefer not to go into."

"But lots of people know it."

"Some people. Some friends."

"Like Lisa. I bet she's more than a friend. But not me. All right. Why don't you take me home."

"I thought you wanted to talk." He took her hand from the table and opened it with his small, hard fingers. "Here's the story," he said, flattening her hand palm up on the table and holding it down with his fist. "I was wrestling my father and I had him down. We did that a lot. He liked to do it. Build me up. Because I was small. Premature. The size of a kitten. See?" He threw his shoulders back. "We had been wrestling for a long time, in the basement where my mom made us go. We had a mat. She didn't like it, because he was big. A big, muscular guy. And me—right? We got into one of those sessions where you just keep on and on. Longer than usual. I wouldn't stop. I had him down, I was not going to let him up. He let out a groan and I kept on. And by the time I stopped, right?, and I decided to let go of him, let him up, by that time—he had died." He took his fist off her hand. The muscles of his lips had formed a slit smile. "First question, 'Of what?' Answer, 'Cardiac arrest.'"

"How old were you?"

"Second question. Let's see if you can just go right down the line with all the key questions and I'll answer and then you make the key statements. You, me, you, me." He beckoned her. "How old was I? I was fourteen."

"Why are you talking to me this way? I've never seen you this—"

"This unpleasant. Right. It's definitely the unpleasant side of me."

"I thought . . ."

"You thought I was just a nice guy. A boyish kind of a guy. The nicest guy you could have run into, under the circumstances." He had her hand back down on the ridged wood, hard enough to hurt. His forehead had popped out in sweat.

"Michael . . ."

"Wait a second. You haven't made the definitive statement."

"What is that?"

"Come on," he said, beckoning again.

"Michael, I'm tired and you're making me unhappy. I don't like this feeling you're giving me. I want to go home. I need to be there." For the first time she felt vaguely ashamed that Michael knew her the way he did, already knew things about her, knew why she had to get to her house.

"'It wasn't your fault.' You're supposed to say, 'It wasn't your fault.'"

Suddenly, as she inspected his dark eyes—brighter than she had seen them before, and smaller, as Steve's had been when he realized he had said *firstborn*—her nervousness fell away. Her fingers curled. She shut them on his and pressed back, hard. "Why would I say that?" she said.

He squinted at her.

"Why would I say that?" She leaned forward, his head filled her vision, she began to speak, right to the eyes and the twisted mouth. "When you did kill him. Why would I say you didn't? Is that what people say to you? It isn't your fault?"

"They do."

"They say that to me, too," she said.

She tore off a piece of bread. As she chewed, she thought she might be smiling as she had before, when Steve said *firstborn*, or as Michael had been smiling when he beckoned her with his hands. She couldn't be sure just what she might look like. Michael didn't turn away. He kept looking, nodding in the rhythm of the owl balloons above them. Their hands were hurting each other. Their faces were close. She swallowed the bread. Before this she had never smelled sweat on him. Under the owls' eyes they began to kiss each other, their teeth scraped, they were two people who would kill, and not go crying for mercy, they were criminals, both of them were, they went on kissing, they were criminals.

Terrarium (2018)

. . . everything is meant for you,
And nothing need be explained.

—WALLACE STEVENS,
"A Rabbit as King of the Ghosts"

I

Cherries

Aliens: Saving the Child

In *Aliens*, she saved the child. That's the key thing, we all agreed in 1986, we mothers with our coffee at the soccer game, even the ones who couldn't stomach that kind of movie, who never would glory with Ripley at the moment when she climbed into the cargo loader and said to the insect-reptile queen, "Get away from her, you bitch," though even the mothers who had not subjected themselves to a film so gruesome agreed that the director would go far, with his mixture of techno-fascism and the tender drives of the female, having rightly judged the effect of hissing acid, claps of blood, and slimy passageways—but ridiculous to indulge in imagined carnage when we live as we do, our children stalked at the borders of the soccer field, our generals marking off sectors of the map as burrows of a tribe to be smoked out and disemboweled, though no one would have said that particular thing in 1986, because it was warheads, not land mines, it was all radiation, not the rudimentary enemy on foot, not limbs blown off in markets with the candy-pull of the alien's egg canal when Ripley lobs shells into it, it was the eighties, that lull between wars, when if we prayed we prayed about nuclear winter, and our children on foot, not having found us in time, climbing a rubble on their sturdy legs, hurt but alive, temporarily saved, because from the ads for Save the Children on TV we could imagine everything but their deaths: the wandering and grubbing, gangrene in the baby fat, the fevers, the curling up when they went to sleep, the dream that we would come in time, as no one did for the captives on LV-426 cocooned in the Alien's sticky web, or for the deathward toddlers of Japan, who lay still, half fused to the tatami mat, cried only feebly for the mother's hands of charcoal, the father's carrying shoulders, ash now on the ramp to the Meiji Bridge, but then—one of the mothers saying of course salvation is the theme of the movie as it is of all art after all, is it not, and of religious myth—then, at the soccer game, over the halftime oranges, we were brooding, the mothers, on a hero, a female bent on rescue, who would not be carried on an Alien's talons at the end, a hero who would not fall or fail, would return in time, would ascend the burning scaffold shaken by lightning, where the smoke would clear to reveal the Alien rowing its appendages as the hero escaped with the child, but the ordeal of rescue would not be over, for the Alien too would crawl aboard the escaping craft, and travel unseen to the mother ship, but there the hero would not be undone in the manner of mothers on earth, but would strap herself into the cargo loader and join in combat with the Alien, the final combat by which she saved the child.

Helen of Troy

That was my high school friend. The victim was. One of the victims. Ronnie Ritchie was the most popular girl all four years. Veronica. Name saved for a wedding day. This was when there were *Archie Comics* in every house. Ronnie was nice, too, nice to everyone. All the boys wanted to go out with her, anticipating a heavenly kindness, but she spent her time with only one, Steve Vance. And with her friends, the popular girls. I was in the group, more or less by accident because my big sister had passed through the school before me as a popular girl.

Only half realizing she was beautiful, when *cute* was the word— never mind that everyone could see Elizabeth Taylor was beautiful and even Natalie Wood, who wasn't that much older than we were, was some way beyond cuteness—we were always thinking how cute it would be if Ronnie would cut her long coal-black hair and curl it towards her face. We'd make a frame for her face with our hands when we proposed the haircut. Just feathered in, like this. As it was, Ronnie didn't set it; she would pull it over her shoulder and cut the back straight across.

We all lived on farms, or if in the growing town, in ramblers, the flat brick houses called *midcentury* now. Ronnie lived in a rambler with no landscaping, but she had a car. It was a dented Swept-Wing Dodge that belonged to her parents, but often she could drive it to school because her father was a drinker home missing work and her mother didn't go out.

Most of us came on the bus; not many families had more than one car, though people outside town would have a truck parked somewhere, too dirty to take on dates. Boys kept their parents' cars clean. There were dirt roads everywhere where you could park and make out. You didn't sleep with your boyfriend at that time, but there was a feeling that Ronnie and Steve might and if they did it was all right. They broke up and got back together all the time. A lot was going on. At slumber parties tears fell for them. Steve was popular because he played football and because of Ronnie. He was not in any of our classes because he took shop. If you tried to talk to him, he was quiet and unsmiling and didn't look at you, as if that could keep you from looking at him and recalling his brothers, who were always in trouble and even in jail. Steve Vance! somebody would start in, if for some reason Ronnie wasn't at the slumber party. Steve Vance is so cute I can't stand it. Me neither. If only. But he'll never look at anybody but her. No. He won't. And she's the same way. My mom says he's a little bit scary. Oh, your mom. They really love each other.

All the teachers liked Ronnie, but they could only give her grades just good enough to pass every year. Other girls helped her with the themes she had to write and the skirts she sewed for home ec, because her mother was no use to her at home, and when she had trouble with the Dodge in the parking lot boys would leave the bus line and crowd around to help. She went to most of the slumber parties, bringing her 45s and her baby-doll pajamas just like anybody, in her red overnight case with the mirror, and listening to the story of The Hook, though not telling stories herself because she couldn't think of any. She was an only child, but she would give you anything of hers, her records and magazines and her necklace if you admired it.

We didn't go to her house. We knew what Mr. Ritchie looked like out in the half-bare yard with the mower when he was sober but we never saw her mother, Bobbie.

When we graduated, Ronnie got a job at Dulles Airport, which had just been built, in a little office in a hidden hallway. Over the years my parents would take me by her office when they were at the airport picking me up from school and we would hug and my parents would hug her. That sweet girl. Whatever is going to become of her. She was still Steve Vance's girlfriend, but she had to work and take care of her mother, who never left the house all the while her father was lying there with his cirrhosis. Her mother died before he did.

Then out of the blue she married a pilot and moved to Chicago. Out of nowhere. No wedding, just a card with a silver border that somebody acting for Bobbie Ritchie printed up, saying the Ritchies' daughter Veronica had been wed on a certain day to J—— B——, a name we all wish to forget.

Steve Vance lost control of himself and shot up a side of the neighbor's dairy barn where he had work. He was a hard worker, but it wasn't easy for a Vance to get a good job. Lucky the milking was over with and the herd out in the back field, people said, sympathizing.

MAYBE SIX OR SEVEN YEARS after Ronnie got married I was in Chicago for my radio job and I took a cab out to see her in Oak Park. She was thinner but more beautiful, if that was possible. Although it was the end of the sixties she had on a full skirt from home ec. Their house was small, not a house you would think a pilot would have. She said they had just moved there and he was working for a new airline I might not have heard of. I couldn't ask the one question, Why did you get married like that? You weren't pregnant. She hugged me and answered the questions I did ask, but she couldn't seem to think of any to ask me, so I played with her little girls in their room. Both of them were black-haired with flower faces pale against the hair, and subdued, just as Ronnie had always been, so at first I didn't give much thought to anything except their sweet beauty. The older one told me in a whisper that she was five. The little one held up three fingers.

The pilot came home at dinnertime and Ronnie had cooked in the afternoon so everything was ready. He was not as tall as I had expected, thinking of Steve Vance. Hardly any taller than Ronnie. He was wearing his uniform and shook hands with me as if I had paid him a visit in the cockpit. His grip was so hard I laughed when I got my hand back. The muscles came from working out, he said. You have to be strong to fly a plane. You have to bench-press.

While we were sitting at the table, there came a knock on the door.

"Your admirer is here," the pilot said, twisting his face. I thought, *I wouldn't want to get in a plane he was flying.*

"Mr. Purefoy," Ronnie said to me. "Our neighbor. They brought us food when we first moved in, like at home. I bet he wants to meet you. I told him my friend was coming and you were the Latin queen. He teaches Latin at the Catholic school." She smiled at me across the table because she had failed Latin. She started to stand up.

"Think you'll go to the door?" the pilot said. "Sit down. Sit down." She did. "Eat your dinner."

None of us could eat, but we tried for a while longer before the two little girls got up to clear the table. "Leave her plate," he told them. "Eat all of it," he said to her. If you see something like this you have to notice. If you noticed, why didn't you save her?

IN JAIL BEFORE THE TRIAL the pilot suffered from headache and was thought to have a tumor in his brain. There was one but it was hardly anything. Not even his lawyer thought it could account for what he did, we heard later, but it allowed him to plead guilty and be taken to a psychiatric facility for an indefinite period.

After the trial Steve Vance drove up to Chicago, identified himself as a visitor, found the pilot on a bench on the green lawns, and shot him. Steve went to prison for life.

At the time of the family murders a reporter interviewed Ronnie's neighbor Mr. Purefoy on TV. He stood in the driveway with his wife, who held him under the elbow as if he might fall down. "She was not just beautiful, she was a beautiful person," he said. Tears ran down his face. His wife patted the arm she held. She said, "She should have been a model. And those girls were her all over again."

"*Model?*" he said. "She was Helen of Troy."

We were in a land of guns. Men with guns, attacks, death, attacks in broad daylight, attacks called domestic, death, clouds of sulfur, children's heads exploded. The slaughter of children in myths and holy books passed through us as we read or did not read them. Nobody read the *Aeneid*, let alone what the Greeks had had to say. Yet at heart we were classicists, we still liked to think beauty was to blame.

Dogs of War and Peace

When smoke filled the downstairs, a dog in our city awakened the family upstairs, nosed them from their beds, and barked them all out of the house moments before the staircase caught. A year later, the paper sent a reporter out to interview the family in their new house. Where was the dog? "We had to get rid of him. He peed in the house, he growled at everybody. He was old."

On the field of the Battle of Marengo, where almost fifteen thousand lay still or writhing, Napoleon came upon a dog killed in the act of licking his dead master's face. "It was the most moving scene of battle I have ever witnessed," Napoleon said.

One of his generals told a story of a dog, a Great Dane, taken to war by a French officer who was persuaded to defect to the Russians. The dog didn't know the difference, one uniform worn by his master being the same to him as another. After the Battle of Dresden, the dog was captured as he raced up and down the streets of a village in search of his master, who had been carried off the field to have both legs amputated and meet his death. Some time later, the Russians sent an envoy to the village to claim the dog. They didn't want him left in the hands of his French captors, when his master had so firmly chosen Russia over France. His big studded collar lies in a glass case in a Dresden museum.

The great Saadat Hasan Manto wrote a story, "The Dog of Tithwal," in which the two sides send a dog back and forth carrying messages until finally both sides decide the dog is a traitor and begin firing on it.

Perhaps it is merely a dictum of stories that the dog will outshine the humans. Up to a point his nature is malleable—for that, hidden in the wild animal, is what our kind must have discovered early, that and his virtues of unswerving loyalty and courage, and the suggestion in the hopeful canine smile that these things may be put at the service of the human will. Once his devotion is established, he will serve forever.

Queen Victoria bestowed a medal on a dog named Bobbie for his (or her, the records vary) bravery in Afghanistan. This was when the British were fighting what they called the Second Afghan War. Bobbie survived the Battle of Maiwand and returned to England, where a cab ran over him.

In Afghanistan in recent times, two hundred forty-four dogs, in the United Nations Mine Dog Program, were sniffing for mines.

Some time during the Vietnam War, dogs were designated "equipment," and when the troops went home, dogs who had been the happy possessors of masters whose voices could stop them in mid-leap, and for whose scent they knew to search without ceasing—dogs in the hundreds remained behind as strays or food.

In World War II, Americans put their dogs in the back seat and drove them to centers to be donated to the Quartermaster General, to be trained in what became known as the K-9 Corps. Those dogs, the ones that survived, came back with the GIs to their proud owners by ship, heroes.

Book Review

Once I had a lover. None of us said *boyfriend* or *girlfriend* the way they do now, like children. We claimed our youth as a final stage, beyond it a void. We had lovers. We were bohemians, just a moment before hippies. Just as the war was getting under way.

In our studio apartment in a former hotel we played loud music on a saved-for turntable, we cooked on a hot plate, we locked ourselves out and climbed in over the transom—a phrase that now means something else to me—which could be pushed open from the hall in case a guest of the old hotel had locked himself in and slit his wrists. We fought almost every day, we read whole books in a day. Certain short stories had more importance than anything we ourselves or anybody of our acquaintance might say or do. We would not go outside on a Sunday before we had read the book review section from cover to cover.

In a famous story, a book critic gets shot in the head. Why is the story so exhilarating, when there is a death and the victim is only a sad, mean-spirited book critic, knowing himself scorned by writers he might have idolized when he was young?

If I were to write a truthful review of this book I'm reviewing, I'd have to begin it this way. It is because of my lover that I read this book at all. It isn't a book I would pick up off the tables so crowded with tempting designs. A deli of paperbacks, with a tempting smell, fresh as rolled-out pasta. Nestled among the piles was this book. I saw a name I knew: a writer about whom I had information of my own, from of old. Once long ago he had lived in the old hotel, across the hall from the studio where we lived.

At that time he was a drunk. The writer of this book, not my lover. He would fall down on the unraveling hallway carpet after failing to get his door unlocked. My lover was always hearing the thuds and going out into the hall to help him up and into his own apartment. Once he even went in over the transom himself, when the guy had no key, and opened the door for him and lugged him in. There was a buried kindness in my lover, surfacing only for those who did not expect or hope for it.

I knew the writer to say hello to, when he was sober. We were all in our twenties. In fact we were all writers; every bartender, every bank guard by day, every waitress had something in the typewriter, notching up on the carriage return or frozen there.

I laughed more than I cried, and although I was beginning to cry in secret because of things that went on with my lover, in a small circle I had a reputation for cheerfulness. Something told me that I could play with life and it would play back, more or less like a tennis partner. I would not have phrased it that way; I went miles to avoid a sports cliché, writing for the newspaper in a high-minded way I did not see as old-fashioned and hoped would catch the attention of those above me, mostly men who would eventually settle me in the Style section and finally get rid of me.

Away from my typewriter I was engrossed in my relationship with life, and took pleasure in speaking cynically of it as I sat around drinking with men from the paper. In the high booths, in the semi-dark, smoking my Salems while music pulsed out of the grilles of jukeboxes already becoming items of décor, I sat offering life insults without end, when it was a golden fruit in my hand, hard and sweet as gold and sweet and succulent as fruit: it was my youth.

"Would you like to sample the caramel pecan tart?" I'm in Starbucks, looking out at the filmy rain. For a while the baristas brought around samples and filled out marketing surveys while you were reading. Try this. Try the tipless mug, the game for smart people.

In Chicago it did not rain in the steady way it does in Seattle, but rain made an impression there, as it does not here. Oh, on some mornings the trees along Lake Michigan were dripping, and the grass was slippery, and people walked dogs with no thought of where they left their messes, and the war was raging. When the sun came out, thin little boys from the projects, who would live to enlist, were leaping off the rocks into Lake Michigan.

It was almost fall, almost the time of the Democratic National Convention. To those of us protesting the foregone nomination of that year, the convention was just one battle of our fight to make the country our own, the fight that would go on logically, with the old giving way to the new as it logically must, and without bloodshed except such blood as we were willing to shed on the streets, because bloodshed was our subject, the thing changing and to be changed by our signs, our shouts. That was the chanted conviction.

My lover was not as engaged as I. Not in the struggle and not in our love. It would take me years to know this.

The writer of this book has, in his jacket photo, large puzzled eyes, heavy-lidded eyes propped wide with the attempt to communicate a love-hate to whoever is looking at him. Tired but glowing eyes that would do an actress credit. I say *actress* even though it's supposed to be *actor* now. Eyes of the actress: a different thing. As a ship must be *she.*

If I am sitting in Starbucks looking out and a man I often see, a street person, comes and sits down at one of the outside tables to smoke a cigarette, and he has comb-tracked wavy white hair streaked with yellow, and a neat but too-long beard, and I see his not-clean jacket and pants, and the positions of his hands, one jiggling the cigarette while the other, on the wrought-iron table, is engaged in something I could only describe as writhing, if I see this man look around, see him clench his jaw, I will have to face the fact that even if I put every truth I have in me into it, the book review I am trying to write could have no effect on him. It will never come to his notice that the book has a war in the center of it, his own war and that of half the street drunks in Seattle. On Veteran's Day he will be selling the little red poppies you can pin on.

And neither will the book under review, or any book, reach him. None of them will serve a man on a wet chair who does not come in for coffee, or save him from the moment when he carefully refolds his newspaper with its headline, "Local Troops Mobilize for Afghanistan," and passes his hand over the waves of his hair as he surveys the sidewalk deciding whether to go up it or down it. Because this is the decision to be made. Because it is the body that lives, that has to go somewhere.

Once I had a lover. To think of our pride in the word, in our little year, in ourselves when we had done nothing. Years later when wheeling my one-year-old in the park, I saw a tree. I went to stand under it, because it was a replica of the trees by the lake at a particular spot on the lakeshore there in Chicago, in the rain of Chicago. Now it was raining the rain of a different city, but I said to my baby, Look at the tree. Look, look, he said. That was one of his first words, Look! Tree. Beautiful tree. Tree dripping with the tears of a year in his mother's life. I wheeled him under, and the drops, bigger because the leaves had gathered and spooned them, splashed on his thin-haired head. He liked that, looking up, squinting and laughing.

The writer of this book: a boy in Chicago wasted on beer and dope, always alone. *Dope* we called it, tougher than *pot*, deeper than *weed*. He got up late; we heard the typewriter late in the afternoon. Did he go to rehab? Did they have rehab in those days? When we had separately gone away, did he take down the poster of a clenched fist from his door and join the army? How did he finally come, forty years later, to write this book, which doesn't seem to match up to the blurbs on the back of it? At least I don't see much *gritty* or *profane*, much with an *edge*. It's an emotional story, like those big eyes. The war is in it, but it's a love story. If a woman had written it, they would say it was sentimental. We. We would say that.

He was always alone; no one came to see him. Who did he love?

Got a tombstone hand and a graveyard mind
Just twenty-two and I don't mind dying
Who do you love?
Who do you love?

Or, for some editors, whom do you love?
Look at those eyes. They looked at me once, over my lover's shoulder, and there was no anger in them, even though my lover was explaining that the janitor wasn't going to clean up the hall carpet any more when

the guy vomited. "You need to do it yourself." Except I don't think we used the *you need to* construction at that time because the movement hadn't really begun in which we would all point out each other's responsibilities and confess our own in that solemn, communitarian way.

Those muddied, weary eyes looked over his shoulder, found me, standing there. They widened. They warned me, saying, "What are you looking at? Look at you. You write for the Style section. Do you think he loves you?"

Certainly I thought he did. Yes, I did, I thought our exhausting quarrels were a prelude to the joy and relief of agreement, the union. Just as I thought the war would be brought to an end and a lesson learned.

That boy lying in vomit has written a book I am reading—propped open on the little round Starbucks table—at the same time as I am writing this review of it. People wouldn't want to know how often reviewers do this. I'm writing it not for him, the young writer on the floor or the gray-haired writer on the back of the book, or for the veteran who walked away, or for any reader of any book, but for one person, the other boy, the one who was kind in the hallway, but not to me. For you, lost one, for you.

The Witch

In a neighborhood designed as a village square, tall women, young and fair-haired, descend all morning from SUVs. Black, dignified, almost noble vehicles, big enough, Esther thinks, for the new massive type of coffin with chrome fixtures. Not like the narrower poplar one in which her husband Lou has just been lowered on creaking cables.

In the café where Esther is sitting the tall young women line up, some of them with small children wearing miniature backpacks or sucking on bottles, to talk to each other and laugh with men in line as they order their coffee. Esther knows, from eavesdropping, that their husbands are lawyers, as was her own. Some of them are lawyers themselves, stopping here on the way to day care or taking the morning off for an activity at their child's school.

Once Esther herself was as tall as these mothers, though without, at any time, a child. Now she is a woman considerably shorter, with cataracts, sitting in a café reading a story in the paper about amputees in Afghanistan. With her magnifying glass she studies a grinning child sitting crossways on a donkey with her stump leg tied in a fringed cloth. As time goes on, the difficulty for these children will come in finding ever-larger prostheses, the article says, and marriage partners.

Somewhere, Esther repeats to herself from the leaflet copy she used to write, men, old men, old men in federal buildings, are scheduling the blowing off of a child's leg. Mercy! In front of the TV at home Esther will call for mercy, allowing herself to shout in the absence of her husband, Lou. Of mercy, he was her example. He never changed from the man she met on a picket line. Not all the old lawyers work in federal buildings. Some grow as disheveled as their clients, and begin to lose memory, and root in bulging briefcases for the stuff the younger ones get from laptops. And to be fair, some of the ones with laptops worked with Lou, and if they took a lint brush to him before he went into court, still they revered him until the day he died and on after that.

She suspects she is making a face, of infantile disbelief. Refusal of the facts.

Watching the news during his illness, with the bright, kindly expression that had always belonged to him, Lou had taken to saying weakly, "Let them all go to hell." She cannot conjure his face with its pure white stubble; it has to flash on her, as now.

At the next table a woman is telling two little girls a story. One of them is her daughter and the other, lurking to one side, the friend or follower of the daughter. The mother's hand droops on her daughter's hair, the ring finger weighed down by a diamond like a little doorknob.

"Tell, tell!" says the daughter. "Tell 'The Story of You.'"

"'The Story of You,'" the mother begins with a smile that includes Esther. "Once there were two little girls and they went to ride ponies. 'Don't be scared,' said César, the . . . oh, the man who took care of the ponies. 'I will hold the rope very, very tightly.' And they rode *all* around the arena and when they got home they said, 'Mommy, we want snacks!'"

"Yah, we want snacks!" the daughter cries with a puzzled, dissatisfied face. The daughter has on overalls like the ones Esther buys for her grandnieces, but the friend is wearing a dress. "Emily, what shall we do? I think your mommy forgot. No? You can ride the pony in your dress? Your legs won't get all rubbed? But now, Emily, I'm not sure they'll let you. Oh, I know, Kirsten honey. Kirsten wants them to let you. Now, when the girls got home, they had—graham crackers!"

"Graham crackers, yah, yah," cry the children, knitting their fair eyebrows at Esther, who is staring down the tunnel of years of desiring and awaiting, longing and planning and pining for just such a little girl as these.

The daughter looks at Esther, whips her glance away. She whispers to her mother, "*There's a witch.*" The mother looks. She shakes her head gently. But yes, a witch.

"Graham crackers!" shouts Esther in a voice that would have made the good, the merciful Lou jump out of his skin, a voice she herself hears as the bray of a donkey in Afghanistan. "That's what I say!" Coffee runs down the newspaper and scalds her thigh. "*Graham crackers!*" She struggles to her feet, while the mother places her palms on the children's cheeks and turns their faces to the window.

Crisco

You could live, then, far enough away from any city that it didn't exist. We lived seventy miles from Washington, sheltered in farmland. Our father raised alfalfa and stood guard over the family because the Rosenbergs had sold out our country. Spies. Nothing was lower, more cruel, more shocking than spying. Handing over to another country something that was ours alone.

An afternoon paper was better than a morning paper, our father said. More things happened in the morning hours than happened overnight. For some time I thought the *Evening Star*, the paper delivered to our mailbox in the afternoon, contained the whole story of every day.

Those two hunched people in coats were going to sit in two electric chairs, our father explained to our big brothers. Why? They had to. I was a baby then and my sister Madeleine was only five, but she heard, she remembers the Rosenbergs. She remembers getting newsprint on her hands from a photograph on the front page, and our mother grabbing the newspaper and heading out to the pit by the barn where we burned trash. Those two people in the photograph: Madeleine dreamed of them, and she remembers our mother coming in the dark to sit on her bed. "Someone else will take good care of their children."

Madeleine got to high school four years ahead of me, with our brothers, Dave and Nicky, already gone, enlisted. High school was more important then than it is now. There you were in closer range of adulthood than you are now, at least girls just ahead of me were, in their ironed blouses and white socks, with their permanents, their teeth staying however they grew in. Some of course were beautiful, like Madeleine, who was also slim, for the time, and tall, five eight in high school. Teachers would come up to our mother at the PTA meeting and talk about the color of Madeleine's hair.

When they were seniors the hero of the basketball team was her boyfriend, something everybody in the county knew, even grade school kids. John McCay, a tall prince knocking at our door. That year, because of an article in the newspaper, people went around calling him "Crisco." Word of him on the court, and of our championship team, had traveled as far as Washington. It was his plan to join the army as soon as he graduated, because of what was going on—the conflict, we said. This too was well-known, and the *Evening Star* sent the reporter out to write about him, what we would call a profile now. Those were just coming in.

The reporter invited John and Madeleine to the old inn near us, where she was staying, and they had an expensive dinner of roast beef and mashed potatoes and peas. She took her own pictures; she pulled a flash camera out of her pocketbook and got a shot of the two of them talking to the waiter they knew from school, who had played basketball. The napkins were cloth, so he had John sign his name on the back of the order pad.

The reporter stayed for two days and I got to meet her when Madeleine invited her to our house. "I'm sure thankful to be here and meet you lovely people and these beautiful well-behaved dogs," she said as our collies wagged their slow tails. She was from farther south, South Carolina. "I have so much fun every day," she said to our stern father, holding up her newspaper badge for him to see. "Oh dear, look at me, worse than a driver's license." I was in the eighth grade and I thought if somebody like that, who thought up the wrong thing to say and fussed with her compact, could be a reporter, I could be one—and for many years I was one, or a journalist, as we like to say now.

"She did talk about her work," Madeleine told me when I asked. "Who, what, when, where, why." Was that all? "Well, she said you have to do that in her job. Know what the story is. She said that to John when he was shy." But how, that was my question, how do you know what the story is? And if you do, how do you pull it, like a Slinky in the toy bin, out of the mess of everything else? Madeleine didn't know either. "She kept calling him *honey*," she said.

The reporter had her pictures of John, but on the second day she wanted one of the two of them out in nature, two long-legged kids sitting on a fence. She wanted a breeze, she said, blowing that fair hair of Madeleine's, so they took her up to Hillcrest Farm, where the Hill family raised horses behind miles of white cross-board fence.

I asked Madeleine, "Did you see the horse?" She had forgotten I knew about the horse. One night she and John had driven up the tractor ruts along the back fields of that farm, and parked to watch the stars. One star in particular they called their own. After a while they got out to cool off in the night air, climbed the fence, and walked into the field. When they were some way in, John stopped and held up his hand. A sound came from over the curve of the hill, where the woods were. "What is it?" "Horse," John said, and they both knew. The snort of a horse can be a farm sound, or it can raise every hair on your body. "Run!" John grabbed her hand and they raced down the hill. In the car they told each other over and over again what horse it was. The loco horse. So that's where he is. That's where they put him.

The horse was a gelding, but that had not fixed what was wrong in his brain. They had tried to make him a show horse, but he was dangerous, he killed another horse. There was a stir in the county paper, but it died down. He was a biter; he went after one of the tenants on Bob Hill's place and put him in the hospital. Of course nobody would buy him, but he was a beautiful animal and that saved him: they could have shot him but they didn't, they put him out on the back of the farm where they didn't think anybody went except on a tractor.

The reporter didn't hear any of that, of course. The piece she wrote began with how green and peaceful the countryside was, how, right in Washington's back yard, things stood still. Except in the high school gym. Sitting on the bleachers watching John McCay shoot, she said, left you more breathless than the scenery. The ball didn't touch the rim. Again and again it just poured through the net like melted Crisco.

"Crisco," said the caption under the one picture the paper used from her visit, with the ball just leaving John's fingertips. Friends who were seeing off the five who left for basic training that summer yelled the name. Even Madeleine joined in. "Crisco!"

John went overseas and Madeleine had to go away to have a baby. Our mother said not to keep it from him, but Madeleine decided that one thing herself. As it turned out, before she left the home he lost his leg. It took another year for him to get home, via hospitals in Japan and Washington, and when he did they got married. They found the couple who had adopted the baby, and Madeleine went to visit them. She got down on her knees on the kitchen floor, to beg them to let her have the baby back. "He had on rolled-up overalls," she told us. "He can already stand up, holding on. But the husband wouldn't put him down. He looks just like Nicky." That was the younger of our two brothers, the short, restless, joking one. "Calmer than Nicky, though. He looked at me. Oh, Mom, Daddy"—our father had forgiven her—"I wonder if he knew me." Here John made a move to get up on his crutches, but he sat back down. His prosthesis was away in the shop. "But he was sleepy, oh he was rubbing his eyes, and they went to put him in his crib. She came back and talked to me. That's when I begged. But she cried and said they couldn't. They couldn't."

What was the story? Was it us, our family with our dogs and our alfalfa? Was it the war, in which one brother fought—though Dave said he didn't fight, just slogged in wet boots ahead of his men, with leeches on him, looking for people—and the other died, Nicky who could never be still, and people on the other side did the same, in flames, holding on to their own baby with its bubbling skin? If you were a boy from around here born in the forties you went to war in the sixties, was that the story? Was it the period in between, the fifties with its spies? Was it Madeleine down on her knees, or Madeleine and John and their love? Or the marriage it became, with bills and children and gained weight and church and hospitals? Or was it a mad horse in a field, or the evening star?

Cherries

While the mother was picking out apples with her back turned, the baby fell out of the grocery cart into the bin of cherries. I was in Produce; I saw it all. The baby, one year old and fat with diaper, had twisted his body enough to pry a knee out of the leg hole. When he heaved himself up, quick as Narcissus he rolled out of the cart—dragged by the large infant head and reaching arms, down into the cherries.

He was pop-eyed with victory. But where was he? He was a fierce baby with the bruise of the explorer already on his forehead. A week's shopping weighed down the cart—ears of corn, blocks of cod, a gallon of milk—so it didn't clatter over. The bin was at the right slant not to dump the baby out. No howl, not a sound of protest escaped him. The only sound in that part of the store was the Beatles and the small rubbery grunts of cherries.

He did look around him, in that moment infants take to sense whether a thing has finished happening. But already his fingers were closing on the cherries. The mother had not yet discovered him. All the other women in Produce, and one man, stood with our arms still up in a preventing motion, as the mother turned around.

"Oh my God," she said, entirely to herself, with no appeal for notice. A mother can be like that. In the final analysis, there is only herself and her baby.

She ran to scoop the baby out of the cherries. This enraged him. How dare she come where toys are juice, where reds are flesh, where blacks are joy, and roughly grapple him against her body? How dare she clutch him, wipe his lip to soreness, pry in his mouth, dislodge the juicy thing in his cheek with her finger, and fumble sweet-smelling globs out from under the bib of his overalls? How dare she hold him up and away from her dripping red juice, while people circle their carts around her and laugh?

The baby had no way of knowing they were admiring him and laughing for that reason, suddenly aware of babies, cherry season, summer. He lifted his wronged soul to heaven in a hoarse, masculine yowl.

This happened in the summer before the war. The war was on its way. But that day in the store there was no reason to know of or think about any other baby, let alone one being born in the opposing city. How could we know another boy fierce for every delight was coming into the world amid groans and laughter, the summer we watched the rescue of a baby of our own from the cherries? And even though this year we have the news of the other one, with his life-span of a year, here we are recalling the one in the cherries instead.

What We Found

From another dimension we came, our race. We joined your world, which was radiant with the light of your star, as we could tell without eyes. Of the many creatures we found, we learned you were the ones from whom we would have to be born. When we grew eyes we saw the copies made by you of everything we found. We heard, though we had come from the infrasound and it was almost lost to us when we heard. We could hear the sound your world made, a hum, louder in the afternoons. We found we could be you, we sang your songs, we ate your animals. We studied, we learned how to explode your bodies. We made war, we grew frail, our skin hung loose, we died. It made no difference to us. Our own kind marveled at what we found.

2

The Infralife

The Tamarins

A red-haired baby had disappeared. The hair was important because it would be hard to snatch a red-haired baby and escape notice while you were trying to get away.

For one moment the nanny had stepped forward to look at the tamarins: tiny golden monkeys behind glass in the Tropical House. Actually red-gold, as the nanny wild with tears told the policewoman, and that was one reason she had stepped closer to look, because they were so beautiful, the same flame-color as the baby's hair.

The nanny was sixteen. She was more a summer babysitter than a nanny; she wasn't old enough to be a nanny. Still, the mother who had hired her called her the nanny. It was a beautiful day in summer; she had not been to the zoo for years.

How long did she look? For a few seconds at most. For the monkeys were so small they could have sat on the palm of your hand. There they sat, or not so much sat as bloomed, silk blossoms on the limb of the artificial tree. One looked right at her out of a tense preoccupation, round-eyed, as if she had interrupted something it had to memorize. Unimaginably small.

Unimaginably. Someone had lifted the baby out of the stroller. Someone who must have been following her, someone without conscience, someone desperate.

Why take a baby to the zoo in the first place? Because the mother suggested it. She had made the suggestion to the nanny, for one of these golden afternoons, a mother who did not, sometimes, seem certain what age her baby was.

For half an hour the nanny had been pushing the stroller with one arm and carrying the baby with the other, holding her close to quiet her after her bottle. She had just laid her carefully down, asleep, and locked the seat belt that keeps a baby from lurching out onto its forehead—as the mother of this baby had once allowed it to do, leaving a brownish plaque in the satin of the forehead.

Of course the nanny had fastened the seat belt. No, she could not be mistaken.

And the plastic lock should have made a click. But there had been nothing. This was a baby who, once asleep, stayed asleep when you picked her up and walked with her in your arms and laid her down.

The nanny actually began to push the stroller. But there was no weight in it. The baby was gone.

She screamed. And the mother, who, according to police documents, had only with the greatest reluctance turned her baby over to a babysitter, was an unstable woman who could not stop screaming, herself, and was to disturb many lives.

Fifteen years can go by in such lives, as in any life. The nanny has grown up, married. She has a son. She has managed everything: carry-on, diaper bag, magazines to be torn up by baby fingers, extra blanket. She is in the window seat, reading the emergency instructions.

In the aisle a man of about thirty, her own age, studies his boarding pass. His disbelief is exaggerated; it is not so frankly unbelievable, after all, that he, in his suit, should be seated next to a baby. "Shit!" he says.

The woman bends over the dark head of her sleeping son. The man sits down, crossing his legs into the aisle. If he had glanced over, he would have met her large, tense eyes. But he would not hear the voice she hears, at its loudest whenever anyone is angry, or blind to the singularity, the sanctity of this baby to whom she has given birth, or of any baby, any unrepeatable baby: the echo of her own voice crying over and over, "It was just for a second. I took a step. Like this," as people roughly take hold of her as if the step might be the first in an attempt to run away, and many pairs of eyes scour her face, as the years before she can live as a person again begin to tick their first seconds. "That's all I did. I looked at the tamarins."

Ghost

"I don't look like much, do I?" A bald woman was standing at my table. I was at a window table in Palms, a café where the late-afternoon sun passed through palm trees in tubs and made a leafy pattern on the floor. I was waiting for my friend Barb, who was coming over from the hospital across the street as soon as she finished her chemo.

Pigeons, lavender and white and speckled brown, milled around the sidewalk tables on the other side of the glass, inside a half circle of the same brown-edged tropical palms I had been pitying in the café because they were so far away from their rightful life, like cars up on blocks. Palms was a sunny, shabby place where diners tired and bemused by lengthy medical appointments across the street, or not hungry, or touched by the birds' low, rippling plaint, gave in and fed them.

"I don't look like myself, that's for sure," said the bald woman.

Then I saw it was Barb.

"Of course you do!" I leapt up so fast the pigeons scattered. Hugging her was pressing a little clutch of cat bones to my chest. "I'm so glad you could meet me! What shall we have?"

She said, "You mean eat?"

"Something light?" I was feeling for what she might be able to eat and what would be involved in keeping up my end.

A wave ran through her, from the top of her head down through the ribbon-arms hanging out of the armholes of her skimpy yellow shift, to her white ankles that looked as if they would give like wax if you pressed them. "I don't want to do *anything at all*," she confided as she slipped into the chair, "and I don't."

Barb was one who had always gone around in linen pants and heels, driving a Volvo station wagon, staying on top of her job as a real estate agent as well as the many activities of her children.

She had no eyebrows or eyelashes to shield her big eyes, nor did she wear one of those jersey turbans, and her scalp had a veiny glow as if she had scrubbed at it with a loofah. She held herself by the upper arms as you might hold a child to stop it wriggling. "I could have been perfectly happy all along doing nothing."

"You could." I went along with her, as you would with a child. She was the size of a child.

"I could be happy right this minute despite the well."

"The well," I agreed.

"*The well.* There was a time when I would have hated you, for instance, without even knowing you."

"You *know* me! Oh, Barb, it's been a while, I know. I feel terrible. Oh, I never meant to be such a poor excuse for a friend."

"Never mind about that. That's the least of your problems," she said cheerfully, looking at me through the goblet of white wine that had been set before her without anyone having come to our table to take our order. Then I realized that of course she must be a regular. She drained the glass as the pigeons flew up and sailed over the traffic, as one, to the spotted sills of the hospital. Watching them, she leaned back and threw her arms wide, revealing a child's smooth armpits.

"What *is* my problem?" I said. "What is it?"

If she said I had led a meaningless life, I would not argue. So much had gone wrong. What had made me take part in so much that did me no credit, and so little that I had once aspired to?

"One minute." She held up a finger and stood up.

While she was gone, shame, remorse, and resignation worked up to a kind of charge in me. Oh, I could feel the arrival of an urgent but joyful moment. For me, it was not too late.

But she did not come back. Music came out of big dusty speakers the restaurant had hung from the ceiling. It was evening. Now there was a hostess at the counter leaning on her elbows, looking out the window with eyes half closed. I went to ask if she could go with me into the ladies' room. I wanted her with me just in case.

Barb was not there. The hostess opened the door of every booth, and did not make light of the situation. When I tried to pay for Barb's glass of wine she said no. How good some people are, in the world.

"Have a good evening," she said. "OK?" She was watching me. "I hope you find your friend." The sight of me had creased her forehead. She thought I was one of them, the ones from the hospital across the street, who come and go all day, endangered and confused.

Stay

Once there was a big farm in our county where the Greeleys raised prize Angus. When her parents died Gwen Greeley kept fifty acres for herself and leased out the rest. Her mother had been a member of the hunt and raised a few hounds, finding she was good with dogs, but people always said her daughter Gwen was the one who had a real way with them and could get one to talk if she wanted to. Gwen had remained unmarried and dedicated herself to them, in compensation as people said, though our mother said that when you saw Gwen work with her dogs—in addition to foxhounds the Greeleys had always kept black and tan coonhounds, a superior dog, and better with some midnight fence-jumper mixed in—you might think it could have been the other way around, a husband to compensate if she had no dogs.

If you had a dog of Gwen Greeley's, or a dog of your own trained by her, you had a good dog. She had trained Rusty, the first dog I remember, a red setter old when we were little. "You know setters can be smart or they can be brainless," our mother said, "and when he was a pup he was the brainless kind. Gwen Greeley got him to the point where he could look at you and know what you wanted. He was a third parent to you babies. He would sit till the sun went down if you told him to stay."

If she heard of unwanted puppies Gwen would take them off a farmer's hands before he drowned them. Not many local people took advantage of the offer, though few at that time would have a dog fixed. Word of her made its way to Washington, D.C., and city people of all kinds would drive out on a weekend to get a puppy. Of course kennels and breeders existed, but they weren't the everyday things they are now. You could get a coonhound from Gwen, but her interest wasn't in breeding, coaxing out some trait or other for an outcome. She took whatever showed up in a dog.

We were born around that time and got all this from our parents later. Gwen had kept a tractor in the barn and turned the empty stable into a kennel. The tenant farmer on the place remained in his house, too arthritic to work but able to rattle his truck out onto some field every day in a mime of work. The truck had a winch. He would pick up branches while Gwen took a chainsaw to a corner of the woods, hauled and bucked up the trees and stacked the wood for fenceposts.

She had money but she was the kind of woman who set her own fence. There are women like that in every decade, but I believe that in the fifties, and in that place, our county, it was rarer to find one than it might be today. She got rid of the big tractors but held on to the little Farmall and all of its parts, one of which was a posthole digger. Only someone who has set fence will know what is called for physically in fencing five acres. She had some chain link in the two kennel runs to keep certain dogs apart but let them see each other, but she wouldn't have metal fence on the land, where she had enclosed the five acres so dogs could run free and chase squirrels. It's hard to keep dogs in with a wood fence, but it was known in the county that Gwen Greeley's dogs did not jump one or dig under it. There was barking to be heard at times, but the whole layout over there was in good order, our father remembered.

Dog training was not the business it is now. The people who could afford to board their dogs in a kennel could not expect to use Gwen's if they went away on vacation, which people around there weren't in the habit of doing anyway. You could board a dog only for training, and that was a hobby, especially for a woman, rather than an enterprise. She did it as a favor if she liked the dog. It wasn't even called training. It was having a poor hunting dog or a young dog with an itch to chase cows calmed down by Gwen. She had made a little ring of a cattle-loading corral, and with no fuss, after a week or so with a dog she would have it sitting still in the presence of a squirrel.

•

CRANE EWING WAS A YOUNG man then. In high school he had gone away to New England, "to a boarding school" our parents always said with some pity. The name of it meant nothing to us. His mother was our mother's friend Louisa, twenty years older than she was and gone now. When Crane was in school Louisa pined—he was the only child—but the school was a tradition on his father's side, to be followed by a certain college and then law school and a looked-for entry into John Ewing's law practice in town. In time Crane was near the end of all that and was said to have a fiancée up there. Whenever he set foot in town, people talked about him. His looks had given him a local fame. Not looks, beauty, our mother said when she was reminiscing. This was years later; home from our colleges, we sat at the dinner table and smiled. Beauty! She defended herself; she didn't mean the black-haired handsomeness that could have tipped Crane Ewing over into Hollywood—"Really!" she said sadly when we laughed—from the school plays his mother went up to attend. He was too smart for that, and set to follow in his father's footsteps. Beauty was a different thing. Louisa Crane had possessed it, in the time when, if a woman was called a beauty, nothing more had to be said of her.

But Crane drowned. He drowned in a sailing accident on a cold bay, and after a disputed amount of time had passed they found him and pulled him off the bottom. Maybe because of the sight of his face (so white, and not bloated, as Louisa told our mother), they went to work on him, and somehow brought him back enough that he could go into the hospital and lie there for two months. He emerged from his coma and stayed for a long period of nursing, and then, half a year later, they brought him home. There he made a steady improvement, but his old self did not come back to him. He was slow and clumsy and down to skin and bone, having lost his muscles, his whole upright outline really, from lying in bed. He tried but he couldn't stand up straight. He couldn't see well enough to read, his mother said, though the word was that he couldn't read, or pronounce his words, or remember anybody much except his parents.

At home he would sit on the floor with the dog for hours doing nothing. The Ewings always had German shepherds, alert animals, and his mother was surprised this one would stay there on the rug for any length of time when things were going on out the window for him to check on. She remembered how her son had felt about their dogs, how all the way into law school, despite all his girls and boats and studies, he had missed them. The one from his grade school days had sickened while he was away and he had made the trip home in time to see her alive.

One day Louisa drove to Gwen Greeley's place and talked to her in the house for a long time. The next time she went she had Crane with her. Gwen was going to take him around the place, but he got himself over to the old stable and met the dogs on his own while his mother and Gwen were talking. Gwen agreed to employ him to clean the kennels and work with dogs and pups if he proved able.

He could go back and forth, but he had to be driven. Eventually he expressed a wish to stay there, near the dogs. His mother hesitated, but he wasn't asking for anything else in his mumbling way and finally she spoke to Gwen, who moved the Farmall to one side and framed up a little room in the barn, with a toilet and shower where farm washtubs had once been. His mother began coming with his clothes washed and foods she said were his favorites though he did not show much interest in food except the potatoes Gwen was always frying up. Gwen had a back porch overlooking the pond and woods, and after a year of this she closed it in and the three of them, his parents and Gwen, settled Crane there. More or less of its own choice, one of the dogs began to stick close to him, became his, and moved into the house. This was one of three or four coonhounds Gwen had kept for herself, a dog named Shady.

It took his fiancée, Elizabeth, two and a half years to feel ready, as she wrote the Ewings, to visit Crane. It was the first time she had seen him since the period in the nursing home after he drowned, when they were tackling his bedsores and what they called "activities of daily living." Fortunately his beauty, our mother said, had survived where so much else had passed into cold water. Despite that, her first sight of him, coming at his slow pace from the kennel with a black hound, must have soothed her conscience, as she was engaged to be married in a few months. "I've taken my ring off," she told Louisa when she first arrived. "That wouldn't matter," Louisa said, perhaps unkindly.

But in her two days with the Ewings Elizabeth became distraught.

"Oh, that dog! Shady! That dog sleeps in his bed, all wrapped up with him. I don't know, I don't know. I mean, it isn't just like a dog sleeping in your bed. Oh God." Louisa took her back to the train the next day, and stopped on the way back to see our mother, who listened with sympathy, although it was uncommon then for women to confess any awareness of anything perverse. Everything was just plain strange, the girl had ventured to say in the car. You had a woman in her forties who dressed like that and worked like that and had an obsession with dogs, and then you had a man who had some of the same knack with them, after what happened, and thank God for that, but he was disabled in many ways of course, and had to be treated in a certain way, taught, warned, instead of allowed whatever came into his mind, what was left of his poor mind, he who had been going to be a lawyer! "There's a lot left of his mind," Louisa said.

And then, as my mother loved to tell her grandchildren when we saw the old woman Gwen and her bent husband in town, they lived happily ever after.

Tarp

I saw universal love," said Cheryl. No one took the bait, no one said, "What did it look like?" Cheryl was a bond they had, after six weeks. She could bring on a silent fury in most of them, including the four other women.

Conklin said casually, "Burroughs said what he got from heroin was 'the crackle of the universe.' Don't worry if that excites you. It would anybody, don't you think?" A murmur of agreement. He said, "No, proud fellowship of the ring." That was their circle of chairs. "The fact is that it would not. Most people are not looking for the crackle. They're doing whatever else. You here in this room—you're a rare lot." He laughed in his bitter way. Conklin was a writer in his spare time; he was Australian and the accent was a help to him in this setting. They had to listen to catch everything.

Cheryl belonged to some screwy Pentecostal church, but she had gone beyond the church into universal love. Something that sounded to Rob like PCP had taken her there, with whoever her righteous attitude had antagonized apparently not suspecting that she was the type to fall, in time, all the way into the hell she believed in, to the point of checking out mentally.

"I had that happen," his friend Rocky said in reply to what Cheryl said. "Universal love. It was like a tarp came down over my brain." Rocky was someone you could actually believe had seen universal love. His third wife was his for life and willing to put him in here a third time. Everybody liked him; he exuded an undespairing carelessness and gave away both cash and cigarettes when he had them. He was the only one in there Rob had any feeling for, though Rob was popular himself. Wherever he went they liked him. The apple pickers had loved him. He took dares on the ATVs, and cleaned whatever campsite or hut he was offered. He would put a complaint about insecticide into English if one of the young guys wrote it up. It would never get sent, though. They would all drink off and then sleep off their wrath.

Rob ran into Cheryl wandering in the hallway where her room was. He was there because the Coke machine was there, relic of former days. Now there were cans of weak orange juice in it, at times. "Hi," he said, a nice guy who said hello.

As soon as she saw him Cheryl sat down heavily on the floor of the dim hallway. Her eyelashes, long but hard to see from the front because they were blond, did not curl upward but cast a blur over her big eyes bloodshot from crying. Rob could feel things, like when somebody in the circle just wanted to give one of those round eyes a punch. Even Conklin. Conklin had his less-than-favorites and did not schedule the group hug others encouraged.

Some members of Cheryl's church were not hard-liners, or at least they had come to visit on the one day in three months you could see people, and brought her scriptures and mottos decoupaged onto plaques. She had a collection Conklin took away from her because of the wall hooks on the back. She could have been a pretty girl if she cut the hair stringing down her back and what, maybe wore something presentable instead of a felt skirt with a scalloped edge.

"Robbie, sit here with me," she said, patting the floor. No one called him Robbie. He thought briefly of pushing her into her room and onto the bed with that skirt up, but he had no desire to get near her and none, any more, to commit a crime. He had been in jail. He had been a roughneck, but here off and on came this gentleman, he had noticed.

He was wearing jeans and a black T-shirt. He was lean and hard from loading crates of apples. He kept working, he worked hard when he was high. He liked to work in the Okanogan with people who didn't know him. He was always polite and helpful. When they saw his tent he got invited into the little prefab structures the growers had put in for them over the years.

"Oh, Robbie," Cheryl said. "I'm so tired." She had a way of sniffing and turning her lower lip down and partly inside out like a little kid, crying without tears. Somebody had given her stuff the first time without her consent. Probably she went out somewhere and met some guy and drove him crazy with her Jesus talk, Rob thought. "I'm so tired, and my mind . . . I wish I had a tarp for my mind," she said.

"But you saw universal love." The mean guy was still in there. He saw somebody whirling her into a tarp and slinging it out the window.

"That's right, I did, one day," she said. "Oh, Jesus. Jesus. Lord Jesus, why aren't you here?" She wiped her eyes and looked up at Rob for a full ten seconds. Finally, in a whisper, she said, "Are you Jesus?"

He didn't answer, he was looking at the cobwebs hanging over the vending machine. They were each supposed to take the initiative and clean up any mess they saw in the building. He jumped against the machine several times to swat at the cobwebs, but they merely swayed in the air. "I guess I'm not," he said, brushing his hands, but her big eyes kept staring and he said, "OK OK, so what if I am?" but he did not, at that time, sit down and save her.

Two Dogs

People did not expect to be robbed in the pouring rain. In this neighborhood they didn't expect to be robbed at all, because they had fences, dogs, alarms. But this house had no alarm decals and he thought the dog was gone. It seemed the kid who had been playing with the dog the day it came through the hedge to see him was gone.

Here they all let their dogs wander up and down the street. It was making friends with the dog that got him interested in this particular house, and then seeing the dog again a few weeks later when he was around at night. At that point he was just watching, out in the rain after a fight with his aunt, checking out the possibilities. He wasn't going in. Even a friendly dog was different at night if you surprised it.

This dog had left its own yard and come through a hole in the hedge to him when he was bagging leaves. It had rolled over on its back in the leaves to show him its belly. It was one of those small, grinning female dogs with wiry hair, maybe not even a breed, not like the big animal with a deep bark at the house where he was working, that had to be held by its choke chain and penned up indoors while he worked.

Indoors was a different life, for a dog. Outside, a dog might make a run at him, but it would stop if he himself stopped whatever he was doing and stood still and talked to it. Inside, a dog stood guard. His own dog had bitten men who came to the house to get stuff from his father.

The kid came up to the hedge and called the dog back. He couldn't remember the name the kid called. A dumb name. All the dogs in the neighborhoods where he raked had dumb names.

The second time he was there the lights in the house had been out for an hour and he was tired of waiting in the rain. He wasn't making any kind of a plan because he was asleep on his feet. He was almost ready to get back to the bus stop—even a couple of blocks away from this neighborhood, into which no bus came, the bus stops had roofs—when the back door of the house opened. A woman appeared. Behind her a man's voice was shouting. She had on an untied bathrobe and she ran down the deck steps, splashed through a puddle to the hedge, and pressed through it into the yard next door. Right behind her came the little dog, shaking itself in the rain. The woman paused and folded her arms and held herself, and then she tapped on the door. The big dog inside began to bark, the light came on, in a minute the door opened. A couple stood in the yellow light, the couple who had hired him for two hours to rake their leaves, and they beckoned the woman in with the little dog behind her.

That time he wasn't sure, he was just looking. He had a piece of a Whopper for the dog if it came up the stone steps to the gate where he was. It knew him, he knew that. But if it ran up the steps barking, he would run. No one could catch him, he was so fast and light—five four and thin.

Dogs came and went, dogs died. They were run over or they disappeared, like his own dog. He wasn't sure now, but he thought his father had taken the dog, after it grabbed meat off the table and tore into it behind the couch. "That dog's a robber," somebody said. It had been marked across the eyes like a raccoon. It was necessary after thinking of the dog, his own dog, to pass off the feeling of shoulders and a head, his father's thin head, blocking the view of the dog yelping on the floor. An arm, a hand. He shook himself. A hand with long fingers, strong, that took hold and did something to the bones in his elbow more than once, a little thing, almost worse than the same hand chopping like a board.

Sooner or later a dog was gone for good. If he waited long enough to try this house, the dog in there would be gone.

Now he was back. It was raining, like the last time. He couldn't see into the garage to tell if there was a car in there, but looking at the house he was pretty sure the people were gone. No lights on, not even a lamp on a timer. You could tell when it was timers. A block away he had stashed his shoes under a car that was always there at night; he was going in barefoot. He worked for fifteen minutes in the rain, prying the lock. You had to be patient. Water meandered down his scalp and into his eyelashes. Finally he had it.

Here was a small room with clinking tiles on the floor, cold on his wet feet, and then a kitchen, with a clock on the stove glowing green. Two a.m. The rain drummed against the window. Water was still dripping off his chin and down the backs of his hands.

Slowly he turned his body, standing in one spot, finding the door, gradually seeing into a wide hallway where the stairs would be. The small things—cameras, jewelry—would be upstairs. The house was cold, the heat must be off. Halfway across the kitchen something stuck him in the heel. Broken glass. He felt away from it with his foot. In the hall his hand encountered a bulky shape, a stiff, bristling column—and then string. He moved both hands over the shape. It was a rolled-up rug, leaned upright against the wall.

Turning, he put a foot in front of him, not quite leaving the rug with his hand. The house led him. He followed it, his fingertips on the wall taking part of his weight, keeping his feet from the creaking places he could avoid if he concentrated. He knew how to make very little noise. It was good, in that way, to be small and light.

The front hall was as big as a room, and on the wall his fingers found a picture so big that at first he thought the frame was a window. Then one of those doorbells with long brass pipes, a whisper of ringing down inside the one he brushed. At knee level another shape, dusty to his fingers. Boxes. The cardboard smell filled his nose, making him think he might sneeze. That was the kind of thing that would happen in a movie, a funny movie.

In the front room, more boxes, furniture. His eyes were seeing again. The stairs creaked, even though he was almost floating as his feet touched them.

He felt certain, in the silence and the cold, that there was nobody in the house. No dog. He was watching and listening to himself. "You quit that," he told himself, in his aunt's sharp voice. At the top of the stairs he saw into the first room. A kid's bed, more boxes, another rug rolled up and propped by the door. In the hall the chemical smell condensed into the smell of booze. Riding over it came something strong, cheesy, so strong it became the only smell.

Vomit.

The hair on his arms lifted. He leaned into the room at the front, holding the doorframe. He saw a desk in the corner, a chair. In the chair was a man. He had glasses that glinted, and a hand on the desk with something in it.

Here it is, said his body and brain at once, because the thing was a gun. His joints relaxed painfully. "Gonna shoot me?" he said, very low. There was no answer, and he began to back away, in the same floating way he had arrived.

"No," the man said. "No wait, I'm not gonna shoot you." The smell of vomit was strong in the room, along with booze. "But let me look at you," the man said. "Hey, I'm just looking, that's all. It's good. It's good to see you." He spoke very slowly in a dead-drunk way. The boy took hold of the door. "You're barefoot," the man said. "That's interesting. That's very smart. There's a lot . . . a lot we don't notice, that's for sure. We don't notice *shit*. We don't know who, we don't know what, we don't know when." He let his wrist drop the gun onto the desk with a sound like a pan lid, and took off his glasses so he could rub his eyes with the other hand.

He could see the man's eye sockets but not his eyes. He could have jumped for the gun, but he let his knees sink forward and raised his cut heel. He was not dead yet, he was very light, he was ready to fly.

He twisted so fast it hurt, away from the door. As he hurled himself down the stairs he heard the gun go off, and he hung in the middle of his jump waiting for the bite in his back. When it did not come he said to himself, *Outta here. Out. Out.* But on the landing, he turned around. He stood listening. He heard something. Maybe a groan. That must have been when he did what he did.

He must have gone back, floated the stairs. He didn't remember that part. In the dark, blood was not red. Unhurriedly it would spread across a bare floor.

His lawyer said he went back. But why would he have gone? Would he have shaken the man and yelled to him? Would he have stayed in the room with him?

Housebreaking: that was the crime for which he was sent to jail. Not the shooting. The man did not die.

Was there any way he could have been stupid enough to pick up a phone and call 911? This was what his lawyer said he did. He was lucky his father was dead, his father would have kicked him down the stairs for a thing like that.

In the courtroom the man had to say exactly what happened, and even then they didn't want to believe him, because they knew who they wanted to pin it on. Even so, the man had to read a letter out loud that he had written to his son, the kid who had lived there with the dog. The man sat in the courtroom not drunk at all, with the glasses neatly on his face, and read the letter that proved he and nobody else had fired the gun at his own head. And missed, missed the place. "I must have wanted to miss," said the man.

He stared and stared across the room at the boy, and said the whole thing was a circus and he had pressed no charges and none of them should be in court, and then he shouted at one of the lawyers when she tried to wind everything up so it wouldn't go over into the next day.

Years later his memory of the man in the courtroom was less sharp than his memory of the man sitting at the desk, in the smell of booze, saying, "Let me look at you." And stronger than either was the memory of the dog that had lived there and rolled over in the leaves, and of the dog with the marked face, that had been his until his father went out the door with it one day and came back without it. There were other parts that were missing. He tried to remember what he had done when the man said, "It's good to see you." There was an answer he might have made, like say he was a fireman coming through the window. There was an answer but it was lost with the dogs.

3
Earthly Love

Hero

I keep a ball spindle high chair in a closet. It's a beautiful chair and who knows how many babies are in its history, but my own baby fell out of it. He stood up and fell. Where am I? A few feet away cutting his carrots.

I don't lend the chair. When I happen to open the closet it looks out at me like a dog I have shut in. The dog we had then was lying by the breakfast table and broke the baby's fall, such a good dog that when he landed on her she just scrambled up carefully and moved, but he cried so hard we took him to the ER, where they said he was unhurt. I have always wondered if something happened in that fall, some knowledge of empty space that determined the course of his life, that he would never try out for a sport or even learn to swim, that he would take a dog for his life companion, even for a parent instead of us.

Ben. The baby is now a man of thirty-seven. Where is he? He is lost. He had gone to live with four other people and a dog in the loft of an empty building near the stadium. Five singles, they were to begin with, and I can't express to anyone, even my husband, what I felt as they formed in the space of months into two couples, leaving one out, our son.

Ylva caused it. Ylva, pronounced Eelva, or Ulva if you could make a Swedish sound as our son had learned to do. Because of her, he is gone. But I must not blame her. I preceded her in the chain of causes. "It was your grandmother's fault," my husband will say, because she was the owner of the chair he fell out of into the life he had.

The police tell us to avoid the word *gone*, because although we do not know where he is and have not for some time, it must be factored in that we're the parents. Somebody else might or may know more. Sometimes it takes longer, if you go away, to work your way back to your parents. You might check in with a friend instead, after a certain length of time. What length? It varies. Weeks? Weeks have gone by. Months? Often months, with the young. But he is not young, and it's three years. I tell them I'm sorry to keep on like this, repeating the age of our son, describing his dog, his circumstances. How out of nowhere, in a life mysteriously blocked at every turn, the day had come when he recovered himself, found a source of—oh, found love—! It's all right, the cop interrupted me. All mothers are persistent.

All mothers: I am one of thousands. Lucky, in the world the cops live in, to be the mother of someone who reached adulthood at all. They will remain in touch with us, as they will with Ylva and her boyfriend and the other couple.

And there's the dog, Hero. Someone thinking about killing himself would have a hard time dealing with the problem of a big dog that belongs to him or in this case has been entrusted to him by someone he loved. Still, a dog cannot be relied on to stand in the way of suicide. Though where the dog is, after appearing in phone-videos taken on the bus to D.C. with a group of them who had been in the local Occupy, is another unknown.

Peter has begun to treat the whole thing as having been foreseeable—if not foreseen by us—or even preventable, had we acted in time. "What did we *do*?" he said for months, but he no longer says that, and no one but me knows he was ever dripping sweat and crying and hitting his head with his fists over his son.

I won't answer; I'm afraid to lose patience for fear Peter will leave the sort of building he has built around himself to hold his son's disappearance, or the building will fall into a sinkhole.

Sinkholes are opening all over the world, you can see them online, but that's not a subject to raise at the police station. Our faces must wear a petitioning eagerness, what we say must be cloaked in full normality, what appeared to our half-sleeping minds in bloody water and rocks when we woke up the morning after we heard from the dog's owner must not come into it.

Others from our city's Occupy encampment, if they are young, are still here, though not in drenched tents; they've gone back to houses or apartments or at least found some indoor place, and moved on to related actions. They didn't just wander off. But he, our son—"homeless" rather than "student" in the detectives' encampment count—was a thirty-four-year-old man. He had temporary places to stay because he knew priests—we had thought he might grow up to be a priest—but he could also be found at times sitting against a doorway or in an empty loading zone or in Tent City wherever it was encamped. He always had books with him.

Five of them formed a group. They pitched four tents with the flaps opening onto a table-sized courtyard. The two Swedish girls, Ylva and Margit, shared a tent; each of the three men had his own tent. Ben's was a two-man tent we had given him when he started sleeping outdoors.

Ben. He was thirty-four when we last saw him but looked like a boy of seventeen, because of his innocence. Not slow, as his teachers sometimes thought at first, seeing the round face and wide eyes, and the trouble with reading. No, he got a degree in physics, he played the piano. But few friends, no girlfriend. Breakdowns. Intervals spent in what we called "facilities."

I sat in their tent. I thought it was theirs because Ylva was there the whole time and she was holding his hand. The dog was lying on the sleeping bag, against his leg, and he and the dog looked at me together, with shining eyes. My son was radiant. There is no other word. I thought, *At last, at last.*

Ylva had light green eyes in a heart-shaped face, a transfixing face, one of those you look at until you look away in embarrassment as though you had touched it. It was like one of those faces we used to see from the highway, looming behind trees on the giant screen of a drive-in, silently speaking from red lips. What it must have been to Ben, that she looked at him, drew him to her. I could see she was taller than he was; she had come up on her knees when I entered the tent. I said to her, "I'm so glad to meet you." She had a tiny camping stove and she let go of his hand to give me, and then Ben, mugs of warm tea. I sat cross-legged as they were doing. There was no noise coming from outside; there was stillness and the filtered light you get in a tent. We could have been somewhere in a desert, drinking tea.

A boy with black curly hair raised the flap and gave the three of us an intense look. "Excuse me," he said in a formal way, and disappeared. I said to Ylva, who had been asking about our family, "I hope you don't think we're the one percent."

Her reply was gentle. She was so gentle, in the tent that day, that I began to think, *How am I causing her this concern?* Could she see something about me? Did she know I had let him fall out of his high chair? She was that way with him, too, concerned and gentle. Loving. Her green eyes had looked into his soul and she had saved him.

"Don't worry," she told me, "in Gothenburg, my father owns a factory."

"What kind?"

"They make the parts for the tractor. Different tractors that we have there. Not so many now."

I didn't say a factory could fail. I didn't say a day could come when we won't have fields, or crops, or need for a tractor. I had almost entirely purged my pessimistic remarks by this time. I had the fear of course that hearing such things in our house, things that we threw in like the darker flavorings without even tasting for them, had had an effect on Ben. She was reassuring me. "They have a good wage there of course. Though not enough. In our family, there is more than enough." I could see that, and see the parents who must have produced this girl, who had come with her friend and her tent to help America.

The dog Hero: if you kept months of lint from your dryer filter and put it on a tall dog frame you would have this dog. An Irish wolfhound mix, Ben said with pride. "He is mine," Ylva said in, that murmuring way she had, as if to quiet you, like a priestess but a gentle one, who loved animals and people. "My friend got sick and had to leave. My little *hjälte*, he gave to me."

Occupy had dispersed and our son was not living in the building down by the stadium any more either, but somewhere in his tent. Different places, he said, the two times I saw him from the car, walking the dog. Both times I double-parked and jumped out and held in my arms for a moment a damp coat with his body in it, and then he talked to me in his vague way and I petted the dog's soft rained-on fur. The dog gave me a look from his big golden-brown eyes as if he would tell me their story if he could. "How are your friends?" I said. "OK." Ben would only look back at me for so long. He kept shaking his head. He felt sorry, sorry for me, sorry for what he was. Oddly, not for himself, or I didn't think so. I don't think he pitied himself. Maybe he could have managed, if he had. It was *everything*, that he was sorry for. I told Peter that. I didn't say how thin he was, and not taking care of his hair, or that although as always he was polite, people would probably avoid him if he asked for anything. From me he took a little money, very little. It took only a few months to get from the lit-up interior of the tent with Ylva to these two meetings on the sidewalk. And then I no longer saw him, he was gone.

I got a phone call. A woman's voice said she thought her dog might have been the one I was looking for. She had found him in a shelter and had him for three years before he died.

Nero! she said. He had worn a red fabric collar with a faint name on it in magic marker. She and her husband didn't want to confuse him; they went ahead and called him by the name. But he was no Nero! He was the gentlest of dogs. She wanted me to explain how he had come by that name, but words were not coming to me as she talked. I didn't say, "No, it was Hero," I could only listen.

He was a good dog, immediately loyal, obedient to their wishes, even unspoken ones. She hoped she was not making me feel worse. She knew how it must have felt to lose such an animal. He must have been stolen, she and her husband decided. He was young when they got him, and when he died she was so surprised and bereft she called the shelter and had them look for his records. They couldn't find any, but they told her the wolfhound breed dies young—or not young, actually old at six or seven—though being mixed with another breed could make them last a little longer. Nobody remembered a collar saying Nero. "Was it a funny *N*?" I finally said. She didn't have the collar any more. The one she hung up forever on her wall was the leather one she and her husband had given him when they brought him home.

"I wonder if it could have said *Hero*," I said. "Why it could! Oh that's a relief to me!" she said. "Hero!" How did she get my number. Well, that's the funny thing, she said. Once the shelter had kept a list tacked up on a bulletin board, people looking state by state for their dogs. Computers had made checking easier, but they never had time to do it. They found two lists for her with a big gray dog on them. One was dated a few months after Ben disappeared, or after we no longer heard from him. Two people in the country were looking for a big gray dog. She called us both.

The dog came to them, they told her at the shelter, when Animal Control brought him in after getting a report that someone had seen him sitting alone on the bank of the Potomac.

My brain kept saying, *No, Ben could never have done that, left his dog.*

Then I heard his voice speak. He was talking to Animal Control on the phone. "There's a dog by the river," he said. "He's just sitting by the river. He's been there for a while. You'll see him." He must have given a location. He must have handed back the phone he had borrowed, and walked with Hero until they got to the river. I saw him sit down on the ground with him and tell him to stay. I saw him stand up, and the dog look up at him.

"Oh, I'm crying too," the woman said kindly. "I'm so sorry. I know how you must have felt about a dog like that." She didn't say, "How did he get to this part of the country?" or anything like that. She seemed to know not to. We cried on the phone about Hero.

Afternoon Tango

The husband and wife are learning the tango. They dress for the class as they do for church. Before he gets into his shirt she straps his arm into the blood pressure cuff, which folds the loose skin because the arm doesn't weigh what it did. Embarrassed without the muscle, she thinks, embarrassed at being lifted by her hands at the bare elbow. They are two weeks into the lessons, three months out from the bypass. Out from opened-up, as he says, and fished-around-in. Out from the bedside frozen in prayer. They smile at the whole thing now.

They are the oldest on the floor, the only ones who forget not to talk. She is a steady talker, a habit he knows can't be broken at will. If change comes, it is like weather, with no thought for what might be welcome. Thus his switch to a beef herd: far from the paths worn by the methodical dairy cows, a mere dozen Herefords now, ambling and scattered, for him to see to. Twice a day the dog tries to round them up.

The dance classes are new in town, held in a tall room upstairs in the old municipal building. At the first lesson she thought she might run into former students of hers, but none were in the room. She had heard about the shiny finish on the floor. The boys who put that on, brothers in business together, had both been in her homeroom. But there at the piano was a friend from school after all, the music teacher. She walked right over and told him, "We're here on orders." He hit a loud chord and waved to her husband, who was taking a folding chair off the stack.

The instructors prowl the dance floor, one torso with four limbs. They slide among couples watching their own feet, even the young ones. At the first lesson they helped the six couples, placed them just so in each other's arms, but now it appears they will teach by example, stopping here and there to give a name to what they're doing with their legs. The exit, the volley, the *sacada*. They're a young man in a tight black suit and a girl taller than he is, now firm as modeling clay, now loose as ribbon. She lets her body lie on him upright, take his form like an apron, the wife thinks, if an apron could be on the alert. He has black hair in a ponytail, she has short red slicked-back hair and a pierced eyebrow. Both thin faces are unusually symmetrical and sweet, the wife has pointed out. They could be brother and sister. Large-eyed as calves—though the heads are back and the lids half down in a way more haughty than sweet.

Atras! Cruzada! As if this couple had received orders from on high, for this class of theirs.

"Oh, did I have a dream last night about those two! A nightmare. They were in the CCU. Dancing! Whipping those legs! The nurse kept saying get out of the way, get out of here!" She is whispering because they are supposed to keep quiet and hearken to the piano. "Those two, those faces. But, oh God, you! You were in that bed, you had your eyes closed, oh—!" She tripped on his foot.

The instructors make their circuit of the floor. "Those two can't be from around here," the wife tells her friends on the phone. "It's something, when they get going." Whatever the town might be outside the tall room is nothing to this pair. Forget all that. Move! Halt! Move!

Most of the couples don't talk even when they gather their things and go down to the parking lot, in a daze of interrupted effort and vague hope. "I remember now," she tells her husband, "how tired the kids would be in sixth period. Oh, they never would say. You don't use the word *tired* at that age."

On the first day she had said, "Look at those two, they could be movie stars." When they dance, the instructors—whose faces can relax into ordinary good-looking young faces, however gaunt—wear the expression of stars, or models, those models that glare from the magazine when you're waiting to get your hair done. The tango is done with that same expression: the look of having a plan, private and fierce.

For herself and her husband, planning is on hold for the time being. At the moment, too, almost everything—ranging from the new doctor, a girl who checks off your dance lessons on her list when you go in to see her, to the new collection plates in church, heavy as frying pans— strikes them as funny. Saved up for the children's phone calls. It's enough to come up out of the chair, grab for a phone the size of a tobacco tin. Enough to live. Live and let live has always been her motto. "You tell a cow that," he would say when he was sick, when they hadn't finished selling off the dairy cows and every one would have her nose at the sky bawling because the kid he hired to milk came late.

The pills are on the breakfast table, in a new dispenser with snap lids on top, hard to pry open. "Like the root cellar." This he has said more than once lately, while they sit eating their eggs, three a week. He is not a talker but he has a few subjects, and she knows the root cellar and the effect of it on the boy he was. The door was so heavy he couldn't get it all the way up. "You had to get a stick in there and prop it. If the stick fell out, you'd have to push like the dickens or you were down in there for good."

For both of them, the tango does not so much come down to volley and *sacada* as it does to the moment when the whole thing is comical enough to stop. They dance over to the windows to check the parking lot. There's the truck, with the dog's nose out the window. The dog! In his relief he'll get tangled in his own paws while they're climbing in with him. In no time, though, they'll all be home. They will have attempted the tango long enough. If they can't do it, it's because they don't want to. All they want is to live. Live, as the tango, danced by the stern instructors, commands.

Two Birthdays

Driving to work they were early enough to stop for coffee. First they disagreed about whether the car could be parked so far into the bus zone. He went in ahead of her, snatched a newspaper from the day before, and sat down. She ordered the coffee. The place was new, one of those high-ceilinged rooms with the overhead pipes exposed, dark except for laptops and gooseneck lamps. Collages for sale on the walls, floor the new kind of concrete, ground and polished to a fine texture and then varnished, revarnished, and waxed to a seeming softness when you slid a chair across it.

The chord of disagreement was still holding and while they both looked through the paper a girl of about twenty came in wrapped in a shawl, over a dress showing one of those hems cut in zigzags. The dress was yellow satin. She carried an iridescent gold purse and had on a lot of eye makeup for the morning hours. Waiting for her order, she stood straight, with her chest out and her legs apart, and never touched her hairdo, half of it held up by a big black comb and the other half lying every which way—though shiny and clean—on her shoulders. She might have been an actress on her way to a dress rehearsal, or an art student. She might have been a girl going to work, in the kind of outfit she would be known for in her building.

The shawl was a different yellow, thin and mostly fringe, with the cloth part wrapped tight around the shoulders and tied under the breasts, a sling for two heavy globes recently called out of the warmth of bed, with only their lower halves covered by the yellow satin.

They started to fight again, and in this café they had the worst fight they had had in years. It was L.'s fiftieth birthday. B. had not yet remembered this, nor did he know how his eyes had traced, aloof and yet calculating as those of a sculptor before a slab of stone, every plane of the art student, around and down, into the darkness of the satin sling, and down, down to the exaggerated calf muscles and the bare feet in sequined sandals. "It's my birthday," the girl said to the guy steaming the milk, who gave her a slow sideways smile. He poured with care. L. knew he was making the girl one of those leaf patterns in the foam. He handed her the cup. "So it's free," he said.

Either B. did not hear—but he must have heard, in his trance of examination—or he could not be alerted so early in the morning to the forgotten date. They argued for a while and when L. got up and pushed her chair back, the industrial floor made a hushed groan. "Oh, leave me alone," L. said, as if he might have reached to stop her, whereas in reality all he had done was lean over for a section of the paper lying on the next table. Shaking his head he began to read the local news, while she turned and ran. Out the door and down the street, where it was spring, the leaves of the sycamores uncurling in their first green. Their fat roots buckled the sidewalk, causing her to trip and fall full-length, and prematurely, as the ER doctor would say with a passing kindness, break a hip.

The ambulance would arrive, thanks to a woman walking a little dog, one of those terriers always on the lookout for something at ground level. From half a block away the dog would catch sight of her and hasten on its little claws, straining the leash. The hip would have to be pinned.

B. was older, and stiffer; he should have been the one to break a bone. But he was going to suffer equally: he would have to see her pale in the recovery room on her birthday and he would have to sleep two nights in the hospital in an uncomfortable chair, and that would be the beginning of his awareness of back trouble as well as of a new phase in their marriage when they would take hold of each other at times like two on a pitching raft in an ocean of yellow satin and soft concrete.

Whiteout

They were at a cabin in a whiteout. The radio said "blizzard," but they set out anyway ahead of it, up into the Cascades. In the car they had two hours to trade life stories. The snow hadn't started and she wanted him to get his guitar out of the back and play while she did the driving. He didn't want her to drive his van, and he had to tell her so. I've never seen you drive, I know you don't pay attention, and you're stoned. She said I am not. I do pay attention. You'll see.

They were students in the same new major, ecology. He was going into organic farming and she was going to be a poet. By the time the snow was coming down heavily they had left the car at the fork onto the Forest Service road and hiked in. They knew the cabin, her friend's parents' cabin, was a little way off the road on a bluff above a river, but they couldn't see how high or how close to the cutbank. They unlocked the cabin door around five, when it would have been dark but the snow was making its own light. On the porch you could sense the dropoff where the snow changed contour and there was the glow of an edge, and she was afraid. While he built the fire she took out her roach-clip earring and lit up with a shaking hand. I wish we couldn't see out. We can't, he said. She was the one who had insisted on coming. Come on, really, let's go up there, I've just got this impulse. I want to. They hardly knew each other, although they had spent time in class looking at each other. He blew on the fire and said don't be afraid, but her dread was already going away, and soon she had no thought of anything but getting the stove going and then the sleeping bags rolled out, and then him. She was wild. He told her so in wonder, in the night. You are a poet, he said. A poet of this. It's not what I want to be a poet of, she said. The snow coming down whenever they switched the flashlight on—how could that descending load of white make no sound?—got her pressed so hard against him from chest to foot that the sun coming at last through cracks in the window frost saw them as one form. Later they rubbed out the frost to see the river, so far below them it was a long black shape with no force, relaxing its way through white boulders. He thought so. Oh God this is high up, she said. You could jump straight down. Why didn't we have to climb to get here? Because we came up the mountain in the car. How do we go down? He didn't have snow tires but he soothed her. How can somebody so wild be so chicken. We're fine. I'll take care of you. In the seventies you could tell a woman that. They had boots. The place had stacks of firewood and they had food. Hardly eating anyway they lay three days beside the stove.

We were beauties, too, don't forget that part, she would say when they saw each other again over the years. You were, he said. You were, she said. The verb was a tide going over them.

They would look for each other every time at a particular conference about water. Water was disappearing. She had poems about it. Her books took up space on a shelf and she was well-known as poets go, but disturbed Nature was her material and she had gone on attending the conferences, which grew more grim while the two of them sat down to catch up with their stories in hotel bars, laughing in their booth. They each had a spouse. Spouse: what an ugly word, wrong for the ones we had the luck to find. Each the right mate. *Mate* says it all, they agreed. Good marriages, his quiet, hers stormy. Kids, his successful, hers what he always called seekers. The problem she returned to after a few drinks was dread, cold dread—don't give me *bipolar*, see that *polar*?—and worse, in her case, the meds for it. Could he tell? No. She seemed fine, he said. Very alive. She had signed herself into a couple of places. What did they say. They said not to take pills, except the ones they said. Not to love three men. Well I hope I'm one of them. You are. Naked man at woodstove. God. Eventually, their mood in the bar having risen steadily to a kind of elation, they got down to mistakes made. They had to lower their voices and curb their shouts of laughter at certain episodes of middle age, foretastes of despair, though he admitted that for him despair was a track he could play in the background or not, he wasn't going to say his life was wasted while he went on with his days teaching undergraduates in a ruined prairie city. Prairie, she said. The land ocean! Remember that geography class, that professor, the woman, who said we had to train. Train for saving the earth. No geography departments any more, he said. This is as close to departments as I want to get, she said. Why do you come, he said, knowing.

They never got in the elevator and joined themselves in a room. They never did. The heart sagged in him when he realized they never had or would. The year she didn't show up at the water meeting he didn't ask anybody. She was missing and then she was found. His wife saw it in the paper and he said that's OK I'll read it, though later they both read about the intention or at least the fleeting impulse, in a poem called "Whiteout."

Forced Entry

Before she got to the top step Louisa saw into her bedroom where a man's leg hung off the edge of the bed. A foot in a sock, jeans. At first she thought, *Kent!* But that was not Kent's sock, Kent's narrow foot. Holding the banister she backed down a step. But of course the man must have heard her come in the front door, heard her clattering on the stairs bare of carpet. Living alone in the house she had yanked the carpet up herself, scattering tacks and staples in a frenzy of change.

A voice came from the bed, not words but a groan. She found herself going up. "Who is it?" she called. The groan came again. On the bed, her bed, lay a hefty man with closed eyes and one leg hanging down. He had on a blue work shirt and jeans fastened below the belly. He was so big the mattress sagged. The pillows had been thrown on the floor.

Had she—had she hired somebody? To do work? But how did he get in, and what work? No, she had not called about anything, scheduled anything.

Who was he? What was the matter with him, groaning on the bed?

As she went forward she could feel the pinched look on her face, like that of a minor character in a movie who did not have to be attractive because she was just making an appearance before being killed, because she wasn't really part of what was going to happen in the movie, just a character to be killed.

The fat man opened his eyes, which were the blue of his shirt and forked with red veins. *Help*, the man said out of the side of his mouth. His lips wouldn't close, he could have been saying *hell*.

She picked up the phone on the bedside table and dialed 911. There's someone here who's had a heart attack. I don't know. I don't know who. Yes, breathing. No. No. I live here. I know it's a heart attack. It's obvious. So come *now*. She gave the address.

He had spoken, so he was breathing. She didn't have to start CPR, which she could not remember how to do. Five breaths? Five punches on the breastbone, measured up how far from the last rib? Or now it was thirty punches, and between the nipples. But what if the breasts sagged? Between the nipples could be anywhere.

The man's face was an off shade of red with a bloom of gray over it, like meat left in the refrigerator.

He dropped one arm off the bed and the knuckles hit the table leg. The other arm he kept folded, giving the fist a sentinel position on the fat chest.

The room was cold. Her eyes passed the four open drawers of the dresser and reached the window, pushed open as far as it would go. And there—the top of a ladder.

He must have found the ladder where Kent always left it, lying along the basement windows under a tarp. She had complained that that might not be a good place to leave a ladder. Someone could stand it up and climb it.

I don't want to have to lug it out of the garage. I want it there when I need it. That was what Kent had said.

She had said, So you can climb down in the middle of the night.

Right.

Escape. Instead of walking out the front door.

Right—like a man.

I didn't say that. I bet *she* says that to you. I bet she says, You really should go out the front door like a man.

Just leave the ladder.

And now, like many things predicted by her, since she never gave up her belief that prediction was a way of preventing a thing, that one about the ladder had come true. And she too had done nothing, after all, after Kent was gone. She had left the ladder lying there under the tarp.

OK, she thought. I see. Mister, if you climb in the window of a house, it's going to go wrong. Any movie can tell you that. I could have told you.

When the aid car pulled up she was standing with the door open. She pointed up the stairs and ran up behind the two men. Except one was a woman who looked like a man, but a nice, provisional man, in glasses like Buddy Holly. That one had a red fishing tackle box and a backpack, and the man with her, or boy because he looked no older than Louisa's son had in middle school, carried a defibrillator, shears he was already working with his fingers, a blanket, a cell phone, and a pad of yellow paper.

The one who was a woman asked what happened and when. Louisa said she hadn't been there. The woman gave her a mean look as if to say, What's with you? The man on the bed gave a heavy groan. For a while the two were busy over him, slitting his shirt with the shears and talking loudly into his big ear, which had gone from red to white. Yep, one of them said. Not so—yeah, the other one said.

She stood close to them but out of their way, thinking she might not have the pinched expression any more. Her heart was no longer pounding. She pushed her hair off the sides of her face. A man on a bed, a fat man in a blue shirt who had eaten himself into a heart attack. Who had put the ladder up and climbed it. Climbed in the window of her house.

Now it seemed she was the central character. Her face was wet; her teeth were bared in an expression she could not identify from the feel of it.

She said, Help him. Help my husband.

Seurat

After she fought with Barrett, Chris yanked the keys off the hook and slammed the door. She didn't hit the brakes until the big intersection, where she realized how fast she was going, and without her glasses. She had torn them off and left them on the kitchen table. She could see them lying there in their new frames. She had a vision: she saw Barrett get up and slam the cast-iron frying pan down on them, splashing out the wet colors of his ratatouille that had been simmering on the stove. The bell peppers looked like fire, yellow and red on the table. Dabs of heat such as Seurat, the subject of her thesis, had painted in *Invitation to the Sideshow*, the study for his circus painting. This calmed her.

No, Barrett would not slam a frying pan. He would never do anything to free himself.

Sunday, late afternoon. Pinot on the counter, butter lettuce washed and draining, chanterelles sprawled on terry cloth, their gills almost moving. But not. You did not have to eat animals to have a fine dinner. You should never have taken animals into your body in the first place. Yet if his mother said you had to go to the bullring in Oaxaca and she was paying for everything, you had to go, both of you, even though he couldn't bear to look at what went on and his parents knew it and were testing him, testing both of you, by shouting *Olé!*, both of them, into your heads until by the time you descended out of the glare into the stripes of dark at the toilet lines you were so lightheaded you grabbed hold of him but he was the one who blacked out. And as for caring about animals, what about a dog? Why couldn't you and Barrett have a dog? Because with dogs came germs. And because—Barrett added this to what he had been taught, his list of restrictions—no dog wanted to live in a city. No dog would choose such a thing. But in the city now there were more dogs than children. Some of them must like it. Weren't their pleasures tied up with humans?

Pleasures?

Wasn't there some pleasure, somewhere, that you and he could have? Other than the perfect meal or the exact— This isn't just— Something's wrong. Something is wrong with you. That was what she had said to him. She had thought it so many times she wasn't sure she had said the words until they altered his face. Then she realized, of course. No, no. What a cruel thing to say to someone who had something wrong with him.

That wasn't all. She said more. She said he wouldn't kill an ant but he might kill her. He, who had never done anything to anybody. Who had that mother, with her goading laugh.

It had rained all night and the streets were wet. She slowed down, drove carefully to the University District. Several times she circled the block where they had lived as undergraduates. It was near the campus and on the sidewalks girls with ponytails were coming and going from the sorority houses, talking on their phones, still wearing halters though fall was in the air. The big wet trees already showed entire separate branches of yellow or red, like insertions from another dimension. She parked in front of the house she had lived in, and looked up at the patched window screen of what had been her room. Barrett had lived there too, in the basement. He had glued a square of new screen over the hole in her screen so that a wasp from the huge nest in the laurel couldn't get in and sting her. Nobody in the house wanted to get rid of the nest. The wasps weren't hurting anybody. In that way their housemates in those years were hardly any different from Barrett. Everyone was a vegetarian, so why when Barrett said anything about an animal was it so oppressive? She looked for the nest, which she had been seeing for years when she parked there: dim silver cone as big as a grocery bag, hanging behind the leaves. It must have long been emptied of wasps. She had lived here ten years ago. Wasps didn't maintain their dwelling year after year, did they, like bees? But there it was, after ten years, in tatters as if someone had flung a gray nightgown in among the branches. No one took care of what grew against the house; they were students.

He had lived in the basement. One day she had said, "Come upstairs."

Tears she had stifled during the fight came to her eyes. No! No! No! Your parents can't come. Not again. Yes! Yes, it would kill me to be nice to them, yes! You hate them! Your mother hates us! No I won't get married to please them. No I won't marry you.

She drove around some more, past the sprawling brick churches with all the social programs and the hills of the campus with the big trees on them, remnant of northern forest, or no, these, spreading and deciduous, were not rainforest trees but maybe some kind of diplomatic-gift trees like those in parks all over the city, given in some time period—because they were all tall and old—when countries offered each other without embarrassment solemn, lasting gifts.

On The Ave she drove slowly, looking at all the places where she had begun to make him laugh. None of the restaurants were the same ones. She had the windows open, and despite all the noises she could hear her own tires. Strapped into a large machine with fire in it, rolling, filled her with a sudden uncertainty. The car leapt out of her grasp. Hit a bicyclist. No, a pedestrian. But no, it did not. She didn't do it, she saw it. A thing so plausible, so almost likely. Was she as crazy as Barrett? She passed the movie theater. She would go sit in the dark. She couldn't go back to the house.

Because the students were flowing back into the District for the new quarter, it took time to find a parking place and walk back to the theater, where she found the matinee half over but sat down anyway.

"HEARD THE SIREN AND I went over to check on the guy. Your husband," he said with no question mark. "I was just sitting here watching TV." He looked at his wife. Something about the wife's face said no, he was asleep like he always is. All the while he told the story, the heavy unspeaking wife sat on the couch with her hands palm-down on her thighs. She made Chris think of those bras where the whole bunched-up volume hums of the underwires. If you painted her you would have to get the hum. Chris had spent enough time with paintings that she had given up trying to be a painter herself. She had given it up for Seurat, she said. She had realized.

"Caught the stove on fire," the wife finally said. "Couldn't get it out. That end of the room went up."

If you were a son thinking of your mother, where would your mind place her? In the kitchen. The wife had her own version but Chris did not want it, she wanted the man's account, sloppy, backtracking. "I worried about the guy," he was saying. "He would stand on the porch. You know. Just stand there."

Chris didn't know. "What's that got to do with a fire?" the wife said.

When had he done that, stood on the porch? If she had left the library where she was working and driven up unseen, would she have realized, would she have run up the steps to him? Day and night she was in the library thinking about Seurat. Seurat had died barely past the age she was now, thirty. A Victorian. But a French Victorian, with some breeze passing through the life he was going to live in her thesis, with the plump young Madeleine who will powder herself forever in his portrait, and their baby son, who will die two weeks after Seurat is buried. Something that made him, for the ten years given him to paint, paint pleasure and calm. A boyish face, hesitant behind the beard, but firm ideas. Ideas about color, about the optical shocks in beauty. A happy man in an unhappy life? The nineteenth century. Diseases everywhere, as Barrett was always saying. VD. Rudimentary anesthesia. Infants dying. But did the Victorians set their houses on fire? Did they try to burn themselves up because of their parents?

"He's burned some for just a stove fire," said the wife. "On the arms. Not so bad, but as a nurse I'd say they'll admit him. He's shook up. I'll give you a ride over there, you better not drive. Do you want to take a look at your place? It's not so bad. I'm Lorna, by the way."

Chris tried to stand up, but her knees were weak. Where had she been, in her house next door, in her own life? What had she done, in her own thirty years, facing none of the threats known to the obsessed and doomed Seurat, ecstatic yet steady in his mind?

"No, let's go now. I want to see him. Poor thing. Poor thing."

The ache she felt on the trip to the hospital with her neighbor was like the exaggerated sadness of graduation, with the future unrolling in it. Soon after they were married she had an episode of clairvoyance, they both said so, that was more than the scenarios that had flicked her in the past. In a dream she saw the twin towers burn. He knew she had seen it ahead of time because they were in the habit now of telling each other their dreams. His were of getting lost, going over cliffs, hers, after the one of the towers, more settled and calm. She was pregnant; she had turned in her thesis, her adviser had okayed the science, the optics, her weak point. The radiant flakes of gaslight in the study for the sideshow painting, the tiny patterns in all things, slipped from her thoughts, though in the spring before the Kentucky Derby of that year she saw in half-sleep the winner's circle with the garlanded black horse painted in the manner of Seurat.

Raccoon

Dark at four in the afternoon, tire tracks on the thin snow. Thomas stood in the mute wind of separateness that would engulf him whenever he stepped out of the car in this city. There was no actual wind, only the smell of snow faintly sweet like nitrous oxide, the snow of every country.

This was a gracious neighborhood overlooking the lake, with so many trees that you could see that steep forest really had preceded the city. He thought he had a long way to go from his parking place, and he was more tired than he would have been at home. Doctors and everyone else here worked long hours with an energy he despaired of matching. He turned to see his footprints, and coming soundlessly behind him was an animal. A raccoon. His mind said *huge*, but that could simply be the size they were here. This was the first one he had seen, but there were said to be droves of them in the city. They got into the papers for menacing children and tearing into housecats. The raccoon had stopped too. It stared without fear, glared, he would say if he found somebody to tell when he got inside, and then it began to advance, leaving prints of its thin hands inside his shoeprints.

He ran. Many stairs to the door. You had to reach into the wreath for the brass knocker. Mrs. Haglen, the medical director's wife, opened the door. Here with lit-up rooms behind her she seemed bigger than when he had shaken her small hand at a reception. "Come in!" she cried as if there were a choice to it. She would not have seen the masked face, the high-arched back of an animal go by her door making a shadow under the streetlamps like a man walking on his feet and the palms of his hands.

In the warmth of the foyer with its mellow wood and candles and swags of evergreen he could think in a logical way about the raccoon. The growing population of them was said to carry dangers. Whatever the animal's instincts might lead it to do in actuality, the papers were making a case against it because of rabies. More raccoons had rabies than you would expect statistically. Worse in England, where they were not native and were trapped and disposed of as invaders when they appeared, with no need for mention of children or cats.

Mrs. Haglen was feeling for his name while he panted, and when he supplied it—"Thomas, from Manchester. In Pathology, visiting fellow with Dr. Cheng"—she gave him a smile that seemed to sympathize with the task of getting free of an overcoat, and quickly turned the sleeves right side out before she handed it to a little boy.

Below a chandelier hung with bells sat a beautiful blond fat girl at a punchbowl. The dining chairs, more than he could quickly count, had been placed along the walls as in a choir. Two remained, at the head of the long table where nobody was drinking punch because everybody had gathered at a sideboard at the far end, where they had a bar. The chair beside the girl was empty.

"Pardon me," he said. She raised large eyes to him, gulfs with bits of sun in them, and flecks where the pure blue went deeper. Her cheeks rose in a smile, and he leaned forward almost tottering. "May I sit down?"

Although her bulk filled the chair to its arms she seemed afloat in a mist of filaments from the pearl-gray shawl around her shoulders. "Please do," she said. She had on a dress—satin, he would have said—close to the color of the red punch. She was filling glass cups and with the ladle slowly dropping cranberries and an orange slice into each one. She made a half ring of the glasses and rested, one white hand on the table. "Will you have some?" she said, the aquamarine eyes opening wide as if an answer he might make would be of warm interest to her. She had a pleasant voice in the low range. The pitch of his wife's speech came to him. "Don't forget your." "Where have you left your." "Whatever did you mean by your."

"I will," he said. "Do you sing? Your voice," he added as he seated himself, to keep her from thinking he meant her size.

"I do sing," she said.

"What roles?"

"Oh, not opera. I am a jazz singer."

She would be nineteen or so, he decided, yet already she could say "I am a jazz singer."

"Your daughter," he said to Mrs. Haglen, once he had given up the chair and tried to find someone he knew. He felt on the verge of tears. At least he was on the verge of saying, "I've fallen in love with her," but he didn't because if Mrs. Haglen remembered him at all, she knew he was the visiting fellow who was not making a success of it and whose wife had stayed back in England. "She has quite bowled me over."

"She does that," Mrs. Haglen said. "She's very fit," she added.

"Yes there's something about her."

"No, I mean she is physically fit. She walks everywhere. Leo has given her a Fitbit."

"Tell me about her singing."

"She is a jazz singer."

"But what does she sing?"

"Ask her and she'll tell you," said Mrs. Haglen.

"I must tell you, she—I—all I can say is as soon as I saw her I—"

"My dear, she's almost forty. I have to say that to you boys." He looked down at himself, his thin body. He was twenty-eight. "Her partner." Mrs. Haglen made a discreet gesture through the arch into the living room, where a tall gray-haired man was moving the piano bench. "You're married I believe," she added with no reproof.

"I am, I was, we were married but we shan't go on. She isn't coming here. I'm not going back."

He wasn't going back. With Mrs. Haglen he turned to look at her daughter, where she sat in her cloudy shawl. She looked back from a region where, curved as the punchbowl, as a pearl, an egg, a snowball, she reigned.

"What is her name?" he said. He had forgotten to introduce himself.

"Celeste." Of course. Of course, Celeste.

A low chord sounded as Celeste crossed the living room to stand by the fireplace. She had left the shawl on her chair, and her round arms, smooth even at the elbow where they folded in a deep dimple, were bare. The red dress touched the floor. Thomas waited to hear what a jazz singer would choose to sing. He knew opera, but not jazz.

A hush fell and she began to sing his favorite hymn, from the days of chapel in school.

O come, O come, Emmanuel
And ransom captive Israel.

SHE SANG WITHOUT RAISING HER arms, without moving except to breathe. Her voice was rich and grave. Her sobriety gave it an unearthly beauty, he thought. Captive Israel. Now Israel was the keeper of captives. People and land. The world was dark and awry. The earthquake in Japan had jarred the earth on its axis. New quakes, shudders of pain, rose up out of undergirdings of rock being crushed for oil. Why was he preparing to be a doctor—not even a doctor, a pathologist—when what he wanted was to offer himself, sacrifice himself for the earth. As she sang he felt he could offer himself to be bitten by a rabid animal, to show, to show— Yet he was going to be afraid to step out of the light of the windows and walk to his car alone, because the animal was there. He had just seen a movie about the Kennedy assassination. Assassinations were as old as the human race. "Close the path to misery," sang Celeste. The path to misery. Close it. Close it. Her voice was going to echo in his brain. Emmanuel really had to do with a war after which the Assyrian would come down, if he remembered his history. He had won a prize in history, for a paper on Herodotus. Oh if a winged animal were to come, he would welcome it.

The Flag of the Nude

A thin old man got up and stepped to the microphone. His fame was such that many in the audience had come only to see and hear him, but had not been sure from their faraway seats which of the men in chairs on the stage was he, even though they had, in their backpacks or on their laps, books with a famous old photograph of him on the back cover. But that man was young. The man at the lectern was far gone; he was like a left-behind bird that has to migrate across a sea and has flown to the top of the last tree on shore. His voice was hoarse, and not deep. He kept drinking from his water glass and made no effort to adjust the squawking microphone during his speech. When he held up his arms to make a point, the audience flinched at the half-empty suit-sleeves ending in papery hands. His fame seemed not to have come with him onto the stage.

It might have been better, some in the audience thought, to be somewhere else speaking seriously of him than to be here in this echoing auditorium where he actually was and yet was not. Was this the man who had so scandalously carried off the married woman, a famous artist from a repressive country where fame was an undesirable thing at the time? But the woman had fallen ill before any official could pound on her door in the night. Years before, she had flown to the top of the tree, leaving him to his many lesser loves.

He had made clear that he would not read from his own work. In the speech, filled with pauses and stares, he recited from memory verses from a greater poet, long dead, with whom he had no quarrel as he did with living ones. More than a few knew the poem and smiled in acknowledgment as he kept repeating—breaking up a poem with repetitions of words and whole lines being a habit he was known for—a line ending in the word *nude*. He leaned so close to the mike his lips touched it like a singer's, making it feed back. "'Flying the flag of the nude.'" What was being claimed about the poet who wrote this was anybody's guess.

It was not clear exactly when he had finished with his speech, though a hush fell. People said later that it seemed to be the silence of an utter end. The program itself was not at an end, but the delayed applause was long, and while it was going on people got out of their seats and swarmed to the proscenium, where some of the young men began hoisting themselves up onto the stage. His hosts had formed a jostling half circle around him, but like a man feeding chickens he bent towards the crowd surging forward.

A young woman with black hair twisted and coming loose from its clasp on her small head reached the stage and held up both arms. He spread the circle of his protectors, and with others lifting from below he raised her up. She had a white face, eyebrows plucked to a stroke, and lips painted a blue-red. The crowd fell back on either side of him with the rustle of an opened robe, making a space for her to stand. Slowly she drew one hand out of his, to bend over, her flesh weighing down the low neck of her dress, and with one finger tuck the strap of her shoe onto her heel. Everyone who was close enough saw the man's tired eyes grow deep and bright, they saw the creased skin of his forehead flush and come out in sweat, they saw the tug he gave his sparse beard. And then he was down from the last tree and the two were flown, into the night sky above that city, into the many unsuspected years.

The Bull

The voice of a bull is not the voice of the cow. The bull growls, a rumble like a train in a tunnel if a train could brood, menace, resent, and pine. He calls, groans, and screams. Pastured away from the herd, a bull who has been a silent lord in their midst bawls his rage and croons his mourning.

Severn Hatch had the farm that you saw on Google Earth as a green eye-patch on a huge gray face. The face was the rooftops of six thousand houses, the farm a round-edged square. From above it made its statement, *I won't sell*; from the roads bordering it, or streets as they were now, it was a kind of theme park. It had a gate and a painted sign, SEVERN, swinging from a post, it had a grate for keeping cattle in, a barn, a silo, and a pond. It had tractors that could be heard in the mornings, and a bull. Hatch kept his bull long after the herd was gone.

The place and the man were named for a town in North Carolina where Severn Hatch had been born, on his grandparents' farm, where his young parents were waiting out the Depression. After giving birth his mother had died in her childhood bedroom. Along with both of her parents, who were already known to the bootleggers, his father had fallen by the wayside. But after a few years the father dragged himself up to Virginia where his own people were. He sent for his son, at eight already lost to the dazed grandparents and the Carolina schools. Schools did not try to hold on to a child as they do now. He never remarried, and his son never returned to school or married either, living on by himself on the dairy farm built up by the father.

Hatch never sold an acre. He sold his herd a few at a time as the demands of milking got too much for him and as tenants came and went in the little house his father had built and kept up. A dairy that size had to have a tenant or a hired man. Every few years he went as his father had done and painted the house, working with whoever the tenant was, until he couldn't find one for the job.

Severn Hatch's last Holstein bull could get past a fence and did so, as bulls do, with some regularity. When his fields had bordered another herd's fields—for the change to house-lots proceeded in a slow, circling way at first—he was just a visitor. "Lucky to have him stop by and improve the herd," Hatch would say when a neighbor complained. And in truth the bull came from a good line and there were still a couple of farmers in the southwestern part of the state who used him as a sire, and that was why Hatch said he kept him, even though eventually he had to drive out some way to get feed and salt blocks.

In the early days the bull could be brought in from his searching, run back onto his own land by Hatch, a waving stick and a good dog. Now he was taller than a man and weighed something over a ton. Older and craftier, he was harder to get back in.

Up in his seventies Hatch could be seen in the Walmart parking lot searching for his bull. He drove all over now instead of walking the fields and roads in a grid that had at one time taken him all day. Nobody outside a few stores knew him, so nobody knew his purpose, though everybody knew the farm, noted on zoning maps as "Sever Farm, Landmark," and the bull on the highway or growling up a ramp into a battered truck at Walmart was part of county lore. People would get out of the way, but many did not know to be afraid of an animal. Hatch's clothing did not give him away as the owner, as people of all ages dressed like farmers by then, even in the electronics parks.

At the far end of that parking lot one day he had a stroke. He was found lying down beside his truck, and when he woke up in the hospital he started raving about his bull. He got his words back right away, but all he did was call out "Tarnation!" The nurse figured out it was a name.

She put it all together. She became the one he talked to in his dread, over the next days when no news of the bull reached them. She was a popular nurse known in the hospital as Kimberly One, because she claimed to be the first person in the United States to bear the name. "Tarnation. I've heard of that guy," she said. "My grandpa farmed here."

"He's got to eat," Hatch said. "Got to have feed. Got to have pills."

"You worry about your own pills," Kimberly said. "I'll find out where he is. Somebody has him, I know."

"Who would that be?" said Hatch rudely. "Holstein bull is a dangerous animal."

"Is he mean?"

"Mean he is not. Ah!"

"What? What hurts?"

"Everything," said Hatch. "How old are you?"

"I'm fifty-six."

"He's cute," she said at the nurse's station.

"To each his own."

"No, really, there must be some news of this critter."

They did find out. The bull had been bumped and thrown by a semi coming off the freeway. By some miracle he was alive at a large animal vet in the next county, with some stitched-up gashes but no bones broken. Hatch left the hospital in his pressure socks—they had taken his shoes from him—but Kimberly caught up with him in her car and drove him so fast they got stopped for a warning. It was a clear day in March and the construction sites thinned out as they drove until they were passing between fields starting to show the green of some leaf crop. She said, "What's that?"

Hatch said, "Couldn't say," though he knew every green thing in state soil. Despite the seat belt she had made him put on, he had himself pressed against the door.

To Kimberly's eyes the bull was as big as an elephant in the hoist, gleaming stark black and white against the bandages and tape. At Hatch's approach he rolled his eye back and then swung his huge head to see, knocking the vet's assistant to his knees in the straw. The head was entirely black, with long eyelashes shadowing the ball-eye with its wet red corner. Streaks ran down from the eyes as if he had cried. Getting to his feet, the assistant had had a look at Hatch's wet socks. He addressed himself to Kimberly, making the sign of writing a bill. "Come on in when you're done with your visit."

"He's beautiful," Kimberly said. "I bet you're gonna say don't touch him."

"Better not." Hatch placed his fingers behind the black jaw and bowed his head. "Heart going," he said after a time. "Fever."

"I think he's just worked up," said Kimberly. "Because you caught up with him. Everything he's been through and then you show up. You love this guy."

Hatch said, "That's a strong word."

"Not so strong as all that," said Kimberly.

Orogeny

Through the half-open door to the tiny bathroom I'll see my father watching the swirl of the flush and then the activity in the bowl for a long time before he comes out wearing a look of consternation. "Hello there!" he'll say, surprised. Had I been there when he went into the bathroom? "I don't know about that in there. That can't be entirely right."

Of course I'll say, "What?"

The room is furnished with his own furniture, his own bedroom rug atop the carpet, with the leather reclining chair from his study. Even on the farm there was a room called his study. On the hassock is a blanket that he wraps around his feet in all seasons. He has a wall clock, a draft-horse calendar, a begonia, and an empty bud vase, and on his lamp table a book of aerial photographs of American farmland and a moldy atlas from the thirties. He'll get around the bed and across the room with his cane, rechecking his zipper all the way, slump the chair back, and once he's in it, wave to me rather than answer. He's still big, he looks as though he should be powerful.

"The toilet? Is everything working?" I say. They're very prompt when there's anything to clean or fix. And although I refuse to judge the place, as everyone advises, by whether or not there is a smell of urine, I can't help saying to myself again that there is not.

I know he comes out of the bathroom in one of two moods. Sometimes he'll say, "I thought that was going to go on forever," his brow wrinkled, his hands fumbling vague, disapproving circles that mean the water in the toilet, which caught his attention a few weeks ago, according to my sister who lives nearby and sees him all the time. Other times he'll just grin at me, father to daughter. A disquiet that is almost dread, or the purest cheer and goodwill: nothing in between.

If it's dread I'll say something like, "It does just go on and on, doesn't it?" Something *idiotic*. "That one in particular," I'll add. "Or I wonder if they're all like that in this . . . building." I don't name the place and neither does he, though if we go out we refer to it as if it were a well-known, popular, but to us rather silly and outgrown landmark. It can be an apartment. It can be a hotel on a trip he must be making. His "commute," he calls it, that has gone on much longer than it should have. This fact so confounds him when it occurs to him—you can see his face freeze, eyes squint—that he doesn't know where to begin on questioning it. Where he actually is and how long he has actually been here are wholly outside the bounds of conversation. He still has conversations. He is still polite and if he's at ease he can rib visitors and he can quote a few poems and he can pun.

He can still play a tune on the harmonica. He was raised on a dirt farm in Indiana, putting up hay with a team and riding a horse to school after getting up at four-thirty to help with the milking. But he left the farm, he got a PhD in geography. He taught for a while before the war came, and then he moved to Virginia and commuted to Washington, D.C., to work for the army. To the staff here, of course, all that has no more weight than past beauty.

When he retired as a geographer, he went back to farming, this time with beef cattle so there would be no milking at four-thirty in the morning.

The thing he says most often, "Look at that!," is perhaps more what a geographer would say than a farmer.

His hearing is good but his vision is getting worse. "Look at that cemetery," he says cheerfully, pointing at the big calendar on the wall. The scene is of a team of Belgian horses in harness. I try to think, then I make the same jump, and see it on the calendar: the squares of the days. Gravestones.

The last trip he made was two years ago, across the country with me on the train. He loved train travel, but it was clear as soon as the train pulled out of the station that he couldn't get his balance, or find his way up and down the cars, or even, in the night, from the lower bunk to the bathroom in our compartment. At the tables for four in the dining car he found inexplicable things to say to strangers, things I would try to smooth into the talk. I didn't want to make that conspiratorial face that says, "He's out of it." Because he wasn't out of it. He was in it, being carried downstream faster than the train was moving, with his feet out in front of him.

"Traveling with your daughter?" someone would say.

"Now why would you ask me that?" A savage frown. This was not long after my mother's death, when he had begun tearing out those cards and envelopes they insert into magazines—he subscribed to *Farm Journal*, *Progressive Farmer*, and *National Geographic*—and trampling them on the floor, and slitting his eyes at people on the sidewalk, and hanging up on neighbors who called.

All of that passed.

For three days on the train he barely spoke. Out the train window, Montana is just shifting, daylong bands of muted color. Across the expanse of gray-green land lay a purplish sky, although it was still daytime, with a silver band of lightning running miles along the horizon, so far away we heard no thunder. In the part of the state where the flat land starts to heave a little in preparation for the Rockies he woke up, looked out the window. He looked for a long time and suddenly he cried out, "Orogeny!"

Orogeny is mountain building, the pushing up of soil and rock into new landmass, part of the steady action, the behavior, of the earth. A mountain is born; through ceaseless motion a mountain is worn away. As he explained this he spoke with a teacher's firm enthusiasm, and a teasing note, such as teachers employ with rows of closed faces in front of them. Then he leaned back with a deep sigh, as if the changeful earth outside the train, with its ancient oceanbeds we had just crossed, its distant, mute storms, offered him a satisfaction. With that, he was finished with speech for the rest of the trip.

Most of the things that we expect will please him do not. The trip across his beloved plains did not. Long before we had covered the three thousand miles from Virginia to Seattle he had spiraled into constipated, snoring, twitching oblivion. When it was time to get off the train he rocked to his feet and said, "I'm glad that's over. It's always good to get back home."

In this place where he lives, what does please him? A greeting card showing a baby monkey is enshrined in front of my mother's picture; a baby bat on the palm of someone's hand on TV starts a tear down the creases of his wondering smile.

That baby who sits in the tire, in the ad, yanks him upright, shocked. "He's not really floating in that tire, Dad." But there *is* water under the baby, a river the ad suggests might whirl a tire away, and my father agrees, he is the perfect audience for such an idea, his mouth hangs open, disaster is in the room with us.

Television stirs him. A maelstrom of deeds and events whirls through his room. The week I'm sitting with him a serial murderer is tracked down and cornered, executives go into hiding, bombs go off. Random soap operas make him grip the chair arm. I try to reminisce, but he has shed the major portion of his life, the part that included his family. Watching television, he is as involved in the sponge wiping a clear space in the soap scum as he is in the car chase, the river flooding a town in Colorado.

That reminds me to get out the National Geographic videos. We always watch the three that are his favorites, "Cyclone," "Nature's Fury," and "*Titanic*."

At three-thirty in the afternoon in his room the *Titanic* slips under again, and five minutes later, or after seventy-four years, the research ship homes in on the wreckage.

In the next video cars tumble and bob down a river that had been the street of a town. A big house comes off its foundation and shakily takes on water, like a jar dipping to the bottom of a dishpan. A woman's voice says the white things flying through the air ("like typing paper!" she says) are garage doors.

He possesses facts of his own. "A tornado will run southwest-northeast. It'll funnel counterclockwise. Yep, you'll see a whole family of them at once, little and big." Sometimes he goes back to country talk.

As a child in Indiana he helped his father dig the storm cellar, and many times the family crowded into it while a tornado roared over. Once, just before they yanked the door down over them and latched it, he saw the porch steps jump, and the whole porch lift off the house and swing away to the woods, where they found it later. If he ever found himself somewhere that had that smell, that *earthen* smell in the storm cellar, he used to tell us, he would feel the hair rise on his head.

If casualties are mentioned, he shakes his head in commiseration. "We're nowhere near there," he says. "We're safe and sound."

I don't anymore say, "This isn't the news, it's a film."

Anyway, on that particular morning we watched a river race through the streets of a Colorado town as it was happening, on the news. "Don't let go of that!" he yelled out to a man clinging to a telephone pole. "Why don't they *get* him?"

For months after a tornado, he told us, men out in the cornfield would find junk and wreckage. And treasures. Unbroken china. Family Bibles. I think of those big gold-stamped thin-paged books, which must have lain open in farmhouses, easily lifted by the whistling gale from their place of honor. As a boy he took one back to a house four miles away, with half the pages torn out. He hasn't opened his own Bible since my mother died. He was a bitter widower, in the early days. "*God*," he said in a terrible voice, when the pastor told him God's comfort would come.

That early attitude is past and gone, though you couldn't really say it has been replaced. It has been smoothed.

What we call weather, says a gentle voice on the video, is only the planet's attempt to balance heat and moisture. After all the chaos and din, the camera is drifting peacefully over the flat farmland of the Midwest, his home.

"Did I milk?" he bursts out.

"No."

"Well, did I milk *last night*?"

"You don't have to milk. Honestly."

"What do you mean don't have to?" He struggles up out of the recliner.

When he went back to farming he raised beef cattle. He hasn't milked since he was a boy, not for seventy-five years.

Most tornadoes have short paths, but some have been known to travel for three hundred miles, touching down again and again. Everything in a house can be sucked out by the pressure of the funneling wind. If you saw it from above you would see the debris whirled up into the funnel go in streams, around and around in a fingerprint as big as God's.

4

What We Found

Where We Grew Up

You learned how to run on gravel barefoot, what to say when people's fathers were drunk at the horse show, when a pattern in dirt was a copperhead, where the snapping turtle heavier than a bag of feed would lurch down the bank, come up beak streaming, and hold on, if your feet were dangling, till lightning struck.

No matter when you went back, it was too late. The true decree or the false, now, you can't have either, let them clamor in dreams as they may, let them tear aside the rushes, plunge in, come up gnashing, let them search for the wavering sign of you in the deep sunlit end of the pond till the cows come home.

Harvest

I remember now how I liked having lice. Maybe because as soon as I had them we were getting rid of them with RID and so I didn't have to think of always having them always living with an itch close to madness which even then I recognized as madness—to want to scratch your head off want to stand on your head so frenzied is the itching and yet almost a frenzy of pleasure—and then because everyone else had them at the same time and the mothers saw to it the heads in every house came under the searching fingers of the district nurse, and the blame was shared because the first cause could never be found, although certain girls got a longer look, the tenant farmers' girls, but having lice was fun when you caught a crop of them in the fine-tooth comb or when you took a hair between finger- and thumbnail, and rasped off the nits, and rolled them on your fingertips and dropped them on the rug where would they hatch and crawl back up onto the next person? But the feel of the nits popping off—I thought of this today stripping rosemary off the stem—oh it gave you as a kid with nothing serious to do and no say over your own body a high, a feeling of triumph, of harvest.

Visiting Revivalist

This was not a tent preacher, but the kind who labored all summer on the highway, county by county, pulpit by pulpit. He held our pastor's Bible over his head and kissed it coming down, and slumped it open flat and backed away, shushing it with both hands. He began to whisper a chapter of Amos, the one with locusts and fire and the Lord standing with a plumb line. Already in tears he was reading sideways under his whirling arm. He read us the whole land rising like the Nile and then sinking, and the labors, which would be in vain, the men staggering from sea to sea, and then he raised his black sleeves and began to crouch and stomp, blame evil and praise good. Every few words he rose on tiptoe and sank, to a beat we knew from the lame cow that labored to the salt block. And when in an hour he threw the black sleeves around himself, it was not over, for an age of prayer ensued, an age of pacing and weeping, making the chancel floorboards creak like a wheelbarrow hauling rocks to the fencerow. We stuck to the pew. Our thighs left a print when we leapt up to sing "Awake, Awake to Love and Work." Then *another* prayer, this one shorter, though how he kept gasping drops of his own sweat—oh the labor that filled all grown-up life—embarrassing our pastor up there with his legs crossed and jaw held in two fingers and a thumb. At last he stopped, on a double amen, to fasten us to what he had prayed, like the five Nevers at the end of *King Lear*, like the old words he kept throwing in like more salt, such as the word *mortals* for us, the children, who could not die. But the organ drew breath at last. Foot pedals chugged, pipe mouths breathed notes so low that fifty years after the great G-chord set out in common measure it circles back, benign and stern, having passed over the whole land rising like the Nile, time rising around the plumb line, and having held in its great notes of dismissal and come all the way back to lead us, and leading us, yet in league with us, and deep as if rising off the cold floor of the silo, says we may have our lives, we may pass down the aisle and out the doors into the rising land and the men staggering, and begin, and do all we have done.

The Girl Who Told

Around and up goes the poison oak, vine that never dies. Thick as legs clamped to the sweetgum trees in their youth. No one has sawed it out in years; the chain gangs are gone, and no one clears the fencerows by the highway.

The sparrowhawk is on the gate, and over the rows of stubble the same shadow, everything as it was, the same snow stalled in the air. The highway drops to the stone bridge over the railroad track and winds back up to the overlook, where picnic tables set in concrete stood like altars, and in the convict crew the father of a girl on the school bus leaned on his rake and glared, and she never looked.

She was the one who told. A thing he did. Stealing, we all said; something hidden afterwards and she knew where.

Even now the bus rattles downhill, past the house where the crippled vice principal lived, feared for his hulking shoulders and little legs, lurching the hallways year after year, half of him visible in the squints from the early bus, at the bay window waiting for his ride, waiting to mete out the derided justice, the unmarked mercy, keeping the secrets of the half-grown children of that county, secrets that could be told, but never die.

Advice

Once with his dog my father got into quicksand. Or whatever our state had that we called quicksand. Thinking back now I have a question, though of course he can't answer now. He was hunting. He never shot anything, but he hunted when he was invited. His friend was way down the woods. His dog sniffed at the quicksand and skirted it and ran to find the one who had invited him, who came at last and dragged him out with a tree limb. While he waited I know he knew not to thrash and stamp. He knew to stay still, not even wipe the sweat while he thought out what he would do once someone came, and how to get together the force to be pulled by the arms out of the equivalent of cement, sparing the weak sockets of the shoulders. By then he was an oldish man with angina. His four children were gone. We were all out forcing something, giving no thought to his advice, which was always "Proceed as the way opens." The dog was gone a long time. An hour. I hope he advised himself, and I hope it gave him, standing by himself knee-deep in the quiet, not quite ready to shout in the empty woods or fire the .22 in the air, the comfort it always gave us, when we were all at home, deep in the unreleasing magnet sand of our family, and gives us now we will never again set foot there, "Proceed as the way opens."

Freeway Rescues

One year the rented car rolled over, out of Toledo north on the ice to Flint. The upside-down front end buried itself in snow, the back spun out into the traffic. A tire in the back went on rolling, scraping bent metal. The headlights of a semi passed over in a slow arc as it ground its gears. We hung in our seat belts with just a few words between us and some time later climbed up warm arms and into the back seat of a van, our rescuers' van, where I sat on the Bible they had put there, on their way to Bible study on the freeway ice. We waited for the cops, who took a long time to get there because there had been so many spinouts. I was so happy that I planned, after a moment of desire for beer and bar-neon and the strong, forgiving cop, to drive on into Bible study, and never be seen in our previous life again, as if we had really died. Another year we were in Michigan after an ice storm, and the same interstate was so beautiful it stopped our fight. In the aisle of trees each tree was a self, exquisite, perfected in ice, *rectified*, as they say of flowers that break from monochrome into stripe, the life of trees explicit suddenly, as if we had put on glasses, so beautiful along I-75 that we heard a silvery cracking between us, and our son remembers the ice-trees, although he was not born.

River Boat

We were in a little boat on a muddy river. Along with twenty or so others, including the crew of two, we were heading for a fishing village. It was the dry season, and when we reached the village we saw houses on exposed stilts above a narrow strip of beach where mudskippers wriggled in the wet clay. For a few hours we would wander up and down the muddy pier, buy things made of wood or tortoiseshell or an aromatic bagful sieved up from a bin of seeds or roots. We would look at the fish traps, and eat crab in chili sauce reeking of shrimp paste, from big tin trays with limes sliced and spread like packs of cards, dozens of them squandered on decoration. The next day we would be sick, but not sick enough for that to become the memory.

When we tied up, fishermen glanced at us climbing out onto the pier in our enterprise of visiting their village. My husband and I stayed quiet so as not to be mistaken for tourists. Of course we were tourists, though we had lived in the country for a year. Downriver and back through the rubber tree plantations was the city that was our home.

We stopped to look at a boy of about eight who was tossing fish from the traps into baskets, twisting his slim torso and flinging each one with a liquid motion of his loose shoulders. The skin of his back shone like a tent with a lantern on inside. We said he was one of the most beautiful children we had ever seen. All morning on the boat we had been saying that about the children.

In the boat, everyone had been seated on benches the length of the vessel. In the center of the deck stood a little house. At first we thought this might be a bathroom, as the trip would be a long one, but of course it was not, it was the engine house. When necessary the women held their babies, who wore no diapers, out over the water.

Never had so many beautiful children been gathered in one boat. For hours we had them before our eyes, burning themselves into memory, with their shining black hair and their soft dark eyes, their perfect proportions, their laughter, as if nothing could threaten them with boredom or resentment, and their easy, exquisite manners with strangers. Watching them, we fell into a long pause that matched the uneven growl of the engine and the lapping of the brown river against the boat. Gradually, when the parents saw us admiring the children, conversation began. We could speak the language haltingly. We had been taught not to plunge into the American project of interrogation, or ply anybody with compliments, and gradually the mothers, proud and smiling, began in low voices to ask questions themselves.

This was years, many years ago. We were a young couple, and not young in any preliminary way, but squarely in the years of obligation, the years of creating and establishing a household. Where was our family? What were we doing, away from where we belonged? Where were our children?

We were waiting for our adoption to come through. *Adoption* was a word not in use in that country. Not at that time. Of course it existed, like prostitution an ancient and ubiquitous thing. But the word was not in the dictionaries. No one used it, and we had learned to avoid it—as if it were one of those vices overlooked in our own country, like drinking, or exposing women's hair, shoulders, and legs—while shreds of news about a child yet to be born kept flying towards us.

But in the long morning on the water, we found ourselves trying to explain to the mothers. Then, as we should have known it would, the talk eddied as we were enfolded in a musing pity. Because the women we were talking to—*they* were not halfway around the world, indulging in needless river travel and exotic seafood and the sight of mudskippers, which looked in the mud like newborn puppies still in the caul, squirming to be licked. On the boat, in the village when we arrived, *they* were at home where they belonged, with their children.

On the way back to the city in the car, we would stop in the early dark for the red rambutans still hung out on roadside stalls. We would sit on upturned rubber buckets while children brought us coffee thick with condensed milk. We would peel the rambutans and eat, with wet fingers, the matchless fruit. For that year, we were under some injunction to see and taste all we could. But when the year was done, we would change. All we had sought out and marveled to see in cities and villages, jungles filled with birds and leopards, the miles of slim trees giving up the white sap that would become our boots and tires, would pass out of our hands. We would not sigh after heat and trailing orchids and the sound of market cleavers. Equatorial landscape would not smite us as if we had once parted the leaves ourselves and stumbled into Eden. We would not care any longer, like tourists, for any momentary possession. All would belong to the child. The river, the bins of roots and mushrooms, the fish traps. The sound of the muezzin on a morning when the sky was black, as figures gathered on a pier to board a boat. The river boat, the river. The ocean. The sky. We would hold back nothing. All would belong to the child. All, all would be exchanged for the one thing. This was what we had tried to explain on the river boat. This was what could not be explained.

Acknowledgments

With deep gratitude to Jack Shoemaker and the booklovers who give their all at Counterpoint.

Author photograph by Lucien Knuteson

VALERIE TRUEBLOOD is the author of the novel *Seven Loves*, and the short story collections *Search Party*, *Marry or Burn*, and *Criminals*. She's been a finalist for the 2014 PEN/Faulkner Award, a finalist for the Frank O'Connor International Short Story Award, and a recipient of the Barnes & Noble Discover Great New Writers Award. She lives in Seattle.

Printed in the United States
by Baker & Taylor Publisher Services